北京理工大学“双一流”建设精品出版工程

Perspectives in American Literature and Culture

美国文学与文化透视

云 玲　范慧玉◎主编

北京理工大学出版社
BEIJING INSTITUTE OF TECHNOLOGY PRESS

内 容 简 介

本书旨在帮助学生在熟练掌握英语语言技能的基础上，深入理解美国相关的历史、社会和文化背景，洞悉文学与文化之间的相互影响与作用，以及美国文化中的重要思潮，对于我们在全球化时代正确认识中西方之间的关系具有重要的参考价值。本书围绕着美国社会和文化中的一些热点词汇展开，如个人主义、美国梦、政治体制、消费主义、种族关系、女性主义、多元文化、社会暴力、生态危机、疾病和瘟疫，结合对相关美国文学经典作品的阅读阐释，以期帮助学生正确了解美国文化和价值观，从而拓宽视野，提高文化修养，培养思辨能力。

本书可作为高等院校英语专业高年级本科生和研究生的学习用书或者教学辅导用书，同时对于那些对美国文学与文化感兴趣，具有一定英语基础的非专业读者也同样具有参考价值。

图书在版编目（CIP）数据

美国文学与文化透视 ：英文 / 云玲，范慧玉主编.
北京 ：北京理工大学出版社，2024. 6.
ISBN 978-7-5763-4159-1

Ⅰ. I712.06

中国国家版本馆 CIP 数据核字第 2024RP2218 号

责任编辑：李颖颖　　文案编辑：辛丽莉
责任校对：刘亚男　　责任印制：李志强

出版发行 / 北京理工大学出版社有限责任公司
社　　址 / 北京市丰台区四合庄路 6 号
邮　　编 / 100070
电　　话 /（010）68944439（学术售后服务热线）
网　　址 / http://www.bitpress.com.cn

版 印 次 / 2024 年 6 月第 1 版第 1 次印刷
印　　刷 / 三河市华骏印务包装有限公司
开　　本 / 787 mm × 1092 mm　1/16
印　　张 / 16.25
字　　数 / 376 千字
定　　价 / 68.00 元

前言

《美国文学与文化透视》是一本适合高等院校英语专业高年级本科生和研究生使用的教材，旨在帮助学生在熟练掌握英语语言技能的基础上，深入理解美国文化与历史的重要主题。该教材围绕着美国社会和文化中的一些热点词汇，如个人主义、美国梦、政治体制、消费主义、种族关系、女性主义、多元文化、社会暴力、生态危机、疾病和瘟疫，结合相关的美国文学经典作品的阅读，运用马克思主义和辩证唯物主义的观点进行分析，以期帮助学生了解美国文化和价值观，从而拓宽学生的视野，提高文化修养，培养思辨能力。

本教材总共分为十个章节，涉及美国文化的十个热点词汇，针对每个章节，首先进行整体文化背景介绍，然后选择两位作家的两部作品进行导读和分析，最后提出一些思考问题。本教材的安排主要是围绕着美国文化的主题关键词展开，而非传统地按照美国历史发展的时间顺序选取文本。另外，本教材选取的作家都是学界公认的经典作家，这些作家的作品在中国都有各类的译本，并被收录在各种文学选集中。这些作品的价值和经典性经历了长久的时间考验，也在国内批评界获得了较高的评价，在思想性和艺术性上也取得了很高的成就。编者在选材和评论时，坚持社会主义核心价值观以及辩证唯物主义和历史唯物主义的文化观，秉承课程思政和立德树人的思想，对于优秀的西方文化采取批判式接纳的态度，这有利于我们深刻洞察西方文化的悖论，利用西方文化成果更好地为社会主义建设服务。

编　者

目 录

Contents

Introduction: Hot Topics in American Literature

Generally speaking, literature refers to any written texts with artistic value, including the traditional literary genres of poems, fiction and drama. But here, when we discuss literature, we will mostly confine this term to fiction. Culture is also a broad term which covers a wide range of aspects. It is the characteristic of a particular group of people, defined by everything from language, religion, cuisine, social habits, music, and arts. Literature and culture are interrelated and interplayed with each other. They share a deep and intricate relationship, with each influencing and shaping the other. Literature, as an artistic expression of human experiences and ideas, reflects and captures the cultural, social, and historical contexts in which it is produced. Literature also contributes to the development and evolution of culture by challenging norms, promoting new perspectives, and fostering dialogue within society. Meanwhile, culture provides a background for the development of literature and will influence the development of it.

Although compared with literature in other countries, American literature is relatively new and has existed for only more than 400 years. American writers have made distinctive achievements and there are several important American writers who have won the Nobel Prize for Literature. Their works have not only influenced American values but also the world cultures. This book combines the study of American literature and culture together and intends to improve the reader's understanding about their interactions. Focusing on some hot topics in American literature and culture, the book will inspire readers to understand American distinctive cultural elements through an examination of different texts. The book will include the following topics such as individualism, American dream, American political system, consumerism, racial problems, feminism, multiculturalism, social violence, ecological crisis, disease and plague. Hopefully, through reading this book, readers will get more enlightenment about the relationship between American literature and culture.

This book is arranged based on the hot topics in American culture, rather than the traditional chronological order. At the same time, when discussing a specific theme, this book will choose parallel texts for comparative study. This crisscross method enables readers to grasp the development of American literature and culture in an all-round way to get a holistic perspective. The book is divided into ten chapters. The following is a brief introduction to the contents of each chapter.

Chapter 1 will discuss American individualism represented in Benjamin Franklin's *The*

Autobiography and Ralph Emerson's *Self-Reliance.* American people value individuality more than anything else. It is the belief in the primary importance of the individual and in the virtues of self-reliance and personal independence. Through his rags-to-riches story, Benjamin Franklin represents the successful model of American individualism. In *Self-Reliance,* Emerson represents American individualism through emphasizing that one should follow one's heart rather than submit to any authority or religion.

Chapter 2 will focus on the myth of American Dream which is also a symbol of American charm. American Dream is the belief that anyone, regardless of where they were born or what class they were born into, can attain their own version of success in a society where upward mobility is possible. But we know that actually it is only an illusion especially for minority people because the real American dream is hard to achieve and there are too many invisible barriers to overcome. This chapter will discuss the theme of American dream in *Between the World and Me* and *The Great Gatsby*.

Chapter 3 will center on American political system. This chapter will discuss *Catch-22* which is a novel by American author Joseph Heller, published in 1961. It's a satirical and darkly comedic masterpiece set during World War II. Henry David Thoreau's *On the Duty of Civil Disobedience* criticizes American social institutions and policies, such as slavery and the Mexican-American War. He believes that "a government is best which governs least". The purpose of a government is to serve the people, so when a government is unjust, people should refuse to follow the law and distance themselves from the government.

Chapter 4 will discuss American consumerism which refers to the culture and behavior of excessive consumption and materialism prevalent in the United States. Consumerism is based on our belief that material things can bring happiness. In American society, individual value is connected with the things people consume. However, consumption will not bring real happiness to people because no matter how many things people own, they will still lament what they lack. Their soul is eaten away with cares as they compete in the struggle for success. This chapter will discuss two texts. *A Pair of Silk Stockings* is a short story by Kate Chopin, first published in 1897. From the perspective of consumerism, it explores the pleasures and dangers of indulgence and the fleeting nature of material possessions. The second text *White Noise* is a novel written by American author Don DeLillo, published in 1985. It's a postmodern masterpiece that explores the anxieties, fears, and absurdities of contemporary American life.

Chapter 5 will discuss racial problems which refer to the systemic and deeply-rooted issues related to race and ethnicity that persist in the United States. When the black people were first brought into America as slaves in the 16th and 17th century, they worked in southern plantations where they were treated as animals and suffered from racial prejudice. The legacy of slavery, including racial discrimination, segregation, and violence against African Americans, has had a lasting impact on the country. Although the Civil Rights Movement has helped improve the black people's condition, racial discrimination is still a serious problem today. This chapter will focus on two texts. The first is *Uncle Tom's Cabin* which, through vivid and emotional storytelling, exposes the brutality and inhumanity of slavery, revealing the harsh conditions, separation of families, and physical abuse suffered by enslaved individuals. The second text is *Invisible Man* which depicts the social and political inequalities that were embedded in American society, highlighting the discrimination, prejudice, and violence that black people face.

Chapter 6 will focus on American feminism which refers to the movement and ideologies that advocate for gender equality and women's rights in the United States. The development of American feminism has experienced several waves. Women struggled first for suffrage and equal pay for equal work, later seeking equal rights in all aspects of social life. Although the situation of women has improved today, compared with men, job and promotion opportunities are still relatively limited. This chapter will discuss two texts — *A Rose for Emily* and *The Yellow Wallpaper*. *A Rose for Emily* can be analyzed through the lens of gender roles, power dynamics, and the constraints placed upon women in patriarchal societies. *The Yellow Wallpaper* is also about a woman who becomes a victim under the double systems of patriarchy and medical authority.

Chapter 7 will explore multiculturalism which promotes the coexistence of multiple cultural groups within a society. It involves different cultures and ethnicities. The United States of America, due to its immense size and diverse heritages, has one of the most complex cultural identities in the world. America is a country which is called a melting pot and later a salad bowl. The different ethnicities keep their own lifestyles, cultural values, business practices and dialects while trying to integrate into the mainstream society. These people have a strong bond with their homeland while trying to form their new identities in their adopted country. This chapter will discuss two texts, the first is *The Joy Luck Club* and the second is *The Third and Final Continent*. Both of the texts are about American minorities, seeking for home, space and identity, in a mainstream society.

Chapter 8 will explore how social violence is represented in American literature. Violence is a social problem in America. Women and minorities are often the victims of violence. America's epidemic of violence is due to the poor control of drugs, guns and the excessive use of alcohol. This chapter will discuss Flannery O'Connor's *A Good Man is Hard to Find* and Edgar Allan Poe's *Black Cat* to explore the influence of violence on American society.

Chapter 9 will discuss American ecological and literature. This chapter will focus on two texts, one is *The Silent Spring* written by Rachel Carson and the other is *The Bear* by William Faulkner. Regarded as a masterpiece of natural literature, the former is concerned about the damage to the ecosystem caused by the excessive use of chemical fertilizers and pesticides. *The Bear* has greatly stimulated the ecological and environmental awareness of human beings. It allows us to re-examine the relationship between human beings and nature and reminds us to respect and revere nature.

Chapter 10 will involve the discussion of disease and plague. Because of the emergence of COVID-19, illness and plague have become a new focus of attention in literature and culture. Plague literature is a chronicle of human suffering, resilience, and the indomitable spirit amidst adversity. We should remember that the world we know today is shaped by the pandemics of the past. This chapter will discuss two texts. The first is *The Masque of the Red Death* by Allan Poe while the second is *The Scarlet Plague* by Jack London. The former text describes how an unnamable illness kills people in the royal place and reveals the relationship between illness and death while the second text *The Scarlet Plague* deals with the familiar themes, such as the inevitability of death and the futility of trying to escape death.

The above is an overview of all the chapters in this book. Generally speaking, culture is a broad concept that embraces all the aspects of the human life. It includes everything humans do or learn to do as members of a society and it shapes our thoughts and actions. Literature and culture are closely intertwined and will also influence each other. I hope that through this book, readers can deepen their understanding of American literature and culture. Through critical reading and learning, we can take the advantage of western literature and culture and employ them for our socialist cultural construction.

Chapter 1 Individualism

Individualism is a very important concept in American history. It is one of the American traits which have shaped the development of American spirit. It is a political and social philosophy that emphasizes the moral value of the individual. It has been reflected in various aspects of American life, from politics and economics to art and literature. This concept is taken as a part of American core ideology, incorporating the influences of New England Puritanism and the philosophy of natural rights. It is also influenced by the social Darwinism which advocates the idea of the survival of the fittest.

When the first Europeans immigrated to this new land, they believed that they could make a fresh start here. The puritans believed they were the god's chosen people and they were very optimistic, so they try to rely on personal efforts and diligence to live a happy life. What is more, American transcendentalism, which is a philosophical school, also contributes to the development of individualism. The self-reliance and moral perfection they embrace are also vital to the formation of American individualism.

Max Weber thinks the term individualism "embrace the utmost heterogeneity of meanings" (Lukes 45). American individualism has very rich connotations such as independence, self-reliance, pursuit of freedom, etc. People with such characteristics don't want to be fettered by common social traditions and conventions. Pioneering spirit is also important because people with individuality like to take risks. During the late 19th century and the early 20th century, the idea of individualism could be seen in the works of many classical American writers, such as Benjamin Franklin and Ralph Emerson. The myth of individualism also has a relationship with the myth of self-made man which "refers, first of all, to expressive individualism and individual success and describes a cultural type that is often seen as an 'American invention' and a 'unique national product'" (Paul 368). Throughout American history, individualism has been celebrated in various forms. The "rugged individualism" of frontiersmen and pioneers, for example, was seen as a hallmark of American identity and a source of national pride. "Rugged individualism" is associated with traditional American values such as personal freedom, capitalism, and limited government[①]. It is especially related to American frontier experience which is filled with challenges and difficulties.

However, the concept of American individualism has faced a lot of criticisms. Critics argue that it can lead to a lack of social cohesion and a disregard for the needs and well-being of others. Some have pointed out the negative effects of individualism on American society, such as rising

---

① Source: Britannica, *Individualism*, Steven M. Lukes.

income inequality and a lack of social mobility.

Despite these criticisms, American individualism remains a core value in American culture and will continue to shape American identity and influence the way Americans view themselves and their role in the world. From the pursuit of the American Dream to the celebration of personal freedom and right, American individualism remains a defining feature of American life.

One of the main ways American individualism has been reflected in literature is through the portrayal of individualistic characters. From the rugged individualism of frontiersmen in works like James Fenimore Cooper's *The Last of the Mohicans* to the entrepreneurial spirit of Jay Gatsby in F. Scott Fitzgerald's *The Great Gatsby*, American literature has celebrated characters who chart their own paths and pursue their own dreams.

Many writers have explored the darker side of individualism, examining how it can lead to isolation, loneliness, and a lack of community. This is evident in works like Nathaniel Hawthorne's *The Scarlet Letter*, where Hester Prynne's individualistic pursuit of personal desires ultimately leads to tragedy.

In addition, American individualism has been examined in the context of larger societal issues. For example, the works of African American writers like James Baldwin and Toni Morrison have explored the tension between individualism and the collective struggle for civil rights. These writers have highlighted how the pursuit of individualism can sometimes be at odds with the larger goals of social justice and equality.

The selected readings in this unit will help readers understand more about American individualism. Benjamin Franklin's *The Autobiography* is a classic work of American literature that reflects the theme of American individualism. Throughout the book, Franklin emphasizes the importance of self-reliance, personal responsibility, and hard work as key components of achieving success in life. *Self-Reliance* is an essay written by Ralph Waldo Emerson in 1841 that emphasizes the importance of individualism, nonconformity in one's life. Emerson thinks that people should trust their own instincts and intuition, rather than conforming to the expectations of others.

Section One: Benjamin Franklin and *The Autobiography*

Benjamin Franklin (1706 — 1790) is one of the founding fathers of the United States. He is an American printer, publisher, author, inventor, scientist and diplomat. Franklin helped draft the Declaration of Independence and American Constitution, representing the United States in France during the American Revolution and was a delegate to the Constitutional Convention. As a very important writer in the colonial period, he is remembered for the wit, wisdom, and elegance of his writing. Franklin's *The Autobiography* stands as a testament to the life and achievements of a remarkable individual who has greatly shaped the course of American history. It provides an intimate glimpse into the mind of a polymathic genius and serves as a source of inspiration for generations to come.

1. Introduction of Benjamin Franklin

Benjamin Franklin was born in a poor family in Boston in 1706. His father, as a poor candlemaker, couldn't provide him with regular schooling. At 12, he was apprenticed to his brother James, a printer. In 1723, he went to Philadelphia and there rose to prominence as a master printer. Through his hard work and talent, he became a famous printer. Later he got a chance to travel around England, which broadened his horizons. He spent two years in London and returned to Philadelphia in 1726. In the days that followed, he made a reputation for himself and accumulated enough wealth through printing. During the outbreak of the American Revolution, he began to get involved in politics and helped draft the Declaration of Independence. In 1778, he persuaded France to make a treaty with the United States to support the American Revolution. He spent his last years in Philadelphia, serving as a member of the Constitutional Convention until his death in 1790.

As a writer Franklin's reputation rests on his two works, *The Autobiography* and *Poor Richard's Almanac*. *The Autobiography* is both an important historical and literary document. It is not only the first autobiography to achieve widespread popularity but after two hundred years remains to be one of the most enduringly popular examples of the genre ever written. As such, it provides not only the story of Franklin's own remarkably influential career but exhibits his self-made success in the context of emerging American nationhood. *The Autobiography* is a major source for exploring Franklin's ideas on wealth, virtue and individuality.

Published in 1733, *Poor Richard's Almanac* contained all sorts of interesting information such as the calendar, weather predictions, sayings, poems and demographics. It also included recipes, advice, aphorisms, and proverbs about industry and frugality. Franklin considered it a vehicle of enlightenment for common people who could not read books in the colonial period. It was a book for the masses and one of the most secular books in the colonies at that time.

2. Introduction of *The Autobiography*

The Autobiography can be broken down into two main halves. The first half was written as a letter to his son, William. The second half was written several years later, but was ultimately never finished due to his death in 1790. *The Autobiography* has since been considered one of the most influential and famous autobiographies of all time.

In this book, Franklin establishes in literary form the first example of the fulfillment of the American Dream through individual work. Today when we think of the American Dream — the ability to rise from rags to riches through hard work — we will usually think of the model set forth by Franklin in *The Autobiography*. Self-reliant individualism is central in *The Autobiography* which not only emphasizes the idea but also helps Americans cultivate their own sense of self-reliance. To Franklin, to be self-reliant is to have self-discipline, to work hard and above all, not to depend on others because the individual has great potential to develop himself materially as well as intellectually. He also advocates for the notion of self-reliant individualism in religion. A person should not confine himself to a certain church. Religion to Franklin simply meant "doing good to others", and "loving mankind". Franklin's self-fashioning celebrates individualism and free will against determinism, but it also shows that everyone is responsible for their own fate and success in life.

3. Reading Material: *The Autobiography* （excerpt）

IX Continuation of the Account of My Life, Begun at Passy, near Paris, 1784

It is some time since I received the above letters, but I have been too busy till now to think of complying with the request they contain. It might, too, be much better done if I were at home among my papers, which would aid my memory, and help to ascertain dates, but my return being uncertain, and having just now a little leisure, I will endeavor to recollect and write what I can; if I live to get home, it may there be corrected and improved.

Not having any copy here of what is already written, I know not whether an account is given of the means I used to establish the Philadelphia public library, which, from a small beginning, is now become so considerable, though I remember to have come down near the time of that transaction (1730). I will therefore begin here with an account of it, which may be struck out if found to have been already given.

At the time I established myself in Pennsylvania, there was not a good bookseller's shop in any of the colonies to the southward of Boston. In New York and Philadelphia, the printers were indeed stationers; they sold only paper, etc., almanacs, ballads, and a few common school books. Those who loved reading were obliged to send for their books from England; the members of the Junto had each a few. We had left the alehouse, where we first met, and hired a room to hold our club in. I proposed that we should all of us bring our books to that room, where they would not only be ready to consult in our conferences, but become a common benefit, each of us being at liberty to borrow such as he wished to read at home. This was accordingly done, and for some time contented us.

Finding the advantage of this little collection, I proposed to render the benefit from books more common, by commencing a public subscription library. I drew a sketch of the plan and rules that would be necessary, and got a skillful conveyancer, Mr. Charles Brockden, to put the whole in form of articles of agreement to be subscribed, by which each subscriber engaged to pay a certain sum down for the first purchase of books, and an annual contribution for increasing them. So few were the readers at that time in Philadelphia, and the majority of us so poor, that I was not able, with great industry, to find more than fifty persons, mostly young tradesmen, willing to pay down for this purpose forty shillings each, and ten shillings per annum. On this little fund we began. The books were imported; the library was opened one day in the week for lending to the subscribers, on their promissory notes to pay double the value if not duly returned. The institution soon manifested its utility, was imitated by other towns, and in other provinces. The libraries were augmented by donations; reading became fashionable; and our people, having no public amusements to divert their attention from study, became better acquainted with books, and in a few years were observed by strangers to be better instructed and more intelligent than people of the same rank generally are in other countries.

When we were about to sign the above-mentioned articles, which were to be binding upon us, our heirs, etc., for fifty years, Mr. Brockden, the scrivener, said to us: "You are young men, but it is scarcely probable that any of you will live to see the expiration of the term fixed in the instrument." A number of us, however, are yet living; but the instrument was after a few years rendered null by a charter that incorporated and gave perpetuity to the company.

The objections and reluctances I met with in soliciting the subscriptions, made me soon feel the impropriety of presenting one's self as the proposer of any useful project, that might be supposed to raise one's reputation in the smallest degree above that of one's neighbors, when one has need of their assistance to accomplish that project. I therefore put myself as much as I could out of sight, and stated it as a scheme of a number of friends, who had requested me to go about and propose it to such as they thought lovers of reading. In this way my affair went on more smoothly, and I ever after practiced it on such occasions; and, from my frequent successes, can heartily recommend it. The present little sacrifice of your vanity will afterwards be amply repaid. If it remains a while uncertain to whom the merit belongs, some one more vain than yourself will be encouraged to claim it, and then even envy will be disposed to do you justice by plucking those assumed feathers, and restoring them to their right owner.

This library afforded me the means of improvement by constant study, for which I set apart an hour or two each day, and thus repaired in some degree the loss of the learned education my father once intended for me. Reading was the only amusement I allowed myself. I spent no time in taverns, games, or frolics of any kind; and my industry in my business continued as indefatigable as it was necessary. I was indebted for my printing house; I had a young family coming on to be educated, and I had to contend with for business two printers, who were established in the place before me. My circumstances, however, grew daily easier. My original habits of frugality continuing, and my father having, among his instructions to me when a boy, frequently repeated a proverb of Solomon, "Seest thou a man diligent in his calling, he shall stand before kings, he shall not stand before mean men," I from thence considered industry as a means of obtaining wealth and distinction, which encouraged me, though I did not think that I should ever literally stand before kings, which, however, has since happened; for I have stood before five, and even had the honor of sitting down with one, the King of Denmark, to dinner.

We have an English proverb that says, "*He that would thrive, must ask his wife*." It was lucky for me that I had one as much disposed to industry and frugality as myself. She assisted me cheerfully in my business, folding and stitching pamphlets, tending shop, purchasing old linen rags for the papermakers, etc. We kept no idle servants, our table was plain and simple, our furniture of the cheapest. For instance, my breakfast was a long-time bread and milk (no tea), and I ate it out of a two-penny earthen porringer, with a pewter spoon. But mark how luxury will enter families, and make a progress, in spite of principle: being called one morning to breakfast, I found it in a china bowl, with a spoon of silver! They had been bought for me without my knowledge by my wife, and had cost her the enormous sum of three-and-twenty shillings, for which she had no other excuse or apology to make, but that she thought her husband deserved a silver spoon and china bowl as well as any of his neighbors. This was the first appearance of plate and china in our house, which afterward, in a course of years, as our wealth increased, augmented gradually to several hundred pounds in value.

I had been religiously educated as a Presbyterian; and tho' some of the dogmas of that persuasion, such as *the eternal decrees of God, election, reprobation, etc.*, appeared to me unintelligible, others doubtful, and I early absented myself from the public assemblies of the sect, Sunday being my studying day, I never was without some religious principles. I never doubted, for instance, the existence of the Deity; that he made the world, and governed it by His Providence; that the most acceptable service of God was the doing good to man; that our souls are immortal; and that all crime will be punished, and virtue rewarded, either here or hereafter. These I esteemed the essentials of every religion; and, being to be found in all the religions we had in our country, I respected them all, tho' with different degrees of respect, as I found them more or less mixed with other articles, which, without any tendency to inspire, promote, or confirm morality, served principally to divide us, and make us unfriendly to one another. This respect to all, with an opinion that the worst had some good effects, induced me to avoid all discourse that might tend to lessen the good opinion another might have of his own religion; and as our province increased in people, and new places of worship were continually wanted, and generally erected by voluntary contributions, my mite for such purpose, whatever might be the sect, was never refused.

Though I seldom attended any public worship, I had still an opinion of its propriety, and of its utility when rightly conducted, and I regularly paid my annual subscription for the support of the only Presbyterian minister or meeting we had in Philadelphia. He used to visit me sometimes as a friend, and admonish me to attend his administrations, and I was now and then prevailed on to do so, once for five Sundays successively. Had he been in my opinion a good preacher, perhaps I might have continued, notwithstanding the occasion I had for the Sunday's leisure in my course of study; but his discourses were chiefly either polemic arguments, or explications of the peculiar doctrines of our sect, and were all to me very dry, uninteresting, and unedifying, since not a single moral principle was inculcated or enforced, their aim seeming to be rather to make us Presbyterians than good citizens.

At length he took for his text that verse of the fourth chapter of Philippians, *"Finally, brethren, whatsoever things are true, honest, just, pure, lovely, or of good report, if there be any virtue, or any praise, think on these things."* And I imagined, in a sermon on such a text, we could not miss of having some morality. But he confined himself to five points only, as meant by the apostle, viz: 1. Keeping holy the Sabbath day. 2. Being diligent in reading the holy Scriptures. 3. Attending duly the public worship. 4. Partaking of the Sacrament. 5. Paying a due respect to God's ministers. These might be all good things; but, as they were not the kind of good things that I expected from that text, I despaired of ever meeting with them from any other, was disgusted, and attended his preaching no more. I had some years before composed a little liturgy, or form of prayer, for my own private use (viz.,1728), entitled, "Articles of Belief and Acts of Religion." I returned to the use of this, and went no more to the public assemblies. My conduct might be blamable, but I leave it, without attempting further to excuse it; my present purpose being to relate facts, and not to make apologies for them.

It was about this time I conceived the bold and arduous project of arriving at moral perfection. I wished to live without committing any fault at any time; I would conquer all that either natural inclination, custom, or company might lead me into. As I knew, or thought I knew, what was right and wrong, I did not see why I might not always do the one and avoid the other. But I soon found I had undertaken a task of more difficulty than I had imagined. While my care was employed in guarding against one fault, I was often surprised by another; habit took the advantage of inattention; inclination was sometimes too strong for reason. I concluded, at length, that the mere speculative conviction that it was our interest to be completely virtuous, was not sufficient to prevent our slipping; and that the contrary habits must be broken, and good ones acquired and established, before we can have any dependence on a steady, uniform rectitude of conduct. For this purpose, I therefore contrived the following method.

In the various enumerations of the moral virtues I had met with in my reading, I found the catalogue more or less numerous, as different writers included more or fewer ideas under the same name. Temperance, for example, was by some confined to eating and drinking, while by others it was extended to mean moderating every other pleasure, appetite, inclination, or passion, bodily or mental, even to our avarice and ambition. I proposed to myself, for the sake of clearness, to use rather more names, with fewer ideas annexed to each, than a few names with more ideas; and I included under thirteen names of virtues all that at that time occurred to me as necessary or desirable, and annexed to each a short precept, which fully expressed the extent I gave to its meaning.

These names of virtues, with their precepts, were:

1. TEMPERANCE. Eat not to dullness; drink not to elevation.

2. SILENCE. Speak not but what may benefit others or yourself; avoid trifling conversation.

3. ORDER. Let all your things have their places; let each part of your business have its time.

4. RESOLUTION. Resolve to perform what you ought; perform without fail what you resolve.

5. FRUGALITY. Make no expense but to do good to others or yourself; i.e., waste nothing.

6. INDUSTRY. Lose no time; be always employed in something useful; cut off all unnecessary actions.

7. SINCERITY. Use no hurtful deceit; think innocently and justly, and, if you speak, speak accordingly.

8. JUSTICE. Wrong none by doing injuries, or omitting the benefits that are your duty.

9. MODERATION. Avoid extremes; forbear resenting injuries so much as you think they deserve.

10. CLEANLINESS. Tolerate no uncleanliness in body, clothes, or habitation.

11. TRANQUILLITY. Be not disturbed at trifles, or at accidents common or unavoidable.

12. CHASTITY. Rarely use venery but for health or offspring, never to dullness, weakness, or the injury of your own or another's peace or reputation.

13. HUMILITY. Imitate Jesus and Socrates.

My intention being to acquire the habitude of all these virtues, I judged it would be well not to distract my attention by attempting the whole at once, but to fix it on one of them at a time; and, when I should be master of that, then to proceed to another, and so on, till I should have gone through the thirteen; and, as the previous acquisition of some might facilitate the acquisition of certain others, I arranged them with that view, as they stand above. Temperance first, as it tends to procure that coolness and clearness of head, which is so necessary where constant vigilance was to be kept up, and guard maintained against the unremitting attraction of ancient habits, and the force of perpetual temptations. This being acquired and established, Silence would be more easy; and my desire being to gain knowledge at the same time that I improved in virtue, and considering that in conversation it was obtained rather by the use of the ears than of the tongue, and therefore wishing to break a habit I was getting into of prattling, punning, and joking, which only made me acceptable to trifling company, I gave Silence the second place. This and the next, Order, I expected would allow me more time for attending to my project and my studies. Resolution, once become habitual, would keep me firm in my endeavors to obtain all the subsequent virtues; Frugality and Industry freeing me from my remaining debt, and producing affluence and independence, would make more easier the practice of Sincerity and Justice, etc., Conceiving, then, that, agreeably to the advice of Pythagoras in his Golden Verses, daily examination would be necessary, I contrived the following method for conducting that examination.

I made a little book, in which I allotted a page for each of the virtues. I ruled each page with red ink, so as to have seven columns, one for each day of the week, marking each column with a letter for the day. I crossed these columns with thirteen red lines, marking the beginning of each line with the first letter of one of the virtues, on which line, and in its proper column, I might mark, by a little black spot, every fault I found upon examination to have been committed respecting that virtue upon that day.

Form of the pages

	S	M	T	W	T	F	S
T							
S	★	★		★		★	
O	★★	★	★		★	★	★
R			★			★	
F		★			★		
I			★				
S							

continued

	S	M	T	W	T	F	S
J							
M							
C							
T							
C							
H							

I determined to give a week's strict attention to each of the virtues successively. Thus, in the first week, my great guard was to avoid the least offence against Temperance, leaving the other virtues to their ordinary chance, only marking every evening the faults of the day. Thus, if in the first week I could keep my first line, marked T, clear of spots, I supposed the habit of that virtue so much strengthened and its opposite weakened, that I might venture extending my attention to include the next, and for the following week keep both lines clear of spots. Proceeding thus to the last, I could go through a course compleat in thirteen weeks, and four courses in a year. And like him who, having a garden to weed, does not attempt to eradicate all the bad herbs at once, which would exceed his reach and his strength, but works on one of the beds at a time, and, having accomplished the first, proceeds to a second, so I should have, I hoped, the encouraging pleasure of seeing on my pages the progress I made in virtue, by clearing successively my lines of their spots, till in the end, by a number of courses, I should be happy in viewing a clean book, after a thirteen weeks daily examination...

I entered upon the execution of this plan for self-examination, and continued it with occasional intermissions for some time. I was surprised to find myself so much fuller of faults than I had imagined; but I had the satisfaction of seeing them diminish. To avoid the trouble of renewing now and then my little book, which, by scraping out the marks on the paper of old faults to make room for new ones in a new course, became full of holes, I transferred my tables and precepts to the ivory leaves of a memorandum book, on which the lines were drawn with red ink, that made a durable stain, and on those lines I marked my faults with a black-lead pencil, which marks I could easily wipe out with a wet sponge. After a while I went through one course only in a year, and afterward only one in several years, till at length I omitted them entirely, being employed in voyages and business abroad, with a multiplicity of affairs that interfered; but I always carried my little book with me.

My scheme of ORDER gave me the most trouble; and I found that, though it might be practicable where a man's business was such as to leave him the disposition of his time, that of a journeyman printer, for instance, it was not possible to be exactly observed by a master, who must mix with the world, and often receive people of business at their own hours. Order, too, with regard to places for things, papers, etc., I found extremely difficult to acquire. I had not been early accustomed to it, and, having an exceeding good memory, I was not so sensible of the inconvenience attending want of method. This article, therefore, cost me so much painful attention, and my faults in it vexed me so much, and I made so little progress in amendment, and had such frequent relapses, that I was almost ready to give up the attempt, and content myself with a faulty character in that respect, like the man who, in buying an ax of a smith, my neighbor, desired to have the whole of its surface as bright as the edge. The smith consented to grind it bright for him if he would turn the wheel; he turned, while the smith pressed the broad face of the ax hard and heavily on the stone, which made the turning of it very fatiguing. The man came every now and then from the wheel to see how the work went on, and at length would take his ax as it was, without farther grinding. "No," said the smith, "turn on, turn on; we shall have it bright by-and-by; as yet, it is only speckled." "Yes," said the man, "but I think I like a speckled ax best." And I believe this may have been the case with many, who, having, for want of some such means as I employed, found the difficulty of obtaining good and breaking bad habits in other points of vice and virtue, have given up the struggle, and concluded that "a speckled ax was best"; for something, that pretended to be reason, was every now and then suggesting to me that such extreme nicety as I exacted of myself might be a kind of foppery in morals, which, if it were known, would make me ridiculous; that a perfect character might be attended with the inconvenience of being envied and hated; and that a benevolent man should allow a few faults in himself, to keep his friends in countenance.

In truth, I found myself incorrigible with respect to Order; and now I am grown old, and my memory bad, I feel very sensibly the want of it. But, on the whole, though I never arrived at the perfection I had been so ambitious of obtaining, but fell far short of it, yet I was, by the endeavor, a better and a happier man than I otherwise should have been if I had not attempted it; as those who aim at perfect writing by imitating the engraved copies, though they never reach the wished-for excellence of those copies, their hand is mended by the endeavor, and is tolerable while it continues fair and legible.

It may be well my posterity should be informed that to this little artifice, with the blessing of God, their ancestor owed the constant felicity of his life, down to his 79th year, in which this is written. What reverses may attend the remainder is in the hand of Providence; but, if they arrive, the reflection on past happiness enjoyed ought to help his bearing them with more resignation. To Temperance he ascribes his long-continued health, and what is still left to him of a good constitution; to Industry and Frugality, the early easiness of his circumstances and acquisition of his fortune, with all that knowledge that enabled him to be a useful citizen, and obtained for him some degree of reputation among the learned; to Sincerity and Justice, the confidence of his country, and the honorable employs it conferred upon him; and to the joint influence of the whole mass of the virtues, even in the imperfect state he was able to acquire them, all that evenness of temper, and that cheerfulness in conversation, which makes his company still sought for, and agreeable even to his younger acquaintance. I hope, therefore, that some of my descendants may follow the example and reap the benefit.

It will be remarked that, though my scheme was not wholly without religion, there was in it no mark of any of the distinguishing tenets of any particular sect. I had purposely avoided them; for, being fully persuaded of the utility and excellency of my method, and that it might be serviceable to people in all religions, and intending some time or other to publish it, I would not have any thing in it that should prejudice any one, of any sect, against it. I purposed writing a little comment on each virtue, in which I would have shown the advantages of possessing it, and the mischiefs attending its opposite vice; and I should have called my book *The Art of Virtue*, because it would have shown the means and manner of obtaining virtue, which would have distinguished it from the mere exhortation to be good, that does not instruct and indicate the means, but is like the apostle's man of verbal charity, who only without showing to the naked and hungry how or where they might get clothes or victuals, exhorted them to be fed and clothed.

But it so happened that my intention of writing and publishing this comment was never fulfilled. I did, indeed, from time to time, put down short hints of the sentiments, reasonings, etc., to be made use of in it, some of which I have still by me; but the necessary close attention to private business in the earlier part of thy life, and public business since, have occasioned my postponing it; for, it being connected in my mind with a great and extensive project, that required the whole man to execute, and which an unforeseen succession of employs prevented my attending to, it has hitherto remained unfinished.

In this piece it was my design to explain and enforce this doctrine, that vicious actions are not hurtful because they are forbidden, but forbidden because they are hurtful, the nature of man alone considered; that it was, therefore, everyone's interest to be virtuous who wished to be happy even in this world; and I should, from this circumstance (there being always in the world a number of rich merchants, nobility, states, and princes, who have need of honest instruments for the management of their affairs, and such being so rare), have endeavored to convince young persons that no qualities were so likely to make a poor man's fortune as those of probity and integrity.

My list of virtues contained at first but twelve; but a Quaker friend having kindly informed me that I was generally thought proud; that my pride showed itself frequently in conversation; that I was not content with being in the right when discussing any point, but was overbearing, and rather insolent, of which he convinced me by mentioning several instances; I determined endeavoring to cure myself, if I could, of this vice or folly among the rest, and I added Humility to my list giving an extensive meaning to the word.

I cannot boast of much success in acquiring the reality of this virtue, but I had a good deal with regard to the appearance of it. I made it a rule to forbear all direct contradiction to the sentiments of others, and all positive assertion of my own. I even forbid myself, agreeably to the old laws of our Junto, the use of every word or expression in the language that imported a fixed opinion, such as certainly, undoubtedly, etc., and I adopted, instead of them, I conceive, I apprehend, or I imagine a thing to be so or so; or it so appears to me at present. When another asserted something that I thought an error, I denied myself the pleasure of contradicting him abruptly, and of showing immediately some absurdity in his proposition; and in answering I began by observing that in certain cases or circumstances his opinion would be right, but in the present case there appeared or seemed to me some difference, etc. I soon found the advantage of this change in my manner; the conversations I engaged in went on more pleasantly. The modest way in which I proposed my opinions procured them a readier reception and less contradiction; I had less mortification when I was found to be in the wrong, and I more easily prevailed with others to give up their mistakes and join with me when I happened to be in the right.

And this mode, which I at first put on with some violence to natural inclination, became at length so easy, and so habitual to me, that perhaps for these fifty years past no one has ever heard a dogmatical expression escape me. And to this habit (after my character of integrity) I think it principally owing that I had early so much weight with my fellow–citizens when I proposed new institutions, or alterations in the old, and so much influence in public councils when I became a member; for I was but a bad speaker, never eloquent, subject to much hesitation in my choice of words, hardly correct in language, and yet I generally carried my points.

In reality, there is, perhaps, no one of our natural passions so hard to subdue as pride. Disguise it, struggle with it, beat it down, stifle it, mortify it as much as one pleases, it is still alive, and will every now and then peep out and show itself; you will see it, perhaps, often in this history; for, even if I could conceive that I had completely overcome it, I should probably be proud of my humility.

4. Questions for Discussion

(1) What kinds of virtues are mentioned in the except? How do you understand them?

(2) How is Franklin's individualism represented in the except?

Section Two: Ralph Waldo Emerson and *Self-Reliance*

Ralph Waldo Emerson (1803—1882) was a very important writer in the 19th century. He was an American essayist, lecturer, philosopher, abolitionist and poet. He was regarded as a leader of transcendentalism and the champion of American individualism. *Self-Reliance* remains one of Emerson's most well-known and celebrated works, embodying the core principles of American Transcendentalism.

1. Introduction of Ralph Waldo Emerson

Ralph Waldo Emerson was born in a minister's family in Boston, in the year of 1803, He graduated from Harvard University at the age of 18 and taught in Boston for three years. In 1829, he became a minister of the Second Church of Boston and married Ellen Tucker. But unfortunately, his wife died 17 months later. In 1832, he left for England and France and made friends with famous writers like William Wordsworth and Taylor Coleridge. In 1833, he returned to the United States and settled in Concord, Massachusetts.

Emerson produced a lot of important works in his life. His most original and significant work is *Nature* which, published in 1836, offers the essence of his philosophical ideas. He opposed popular materialism and Calvinism, calling for individual freedom and independence. He delivered a speech The American Scholar before the Phi Beta Kappa Society of Harvard, which is a college fraternity composed of the first twenty-five men in each graduating class. In the speech, he called on American writers to be independent and opposed the imitation of British writers' styles and topics.

Emerson died on April 27, 1882, in Concord. His beliefs and idealism have strong influences on the works of his contemporary writers like Henry David Thoreau and Walt Whitman, as well as numerous others. His writings are considered major documents of 19th-century American literature, religion and thought.

2. Introduction of *Self-Reliance*

Published first in 1841 in *Essays* and then in the 1847 revised edition of *Essays*, *Self-Reliance* took shape over a long period of time. Throughout his life, Emerson kept detailed journals of his thoughts and actions and returned to them as a source for many of his essays. Such is the case with *Self-Reliance*, which includes materials from journal entries dating as far back as 1832. In addition to his journals, Emerson drew on various lectures he delivered between 1836 and 1839.

The essay has three major divisions: the importance of self-reliance (paragraphs1 – 17), self-reliance and the individual (paragraphs 18 – 32), and self-reliance and society (paragraphs 33 – 50). As a whole, it promotes self-reliance as an ideal, even a virtue, and contrasts it with various modes of dependence or conformity. In his essay, Emerson defines individualism as a profound and unshakable trust in one's own intuitions. Embracing this view of individualism, he asserts, can revolutionize society, not through a sweeping mass movement, but through the transformation of individual life at a time and through the creation of leaders capable of greatness.

In the essay, he urges his readers to follow their individual will instead of conforming to social expectations. Emerson considers self-reliance as an ideal. He believes that one should trust himself, be confident and responsible for his own choice. He believes that in every man, there is the potential for great genius and contribution, but that potential can only be realized through individualism and embracing one's own strengths and instincts.

3. Reading Material: *Self-Reliance* (excerpt)

I read the other day some verses written by an eminent painter which were original and not conventional. The soul always hears an admonition in such lines, let the subject be what it may. The sentiment they instill is of more value than any thought they may contain. To believe your own thought, to believe that what is true for you in your private heart is true for all men, that is genius. Speak your latent conviction, and it shall be the universal sense; for the inmost in due time becomes the outmost, and our first thought is rendered back to us by the trumpets of the Last Judgment. Familiar as the voice of the mind is to each, the highest merit we ascribe to Moses, Plato, and Milton is, that they set at naught books and traditions, and spoke not what men but what they thought. A man should learn to detect and watch that gleam of light which flashes across his mind from within, more than the luster of the firmament of bards and sages. Yet he dismisses without notice his thought, because it is his. In every work of genius, we recognize our own rejected thoughts: they come back to us with a certain alienated majesty. Great works of art have no more affecting lesson for us than this. They teach us to abide by our spontaneous impression with good-humored inflexibility then most when the whole cry of voices is on the other side. Else, tomorrow a stranger will say with masterly good sense precisely what we have thought and felt all the time, and we shall be forced to take with shame our own opinion from another.

There is a time in every man's education when he arrives at the conviction that envy is ignorance; that imitation is suicide; that he must take himself for better, for worse, as his portion; that though the wide universe is full of good, no kernel of nourishing corn can come to him but through his toil bestowed on that plot of ground which is given to him to till. The power which resides in him is new in nature, and none but he knows what that is which he can do, nor does he know until he has tried. Not for nothing one face, one character, one fact, makes much impression on him, and another none. This sculpture in the memory is not without pre-established harmony. The eye was placed where one ray should fall, that it might testify of that particular ray. We but half express ourselves, and are ashamed of that divine idea which each of us represents. It may be safely trusted as proportionate and of good issues, so it be faithfully imparted, but God will not have his work made manifest by cowards. A man is relieved and gay when he has put his heart into his work and done his best; but what he has said or done otherwise, shall give him no peace. It is a deliverance which does not deliver. In the attempt his genius deserts him; no muse befriends; no invention, no hope.

Trust thyself: every heart vibrates to that iron string. Accept the place the divine providence has found for you, the society of your contemporaries, the connection of events. Great men have always done so, and confided themselves childlike to the genius of their age, betraying their perception that the absolutely trustworthy was seated at their heart, working through their hands, predominating in all their being. And we are now men, and must accept in the highest mind the same transcendent destiny; and not minors and invalids in a protected corner, not cowards fleeing before a revolution, but guides, redeemers, and benefactors, obeying the Almighty effort, and advancing on Chaos and the Dark.

What pretty oracles nature yields us on this text, in the face and behavior of children, babes, and even brutes! That divided and rebel mind, that distrust of a sentiment because our arithmetic has computed the strength and means opposed to our purpose, these have not. Their mind being whole, their eye is as yet unconquered, and when we look in their faces, we are disconcerted. Infancy conforms to nobody: all conform to it, so that one babe commonly makes four or five out of the adults who prattle and play to it. So, God has armed youth and puberty and manhood no less with its own piquancy and charm, and made it enviable and gracious and its claims not to be put by, if it will stand by itself. Do not think the youth has no force, because he cannot speak to you and me. Hark! In the next room his voice is sufficiently clear and emphatic. It seems he knows how to speak to his contemporaries. Bashful or bold, then, he will know how to make us seniors very unnecessary.

The nonchalance of boys who are sure of a dinner, and would disdain as much as a lord to do or say aught to conciliate one, is the healthy attitude of human nature. A boy is in the parlor what the pit is in the playhouse; independent, irresponsible, looking out from his corner on such people and facts as pass by, he tries and sentences them on their merits, in the swift, summary way of boys, as good, bad, interesting, silly, eloquent, troublesome. He cumbers himself never about consequences, about interests; he gives an independent, genuine verdict. You must court him: he does not court you. But the man is, as it were, clapped into jail by his consciousness. As soon as he has once acted or spoken with eclat, he is a committed person, watched by the sympathy or the hatred of hundreds, whose affections must now enter into his account. There is no Lethe for this. Ah, that he could pass again into his neutrality! Who can thus avoid all pledges, and having observed, observe again from the same unaffected, unbiased, unbribable, affrighted innocence, must always be formidable. He would utter opinions on all passing affairs, which being seen to be not private, but necessary, would sink like darts into the ear of men, and put them in fear.

These are the voices which we hear in solitude, but they grow faint and inaudible as we enter into the world. Society everywhere is in conspiracy against the manhood of every one of its members. Society is a joint-stock company, in which the members agree, for the better securing of his bread to each shareholder, to surrender the liberty and culture of the eater. The virtue in most request is conformity. Self-reliance is its aversion. It loves not realities and creators, but names and customs.

Whoso would be a man must be a nonconformist. He who would gather immortal palms must not be hindered by the name of goodness, but must explore if it be goodness. Nothing is at last sacred but the integrity of your own mind. Absolve you to yourself, and you shall have the suffrage of the world. I remember an answer which when quite young I was prompted to make to a valued adviser, who was wont to importune me with the dear old doctrines of the church. On my saying, what have I to do with the sacredness of traditions, if I live wholly from within? My friend suggested — "But these impulses may be from below, not from above." I replied, "They do not seem to me to be such; but if I am the Devil's child, I will live then from the Devil." No law can be sacred to me but that of my nature. Good and bad are but names very readily transferable to that or this; the only right is what is after my constitution, the only wrong what is against it. A man is to carry himself in the presence of all opposition, as if everything were titular and ephemeral but he. I am ashamed to think how easily we capitulate to badges and names, to large societies and dead institutions. Every decent and well-spoken individual affects and sways me more than is right. I ought to go upright and vital, and speak the rude truth in all ways. If malice and vanity wear the coat of philanthropy, shall that pass? If an angry bigot assumes this bountiful cause of Abolition, and comes to me with his last news from Barbadoes, why should I not say to him, "Go love thy infant; love thy wood-chopper: be good-natured and modest: have that grace; and never varnish your hard, uncharitable ambition with this incredible tenderness for black folk a thousand miles off.

Thy love afar is spite at home." Rough and graceless would be such greeting, but truth is handsomer than the affectation of love. Your goodness must have some edge to it, — else it is none. The doctrine of hatred must be preached as the counteraction of the doctrine of love when that pules and whines. I shun father and mother and wife and brother, when my genius calls me. I would write on the lintels of the door-post, *Whim*. I hope it is somewhat better than whim at last, but we cannot spend the day in explanation. Expect me not to show cause why I seek or why I exclude company. Then, again, do not tell me, as a good man did today, of my obligation to put all poor men in good situations. Are they my poor? I tell thee, thou foolish philanthropist, that I grudge the dollar, the dime, the cent, I give to such men as do not belong to me and to whom I do not belong. There is a class of persons to whom by all spiritual affinity I am bought and sold; for them I will go to prison, if need be; but your miscellaneous popular charities; the education at college of fools; the building of meeting-houses to the vain end to which many now stand; alms to sots; and the thousandfold Relief Societies; though I confess with shame I sometimes succumb and give the dollar, it is a wicked dollar which by and by I shall have the manhood to withhold.

Virtues are, in the popular estimate, rather the exception than the rule. There is the man and his virtues. Men do what is called a good action, as some piece of courage or charity, much as they would pay a fine in expiation of daily non-appearance on parade. Their works are done as an apology or extenuation of their living in the world — as invalids and the insane pay a high board. Their virtues are penances. I do not wish to expiate, but to live. My life is for itself and not for a spectacle. I much prefer that it should be of a lower strain, so it be genuine and equal, than that it should be glittering and unsteady. I wish it to be sound and sweet, and not to need diet and bleeding. I ask primary evidence that you are a man, and refuse this appeal from the man to his actions. I know that for myself it makes no difference whether I do or forbear those actions which are reckoned excellent. I cannot consent to pay for a privilege where I have intrinsic right. Few and mean as my gifts may be, I actually am, and do not need for my own assurance or the assurance of my fellows any secondary testimony.

What I must do is all that concerns me, not what the people think. This rule, equally arduous in actual and in intellectual life, may serve for the whole distinction between greatness and meanness. It is the harder, because you will always find those who think they know what is your duty better than you know it. It is easy in the world to live after the world's opinion; it is easy in solitude to live after our own; but the great man is he who in the midst of the crowd keeps with perfect sweetness the independence of solitude.

The objection to conforming to usages that have become dead to you is, that it scatters your force. It loses your time and blurs the impression of your character. If you maintain a dead church, contribute to a dead Bible-society vote with a great party either for the government or against it, spread your table like base housekeepers — under all these screens I have difficulty to detect the precise man you are. And, of course, so much force is withdrawn from your proper life. But do your work, and I shall know you. Do your work, and you shall reinforce yourself. A man must consider what a bindman's-buff is this game of conformity. If I know your sect, I anticipate your argument. I hear a preacher announce for his text and topic the expediency of one of the institutions of his church. Do I not know beforehand that not possibly can he say a new and spontaneous word? Do I not know that, with all this ostentation of examining the grounds of the institution, he will do no such thing? Do I not know that he is pledged to himself not to look but at one side, — the permitted side, not as a man, but as a parish minister? He is a retained attorney, and these airs of the bench are the emptiest affectation. Well, most men have bound their eyes with one or another handkerchief, and attached themselves to some one of these communities of opinion. This conformity makes them not false in a few particulars, authors of a few lies, but false in all particulars. Their every truth is not quite true. Their two is not the real two, their four not the real four; so that every word they say chagrins us, and we know not where to begin to set them right. Meantime nature is not slow to equip us in the prison-uniform of the party to which we adhere. We come to wear one cut of face and figure, and acquire by degrees the gentlest asinine expression. There is a mortifying experience in particular, which does not fail to wreak itself also in the general history; I mean "the foolish face of praise," the forced smile which we put on in company where we do not feel at ease in answer to conversation which does not interest us. The muscles, not spontaneously moved, but moved by a low usurping willfulness, grow tight about the outline of the face with the most disagreeable sensation.

For nonconformity the world whips you with its displeasure. And therefore, a man must know how to estimate a sour face. The by-standers look askance on him in the public street or in the friend's parlor. If this aversion had its origin in contempt and resistance like his own, he might well go home with a sad countenance; but the sour faces of the multitude, like their sweet faces, have no deep cause, but are put on and off as the wind blows and a newspaper directs. Yet is the discontent of the multitude more formidable than that of the senate and the college. It is easy enough for a firm man who knows the world to brook the rage of the cultivated classes. Their rage is decorous and prudent, for they are timid as being very vulnerable themselves. But when to their feminine rage the indignation of the people is added, when the ignorant and the poor are aroused, when the unintelligent brute force that lies at the bottom of society is made to growl and mow, it needs the habit of magnanimity and religion to treat it godlike as a trifle of no concernment.

The other terror that scares us from self-trust is our consistency; a reverence for our past act or word, because the eyes of others have no other data for computing our orbit than our past acts, and we are loath to disappoint them.

But why should you keep your head over your shoulder? Why drag about this corpse of your memory, lest you contradict somewhat you have stated in this or that public place? Suppose you should contradict yourself; what then? It seems to be a rule of wisdom never to rely on your memory alone, scarcely even in acts of pure memory, but to bring the past for judgment into the thousand-eyed present, and live ever in a new day. In your metaphysics you have denied personality to the Deity: yet when the devout motions of the soul come, yield to them heart and life, though they should clothe God with shape and color. Leave your theory, as Joseph his coat in the hand of the harlot, and flee.

A foolish consistency is the hobgoblin of little minds, adored by little statesmen and philosophers and divines. With consistency a great soul has simply nothing to do. He may as well concern himself with his shadow on the wall. Speak what you think now in hard words and to-morrow speak what to-wall. Speak what you think now in hard words, and tomorrow speak what tomorrow thinks in hard words again, though it contradicts everything you said today. —"Ah, so you shall be sure to be misunderstood." — Is it so bad, then, to be misunderstood? Pythagoras was misunderstood, and Socrates, and Jesus, and Luther, and Copernicus, and Galileo, and Newton, and every pure and wise spirit that ever took flesh. To be great is to be misunderstood.

4. Questions for Discussion

(1) How do you understand the following sentences in terms of American individualism?

1) To believe your own thought, to believe that what is true for you in your private heart is true for all men — that is genius.

2) A man should learn to detect and watch that gleam of light which flashes across his mind from within.

3) A man is relieved and gay when he has put his heart into his work and done his best; but what he has said or done otherwise shall give him no peace.

(2) Use the examples given in the text to illustrate Emerson's statement "To be great is to be misunderstood".

(3) What does Ralph Waldo Emerson mean by "Whoso would be a man must be a nonconformist"?

(4) What was Emerson's opinion on consistency and conformity?

Chapter 2 American Dream

American Dream is a term coined by James Truslow Adams in 1931. In his book, *The Epic of America*, he points out that life should be better and richer and fuller for everyone, with opportunity for each according to ability or achievement regardless of social class or circumstances of birth. Lionell Trilling wrote in his book *Liberal Imagination*, "Ours is the only nation that prides itself upon a dream and gives its name to one, 'the American Dream'"(252).

Jennifer Hochschild defines the American Dream as a set of "tenets about achieving success". (15) As a national ethos, it consists of a set of ideals, including democracy, equal rights, liberty, opportunity and freedom. Everybody should have the equal opportunity to get rich and become prosperous and successful as long as he works hard. The social upward mobility is also available for everyone whatever you are men or women, black, or white or from other ethnic origin.

American dream is guaranteed by American Declaration of Independence and American Constitution. It is essentially an idea that suggests anyone in the US can succeed through hard work and has the potential to lead a happy, successful life. Many people have expanded the definition to include things such as freedom, fulfillment and meaningful relationships. Critics also point out the vague and deceptive nature of American dream. As Bloom said "The major American writers who have engaged the dream — Emerson, Whitman, Thoreau, Mark Twain, Henry James, Willa Cather, Robert Frost, Wallace Stevens, Ernest Hemingway, Scott Fitzgerald, Hart Crane — have been aware of this haziness and of attendant ironies (Introduction xv)". Critics often point out some examples of inequality rooted in class, race, religion and ethnicity that suggest that the American dream is not attainable for everyone. This is especially important for immigrants, because many of them fled extremely difficult circumstances in their native countries to seek a new life in the US.

Despite its enduring appeal, the American Dream has also been subject to criticism and scrutiny. Blooms have called this "American Nightmare" (xv). Some argue that it is a myth that obscures the reality of economic inequality and social injustice in America, and that it perpetuates a culture of individualism and competition at the expense of community and cooperation. Others argue that the American Dream is still achievable for those who are willing to work hard and seize opportunities, but it requires systemic changes to address issues such as income inequality, access to education, and racial and gender discrimination.

The American Dream and American literature have a long and intertwined history. American literature has often reflected and challenged the idea of the American Dream, exploring the complexities of achieving success and the costs and consequences of pursuing it.

From the early colonial period to the present day, American writers have explored the themes of individualism, self-reliance, and the pursuit of success. One of the earliest examples is the Puritan literature of the 17th century, which emphasized the importance of hard work, frugality, and moral virtue as a means of achieving success and salvation.

The 19th century saw the rise of Romanticism in American literature, which celebrated individualism, imagination, and the natural world. Writers such as Ralph Waldo Emerson, Henry David Thoreau, and Walt Whitman have explored the ideas of the self-made man and the importance of following one's own path in life.

In the 20th century, American literature continued to grapple with the complexities of the American Dream. *The Great Gatsby* by Francis Scott Fitzgerald, published in 1925, is perhaps the most famous novel about the American Dream. The novel explores the corruption and disillusionment that may accompany the pursuit of wealth and status.

The 1950s and 1960s saw the rise of the Beat Generation and the counterculture movement, which rejected mainstream American values and embraced a more rebellious and unconventional way of life. Writers such as Jack Kerouac, Allen Ginsberg, and William S. Burroughs explored themes of nonconformity, freedom, and individualism in their works.

In recent years, American literature has continued to explore the complexities of the American Dream, particularly in the context of issues such as race, class, and gender. Writers such as Toni Morrison, James Baldwin, and Ta-Nehisi Coates have explored the ways in which systemic inequality can make the American Dream more difficult, if not impossible, to achieve for certain groups of people.

In conclusion, the American Dream and American literature have been closely intertwined throughout American history. American literature has explored the complexities of achieving success and the costs and consequences of pursuing it, and has challenged and critiqued the idea of the American Dream in various ways. Through its exploration of these themes, American literature has helped to shape and define the American Dream, both as a concept and as a lived reality.

Section One: Ta-Nehisi Coates and *Between the World and Me*

Ta-Nehisi Coates is a renowned author, journalist, and social commentator who has gained recognition for his insightful and thought-provoking writings on issues of race, politics, and social justice in America. Howard Rambsy Ⅱ (a famous professor of literature) praised him for his wide acceptance and commented that "Rarely has a book by a black writer generated so much attention in the young twenty-first century" (196). *Between the World and Me* is a critically acclaimed book by Ta-Nehisi Coates, published in 2015. It is a profound and impassioned exploration of race, power, and identity in America, shedding light on the Black experience and fostering a deeper understanding of the complexities of race in modern society.

1. Introduction of Ta-Nehisi Coates

Ta-Nehisi Coates was born on September 30, 1975, in Baltimore, Maryland, and grew up in a predominantly African-American community that was marked by poverty, violence and social inequality.

Coates began his career as a journalist, writing for a number of publications, including *The Village Voice, The Atlantic, and The Washington Post.* His writing on topics such as race relations, police brutality, and the legacy of slavery in America garnered widespread attention and critical acclaim, earning him numerous awards and accolades.

In 2015, Coates published his first book, *Between the World and Me,* which was a finalist for the National Book Award and won the National Book Critics Circle Award. The book is written as a letter to his teenage son, and explores the experiences of being a Black man in America, drawing on Coates' own experiences and the history of racism and oppression in the country.

Coates has since published several other books, including *We Were Eight Years in Power: An American Tragedy*, which examines the legacy of the Obama presidency in the context of racial politics in America, and *The Water Dancer,* a novel that combines elements of historical fiction and magical realism to tell the story of a young enslaved man who escapes from a plantation.

Throughout his career, Coates has been a powerful and influential voice in discussions of race and social justice in America, challenging his readers to confront uncomfortable truths and to engage with the difficult work of creating a more just and equitable society.

2. Introduction of *Between the World and Me*

Between the World and Me is a critically acclaimed book by Ta-Nehisi Coates, published in 2015. It is written as a letter from Coates to his teenage son, Samori, and explores the experiences of being a Black man in America. The book is a deeply personal meditation on race, violence, and identity, drawing on Coates' own experiences of growing up in Baltimore and his observations of the racial dynamics of American society. (a professor of African literature) called this book a "black protest novel" and commented that the book "is structured as Coates's letter to his son in the wake of a series of state-sanctioned violent assaults against black people, from Marlene Pinnock to Tamir Rice to Eric Garner. The book was met with near unprecedented success. It was easily among the most talked-about and widely reviewed books of 2015; it won the National Book Award for nonfiction; and Coates received a MacArthur Fellowship not long after its publication" (Williams 180).

The book is structured around three parts, each of which focuses on a different aspect of the Black experience in America. In the first part, Coates reflects on the physical and emotional violence that Black people face in America, from police brutality to the legacy of slavery and segregation. In the second part, he discusses the impact of American history on the Black experience, exploring the role of slavery, segregation, and discrimination in shaping the lives of Black people in America. In the final part, Coates reflects on the importance of community, family, and culture in the face of systemic racism and oppression. The book won the National Book Award for Nonfiction in 2015, and has since become a seminal work in discussions of race and social justice in America.

Between the World and Me offers a scathing critique of the American Dream and its failure to provide equal opportunities and justice to Black people. Coates argues that the American Dream, which promises a land of freedom and equality, has never truly existed for Black people in America.

In the book, Coates repeatedly emphasizes the ways in which Black people have been denied access to the American Dream. He also highlights the violence and police brutality that have been used to maintain the systemic inequalities, and argues that the American Dream has always been a myth for Black people.

Coates is particularly critical of the idea that hard work and perseverance will lead to success in America, which is a central tenet of the American Dream. He argues that this idea ignores the systemic barriers that have been put in place to prevent Black people from achieving success. He also notes that even when Black people have achieved success, they are still subject to racism and discrimination, and are never truly free from the threat of violence and oppression.

3. Reading Material*: Between the World and Me* (excerpt)

Son,

Last Sunday the host of a popular news show asked me what it meant to lose my body. The host was broadcasting from Washington, D.C., and I was seated in a remote studio on the far west side of Manhattan. A satellite closed the miles between us, but no machinery could close the gap between her world and the world for which I had been summoned to speak. When the host asked me about my body, her face faded from the screen, and was replaced by a scroll of words, written by me earlier that week.

The host read these words for the audience, and when she finished, she turned to the subject of my body, although she did not mention it specifically. But by now I am accustomed to intelligent people asking about the condition of my body without realizing the nature of their request. Specifically, the host wished to know why I felt that white America's progress, or rather the progress of those Americans who believe that they are white, was built on looting and violence. Hearing this, I felt an old and indistinct sadness well up in me. The answer to this question is the record of the believers themselves. The answer is American history.

There is nothing extreme in this statement. Americans deify democracy in a way that allows for a dim awareness that they have, from time to time, stood in defiance of their God. But democracy is a forgiving God and America's heresies — torture, theft, enslavement — are so common among individuals and nations that none can declare themselves immune. In fact, Americans, in a real sense, have never betrayed their God. When Abraham Lincoln declared, in 1863, that the battle of Gettysburg must ensure "that government of the people, by the people, for the people, shall not perish from the earth," he was not merely being aspirational; at the onset of the Civil War, the United States of America had one of the highest rates of suffrage in the world. The question is not whether Lincoln truly meant "government of the people" but what our country has, throughout its history, taken the political term "people" to actually mean. In 1863 it did not mean your mother or your grandmother, and it did not mean you and me. Thus, America's problem is not its betrayal of "government of the people," but the means by which "the people" acquired their names.

This leads us to another equally important ideal, one that Americans implicitly accept but to which they make no conscious claim. Americans believe in the reality of "race" as a defined, indubitable feature of the natural world. Racism — the need to ascribe bone-deep features to people and then humiliate, reduce, and destroy them — inevitably follows from this inalterable condition. In this way, racism is rendered as the innocent daughter of Mother Nature, and one is left to deplore the Middle Passage or the Trail of Tears the way one deplores an earthquake, a tornado, or any other phenomenon that can be cast as beyond the handiwork of men.

But race is the child of racism, not the father. And the process of naming "the people" has never been a matter of genealogy and physiognomy so much as one of hierarchy. Difference in hue and hair is old. But the belief in the preeminence of hue and hair, the notion that these factors can correctly organize a society and that they signify deeper attributes, which are indelible — this is the new idea at the heart of these new people who have been brought up hopelessly, tragically, deceitfully, to believe that they are white.

These new people are, like us, a modern invention. But unlike us, their new names have no real meaning divorced from the machinery of criminal power. The new people are something else before they were white — Catholic, Corsican, Welsh, Mennonite, Jewish — and if all our national hopes have any fulfillment, then they will have to be something else again. Perhaps they will truly become American and create a nobler basis for their myths. I cannot call it. As for now, it must be said that the process of washing the disparate tribes white, the elevation of the belief in being white, was not achieved through wine tastings and ice cream socials, but rather through the pillaging of life, liberty, labor, and land; through the flaying of backs; the chaining of limbs; the strangling of dissidents; the destruction of families; the rape of mothers; the sale of children; and various other acts meant, first and foremost, to deny you and me the right to secure and govern our own bodies.

The new people are not original in this. Perhaps there has been, at some point in history, some great power whose elevation was exempt from the violent exploitation of other human bodies. If there has been, I have yet to discover it. But this banality of violence can never excuse America, because America makes no claim to the banal. America believes itself exceptional, the greatest and noblest nation ever to exist, a lone champion standing between the white city of democracy and the terrorists, despots, barbarians, and other enemies of civilization. One cannot, at once, claim to be superhuman and then plead mortal error. I propose to take our countrymen's claims of American exceptionalism seriously, which is to say I propose subjecting our country to an exceptional moral standard. This is difficult because there exists, all around us, an apparatus urging us to accept American innocence at face value and not to inquire too much. And it is so easy to look away, to live with the fruits of our history and to ignore the great evil done in all of our names. But you and

I have never truly had that luxury. I think you know.

I write you in your fifteenth year. I am writing you because this was the year you saw Eric Garner choked to death for selling cigarettes; because you know now that Renisha McBride was shot for seeking help, that John Crawford was shot down for browsing in a department store. And you have seen men in uniform drive by and murder Tamir Rice, a twelve-year-old child whom they were oath-bound to protect. And you have seen men in the same uniforms pummel Marlene Pinnock, someone's grandmother, on the side of a road. And you know now, if you did not before, that the police departments of your country have been endowed with the authority to destroy your body. It does not matter if the destruction is the result of an unfortunate overreaction. It does not matter if it originates in a misunderstanding. It does not matter if the destruction springs from a foolish policy. Sell cigarettes without the proper authority and your body can be destroyed. Resent the people trying to entrap your body and it can be destroyed. Turn into a dark stairwell and your body can be destroyed. The destroyers will rarely be held accountable. Mostly they will receive pensions. And destruction is merely the superlative form of a dominion whose prerogatives include friskings, detainings, beatings, and humiliations. All of this is common to black people. And all of this is old for black people. No one is held responsible.

There is nothing uniquely evil in these destroyers or even in this moment. The destroyers are merely men enforcing the whims of our country, correctly interpreting its heritage and legacy. It is hard to face this. But all our phrasing — race relations, racial chasm, racial justice, racial profiling, white privilege, even white supremacy — serves to obscure that racism is a visceral experience, that it dislodges brains, blocks airways, rips muscle, extracts organs, cracks bones, breaks teeth. You must never look away from this. You must always remember that the sociology, the history, the economics, the graphs, the charts, the regressions all land, with great violence, upon the body.

That Sunday, with that host, on that news show, I tried to explain this as best I could within the time allotted. But at the end of the segment, the host flashed a widely shared picture of an eleven-year-old black boy tearfully hugging a white police officer. Then she asked me about "hope". And I knew then that I had failed. And I remembered that I had expected to fail. And I wondered again at the indistinct sadness welling up in me. Why exactly was I sad? I came out of the studio and walked for a while. It was a calm December day. Families, believing themselves white, were out on the street. Infants, raised to be white, were bundled in strollers. And I was sad for these people, much as I was sad for the host and sad for all the people out there watching and reveling in a specious hope. I realized then why I was sad. When the journalist asked me about my body, it was like she was asking me to awaken her from the most gorgeous dream. I have seen that dream all my life. It is perfect houses with nice lawns. It is Memorial Day cookouts, block associations, and driveways. The Dream is treehouses and the Cub Scouts. The Dream smells like peppermint but tastes like strawberry shortcake. And for so long I have wanted to escape into the Dream, to fold my country over my head like a blanket. But this has never been an option because the Dream rests on our backs, the bedding made from our bodies. And knowing this, knowing that the Dream persists by warring with the known world, I was sad for the host, I was sad for all those families, I was sad for my country, but above all, in that moment, I was sad for you.

That was the week you learned that the killers of Michael Brown would go free. The men who had left his body in the street like some awesome declaration of their inviolable power would never be punished. It was not my expectation that anyone would ever be punished. But you were young and still believed. You stayed up till 11 p.m. that night, waiting for the announcement of an indictment, and when instead it was announced that there was none you said, "I've got to go," and you went into your room, and I heard you crying. I came in five minutes after, and I didn't hug you, and I didn't comfort you, because I thought it would be wrong to comfort you. I did not tell you that it would be okay, because I have never believed it would be okay. What I told you is what your grandparents tried to tell me: that this is your country that this is your world, that this is your body, and you must find some way to live within the all of it. I tell you now that the question of how one should live within a black body, within a country lost in the Dream, is the question of my life, and the pursuit of this question, I have found, ultimately answers itself.

This must seem strange to you. We live in a "goal-oriented" era. Our media vocabulary is full of hot takes, big ideas, and grand theories of everything. But some time ago I rejected magic in all its forms. This rejection was a gift from your grandparents, who never tried to console me with ideas of an afterlife and were skeptical of preordained American glory. In accepting both the chaos of history and the fact of my total end, I was freed to truly consider how I wished to live — specifically, how do I live free in this black body? It is a profound question because America understands itself as God's handiwork, but the black body is the clearest evidence that America is the work of men. I have asked the question through my reading and writings, through the music of my youth, through arguments with your grandfather, with your mother, your aunt Janai, your uncle Ben. I have searched for answers in nationalist myth, in classrooms, out on the streets, and on other continents. The question is unanswerable, which is not to say futile. The greatest reward of this constant interrogation, of confrontation with the brutality of my country, is that it has freed me from ghosts and girded me against the sheer terror of disembodiment.

And I am afraid. I feel the fear most acutely whenever you leave me. But I was afraid long before you, and in this I was unoriginal. When I was your age the only people I knew were black, and all of them were powerfully, adamantly, dangerously afraid. I had seen this fear all my young life, though I had not always recognized it as such.

It was always right in front of me. The fear was there in the extravagant boys of my neighborhood, in their large rings and medallions, their big puffy coats and full-length fur-collared leathers, which was their armor against their world. They would stand on the corner of Gwynn Oak and Liberty, or Cold Spring and Park Heights, or outside Mondawmin Mall, with their hands dipped in Russell sweats. I think back on those boys now and all I see is fear, and all I see is them girding themselves against the ghosts of the bad old days when the Mississippi mob gathered 'round their grandfathers so that the branches of the black body might be torched, then cut away. The fear lived on in their practiced bop, their slouching denim, their big T-shirts, the calculated angle of their baseball caps, a catalog of behaviors and garments enlisted to inspire the belief that these boys were in firm possession of everything they desired.

I saw it in their customs of war. I was no older than five, sitting out on the front steps of my home on Woodbrook Avenue, watching two shirtless boys circle each other close and buck shoulders. From then on, I knew that there was a ritual to a street fight, bylaws and codes that, in their very need, attested to all the vulnerability of the black teenage bodies.

I heard the fear in the first music I ever knew, the music that pumped from boom boxes full of grand boast and bluster. The boys who stood out on Garrison and Liberty up on Park Heights loved this music because it told them, against all evidence and odds, that they were masters of their own lives, their own streets, and their own bodies. I saw it in the girls, in their loud laughter, in their gilded bamboo earrings that announced their names thrice over. And I saw it in their brutal language and hard gaze, how they would cut you with their eyes and destroy you with their words for the sin of playing too much. "Keep my name out your mouth;" they would say. I would watch them after school, how they squared off like boxers, vase lined up, earrings off, Reeboks on, and leaped at each other.

I felt the fear in the visits to my Nana's home in Philadelphia. You never knew her. I barely knew her, but what I remember is her hard manner, her rough voice. And I knew that my father's father was dead and that my uncle Oscar was dead and that my uncle David was dead and that each of these instances was unnatural. And I saw it in my own father, who loves you, who counsels you, who slipped me money to care for you. My father was so very afraid. I felt it in the sting of his black leather belt, which he applied with more anxiety than anger, my father who beat me as if someone might steal me away because that is exactly what was happening all around us. Everyone had lost a child, somehow, to the streets, to jail, to drugs, to guns. It was said that these lost girls were sweet as honey and would not hurt a fly. It was said that these lost boys had just received a GED and had begun to turn their lives around. And now they were gone, and their legacy was a great fear.

Have they told you this story? When your grandmother was sixteen years old a young man knocked on her door. The young man was your Nana Jo's boyfriend. No one else was home. Ma allowed this young man to sit and wait until your Nana Jo returned. But your great-grandmother got there first. She asked the young man to leave. Then she beat your grandmother terrifically, one last time, so that she might remember how easily she could lose her body. Ma never forgot. I remember her clutching my small hand tightly as we crossed the street. She would tell me that if I ever let go and were killed by an onrushing car, she would beat me back to life. When I was six, Ma and Dad took me to a local park. I slipped from their gaze and found a playground. Your grandparents spent anxious minutes looking for me. When they found me, Dad did what every parent I knew would have done — he reached for his belt. I remember watching him in a kind of daze, awed at the distance between punishment and offense. Later, I would hear it in Dad's voice — "Either I can beat him, or the police." Maybe that saved me. Maybe it didn't. As I know is, the violence rose from the fear like smoke from a fire, and I cannot say whether that violence, even administered in fear and love, sounded the alarm or choked us at the exit. What I know is that fathers who slammed their teenage boys would then release them to streets where their boys employed, and were subject to, the same justice. And I knew mothers who belted their girls, but the belt could not save these girls from drug dealers twice their age. We, the children, employed our darkest humor to cope. We stood in the alley where we shot basketballs through hollowed crates and cracked jokes on the boy whose mother wore him out with a beating in front of his entire fifth-grade class. We sat on the number five bus, headed downtown, laughing at some girl whose mother was known to reach for anything — cable wires, extension cords, pots, pans. We were laughing, but I know that we were afraid of those who loved us most. Our parents resorted to the lash the way flagellant in the plague years resorted to the scourge.

To be black in the Baltimore of my youth was to be naked before the elements of the world, before all the guns, fists, knives, crack, rape, and disease. The nakedness is not an error, nor pathology. The nakedness is the correct and intended result of policy, the predictable upshot of people forced for centuries to live under fear. The law did not protect us. And now in your time, the law has become an excuse for stopping and frisking you, which is to say, for furthering the assault on your body. But a society that protects some people through a safety net of schools, government-backed home loans, and ancestral wealth but can only protect you with the club of criminal justice has either failed at enforcing its good intentions or has succeeded at something much darker. However, you call it, the result was our infirmity before the criminal forces of the world. It does not matter if the agent of those forces is white or black — what matters is our conditions, what matters is the system that makes your body breakable.

The revelation of these forces, a series of great changes, has unfolded over the course of my life. The changes are still unfolding and will likely continue until I die. I was eleven years old, standing out in the parking lot in front of the 7-Eleven, watching a crew of older boys standing near the street. They yelled and gestured at...who? …another boy, young, like me, who stood there, almost smiling, gamely throwing up his hands. He had already learned the lesson he would teach me that day: that his body was in constant jeopardy. Who knows what brought him to that knowledge? The projects, a drunken stepfather, an older brother concussed by police, a cousin pinned in the city jail. That he was outnumbered did not matter because the whole world had outnumbered him long ago, and what do numbers matter? This was a war for the possession of his body and that would be the war of his whole life.

I stood there for some seconds, marveling at the older boys' beautiful sense of fashion. They all wore ski jackets, the kind which, in my day, mothers put on layaway in September, then piled up overtime hours so as to have the thing wrapped and ready for Christmas. I focused in on a light-skinned boy with a long head and small eyes. He was scowling at another boy, who was standing close to me. It was just before three in the afternoon. I was in sixth grade. School had just let out, and it was not yet the fighting weather of early spring. What was the exact problem here? Who could know?

The boy with the small eyes reached into his ski jacket and pulled out a gun. I recall it in the slowest motion, as though in a dream. There the boy stood, with the gun brandished, which he slowly untucked, tucked, then untucked once more, and in his small eyes I saw a surging rage that could, in an instant, erase my body. That was 1986. That year I felt myself to be drowning in the news reports of murder. I was aware that these murders very often did not land upon the intended targets but fell upon great-aunts, PTA mothers, overtime uncles, and joyful children — fell upon them random and relentless, like great sheets of rain. I knew this in theory but could not understand it as fact until the boy with the small eyes stood across from me holding my entire body in his small hands. The boy did not shoot. His friends pulled him back. He did not need to shoot. He had affirmed my place in the order of things. He had let it be known how easily I could be selected. I took the subway home that day, processing the episode all alone. I did not tell my parents. I did not tell my teachers, and if I told my friends I would have done so with all the excitement needed to obscure the fear that came over me in that moment.

I remember being amazed that death could so easily rise up from the nothing of a boyish afternoon, billow up like fog. I knew that West Baltimore, where I lived; that the north side of Philadelphia, where my cousins lived; that the South Side of Chicago, where friends of my father lived, comprised a world apart. Somewhere out there beyond the firmament, past the asteroid belt, there were other worlds where children did not regularly fear for their bodies. I knew this because there was a large television resting in my living room. In the evenings I would sit before this television bearing witness to the dispatches from this other world. There were little white boys with complete collections of football cards, and their only want was a popular girlfriend and their only worry was poison oak. That other world was suburban and endless, organized around pot roasts, blueberry pies, fireworks, ice cream sundaes, immaculate bathrooms, and small toy trucks that were loosed in wooded backyards with streams and glens. Comparing these dispatches with the facts of my native world, I came to understand that my country was a galaxy, and this galaxy stretched from the pandemonium of West Baltimore to the happy hunting grounds of *Mr. Belvedere*. I obsessed over the distance between that other sector of space and my own. I knew that my portion of the American galaxy, where bodies were enslaved by a tenacious gravity, was black and that the other, liberated portion was not. I knew that some inscrutable energy preserved the breach. I felt, but did not yet understand, the relation between that other world and me. And I felt in this a cosmic injustice, a profound cruelty, which infused an abiding, irrepressible desire to unshackle my body and achieve the velocity of escape.

Do you ever feel that same need? Your life is so very different from my own. The grandness of the world, the real world, the whole world, is a known thing for you. And you have no need of dispatches because you have seen so much of the American galaxy and its inhabitants — their homes, their hobbies — up close. I don't know what it means to grow up with a black president, social networks, omnipresent media, and black women everywhere in their natural hair. What I know is that when they loosed the killer of Michael Brown, you said, "I've got to go." And that cut me because, for all our differing words, at your age my feeling was exactly the same. And I recall that even then I had not yet begun to imagine the perils that tangle us. You still believe the injustice was Michael Brown. You have not yet grappled with your own myths and narratives and discovered the plunder everywhere around us.

Before I could discover, before I could escape, I had to survive, and this could only mean a clash with the streets, by which I mean not just physical blocks, nor simply the people packed into them, but the array of lethal puzzles and strange perils that seem to rise up from the asphalt itself. The streets transform every ordinary day into a series of trick questions, and every incorrect answer risks a beatdown, a shooting, or a pregnancy. No one survives unscathed. And yet the heat that springs from the constant danger, from a lifestyle of near-death experience, is thrilling. This is what the rappers mean when they pronounce themselves addicted to "the streets" or in love with "the game." I imagine they feel something akin to parachutists, rock climbers, BASE jumpers, and others who choose to live on the edge. Of course, we chose nothing. And I have never believed the brothers who claim to "run," much less "own," the city. We did not design the streets. We do not fund them. We do not preserve them. But I was there, nevertheless, charged like all the others with the protection of my body.

The crews, the young men who'd transmuted their fear into rage, were the greatest danger. The crews walked the blocks of their neighborhood, loud and rude, because it was only through their loud rudeness that they might feel any sense of security and power. They would break your jaw, stomp your face, and shoot you down to feel that power, to revel in the might of their own bodies. And their wild reveling, their astonishing acts made their names ring out. Reps were made, atrocities recounted. And so in my Baltimore it was known that when Cherry Hill rolled through you rolled the other way, that North and Pulaski was not an intersection but a hurricane, leaving only splinters and shards in its wake. In that fashion, the security of these neighborhoods flowed downward and became the security of the bodies living there. You steered clear of JoJo, for instance, because he was cousin to Keon, the don of Murphy Homes. In other cities, indeed in other Baltimores, the neighborhoods had other handles and the boys went by other names, but their mission did not change: prove the inviolability of their block, of their bodies, through their power to crack knees, ribs, and arms. This practice was so common that today you can approach any black person raised in the cities of that era and they can tell you which crew ran which hood in their city and they can tell you the names of all the captains and all their cousins and offer an anthology of all their exploits.

To survive the neighborhoods and shield my body, I learned another language consisting of a basic complement of head nods and handshakes. I memorized a list of prohibited blocks. I learned the smell and feel of fighting weather. And I learned that "Shorty, can I see your bike?" was never a sincere question, and "Yo, you were messing with my cousin" was neither an earnest accusation nor a misunderstanding of the fact. These were the summonses that you answered with your left foot forward, your right foot back, your hands guarding your face, one slightly lower than the other, cocked like a hammer. Or they were answered by breaking out, ducking through alleys, cutting through backyards, then bounding through the door past your kid brother into your bedroom, pulling the tool out of your lambskin or from under your mattress or out of your Adidas shoebox, then calling up your own cousins (who really aren't) and returning to that same block, on that same day, and to that same crew, hollering out, "Yeah, nigger, what's up now?" I recall learning these laws clearer than I recall learning my colors and shapes, because these laws were essential to the security of my body.

I think of this as a great difference between us. You have some acquaintance with the old rules, but they are not as essential to you as they were to me. I am sure that you have had to deal with the occasional roughneck on the subway or in the park, but when I was about your age, each day, fully one-third of my brain was concerned with who I was walking to school with, our precise number, the manner of our walk, the number of times I smiled, who or what I smiled at, who offered a pound and who did not — all of which is to say that I practiced the culture of the streets, a culture concerned chiefly with securing the body. I do not long for those days. I have no desire to make you "tough" or "street," perhaps because any "toughness" I garnered came reluctantly. I think I was always, somehow, aware of the price. I think I somehow knew that that third of my brain should have been concerned with more beautiful things. I think I felt that something out there, some force, nameless and vast, had robbed me of ... what? Time? Experience? I think you know something of what that third could have done, and I think that is why you may feel the need for escape even more than I did. You have seen all the wonderful life up above the tree-line, yet you understand that there is no real distance between you and Trayvon Martin, and thus Trayvon Martin must terrify you in a way that he could never terrify me. You have seen so much more of all that is lost when they destroy your body.

The streets were not my only problem. If the streets shackled my right leg, the schools shackled my left. Fail to comprehend the streets and you gave up your body now. But fail to comprehend the schools and you gave up your body later. I suffered at the hands of both, but I resent the schools more. There was nothing sanctified about the laws of the streets — the laws were amoral and practical. You rolled with a posse to the party as sure as you wore boots in the snow, or raised an umbrella in the rain. These were rules aimed at something obvious — the great danger that haunted every visit to Shake & Bake, every bus ride downtown. But the laws of the schools were aimed at something distant and vague. What did it mean to, as our elders told us, "Grow up and be somebody"? And what precisely did this have to do with an education rendered as rote discipline? To be educated in my Baltimore mostly meant always packing an extra number 2 pencil and working quietly. Educated children walked in single file on the right side of the hallway, raised their hands to use the lavatory, and carried the lavatory pass when en route. Educated children never offered excuses — certainly not childhood itself. The world had no time for the childhoods of black boys and girls. How could the schools? Algebra, Biology, and English were not subjects so much as opportunities to better discipline the body, to practice writing between the lines, copying the directions legibly, memorizing theorems extracted from the world they were created to represent. All of it felt so distant to me. I remember sitting in my seventh-grade French class and not having any idea why I was there. I did not know any French people, and nothing around me suggested I ever would. France was a rock rotating in another galaxy, around another sun, in another sky that I would never cross. Why, precisely, was I sitting in this classroom?

4. Questions for Discussion

(1) How does Coates draw on his personal experiences to explore broader themes of race and identity in America?

(2) What is Coates' view of the American Dream, and how does it relate to his critique of American society?

(3) How does Coates discuss the role of violence in shaping the experiences of Black people in America, and how does he suggest we address this issue?

Section 2: Francis Scott Fitzgerald and *The Great Gatsby*

F. Scott Fitzgerald is one of the most important American writers in the 1920s, regarded as the literary spokesman and poet laureate of the jazz age. *The Great Gatsby* is a masterful novel that offers a captivating glimpse into the excesses and contradictions of the Jazz Age and remains to be classical in American literature.

1. Introduction of Francis Scott Fitzgerald (1896—1940)

F. Scott Fitzgerald was born on September 24, 1896 in St. Paul, Minnesota. He was the only son of Edward Fitzgerald, a salesman who descended from old American families and had numerous commercial failures. His mother was the daughter of a rich Irish immigrant family. Relying on his mother's rich family background, he attended private schools and went to Princeton University in 1913. In 1917, he gave up his studies because of his poor grades and joined the army in the south. There he met Zelda, a beautiful southern belle, the daughter of a local judge. In 1919, he retired from the army and began to write, hoping to earn enough money to marry Zelda. Published in 1920, his first novel, *This Side of Paradise*, was a great success and established his reputation as a promising novelist. He married Zelda in the same year. In April, 1921, Fitzgerald and Zelda settled at Long Island. The couple threw themselves crazily into all kinds of parties, dancing, drinking and taking trips to Europe. He supported their extravagant life by doing the job of a hack writer and published *The Beautiful and Damned* and two collections of short stories, *Flappers and Philosophers* and *Tales of the Jazz Age*. Through these works, he attracted his readers by showing his contradictory attitudes towards the life of the Jazz Age, combining strong love and profound pain. As John F. Callahan said, "Fitzgerald, who named and chronicled that brash, schizophrenic decade, was no stranger to the dissipation of values and the pursuit of sensation in the Jazz Age of the 1920" (374). As an insider and outsider, he enjoyed the happiness brought by this crazy life. Meanwhile he had a profound insight into the pain and despair behind it. Meanwhile he also predicted the coming failure and doom behind the short-term prosperity of Postwar America. For the next two years, the couple lived in Europe and met a lot of writers of the lost generation, such as Ernest Hemingway, Gertrude Stein and Ezra Pound.

Published in 1925, *The Great Gatsby* is considered to be one of Fitzgerald's best works. In the year of 1934, Fitzgerald published *Tender is the Night*. His later life suffered from financial worries and became more and more tragical. Fitzgerald's wife suffered from insanity and required expensive treatment, so he had to go to Hollywood to work as a scriptwriter. In order to cure his wife and send his daughter to the best private education, he kept on writing until he died of a heart attack in 1940.

2. Introduction of *The Great Gatsby*

After the World War Ⅰ, the United States has experienced great changes. The social wealth of the United States has been accumulated in the war. With the development of industrialization and urbanization, the influx of a large number of immigrants has injected vitality into the economic development of the United States, and the American society has entered a period of prosperity.

The Great Gatsby was published in 1925. The story's main character Jay Gatsby gained a lot of wealth through bootlegging, an illegal business. Jay Gatsby was a mysterious and wealthy tycoon who threw lavish parties in his big mansion every weekend. Nick Carraway, his neighbor, accidentally attended one of his parties and got acquainted with Gatsby. As the novel progresses, Nick became increasingly drawn into Gatsby's complicated world: Gatsby wanted Daisy, Nick's cousin, the girl he once loved. Under Nick's arrangement, Gatsby got chances to meet Daisy and they began an affair. After Daisy's husband, Tom confronted Daisy and Gatsby, Daisy was anxious and accidentally killed Tom's mistress Myrtle Wilson with Gatsby's car. Gatsby took the blame for the accident and was killed by Myrtle Wilson's husband. Finally, very few people attended Gatsby's funeral, including Nick, Gatsby's father and former servants. The rich couple, Tom and Daisy, who shifted the blame to Gatsby, didn't appear at his funeral. Nick was very disappointed with the cruel and indifferent upper-class people like Daisy and Tom and decided to go to the west.

The story is a poignant portrait of the failure of American Dream which measures success and love in terms of money. The novel is a vivid description of the 20th century which was described as a spiritual wasteland by T.S. Eliot. The story exposes the hollow nature of American dream which is illusionary. Jay Gatsby wanted to win back his lost love but he didn't know that it was impossible to recapture the past and also it was difficult to alter one future in a world everyone was judged by his class and social wealth. Gatsby is great because he still values romantic love in a materialistic world where everybody is realistic and chases after money by all means. Gatsby's American dream is quite paradoxical, combining idealism and a lot of commercialism. He doesn't realize that in a realistic world true love is hard to regain.

3. Reading Material: *The Great Gatsby* (excerpt)

Ⅲ

There was music from my neighbor's house through the summer nights. In his blue gardens men and girls came and went like moths among the whisperings and the champagne and the stars. At high tide in the afternoon, I watched his guests diving from the tower of his raft, or taking the sun on the hot sand of his beach while his two motorboats slit the waters of the Sound, drawing aquaplanes over cataracts of foam. On weekends his Rolls-Royce became an omnibus, bearing parties to and from the city between nine in the morning and long past midnight, while his station-wagon scampered like a brisk yellow bug to meet all trains. And on Mondays eight servants, including an extra gardener, toiled all day with mops and scrubbing-brushes and hammers and garden-shears, repairing the ravages of the night before.

Every Friday five crates of oranges and lemons arrived from a fruiterer in New York — every Monday these same oranges and lemons left his back door in a pyramid of pulpless halves. There was a machine in the kitchen which could extract the juice of two hundred oranges in half an hour if a little button was pressed two hundred times by a butler's thumb.

At least once a fortnight a corps of caterers came down with several hundred feet of canvas and enough colored lights to make a Christmas tree of Gatsby's enormous garden. On buffet tables, garnished with glistening hors-d'oeuvre, spiced baked hams crowded against salads of harlequin designs and pastry pigs and turkeys bewitched to a dark gold. In the main hall a bar with a real brass rail was set up, and stocked with gins and liquors and with cordials so long forgotten that most of his female guests were too young to know one from another.

By seven o'clock the orchestra has arrived, no thin five-piece affair, but a whole pitful of oboes and trombones and saxophones and viols and cornets and piccolos, and low and high drums. The last swimmers have come in from the beach now and are dressing upstairs; the cars from New York are parked five deep in the drive, and already the halls and salons and verandas are gaudy with primary colors, and hair bobbed in strange new ways, and shawls beyond the dreams of Castile. The bar is in full swing, and floating rounds of cocktails permeate the garden outside, until the air is alive with chatter and laughter, and casual innuendo and introductions forgotten on the spot, and enthusiastic meetings between women who never knew each other's names.

The lights grow brighter as the earth lurches away from the sun, and now the orchestra is playing yellow cocktail music, and the opera of voices pitches a key higher. Laughter is easier minute by minute, spilled with prodigality, tipped out at a cheerful word. The groups change more swiftly, swell with new arrivals, dissolve and form in the same breath; already there are wanderers, confident girls who weave here and there among the stouter and more stable, become for a sharp, joyous moment the centre of a group, and then, excited with triumph, glide on through the sea-change of faces and voices and colour under the constantly changing light.

Suddenly one of these gypsies, in trembling opal, seizes a cocktail out of the air, dumps it down for courage and, moving her hands like Frisco, dances out alone on the canvas platform. A momentary hush; the orchestra leader varies his rhythm obligingly for her, and there is a burst of chatter as the erroneous news goes around that she is Gilda Gray's understudy from the Follies. The party has begun.

I believe that on the first night I went to Gatsby's house I was one of the few guests who had actually been invited. People were not invited — they went there. They got into automobiles which bore them out to Long Island, and somehow, they ended up at Gatsby's door. Once there they were introduced by somebody who knew Gatsby, and after that they conducted themselves according to the rules of behavior associated with an amusement park. Sometimes they came and went without having met Gatsby at all, came for the party with a simplicity of heart that was its own ticket of admission.

I had been actually invited. A chauffeur in a uniform of robin's-egg blue crossed my lawn early that Saturday morning with a surprisingly formal note from his employer: the honor would be entirely Gatsby's, it said, if I would attend his "little party" that night. He had seen me several times, and had intended to call on me long before, but a peculiar combination of circumstances had prevented it — signed Jay Gatsby, in a majestic hand.

Dressed up in white flannels I went over to his lawn a little while after seven, and wandered around rather ill at ease among swirls and eddies of people I didn't know — though here and there was a face I had noticed on the commuting train. I was immediately struck by the number of young Englishmen dotted about; all well dressed, all looking a little hungry, and all talking in low, earnest voices to solid and prosperous Americans. I was sure that they were selling something: bonds or insurance or automobiles. They were at least agonizingly aware of the easy money in the vicinity and convinced that it was theirs for a few words in the right key.

As soon as I arrived I made an attempt to find my host, but the two or three people of whom I asked his whereabouts stared at me in such an amazed way, and denied so vehemently any knowledge of his movements, that I slunk off in the direction of the cocktail table — the only place in the garden where a single man could linger without looking purposeless and alone.

I was on my way to get roaring drunk from sheer embarrassment when Jordan Baker came out of the house and stood at the head of the marble steps, leaning a little backward and looking with contemptuous interest down into the garden.

Welcome or not, I found it necessary to attach myself to someone before I should begin to address cordial remarks to the passers-by.

"Hello!" I roared, advancing towards her. My voice seemed unnaturally loud across the garden.

"I thought you might be here," she responded absently as I came up. "I remembered you lived next door to — "She held my hand impersonally, as a promise that she'd take care of me in a minute, and gave ear to two girls in twin yellow dresses, who stopped at the foot of the steps.

"Hello!" they cried together. "Sorry you didn't win."

That was for the golf tournament. She had lost in the finals the week before.

"You don't know who we are," said one of the girls in yellow, "but we met you here about a month ago."

"You've dyed your hair since then," remarked Jordan, and I started, but the girls had moved casually on and her remark was addressed to the premature moon, produced like the supper, no doubt, out of a caterer's basket. With Jordan's slender golden arm resting in mine, we descended the steps and sauntered about the garden. A tray of cocktails floated at us through the twilight, and we sat down at a table with the two girls in yellow and three men, each one introduced to us as Mr. Mumble.

"Do you come to these parties often?" inquired Jordan of the girl beside her.

"The last one was the one I met you at," answered the girl, in an alert confident voice. She turned to her companion: "Wasn't it for you, Lucille?"

It was for Lucille, too.

"I like to come," Lucille said. "I never care what I do, so I always have a good time. When I was here last I tore my gown on a chair, and he asked me my name and address — inside of a week I got a package from Croirier's with a new evening gown in it."

"Did you keep it?" asked Jordan.

"Sure I did. I was going to wear it tonight, but it was too big in the bust and had to be altered. It was gas blue and lavender beads. Two hundred and sixty-five dollars."

"There's something funny about a fellow that'll do a thing like that," said the other girl eagerly. "He doesn't want any trouble with anybody."

"Who doesn't?" I inquired.

"Gatsby. Somebody told me —"

The two girls and Jordan leaned together confidentially.

"Somebody told me they thought he killed a man once."

A thrill passed over all of us. The three Mr. Mumbles bent forward and listened eagerly.

"I don't think it's so much THAT," argued Lucille skeptically; "it's more that he was a German spy during the war."

One of the men nodded in confirmation.

"I heard that from a man who knew all about him, grew up with him in Germany," he assured us positively.

"Oh, no," said the first girl, "it couldn't be that, because he was in the American army during the war." As our credulity switched back to her, she leaned forward with enthusiasm. "You look at him sometimes when he thinks nobody's looking at him. I'll bet he killed a man."

She narrowed her eyes and shivered. Lucille shivered. We all turned and looked around for Gatsby. It was testimony to the romantic speculation he inspired that there were whispers about him from those who found little that it was necessary to whisper about in this world.

The first supper — there would be another one after midnight — was now being served, and Jordan invited me to join her own party, who were spread around a table on the other side of the garden. There were three married couples and Jordan's escort, a persistent undergraduate given to violent innuendo, and obviously under the impression that sooner or later Jordan was going to yield him up her person to a greater or lesser degree. Instead of rambling, this party had preserved a dignified homogeneity, and assumed to itself the function of representing the staid nobility of the country side — East Egg condescending to West Egg, and carefully on guard against its spectroscopic gaiety.

"Let's get out," whispered Jordan, after a somehow wasteful and inappropriate half-hour. "This is much too polite for me."

We got up, and she explained that we were going to find the host: I had never met him, she said, and it was making me uneasy. The undergraduate nodded in a cynical, melancholy way.

The bar, where we glanced first, was crowded, but Gatsby was not there. She couldn't find him from the top of the steps, and he wasn't on the veranda. On a chance we tried an important-looking door, and walked into a high Gothic library, paneled with carved English oak, and probably transported complete from some ruin overseas.

A stout, middle-aged man, with enormous owl-eyed spectacles, was sitting somewhat drunk on the edge of a great table, staring with unsteady concentration at the shelves of books. As we entered, he wheeled excitedly around and examined Jordan from head to foot.

"What do you think?" he demanded impetuously.

"About what?" He waved his hand towards the book-shelves.

"About that. As a matter of fact, you needn't bother to ascertain. I ascertained. They're real."

"The books?"

He nodded.

"Absolutely real — have pages and everything. I thought they'd be a nice durable cardboard. As a matter of fact, they're absolutely real. Pages and — Here! Lemme show you."

"Taking our skepticism for granted, he rushed to the bookcases and returned with Volume One of the *"Stoddard Lectures"* .

"See!" he cried triumphantly. "It's a bona-fide piece of printed matter. It fooled me. This fella's a regular Belasco. It's a triumph. What thoroughness! What realism! Knew when to stop, too — didn't cut the pages. But what do you want? What do you expect?"

He snatched the book from me and replaced it hastily on its shelf, muttering that if one brick was removed the whole library was liable to collapse.

"Who brought you?" he demanded. "Or did you just come? I was brought. Most people were brought."

Jordan looked at him alertly, cheerfully without answering.

"1 was brought by a woman named Roosevelt, "he continued. "Mrs. Claud Roosevelt. Do you know her? I met her somewhere last night. I've been drunk for about a week now, and I thought it might sober me up to sit in a library."

"Has it?"

"A little bit, I think. I can't tell yet. I've only been here an hour. Did I tell you about the books? They're real. They're —"

"You told us." We shook hands with him gravely and went back outdoors.

There was dancing now on the canvas in the garden; old men pushing young girls backwards in eternal graceless circles, superior couples holding each other tortuously, fashionably, and keeping in the corners — and a great number of single girls dancing individualistically, or relieving the orchestra for a moment of the burden of the banjo or the traps. By midnight the hilarity had increased. A celebrated tenor had sung in Italian and a notorious contralto had sung in jazz and between the numbers of people were doing "stunts" all over the garden, while happy, vacuous bursts of laughter rose towards the summer sky. A pair of stage "twins" — who turned out to be the girls in yellow — did a baby act in costume and champagne was served in glasses bigger than finger-bowls. The moon had risen higher, and floating in the Sound was a triangle of silver scales, trembling a little to the stiff, tinny drip of the banjoes on the lawn.

I was still with Jordan Baker. We were sitting at a table with a man of about my age and a rowdy little girl, who gave way upon the slightest provocation to uncontrollable laughter. I was enjoying myself now. I had taken two finger-bowls of champagne, and the scene had changed before my eyes into something significant, elemental and profound.

At a lull in the entertainment the man looked at me and smiled.

"Your face is familiar," he said, politely, "weren't you in the Third Division during the war?"

"Why, yes. I was in the Ninth Machine-gun Battalion."

"I was in the Seventh Infantry until June nineteen-eighteen. I knew I'd seen you somewhere before."

We talked for a moment about some wet, grey little villages in France. Evidently, he lived in this vicinity, for he told me that he had just bought a hydroplane, and was going to try it out in the morning.

"Want to go with me, old sport? Just near the shore along the Sound."

"What time?"

"Any time that suits you best."

It was on the tip of my tongue to ask his name when Jordan looked around and smiled.

"Having a gay time now?" she inquired.

"Much better." I turned again to my new acquaintance. "This is an unusual party for me. I haven't even seen the host. I live over there —" I waved my hand at the invisible hedge in the distance, "and this man Gatsby sent over his chauffeur with an invitation." For a moment he looked at me as if he failed to understand.

"I'm Gatsby," he said suddenly.

"What!" I exclaimed. "Oh, I beg your pardon."

"I thought you knew, old sport. I'm afraid I'm not a very good host."

He smiled understandingly — much more than understandingly. It was one of those rare smiles with a quality of eternal reassurance in it, that you may come across four or five times in life. It faced — or seemed to face — the whole eternal world for an instant, and then concentrated on you with an irresistible prejudice in your favor. It understood you just as far as you wanted to be understood, believed in you as you would like to believe in yourself, and assured you that it had precisely the impression of you that, at your best, you hoped to convey. Precisely at that point it vanished — and I was looking at an elegant young rough-neck, a year or two over thirty, whose elaborate formality of speech just missed being absurd. Sometime before he introduced himself, I'd got a strong impression that he was picking his words with care.

Almost at the moment when Mr. Gatsby identified himself, a butler hurried towards him with the information that Chicago was calling him on the wire. He excused himself with a small bow that included each of us in turn.

"If you want anything just ask for it, old sport," he urged me. "Excuse me. I will rejoin you later."

When he was gone I turned immediately to Jordan — constrained to assure her of my surprise. I had expected that Mr. Gatsby would be a florid and corpulent person in his middle years.

"Who is he?" I demanded. "Do you know?"

"He's just a man named Gatsby."

"Where is he from, I mean? And what does he do?"

"Now you're started on the subject," she answered with a wan smile. "Well, he told me once he was an Oxford man."

A dim background started to take shape behind him, but at her next remark it faded away.

"However, I don't believe it."

"Why not?"

"I don't know," she insisted, "I just don't think he went there."

Something in her tone reminded me of the other girl's "I think he killed a man," and had the effect of stimulating my curiosity. I would have accepted without question the information that Gatsby sprang from the swamps of Louisiana or from the lower East Side of New York. That was comprehensible. But young men didn't — at least in my provincial inexperience I believed they didn't — drift coolly out of nowhere and buy a palace on Long Island Sound.

"Anyhow, he gives large parties," said Jordan, changing the subject with an urbane distaste for the concrete. "And I like large parties. They're so intimate. At small parties there isn't any privacy."

There was the boom of a bass drum, and the voice of the orchestra leader rang out suddenly above the echolalia of the garden.

"Ladies and gentlemen," he cried. "At the request of Mr. Gatsby we are going to play for you Mr. Vladimir Tostoff's latest work, which attracted so much attention at Carnegie Hall last May. If you read the papers, you know there was a big sensation." He smiled with jovial condescension, and added: "Some sensation!" Whereupon everybody laughed.

"The piece is known," he concluded lustily, "as *Vladimir Setoff's Jazz History of the World*."

The nature of Mr. Tostoff's composition eluded me, because just as it began my eyes fell on Gatsby, standing alone on the marble steps and looking from one group to another with approving eyes. His tanned skin was drawn attractively tight on his face and his short hair looked as though it were trimmed every day. I could see nothing sinister about him. I wondered if the fact that he was not drinking helped to set him off from his guests, for it seemed to me that he grew more correct as the fraternal hilarity increased. When the *Jazz History of the World* was over, girls were putting their heads on men's shoulders in a puppyish, convivial way, girls were swooning backward playfully into men's arms, even into groups, knowing that some one would arrest their falls — but no one swooned backward on Gatsby, and no French bob touched Gatsby's shoulder, and no singing quartets were formed with Gatsby's head for one link.

"I beg your pardon."

Gatsby's butler was suddenly standing beside us.

"Miss Baker?" he inquired. "I beg your pardon, but Mr. Gatsby would like to speak to you alone."

"With me?" she exclaimed in surprise.

"Yes, madame."

She got up slowly, raising her eyebrows at me in astonishment, and followed the butler towards the house. I noticed that she wore her evening-dress, all her dresses, like sports clothes — there was a jauntiness about her movements as if she had first learned to walk upon golf courses on clean, crisp mornings.

I was alone and it was almost two. For some time confused and intriguing sounds had issued from a long, many-windowed room which overhung the terrace. Eluding Jordan's undergraduate, who was now engaged in an obstetrical conversation with two chorus girls, and who implored me to join him, I went inside.

The large room was full of people. One of the girls in yellow was playing the piano, and beside her stood a tall, red-haired young lady from a famous chorus, engaged in song. She had drunk a quantity of champagne, and during the course of her song she had decided, ineptly, that everything was very, very sad — she was not only singing, she was weeping too. Whenever there was a pause in the song she filled it with gasping, broken sobs, and then took up the lyric again in a quavering soprano. The tears coursed down her cheeks — not freely, however, for when they came into contact with her heavily beaded eyelashes they assumed an inky color, and pursued the rest of their way in slow black rivulets. A humorous suggestion was made that she sang the notes on her face, whereupon she threw up her hands, sank into a chair, and went off into a deep vinous sleep.

"She had a fight with a man who says he's her husband," explained a girl at my elbow.

I looked around. Most of the remaining women were now having fights with men said to be their husbands. Even Jordan's party, the quartet from East Egg, were rent asunder by dissension. One of the men was talking with curious intensity to a young actress, and his wife, after attempting to laugh at the situation in a dignified and indifferent way, broke down entirely and resorted to flank attacks — at intervals she appeared suddenly at his side like an angry diamond, and hissed: "You promised!" into his ear.

The reluctance to go home was not confined to wayward men. The hall was at present occupied by two deplorably sober men and their highly indignant wives. The wives were sympathizing with each other in slightly raised voices.

"Whenever he sees I'm having a good time he wants to go home."

"Never heard anything so selfish in my life."

"We're always the first ones to leave."

"So are we."

"Well, we're almost the last to-night," said one of the men sheepishly. "The orchestra left half an hour ago."

"In spite of the wives' agreement that such malevolence was beyond credibility, the dispute ended in a short struggle, and both wives were lifted, kicking into the night.

As I waited for my hat in the hall, the door of the library opened and Jordan Baker and Gatsby came out together. He was saying some last word to her, but the eagerness in his manner tightened abruptly into formality as several people approached him to say goodbye.

Jordan's party were calling impatiently to her from the porch, but she lingered for a moment to shake hands.

"I've just heard the most amazing thing," she whispered. "How long were we in there?"

"Why, about an hour."

It was... Simply amazing," she repeated abstractedly. "But I swore I wouldn't tell it and here I am tantalizing you." She yawned gracefully in my face. "Please come and see me... phone book... under the name of Mrs. Sigourney Howard... My aunt..." She was hurrying off as she talked — her brown hand waved a jaunty salute as she melted into her party at the door.

Rather ashamed that on my first appearance I had stayed so late, I joined the last of Gatsby's guests, who were clustered around him. I wanted to explain that I'd hunted for him early in the evening and to apologize for not having known him in the garden.

"Don't mention it," he enjoined me eagerly. "Don't give it another thought, old sport." The familiar expression held no more familiarity than the hand which reassuringly brushed my shoulder, "And don't forget we're going up in the hydroplane tomorrow morning, at nine o'clock." Then the butler, behind his shoulder:

"Philadelphia wants you on the phone, sir."

"All right, in a minute. Tell them I'll be right there ... Good night."

"Good night."

"Good night." He smiled — and suddenly there seemed to be a pleasant significance in having been among the last to go, as if he had desired it all the time. "Good night, old sport... Good night."

But as I walked down the steps, I saw that the evening was not quite over. Fifty feet from the door a dozen headlights illuminated a bizarre and tumultuous scene. In the ditch beside the road, right side up, but violently shorn of one wheel, rested a new coupe which had left Gatsby's drive not two minutes before. The sharp jut of a wall accounted for the detachment of the wheel, which was now getting considerable attention from half a dozen curious chauffeurs. However, as they had left their cars blocking the road, a harsh, discordant din from those in the rear had been audible for some time, and added to the already violent confusion of the scene.

A man in a long duster had dismounted from the wreck and now stood in the middle of the road, looking from the car to the tyre and from the tyre to the observers in a pleasant, puzzled way. "See!" he explained. "It went in the ditch."

The fact was infinitely astonishing to him, and I recognized first the unusual quality of wonder, and then the man — it was the late patron of Gatsby's library.

"How'd it happen?"

He shrugged his shoulders.

"I know nothing whatever about mechanics," he said decisively.

"But how did it happen? Did you run into the wall?"

"Don't ask me," said Owl Eyes, washing his hands of the whole matter. "I know very little about driving — next to nothing. It happened, and that's all I know."

"Well, if you're a poor driver you oughtn't to try driving at night."

"But I wasn't even trying," he explained indignantly, "I wasn't even trying."

An awed hush fell upon the bystanders.

"Do you want to commit suicide?"

"You're lucky it was just a wheel! A bad driver and not even trying!"

"You don't understand," explained the criminal. "I wasn't driving. There's another man in the car."

The shock that followed this declaration found voice in a sustained "Ah-h-h!" as the door of the coupé swung slowly open. The crowd — it was now a crowd — stepped back involuntarily, and when the door had opened wide there was a ghostly pause. Then, very gradually, part by part, a pale, dangling individual stepped out of the wreck, pawing tentatively at the ground with a large uncertain dancing shoe.

Blinded by the glare of the headlights and confused by the incessant groaning of the horns, the apparition stood swaying for a moment before he perceived the man in the duster.

"What's matter?" he inquired calmly. "Did we run out a gas?"

"Look!"

Half a dozen fingers pointed at the amputated wheel — he stared at it for a moment, and then looked upward as though he suspected that it had dropped from the sky.

"It came off," someone explained.

He nodded.

"At first I didn't notice we'd stopped."

A pause. Then, taking a long breath and straightening his shoulders, he remarked in a determined voice.

"Wonder if tell me where there's a gas' line station?"

At least a dozen men, some of them a little better off than he was, explained to him that wheel and car were no longer joined by any physical bond.

"Back out," he suggested after a moment. "Put her in reverse."

"But the wheel's off!"

He hesitated.

"No harm in trying," he said.

The caterwauling horns had reached a crescendo and I turned away and cut across the lawn towards home. I glanced back once. A wafer of a moon was shining over Gatsby's house, making the night fine as before, and surviving the laughter and the sound of his still glowing garden. A sudden emptiness seemed to flow now from the windows and the great doors, endowing with complete isolation the figure of the host, who stood on the porch, his hand up in a formal gesture of farewell.

Reading over what I have written so far, I see I have given the impression that the events of three nights several weeks apart were all that absorbed me. On the contrary, they were merely casual events in a crowded summer, and, until much later, they absorbed me infinitely less than my personal affairs.

Most of the time I worked. In the early morning the sun threw my shadow westward as I hurried down the white chasms of lower New York to the Probity Trust. I knew the other clerks and young bond-salesmen by their first names, and lunched with them in dark, crowded restaurants on little pig sausages and mashed potatoes and coffee. I even had a short affair with a girl who lived in Jersey City and worked in the accounting department, but her brother began throwing mean looks in my direction, so when she went on her vacation in July, I let it blow quietly away.

I took dinner usually at the Yale Club — for some reason it was the gloomiest event of my day — and then I went upstairs to the library and studied investments and securities for a conscientious hour. There were generally a few rioters around, but they never came into the library, so it was a good place to work. After that, if the night was mellow, I strolled down Madison Avenue past the old Murray Hill Hotel, and over 33rd Street to the Pennsylvania Station.

I began to like New York, the racy, adventurous feel of it at night, and the satisfaction that the constant flicker of men and women and machines gives to the restless eye. I liked to walk up Fifth Avenue and pick out romantic women from the crowd and imagine that in a few minutes I was going to enter into their lives, and no one would ever know or disapprove. Sometimes, in my mind, I followed them to their apartments on the corners of hidden streets, and they turned and smiled back at me before they faded through a door into warm darkness. At the enchanted metropolitan twilight I felt a haunting loneliness sometimes, and felt it in others — poor young clerks who loitered in front of windows waiting until it was time for a solitary restaurant dinner — young clerks in the dusk, wasting the most poignant moments of night and life.

Again at eight o'clock, when the dark lanes of the Forties were lined five deep with throbbing taxi-cabs, bound for the theatre district, I felt a sinking in my heart. Forms leaned together in the taxis as they waited, and voices sang, and there was laughter from unheard jokes, and lighted cigarettes outlined unintelligible 70 gestures inside. Imagining that I, too, was hurrying towards gaiety and sharing their intimate excitement, I wished them well.

For a while I lost sight of Jordan Baker, and then in midsummer I found her again. At first I was flattered to go places with her, because she was a golf champion, and everyone knew her name. Then it was something more. I wasn't actually in love, but I felt a sort of tender curiosity. The bored haughty face that she turned to the world concealed something — most affectations conceal something eventually, even though they don't in the beginning — and one day I found what it was.

When we were on a house-party together up in Warwick, she left a borrowed car out in the rain with the top down, and then lied about it — and suddenly I remembered the story about her that had eluded me that night at Daisy's. At her first big golf tournament there was a row that nearly reached the newspapers — a suggestion that she had moved her ball from a bad lie in the semi-final round. The thing approached the proportions of a scandal — then died away. A caddy retracted his statement, and the only other witness admitted that he might have been mistaken. The incident and the name had remained together in my mind.

Jordan Baker instinctively avoided clever, shrewd men, and now I saw that this was because she felt safer on a plane where any divergence from a code would be thought impossible. She was incurably dishonest. She wasn't able to endure being at a disadvantage and, given this unwillingness, I suppose she had begun dealing in subterfuges when she was very young in order to keep that cool, insolent smile turned to the world and yet satisfy the demands of her hard, jaunty body.

It made no difference to me. Dishonesty in a woman is a thing you never blame deeply — I was casually sorry, and then I forgot. It was on that same house party that we had a curious conversation about driving a car. It started because she passed so close to some workmen that our fender flicked a button on one man's coat.

"You're a rotten driver," I protested. "Either you ought to be more careful, or you oughtn't to drive at all."

"I am careful."

"No, you're not."

"Well, other people are," she said lightly.

"What's that got to do with it?"

"They'll keep out of my way," she insisted. "It takes two to make an accident."

"Suppose you met somebody just as careless as yourself."

"I hope I never will," she answered. "I hate careless people. That's why I like you."

Her grey, sun-strained eyes stared straight ahead, but she had deliberately shifted our relations, and for a moment I thought I loved her. But I am slow-thinking and full of interior rules that act as brakes on my desires, and I knew that first I had to get myself definitely out of that tangle back home. I'd been writing letters once a week and signing them: "Love, Nick," and all I could think of was how, when that certain girl played tennis, a faint moustache of perspiration appeared on her upper lip. Nevertheless, there was a vague understanding that had to be tactfully broken off before I was free.

Everyone suspects himself of at least one of the cardinal virtues, and this is mine: I am one of the few honest people that I have ever known.

4. Questions for Discussion

(1) How do you understand the word "great" in the title *The Great Gatsby*?

(2) Do you think Gatsby's American Dream is a success or a failure? Why?

(3) What are some important symbols in *The Great Gatsby*? How are they related to the theme of American Dream?

(4) What is the importance of settings like West Egg, East Egg, the valley of ashes, and New York City in this novel?

Chapter 3 Political System

Democracy is closely related to liberty and freedom. Traditionally, there's a natural suspicion that government is the enemy of freedom. The stronger the government is, the more severely individual freedom will be damaged. American people's suspicion towards government went back to the revolution period. Thomas Paine, a famous revolutionary writer expressed his view in his *Common Sense* that "Government even in its best state is but a necessary evil. In its worst state, an intolerable one." (5) Abraham Lincoln also defined the position of the American government in his *Gettysburg Address*, "American people will establish a government, based on the principles of the people, by the people, and for the people." That's to say, instead of ruling over US citizens, the government should be ruled by them. Each American citizen has a vested interest in how he or she is governed. In his speech at Asheville, North Carolina, September 9, 1902, former U.S. President Theodore Roosevelt said: "The government is us. We are the government, you and I."

American democracy and freedom are guaranteed by both American Declaration of Independence and American constitution. American Declaration of Independence emphasizes that the power of American government comes from people, so if it fails to defend the rights of people, citizens are entitled to create a more responsible and better government. American constitution also guaranteed people's rights based on equality and justice.

According to the constitution of the United States, the democratic republic system is divided into three powers, namely legislation, administration and justice. The three rights check and balance each other. The legislative power is stipulated to belong to the United States Congress; the executive power belongs to the president of the United States, and the judicial power belongs to the Supreme Court of the United States. The division of power is also a good representation of American democracy.

American politics and literature have a long and complex relationship, with writers often reflecting and commenting on the political issues of their times. As John D Lindberg commented that "the relationship between literature and politics is a multilane freeway with a traffic flowing freely in both directions: any work of literature is in part a product of sociological and political factors... Conversely, important works of literature or whole literary movements have had profound effects on society by setting up or destroying taboos, conventions and social prejudices, thus contributing to changes in values" (163). From the Revolutionary War and the early struggles for independence to the Civil Rights Movement and contemporary debates over immigration and social justice, American literature has both shaped and been shaped by political discourse and action.

Throughout American history, writers have used their craft to engage with political issues, often advocating for social change or offering critiques of existing power structures. For example, during the Civil War era, writers such as Harriet Beecher Stowe and Frederick Douglass used literature to advocate for the abolition of slavery and to challenge the prevailing racist ideologies of their time. In the early 20th century, writers such as Upton Sinclair and John Steinbeck used their fictions to expose the harsh realities of poverty and inequality in America, and to advocate for labor rights and social welfare reforms.

During the Cold War, writers such as Joseph Heller and Kurt Vonnegut used satire and dark humor to critique the military-industrial complex and the absurdity of war. In the 1960s and 1970s, the counterculture movements of the era gave rise to a new generation of writers who used their works to challenge conventional political and cultural norms, exploring issues such as feminism, civil rights, and the Vietnam War.

In recent years, American literature has continued to grapple with political issues, from the aftermath of 9/11 Terrorist Attacks to the rise of identity politics and the resurgence of nationalist movements. Contemporary writers such as Ta-Nehisi Coates, Jesmyn Ward, and Junot Diaz have used their work to explore issues of race, identity, and inequality in America, while writers such as George Saunders have used dystopian and speculative fiction to reflect on the dangers of authoritarianism and the erosion of democracy.

At the same time, American politics has also been influenced by literary and cultural trends. Political leaders and activists have often drawn on literary and cultural references to frame their messages and to connect with audiences. For example, Barack Obama famously cited writers such as James Baldwin and Toni Morrison as inspirations for his political vision.

Overall, the relationship between American politics and literature is complex and multifaceted, with writers often serving as both critics and advocates for political change, and with political discourse and action often influencing the themes and styles of literary works.

Section One: Joseph Heller and *Catch-22*

Joseph Heller (1923—1999) was an American novelist, playwright, and satirist best known for his novel *Catch-22*, which has become a classic of American literature. Published in 1961, the book is set during World War II and offers a darkly comedic and absurdist portrayal of the military bureaucracy and the absurdity of war itself and remains to be a canonical novel in American literature.

1. Introduction of Joseph Heller

Born in Brooklyn, New York, Joseph Heller served as a bombardier in World War Ⅱ, an experience that would inform much of his writing. After the war, he attended the University of southern California and later Columbia University, where he studied with renowned literary critic Lionel Trilling. Heller worked as a copywriter for a time before turning to writing full-time and publishing his first novel, *Catch-22*, in 1961. The novel was a critical and commercial success, and its title became a widely recognized term for some absurd, circular logic. Heller went on to write several other novels and plays, including *Something Happened* and *Good as Gold*. Throughout his career, he was known for his wit, irreverence, and sharp critiques of American society and politics. Heller's legacy as a writer and satirist continues to influence contemporary literature and culture.

2. Introduction of *Catch-22*

Catch-22 is a satirical novel by Joseph Heller, published in 1961. Set during World War II, the novel follows the experiences of Captain John Yossarian, a US Air Forces bombardier who becomes increasingly disillusioned with the military bureaucracy and the horrors of war. The novel is known for its non-linear narrative structure, its use of dark humor, and its biting critiques of war, capitalism, and American society.

Charlie Reilly wrote in his interview with Joseph Heller that "Heller's novels are fiercely critical of his times. As is often the case with satire, again and again his works involve a startling confrontation with the reader. The world of Heller's fiction is an eerily insane one — perhaps an eerily sane one — filled with preposterous characters mired in outrageous circumstances." (506) The novel's title has become a widely recognized term for a paradoxical situation in which a solution is impossible due to contradictory rules or conditions. The novel popularized this term and brought it into common usage.

Catch-22 has been praised for its extraordinary achievement "in terms of its radical departure from the conventions that had governed previous war novels" (Pinsker 381). It has been widely acclaimed for its literary style and its exploration of themes such as the absurdity of war, the dangers of bureaucracy and conformity, and the corruption of the American dream. In terms of politics, "men with authority in the novel do not focus on a common goal (which Clevinger believes), nor do they recognize the humanity of those they command. They value only the power they hold in the military (or the medical, religious, or commercial professions). To gain more power, these men corrupt and exploit the founding principles of the institutions they serve" (Felty 1). For instance, instead of fighting to stop totalitarian regimes that would eliminate freedom, the military itself has imposed totalitarian rule.

The novel has been praised for its innovative narrative structure and its ability to combine humor and satire with serious social commentary. *Catch-22* remains a classic of American literature and is widely studied in universities and schools.

3. Reading Material: *Catch-22* (excerpt)

I — The Texan

It was love at first sight.

The first time Yossarian saw the chaplain he fell madly in love with him.

Yossarian was in the hospital with a pain in his liver that fell just short of being jaundice. The doctors were puzzled by the fact that it wasn't quite jaundice. If it became jaundice, they could treat it. If it didn't become jaundice and went away, they could discharge him. But this just being short of jaundice all the time confused them.

Each morning they came around, three brisk and serious men with efficient mouths and inefficient eyes, accompanied by brisk and serious Nurse Duckett, one of the ward nurses who didn't like Yossarian. They read the chart at the foot of the bed and asked impatiently about the pain. They seemed irritated when he told them it was exactly the same.

"Still no movement?" the full colonel demanded.

The doctors exchanged a look when he shook his head.

"Give him another pill."

Nurse Duckett made a note to give Yossarian another pill, and the four of them moved along to the next bed. None of the nurses liked Yossarian. Actually, the pain in his liver had gone away, but Yossarian didn't say anything and the doctors never suspected. They just suspected that he had been moving his bowels and not telling anyone.

Yossarian had everything he wanted in the hospital. The food wasn't too bad, and his meals were brought to him in bed. There were extra rations of fresh meat, and during the hot part of the afternoon he and the others were served chilled fruit juice or chilled chocolate milk. Apart from the doctors and the nurses, no one ever disturbed him. For a little while in the morning he had to censor letters, but he was free after that to spend the rest of each day lying around idly with a clear conscience. He was comfortable in the hospital, and it was easy to stay on because he always ran a temperature of 101. He was even more comfortable than Dunbar, who had to keep falling down on his face in order to get his meals brought to him in bed.

After he had made up his mind to spend the rest of the war in the hospital, Yossarian wrote letters to everyone he knew saying that he was in the hospital but never mentioning why. One day he had a better idea. To everyone he knew he wrote that he was going on a very dangerous mission. "They asked for volunteers. It's very dangerous, but someone has to do it. I'll write you the instant I get back". And he had not written anyone since.

All the officer patients in the ward were forced to censor letters written by all the enlisted-men patients, who were kept in residence in wards of their own. It was a monotonous job, and Yossarian was disappointed to learn that the lives of enlisted men were only slightly more interesting than the lives of officers. After the first day he had no curiosity at all. To break the monotony, he invented games. Death to all modifiers, he declared one day, and out of every letter that passed through his hands went every adverb and every adjective. The next day he made war on articles. He reached a much higher plane of creativity the following day when he blacked out everything in the letters but "a, an" and "the". That erected more dynamic interlinear tensions, he felt, and in just about every case left a message far more universal. Soon he was proscribing parts of salutations and signatures and leaving the text untouched. One time he blacked out all but the salutation "Dear Mary" from a letter, and at the bottom he wrote, "I yearn for you tragically. R. O. Shipman, Chaplain, US Army." R.O. Shipman was the group chaplain's name.

When he had exhausted all possibilities in the letters, he began attacking the names and addresses on the envelopes, obliterating whole homes and streets, annihilating entire metropolises with careless flicks of his wrist as though he were God. *Catch-22* required that each censored letter bear the censoring officer's name. Most letters he didn't read at all. On those he didn't read at all he wrote his own name. On those he did read he wrote, "Washington Irving". When that grew monotonous, he wrote, "Irving Washington". Censoring the envelopes had serious repercussions, produced a ripple of anxiety on some ethereal military echelon that floated a C.I.D. man back into the ward posing as a patient. They all knew he was a C.I.D. man because he kept inquiring about an officer named Irving or Washington and because after his first day there, he wouldn't censor letters. He found them too monotonous.

It was a good ward this time, one of the best he and Dunbar had ever enjoyed. With them this time was the twenty-four-year-old fighter-pilot captain with the sparse golden mustache who had been shot into the Adriatic Sea in midwinter and not even caught cold. Now the summer was upon them, the captain had not been shot down, and he said he had the grippe. In the bed on Yossarian's right, still lying amorously on his belly, was the startled captain with malaria in his blood and a mosquito bite on his ass. Across the aisle from Yossarian was Dunbar, and next to Dunbar was the artillery captain with whom Yossarian had stopped playing chess. The captain was a good chess player, and the games were always interesting. Yossarian had stopped playing chess with him because the games were so interesting and they were foolish. Then there was the educated Texan from Texas who looked like someone in Technicolor and felt, patriotically, that people of means — decent folk should be given more votes than drifters, whores, criminals, degenerates, atheists and indecent folk — people without means.

Yossarian was unspringing rhythms in the letters the day they brought the Texan in. It was another quiet, hot, untroubled day. The heat pressed heavily on the roof, stifling sound. Dunbar was lying motionless on his back again with his eyes staring up at the ceiling like a doll's. He was working hard at increasing his life span. He did it by cultivating boredom. Dunbar was working so hard at increasing his life span that Yossarian thought he was dead. They put the Texan in a bed in the middle of the ward, and it wasn't long before he donated his views.

Dunbar sat up like a shot. "That's it," he cried excitedly. "There was something missing — all the time I knew there was something missing — and now I know what it is." He banged his fist down into his palm. "No patriotism," he declared.

"You're right," Yossarian shouted back. "You're right, you're right, you're right. The hot dog, the Brooklyn Dodgers. Mom's apple pie. That's what everyone's fighting for. But who's fighting for the decent folk? Who's fighting for more votes for the decent folk? There's no patriotism, that's what it is. And no matriotism, either."

The warrant officer on Yossarian's left was unimpressed. "Who gives a shit?" he asked tiredly, and turned over on his side to go to sleep.

The Texan turned out to be good-natured, generous and likable. In three days no one could stand him.

He sent shudders of annoyance scampering up ticklish spines, and everybody fled from him — everybody but the soldier in white, who had no choice. The soldier in white was encased from head to toe in plaster and gauze. He had two useless legs and two useless arms. He had been smuggled into the ward during the night, and the men had no idea he was among them until they awoke in the morning and saw the two strange legs hoisted from the hips, the two strange arms anchored up perpendicularly, all four limbs pinioned strangely in air by lead weights suspended darkly above him that never moved. Sewn into the bandages over the insides of both elbows were zippered lips through which he was fed clear fluid from a clear jar. A silent zinc pipe rose from the cement on his groin and was coupled to a slim rubber hose that carried waste from his kidneys and dripped it efficiently into a clear, stoppered jar on the floor. When the jar on the floor was full, the jar feeding his elbow was empty, and the two were simply switched quickly so that the stuff could drip back into him. All they ever really saw of the soldier in white was a frayed black hole over his mouth.

The soldier in white had been filed next to the Texan, and the Texan sat sideways on his own bed and talked to him throughout the morning, afternoon and evening in a pleasant, sympathetic drawl. The Texan never minded that he got no reply.

Temperatures were taken twice a day in the ward. Early each morning and late each afternoon Nurse Cramer entered with a jar full of thermometers and worked her way up one side of the ward and down the other, distributing a thermometer to each patient. She managed the soldier in white by inserting a thermometer into the hole over his mouth and leaving it balanced there on the lower rim. When she returned to the man in the first bed, she took his thermometer and recorded his temperature, and then moved on to the next bed and continued around the ward again. One afternoon when she had completed her first circuit of the ward and came a second time to the soldier in white, she read his thermometer and discovered that he was dead.

"Murderer," Dunbar said quietly.

The Texan looked up at him with an uncertain grin.

"Killer," Yossarian said.

What are you fellas talking about?" the Texan asked nervously.

"You murdered him," said Dunbar.

"You killed him," said Yossarian.

The Texan shrank back. "You fellas are crazy. I didn't even touch him."

"You murdered him," said Dunbar.

"I heard you kill him," said Yossarian.

"You killed him because he was a nigger," Dunbar said.

"You fellas are crazy," the Texan cried. "They don't allow niggers in here. They got a special place for niggers."

"The sergeant smuggled him in," Dunbar said.

"The Communist sergeant," said Yossarian.

"And you knew it."

The warrant officer on Yossarian's left was unimpressed by the entire incident of the soldier in white. The warrant officer was unimpressed by everything and never spoke at all unless it was to show irritation.

The day before Yossarian met the chaplain, a stove exploded in the mess hall and set fire to one side of the kitchen. An intense heat flashed through the area. Even in Yossarian's ward, almost three hundred feet away, they could hear the roar of the blaze and the sharp cracks of flaming timber. Smoke sped past the orange-tinted windows. In about fifteen minutes the crash trucks from the airfield arrived to fight the fire. For a frantic half hour it was touch and go. Then the firemen began to get the upper hand. Suddenly there was the monotonous old drone of bombers returning from a mission, and the firemen had to roll up their hoses and speed back to the field in case one of the planes crashed and caught fire. The planes landed safely. As soon as the last one was down, the firemen wheeled their trucks around and raced back up the hill to resume their fight with the fire at the hospital. When they got there, the blaze was out. It had died of its own accord, expired completely without even an ember to be watered down, and there was nothing for the disappointed firemen to do but drink tepid coffee and hang around trying to screw the nurses.

The chaplain arrived the day after the fire. Yossarian was busy expurgating all but romance words from the letters when the chaplain sat down in a chair between the beds and asked him how he was feeling. He had placed himself a bit to one side, and the captain's bars on the tab of his shirt collar were all the insignia Yossarian could see. Yossarian had no idea who he was and just took it for granted that he was either another doctor or another madman.

"Oh, pretty good," he answered. "I've got a slight pain in my liver and I haven't been the most regular of fellows, I guess, but all in all I must admit that I feel pretty good."

"That's good," said the chaplain.

"Yes," Yossarian said. "Yes, that is good."

"I meant to come around sooner," the chaplain said, "but I really haven't been well."

"That's too bad," Yossarian said.

"Just a head cold," the chaplain added quickly.

"I've got a fever of a hundred and one," Yossarian added just as quickly.

"That's too bad," said the chaplain.

"Yes," Yossarian agreed. "Yes, that is too bad."

The chaplain fidgeted. "Is there anything I can do for you?" he asked after a while.

"No, no." Yossarian sighed. "The doctors are doing all that's humanly possible, I suppose."

"No, no." The chaplain colored faintly. "I didn't mean anything like that. I meant cigarettes or books or toys."

"No, no," Yossarian said. "Thank you. I have everything I need, I suppose — everything but good health."

"That's too bad."

"Yes," Yossarian said. "Yes, that is too bad."

The chaplain stirred again. He looked from side to side a few times, then gazed up at the ceiling, then down at the floor. He drew a deep breath.

"Lieutenant Nately sends his regards," he said.

Yossarian was sorry to hear they had a mutual friend. It seemed there was a basis to their conversation after all. “You know Lieutenant Nately?” he asked regretfully.

“Yes, I know Lieutenant Nately quite well.”

“He’s a bit loony, isn’t he?”

The chaplain’s smile was embarrassed. “I’m afraid I couldn’t say. I don’t think I know him that well.”

“You can take my word for it,” Yossarian said. “He’s as goofy as they come.”

The chaplain weighed the next silence heavily and then shattered it with an abrupt question. “You are Captain Yossarian, aren’t you?”

“Nately had a bad start. He came from a good family.”

“Please excuse me,” the chaplain persisted timorously. “I may be committing a very grave error. Are you Captain Yossarian?”

“Yes,” Captain Yossarian confessed. “I am Captain Yossarian.”

“Of the 256th Squadron?”

“Of the fighting 256th Squadron,” Yossarian replied. “I didn’t know there were any other Captain Yossarians. As far as I know, I’m the only Captain Yossarian I know, but that’s only as far as I know.”

“I see,” the chaplain said unhappily.

“That’s two to the fighting eighth power,” Yossarian pointed out, “if you’re thinking of writing a symbolic poem about our squadron.”

“No,” mumbled the chaplain. “I’m not thinking of writing a symbolic poem about your squadron.”

Yossarian straightened sharply when he spied the tiny silver cross on the other side of the chaplain’s collar. He was thoroughly astonished, for he had never really talked with a chaplain before.

“You’re a chaplain,” he exclaimed ecstatically. “I didn’t know you were a chaplain.”

“Why, yes,” the chaplain answered. “Didn’t you know I was a chaplain?”

“Why, no. I didn’t know you were a chaplain.” Yossarian stared at him with a big, fascinated grin. “I’ve never really seen a chaplain before.”

The chaplain flushed again and gazed down at his hands. He was a slight man of about thirty-two with tan hair and brown diffident eyes. His face was narrow and rather pale. An innocent nest of ancient pimple pricks lay in the basin of each cheek. Yossarian wanted to help him.

“Can I do anything at all to help you?” the chaplain asked.

Yossarian shook his head, still grinning. “No, I’m sorry. I have everything I need and I’m quite comfortable. In fact, I’m not even sick.”

“That’s good.” As soon as the chaplain said the words, he was sorry and shoved his knuckles into his mouth with a giggle of alarm, but Yossarian remained silent and disappointed him. “There are other men in the group I must visit,” he apologized finally. “I’ll come to see you again, probably tomorrow.”

“Please do that,” Yossarian said.

"I'll come only if you want me to," the chaplain said, lowering his head shyly. "I've noticed that I make many of the men uncomfortable."

Yossarian glowed with affection. "I want you to." he said. "You won't make me uncomfortable."

The chaplain beamed gratefully and then peered down at a slip of paper he had been concealing in his hand all the while. He counted along the beds in the ward, moving his lips, and then centered his attention dubiously on Dunbar.

"May I inquire," he whispered softly, "if that is Lieutenant Dunbar?"

"Yes," Yossarian answered loudly, "that is Lieutenant Dunbar."

"Thank you," the chaplain whispered. "Thank you very much. I must visit with him. I must visit with every member of the group who is in the hospital."

"Even those in other wards?" Yossarian asked.

"Even those in other wards."

"Be careful in those other wards, Father," Yossarian warned. "That's where they keep the mental cases. They're filled with lunatics."

"It isn't necessary to call me Father," the chaplain explained. "I'm an Anabaptist."

"I'm dead serious about those other wards," Yossarian continued grimly. "M.P.s won't protect you, because they're craziest of all. I'd go with you myself, but I'm scared stiff. Insanity is contagious. This is the only sane ward in the whole hospital. Everybody is crazy but us. This is probably the only sane ward in the whole world, for that matter."

The chaplain rose quickly and edged away from Yossarian' s bed, and then nodded with a conciliating smile and promised to conduct himself with appropriate caution. "And now I must visit with Lieutenant Dunbar," he said. Still he lingered, remorsefully. "How is Lieutenant Dunbar?" he asked at last.

"As good as they go," Yossarian assured him. "A true prince. One of the finest, least dedicated men in the whole world."

"I didn't mean that," the chaplain answered, whispering again. "Is he very sick?"

"No, he isn't very sick. In fact, he isn't sick at all."

"That's good." The chaplain sighed with relief.

"Yes," Yossarian said.

"Yes, that is good."

"A chaplain," Dunbar said when the chaplain had visited him and gone.

"Did you see that? A chaplain."

"Wasn't he sweet?" said Yossarian. "Maybe they should give him three votes."

"Who's they?" Dunbar demanded suspiciously.

In a bed in the small private section at the end of the ward, always working ceaselessly behind the green plyboard partition, was the solemn middle-aged colonel who was visited every day by a gentle, sweet-faced woman with curly ash-blond hair who was not a nurse and not a Wac and not a Red Cross girl but who nevertheless appeared faithfully at the hospital in Pianosa each afternoon wearing pretty pastel summer dresses that were very smart and white leather pumps with heels half high at the base of nylon seams that were inevitably straight. The colonel was in Communications, and he was kept busy day and night transmitting glutinous messages from the interior into square pads of gauze which he sealed meticulously and delivered to a covered white pail that stood on the night table beside his bed. The colonel was gorgeous. He had a cavernous mouth, cavernous cheeks, cavernous, sad, mildewed eyes. His face was the color of clouded silver. He coughed quietly, gingerly, and dabbed the pads slowly at his lips with a distaste that had become automatic.

The colonel dwelt in a vortex of specialists who were still specializing in trying to determine what was troubling him. They hurled lights in his eyes to see if he could see, rammed needles into nerves to hear if he could feel. There was a urologist for his urine, a lymphologist for his lymph, an endocrinologist for his endocrines, a psychologist for his psyche, a dermatologist for his derma; there was a pathologist for his pathos, a cytologist for his cysts, and a bald and pedantic cetologist from the zoology department at Harvard who had been shanghaied ruthlessly into the Medical Corps by a faulty anode in an I.B.M. machine and spent his sessions with the dying colonel trying to discuss *Moby Dick* with him.

The colonel had really been investigated. There was not an organ of his body that had not been drugged and derogated, dusted and dredged, fingered and photographed, removed, plundered and replaced. Neat, slender and erect, the woman touched him often as she sat by his bedside and was the epitome of stately sorrow each time she smiled. The colonel was tall, thin and stooped. When he rose to walk, he bent forward even more, making a deep cavity of his body, and placed his feet down very carefully, moving ahead by inches from the knees down. There were violet pools under his eyes. The woman spoke softly, softer than the colonel coughed, and none of the men in the ward ever heard her voice.

In less than ten days the Texan cleared the ward. The artillery captain broke first, and after that the exodus started. Dunbar, Yossarian and the fighter captain all bolted the same morning. Dunbar stopped having dizzy spells, and the fighter captain blew his nose. Yossarian told the doctors that the pain in his liver had gone away. It was as easy as that. Even the warrant officer fled. In less than ten days, the Texan drove everybody in the ward back to duty — everybody but the C.I.D. man, who had caught cold from the fighter captain and come down with pneumonia.

Ⅱ — Clevinger

In a way the C.I.D. man was pretty lucky, because outside the hospital the war was still going on. Men went mad and were rewarded with medals. All over the world, boys on every side of the bomb line were laying down their lives for what they had been told was their country, and no one seemed to mind, least of all the boys who were laying down their young lives. There was no end in sight. The only end in sight was Yossarian's own, and he might have remained in the hospital until doomsday had it not been for that patriotic Texan with his infundibuliform jowls and his lumpy, rumple-headed, indestructible smile cracked forever across the front of his face like the brim of a black ten-gallon hat. The Texan wanted everybody in the ward to be happy but Yossarian and Dunbar. He was really very sick.

But Yossarian couldn't be happy, even though the Texan didn't want him to be, because outside the hospital there was still nothing funny going on. The only thing going on was a war, and no one seemed to notice but Yossarian and Dunbar. And when Yossarian tried to remind people, they drew away from him and thought he was crazy. Even Clevinger, who should have known better but didn't, had told him he was crazy the last time they had seen each other, which was just before Yossarian had fled into the hospital.

Clevinger had stared at him with apoplectic rage and indignation and, clawing the table with both hands, had shouted, "You're crazy!"

"Clevinger, what do you want from people?" Dunbar had replied wearily above the noises of the officers' club.

"I'm not joking," Clevinger persisted.

"They're trying to kill me," Yossarian told him calmly.

"No one's trying to kill you," Clevinger cried.

"Then why are they shooting at me?" Yossarian asked.

"They're shooting at everyone," Clevinger answered. "They're trying to kill everyone."

"And what difference does that make?"

Clevinger was already on the way, half out of his chair with emotion, his eyes moist and his lips quivering and pale. As always occurred when he quarreled over principles in which he believed passionately, he would end up gasping furiously for air and blinking back bitter tears of conviction.

There were many principles in which Clevinger believed passionately. He was crazy.

"Who's they?" he wanted to know. "Who, specifically, do you think is trying to murder you?"

"Every one of them," Yossarian told him.

"Every one of whom?"

"Every one of whom do you think?"

"I haven't any idea."

"Then how do you know they aren't?"

"Because…" Clevinger sputtered, and turned speechless with frustration.

Clevinger really thought he was right, but Yossarian had proof, because strangers he didn't know shot at him with cannons every time he flew up into the air to drop bombs on them, and it wasn't funny at all. And if that wasn't funny, there were lots of things that weren't even funnier. There was nothing funny about living like a bum in a tent in Pianosa between fat mountains behind him and a placid blue sea in front that could gulp down a person with a cramp in the twinkling of an eye and ship him back to shore three days later, all charges paid, bloated, blue and putrescent, water draining out through both cold nostrils.

The tent he lived in stood right smack up against the wall of the shallow, dull-colored forest separating his own squadron from Dunbar's. Immediately alongside was the abandoned railroad ditch that carried the pipe that carried the aviation gasoline down to the fuel trucks at the airfield. Thanks to Orr, his roommate, it was the most luxurious tent in the squadron. Each time Yossarian returned from one of his holidays in the hospital or rest leaves in Rome, he was surprised by some new comfort Orr had installed in his absence — running water, wood-burning fireplace, cement floor. Yossarian had chosen the site, and he and Orr had raised the tent together. Orr, who was a grinning pygmy with pilot's wings and thick, wavy brown hair parted in the middle, furnished all the knowledge, while Yossarian, who was taller, stronger, broader and faster, did most of the work. Just the two of them lived there, although the tent was big enough for six. When summer came, Orr rolled up the side flaps to allow a breeze that never blew to flush away the air baking inside.

Immediately next door to Yossarian was Havermeyer, who liked peanut brittle and lived all by himself in the two-man tent in which he shot tiny field mice every night with huge bullets he had stolen from the dead man in Yossarian's tent. On the other side of Havermeyer stood the tent. McWatt no longer shared with Clevinger, who had still not returned when Yossarian came out of the hospital. McWatt shared his tent now with Nately, who was away in Rome courting the sleepy whore he had fallen so deeply in love with there who was bored with her work and bored with him too. McWatt was crazy. He was a pilot and flew his plane as low as he dared over Yossarian's tent as often as he could, just to see how much he could frighten him, and loved to go buzzing with a wild, close roar over the wooden raft floating on empty oil drums out past the sand bar at the immaculate white beach where the men went swimming naked. Sharing a tent with a man who was crazy wasn't easy, but Nately didn't care. He was crazy, too, and had gone every free day to work on the officers' club that Yossarian had not helped build.

Actually, there were many officers' clubs that Yossarian had not helped build, but he was proudest of the one on Pianosa. It was a sturdy and complex monument to his powers of determination. Yossarian never went there to help until it was finished; then he went there often, so pleased was he with the large, fine, rambling, shingled building. It was truly a splendid structure, and Yossarian throbbed with a mighty sense of accomplishment each time he gazed at it and reflected that none of the work that had gone into it was his.

There were four of them seated together at a table in the officers' club, the last time he and Clevinger had called each other crazy. They were seated in back near the crap table on which Appleby always managed to win. Appleby was as good at shooting crap as he was at playing ping-pong, and he was as good at playing ping-pong as he was at everything else. Everything Appleby did, he did well. Appleby was a fair-haired boy from Iowa who believed in God, Motherhood and the American Way of Life, without ever thinking about any of them, and everybody who knew him liked him.

"I hate that son of a bitch," Yossarian growled.

The argument with Clevinger had begun a few minutes earlier when Yossarian had been unable to find a machine gun. It was a busy night. The bar was busy, the crap table was busy, the ping-pong table was busy. The people Yossarian wanted to machine-gun were busy at the bar singing sentimental old favorites that nobody else ever tired of. Instead of machine-gunning them, he brought his heel down hard on the ping-pong ball that came rolling toward him off the paddle of one of the two officers playing.

"That Yossarian," the two officers laughed, shaking their heads, and got another ball from the box on the shelf.

"That Yossarian," Yossarian answered them.

"Yossarian," Nately whispered cautiously.

"You see what I mean?" asked Clevinger.

The officers laughed again when they heard Yossarian mimicking them. "That Yossarian," they said more loudly.

"That Yossarian," Yossarian echoed.

"Yossarian, please," Nately pleaded.

"You see what I mean?" asked Clevinger. "He has antisocial aggressions."

"Oh, shut up," Dunbar told Clevinger. Dunbar liked Clevinger because Clevinger annoyed him and made the time go slow.

"Appleby isn't even here," Clevinger pointed out triumphantly to Yossarian.

"Who said anything about Appleby?" Yossarian wanted to know.

"Colonel Cathcart isn't here, either."

"Who said anything about Colonel Cathcart?"

"What son of a bitch do you hate, then?"

"What son of a bitch is here?"

"I'm not going to argue with you," Clevinger decided. "You don't know who you hate."

"Whoever's trying to poison me," Yossarian told him.

"Nobody's trying to poison you."

They poisoned my food twice, didn't they? Didn't they put poison in my food during Ferrara and during the Great Big Siege of Bologna?"

"They put poison in everybody's food," Clevinger explained.

"And what difference does that make?"

"And it wasn't even poison!" Clevinger cried heatedly, growing more emphatic as he grew more confused.

As far back as Yossarian could recall, he explained to Clevinger with a patient smile, somebody was always hatching a plot to kill him. There were people who cared for him and people who didn't, and those who didn't hate him and were out to get him. They hated him because he was Assyrian. But they couldn't touch him, he told Clevinger, because he had a sound mind in a pure body and was as strong as an ox. They couldn't touch him because he was Tarzan, Mandrake, Flash Gordon. He was Bill Shakespeare. He was Cain, Ulysses, the Flying Dutchman; he was Lot in Sodom, Deirdre of the Sorrows, Sweeney in the nightingales among trees. He was miracle ingredient Z-247.

"He was crazy!" Clevinger interrupted, shrieking. "That's what you are! Crazy!"

"Immense. I'm a real, slam-bang, honest-to-goodness, three-fisted humdinger. I'm a bona fide superman."

"Superman?" Clevinger cried. "Superman?"

"Superman," Yossarian corrected.

"Hey, fellas, cut it out," Nately begged with embarrassment. "Everybody's looking at us."

"You're crazy," Clevinger shouted vehemently, his eyes filling with tears. "You've got a Jehovah complex."

"I think everyone is Nathaniel."

Clevinger arrested himself in mid-declamation, suspiciously. "Who's Nathaniel?"

"Nathaniel who?" inquired Yossarian innocently.

Clevinger skirted the trap neatly. "You think everybody is Jehovah. You're no better than Raskolnikov—"

"Who?"

"— yes, Raskolnikov, who —"

"Raskolnikov!"

"— who — I mean it — who felt he could justify killing an old woman—"

"No better than?"

"— yes, justify, that's right — with an ax! And I can prove it to you!" Gasping furiously for air, Clevinger enumerated Yossarian's symptoms: an unreasonable belief that everybody around him was crazy, a homicidal impulse to machine-gun strangers, retrospective falsification, an unfounded suspicion that people hated him and were conspiring to kill him.

But Yossarian knew he was right, because, as he explained to Clevinger, to the best of his knowledge he had never been wrong. Everywhere he looked was a nut, and it was a sensible young gentleman like himself could do to maintain his perspective amid so much madness. And it was urgent that he did, for he knew his life was in peril.

Yossarian eyed everyone he saw warily when he returned to the squadron from the hospital. Milo was away, too, in Smyrna for the fig harvest. The mess hall ran smoothly in Milo's absence. Yossarian had responded ravenously to the pungent aroma of spicy lamb while he was still in the cab of the ambulance bouncing down along the knotted road that lay like a broken suspender between the hospital and the squadron. There was shish-kabob for lunch, huge, savory hunks of spitted meat sizzling like the devil over charcoal after marinating seventy-two hours in a secret mixture Milo had stolen from a crooked trader in the Levant, served with Iranian rice and asparagus tips Parmesan, followed by cherries jubilee for dessert and then steaming cups of fresh coffee with Benedictine and brandy. The meal was served in enormous helpings on damask tablecloths by the skilled Italian waiters Major de Coverley had kidnaped from the mainland and given to Milo.

Yossarian gorged himself in the mess hall until he thought he would explode and then sagged back in a contented stupor, his mouth filmy with a succulent residue. None of the officers in the squadron had ever eaten so well as they ate regularly in Milo's mess hall, and Yossarian wondered awhile if it wasn't perhaps all worth it. But then he burped and remembered that they were trying to kill him, and he sprinted out of the mess hall wildly and ran looking for Doc Daneeka to have himself taken off combat duty and sent home. He found Doc Daneeka in sunlight, sitting on a high stool outside his tent.

"Fifty missions," Doc Daneeka told him, shaking his head. "The colonel wants fifty missions."

"But I've only got forty-four!"

Doc Daneeka was unmoved. He was a sad, birdlike man with the spatulate face and scrubbed, tapering features of a well-groomed rat.

"Fifty missions," he repeated, still shaking his head. "The colonel wants fifty missions."

4. Questions for Discussion

(1) In what ways does *Catch-22* critique the military industrial complex and its influence on American politics?

(2) How does the concept of "Catch-22" relate to the political tactics used by American politicians to maintain power and control over their constituents?

(3) How does the character of Yossarian represent the disillusionment and cynicism towards American politics and society during the time period in which the book was written?

(4) How does *Catch-22* satirize the American political system of the twentieth century?

Section Two: Henry David Thoreau and *On the Duty of Civil Disobedience*

Henry David Thoreau (1817—1862) was an American author, naturalist, transcendentalist, critic, and philosopher who is best known for *Walden*, a reflection upon simple living in natural surroundings, and his essay, *On the Duty of Civil Disobedience*, an argument for individual resistance to the unfair treatment of civil government. He is considered as one of the most influential figures in American thought and literature.

1. Introduction of Henry David Thoreau

Henry David Thoreau was born on July 12, 1817. in Concord, Massachusetts. His father operated a local pencil factory, and his mother rented out parts of the family's home to boarders. As a gifted student, Thoreau attended Harvard University in 1833. He graduated from Harvard in 1837 and struggled with what to do next. Then, he chose to open a school and became a teacher. He befriended Emerson and became his follower. Through Emerson, he got to know transcendentalism and many of the movement's leading figures, including Bronson Alcott and Margaret Fuller. As his mentor, Emerson gave Thoreau much help and used his influence to promote Thoreau's literary career. Emerson also allowed Thoreau to use his property and built a cottage for himself near Walden Pond, which inspired his most important works. Thoreau spent more than two years there, trying to work as little as possible rather than engage in the pattern of six days on with one day off, spending most of his time on philosophical and literary thinking. There he wrote *A Week on the Concord and Merrimack Rivers* in 1849, drawing from a boating trip he took with his brother John in 1839. He published *Walden* in 1854 and it became an immediate success. *Walden* has inspired and informed the works of naturalists, environmentalists and writers for many years. While living at Walden Pond, Thoreau also had one-night experience of staying in jail after refusing to pay a poll tax. This experience led him to write one of his best-known and most influential essays, *On the Duty of Civil Disobedience*. He was opposed to slavery and the Mexican-American War. He proposed that one should follow his own conscience rather than blindly follow laws and government policies.

Since its publication in 1849, *On the Duty of Civil Disobedience* has inspired many leaders of protest movements around the world. This non-violent approach to political and social resistance has influenced American Civil Rights Movement activists such as Martin Luther King Jr. and Mahatma Gandhi. Thoreau also supported abolitionist movement and wrote an essay to support John Brown, a leader of abolitionism, calling him "an angel of light" and "the bravest and humanist man in all the country". Thoreau died on May 6, 1862 and was praised as "an original thinker", "father of environmentalism" and a man who is far ahead of his times.

2. Introduction of *On the Duty of Civil Disobedience*

Civil disobedience, as one form of civil resistance, is commonly defined as being nonviolent resistance. In July, 1846, Thoreau was put into jail since he refused to pay a poll-tax of $2.00 to a government which he thought unjust. Though this event was insignificant enough, it inspired Thoreau to write one of his famous essays *On the Duty of Civil Disobedience*, which advocated passive resistance to unjust laws.

First published in 1849, *On the Duty of Civil Disobedience* is an essay written by Henry David Thoreau, in which he attempts to convince readers to oppose the Mexican-American War and the institution of slavery as a whole. "The central theme of *On the Duty of Civil Disobedience* is that there is no higher duty than to live according to one's conscience; when an individual's conscience is at odds with the government, breaking the law is justified. Thoreau rejects the traditional political process as a means of change, arguing that representative government gives the individual conscience away to a legislative body operating by majority rule" (Banion 192).

In *On the Duty of Civil Disobedience*, Thoreau articulates his concerns about the relationship between the individual and the state. He argues that the government is chosen by people to achieve certain ends of people and exists to execute citizens' will. Thoreau questions the integrity of the state, suggesting that the self-interests of a few can direct the policies of the government against the will of the people. "Thoreau repeatedly characterizes government as operating according to expediency, whereas the individual citizen is capable of acting according to a higher principle, that of morality or conscience. In advising that the individual has not merely the right but the duty to resist unjust laws, Thoreau postulates a higher, spiritual law that supersedes civil or constitutional law" (Jaskoski1). He believes that under ideal conditions people will no longer need government because they will be truly self-governing, but, until that day arrives, he asks for a "better government".

3. Reading Material: *On the Duty of Civil Disobedience* (excerpt)

I heartily accept the motto, "That government is best which governs least"; and I should like to see it acted up to more rapidly and systematically. Carried out, it finally amounts to this, which also I believe, "That government is best which governs not at all"; and when men are prepared for it, that will be the kind of government which they will have. Government is at best but an expedient; but most governments are usually, and all governments are sometimes, inexpedient. The objections which have been brought against a standing army, and they are many and weighty, and deserve to prevail, may also at last be brought against a standing government. The standing army is only an arm of the standing government. The government itself, which is only the mode which the people have chosen to execute their will, is equally liable to be abused and perverted before the people can act through it. Witness the present Mexican war, the work of comparatively a few individuals using the standing government as their tool; for, in the outset, the people would not have consented to this measure.

This American government — what is it but a tradition, though a recent one, endeavoring to transmit itself unimpaired to posterity, but each instant losing some of its integrity? It has not the vitality and force of a single living man; for a single man can bend it to his will. It is a sort of wooden gun to the people themselves: But it is not the less necessary for this; for the people must have some complicated machinery or other, and hear its din, to satisfy that idea of government which they have. Governments show thus how successfully men can be imposed on, even impose on themselves, for their own advantage. It is excellent, we must all allow. Yet this government never of itself furthered any enterprise, but by the alacrity with which it got out of its way. It does not keep the country free. It does not settle the West. It does not educate. The character inherent in the American people has done all that has been accomplished; and it would have done somewhat more, if the government had not sometimes got in its way. For government is an expedient by which men would fain succeed in letting one another alone; and, as has been said, when it is the most expedient, the governed are most let alone by it. Trade and commerce, if they were not made of India rubber, would never manage to bounce over the obstacles which legislators are continually putting in their way; and, if one were to judge these men wholly by the effects of their actions, and not partly by their intentions, they would deserve to be classed and punished with those mischievous persons who put obstructions on the railroads.

But, to speak practically and as a citizen, unlike those who call themselves no-government men, I ask for, not at once no government, but at once a better government. Let every man make known what kind of government would command his respect, and that will be one step toward obtaining it.

After all, the practical reason why, when the power is once in the hands of the people, a majority are permitted, and for a long period continue, to rule, is not because they are most likely to be in the right, nor because this seems fairest to the minority, but because they are physically the strongest. But a government in which the majority rule in all cases cannot be based on justice, even as far as men understand it. Can there not be a government in which majorities do not virtually decide right and wrong, but conscience? — in which majorities decide only those questions to which the rule of expediency is applicable? Must the citizen ever for a moment, or in the least degree, resign his conscience to the legislator? Why has every man a conscience, then? I think that we should be men first, and subjects afterward. It is not desirable to cultivate a respect for the law, so much as for the right. The only obligation which I have a right to assume is to do at any time what I think right. It is truly enough said that a corporation has no conscience; but a corporation of conscientious men is a corporation with a conscience. Law never made men a whit more just; and, by means of their respect for it, even the well-disposed are daily made the agents of injustice. A common and natural result of an undue respect for law is, that you may see a file of soldiers, colonel, captain, corporal, privates, powder-monkeys, and all, marching in admirable order over hill and dale to the wars, against their wills, ay, against their common sense and consciences, which makes it very steep marching indeed, and produces a palpitation of the heart. They have no doubt that it is a damnable business in which they are concerned; they are all peaceably inclined. Now, what are they? Men at all? or small movable forts and magazines, at the service of some unscrupulous man in power? Visit the Navy Yard, and behold a marine, such a man as an American government can make, or such as it can make a man with its black arts — a mere shadow and reminiscence of humanity, a man laid out alive and standing, and already, as one may say, buried under arms with funeral accompaniments, "Not a drum was heard, not a funeral note, as his corse to the rampart we hurried; Not a soldier discharged his farewell shot O'er the grave where our hero we buried."

The mass of men serves the State thus, not as men mainly, but as machines, with their bodies. They are the standing army, and the militia, jailers, constables, posse comitatus, etc. In most cases there is no free exercise whatever of the judgment or of the moral sense; but they put themselves on a level with wood and earth and stones; and wooden men can perhaps be manufactured that will serve the purpose as well. Such command no more respect than men of straw, or a lump of dirt. They have the same sort of worth only as horses and dogs. Yet such as these even are commonly esteemed good citizens. Others, as most legislators, politicians, lawyers, ministers, and office-holders, serve the state chiefly with their heads; and, as they rarely make any moral distinctions, they are as likely to serve the devil, without intending it, as God. A very few, as heroes, patriots, martyrs, reformers in the great sense, and men, serve the state with their consciences also, and so necessarily resist it for the most part; and they are commonly treated as enemies by it. A wise man will only be useful as a man, and will not submit to be "clay," and "stop a hole to keep the wind away," but leave that office to his dust at least:

> "I am too high-born to be propertied,
> To be a secondary at control,
> or useful serving-man and instrument
> To any sovereign state throughout the world."

He who gives himself entirely to his fellow-men appears to them useless and selfish; but he who gives himself partially to them is pronounced a benefactor and philanthropist.

How does it become a man to behave toward this American government today? I answer that he cannot without disgrace be associated with it. I cannot for an instant recognize that political organization as my government which is the slave's government also.

All men recognize the right of revolution; that is, the right to refuse allegiance to, and to resist the government, when its tyranny or its inefficiency are great and unendurable. But almost all say that such is not the case now. But such was the case, they think, in the Revolution of '75. If one were to tell me that this was a bad government because it taxed certain foreign commodities brought to its ports, it is most probable that I should not make an ado about it, for I can do without them: all machines have their friction; and possibly this does enough good to counterbalance the evil. At any rate, it is a great evil to make a stir about it. But when the friction comes to have its machine, and oppression and robbery are organized, I say, let us not have such a machine any longer. In other words, when a sixth of the population of a nation which has undertaken to be the refuge of liberty are slaves, and a whole country is unjustly overrun and conquered by a foreign army, and subjected to military law, I think that it is not too soon for honest men to rebel and revolutionize. What makes this duty the more urgent is the fact that the country so overrun is not our own, but ours is the invading army.

Paley, a common authority with many on moral questions, in his chapter on the *Duty of Submission to Civil Government*, resolves all civil obligation into expediency; and he proceeds to say that, "so long as the interest of the whole society requires it, that is, so long as the established government cannot be resisted or changed without public inconveniency, it is the will of God that the established government be obeyed, and no longer." — "This principle being admitted, the justice of every particular case of resistance is reduced to a computation of the quantity of the danger and grievance on the one side, and of the probability and expense of redressing it on the other." Of this, he says, every man shall judge for himself. But Paley appears never to have contemplated those cases to which the rule of expediency does not apply, in which a people, as well as an individual, must do justice, cost what it may. If I have unjustly wrested a plank from a drowning man, I must restore it to him though I drown myself. This, according to Paley, would be inconvenient. But he that would save his life, in such a case, shall lose it. This people must cease to hold slaves, and to make war on Mexico, though it cost them their existence as a people.

In their practice, nations agree with Paley; but does anyone think that Massachusetts does exactly what is right at the present crisis?

'A drab of state, a cloth-o'-silver slut,

To have her train borne up, and her soul trail in the dirt."

Practically speaking, the opponents to a reform in Massachusetts are not a hundred thousand politicians at the south, but a hundred thousand merchants and farmers here, who are more interested in commerce and agriculture than they are in humanity, and are not prepared to do justice to the slave and to Mexico, cost what it may. I quarrel not with far-off foes, but with those who, near at home, co-operate with, and do the bidding of those far away, and without whom the latter would be harmless. We are accustomed to say, that the mass of men are unprepared; but improvement is slow, because the few are not materially wiser or better than the many. It is not so important that many should be as good as you, as there be some absolute goodness somewhere; for that will leaven the whole lump. There are thousands who are in opinion opposed to slavery and to the war, who yet in effect do nothing to put an end to them; who, esteeming themselves children of Washington and Franklin, sit down with their hands in their pockets, and say that they know not what to do, and do nothing; who even postpone the question of freedom to the question of free-trade, and quietly read the prices-current along with the latest advices from Mexico, after dinner, and, it may be, fall asleep over them both. What is the price-current of an honest man and patriot today? They hesitate, and they regret, and sometimes they petition; but they do nothing in earnest and with effect. They will wait, well disposed, for others to remedy the evil, that they may no longer have it to regret. At most, they give only a cheap vote, and a feeble countenance and Godspeed, to the right, as it goes by them. There are nine hundred and ninety-nine patrons of virtue to one virtuous man; but it is easier to deal with the real possessor of a thing than with the temporary guardian of it.

All voting is a sort of gaming, like checkers or backgammon, with a slight moral tinge to it, a playing with right and wrong, with moral questions; and betting naturally accompanies it. The character of the voters is not staked. I cast my vote, perchance, as I think right; but I am not vitally concerned that that right should prevail. I am willing to leave it to the majority. Its obligation, therefore, never exceeds that of expediency. Even voting for the right is doing nothing for it. It is only expressing to men feebly your desire that it should prevail. A wise man will not leave the right to the mercy of chance, nor wish it to prevail through the power of the majority. There is but little virtue in the action of masses of men. When the majority shall at length vote for the abolition of slavery, it will be because they are indifferent to slavery, or because there is but little slavery left to be abolished by their vote. They will then be the only slaves. Only his vote can hasten the abolition of slavery who asserts his own freedom by his vote.

I hear of a convention to be held at Baltimore, or elsewhere, for the selection of a candidate for the Presidency, made up chiefly of editors, and men who are politicians by profession; but I think, what is it to any independent, intelligent, and respectable man what decision they may come to? Shall we not have the advantage of his wisdom and honesty, nevertheless? Can we not count upon some independent votes? Are there not many individuals in the country who do not attend conventions? But no: I find that the respectable man, so called, has immediately drifted from his position, and despairs of his country, when his country has more reason to despair of him. He forthwith adopts one of the candidates thus selected as the only available one, thus proving that he is himself available for any purposes of the demagogue. His vote is of no more worth than that of any unprincipled foreigner or hireling native, who may have been bought. Oh for a man who is a man, and, as my neighbor says, has a bone in his back which you cannot pass your hand through! Our statistics are at fault: the population has been returned too large. How many men are there to a square thousand miles in this country? Hardly one. Does not America offer any inducement for men to settle here? The American has dwindled into an Odd Fellow, — one who may be known by the development of his organ of gregariousness, and a manifest lack of intellect and cheerful self-reliance; whose first and chief concern, on coming into the world, is to see that the alms-houses are in good repair; and, before yet he has lawfully donned the virile garb, to collect a fund for the support of the widows and orphans that may be; who, in short ventures to live only by the aid of the Mutual Insurance company, which has promised to bury him decently.

It is not a man's duty, as a matter of course, to devote himself to the eradication of any, even the most enormous wrong; he may still properly have other concerns to engage him; but it is his duty, at least, to wash his hands of it, and, if he gives it no thought longer, not to give it practically his support. If I devote myself to other pursuits and contemplations, I must first see, at least, that I do not pursue them sitting upon another man's shoulders. I must get off him first, that he may pursue his contemplations too. See what gross inconsistency is tolerated. I have heard some of my townsmen say, "I should like to have them order me out to help put down an insurrection of the slaves, or to march to Mexico, — see if I would go;" and yet these very men have each, directly by their allegiance, and so indirectly, at least, by their money, furnished a substitute. The soldier is applauded who refuses to serve in an unjust war by those who do not refuse to sustain the unjust government which makes the war; is applauded by those whose own act and authority he disregards and sets at naught; as if the State were penitent to that degree that it hired one to scourge it while it sinned, but not to that degree that it left off sinning for a moment. Thus, under the name of Order and Civil Government, we are all made at last to pay homage to and support our own meanness. After the first blush of sin comes its indifference; and from immoral it becomes, as it were, unmoral, and not quite unnecessary to that life which we have made.

The broadest and most prevalent error requires the most disinterested virtue to sustain it. The slight reproach to which the virtue of patriotism is commonly liable, the noble is most likely to incur. Those who, while they disapprove of the character and measures of a government, yield to it their allegiance and support are undoubtedly its most conscientious supporters, and so frequently the most serious obstacles to reform. Some are petitioning the State to dissolve the Union, to disregard the requisitions of the President. Why do they not dissolve it themselves, — the Union between themselves and the State, — and refuse to pay their quota into its treasury? Do not they stand in the same relation to the State, that the State does to the Union? And have not the same reasons prevented the State from resisting the Union, which have prevented them from resisting the State?

How can a man be satisfied to entertain an opinion merely, and enjoy it? Is there any enjoyment in it, if his opinion is that he is aggrieved? If you are cheated out of a single dollar by your neighbor, you do not rest satisfied with knowing that you are cheated, or with saying that you are cheated, or even with petitioning him to pay you your due; but you take effectual steps at once to obtain the full amount, and see that you are never cheated again. Action from principle — the perception and the performance of right — changes things and relations; it is essentially revolutionary, and does not consist wholly with anything which was. It not only divides states and churches, it divides families; ay, it divides the individual, separating the diabolical in him from the divine.

Unjust laws exist: shall we be content to obey them, or shall we endeavor to amend them, and obey them until we have succeeded, or shall we transgress them at once? Men generally, under such a government as this, think that they ought to wait until they have persuaded the majority to alter them. They think that, if they should resist, the remedy would be worse than the evil. But it is the fault of the government itself that the remedy is worse than the evil. It makes it worse. Why is it not more apt to anticipate and provide for reform? Why does it not cherish its wise minority? Why does it cry and resist before it is hurt? Why does it not encourage its citizens to be on the alert to point out its faults, and do better than it would have them? Why does it always crucify Christ, and excommunicate Copernicus and Luther, and pronounce Washington and Franklin rebels?

One would think, that a deliberate and practical denial of its authority was the only offence never contemplated by government; else, why has it not assigned its definite, its suitable and proportionate, penalty? If a man who has no property refuses but once to earn nine shillings for the State, he is put in prison for a period unlimited by any law that I know, and determined only by the discretion of those who placed him there; but if he should steal ninety times nine shillings from the State, he is soon permitted to go at large again.

If the injustice is part of the necessary friction of the machine of government, let it go, let it go: perchance it will wear smooth, — certainly the machine will wear out. If the injustice has a spring, or a pulley, or a rope, or a crank, exclusively for itself, then perhaps you may consider whether the remedy will not be worse than the evil; but if it is of such a nature that it requires you to be the agent of injustice to another, then, I say, break the law. Let your life be a counter friction to stop the machine. What I have to do is to see, at any rate, that I do not lend myself to the wrong which I condemn.

As for adopting the ways which the State has provided for remedying the evil, I know not of such ways. They take too much time, and a man's life will be gone. I have other affairs to attend to. I came into this world, not chiefly to make this a good place to live in, but to live in it, be it good or bad. A man has not everything to do, but something; and because he cannot do everything, it is not necessary that he should do something wrong. It is not my business to be petitioning the Governor or the Legislature any more than it is theirs to petition me; and if they should not hear my petition, what should I do then? But in this case the State has provided no way; its very Constitution is the evil. This may seem to be harsh and stubborn and unconciliatory; but it is to treat with the utmost kindness and consideration the only spirit that can appreciate or deserves it. So is all change for the better, like birth and death which convulse the body.

I do not hesitate to say that those who call themselves abolitionists should at once effectually withdraw their support, both in person and property, from the government of Massachusetts, and not wait till they constitute a majority of one, before they suffer the right to prevail through them. I think that it is enough if they have God on their side, without waiting for that other one. Moreover, any man more rights than his neighbors constitutes a majority of one already.

I meet this American government, or its representative, the State government, directly, and face to face, once a year — no more — in the person of its tax-gatherer; this is the only mode in which a man situated as I am necessarily meets it; and it then says distinctly, recognize me; and the simplest, the most effectual, and, in the present posture of affairs, the indispensable mode of treating with it on this head, of expressing your little satisfaction with and love for it, is to deny it then. My civil neighbor, the tax-gatherer, is the very man I have to deal with — for it is, after all, with men and not with parchment that I quarrel, — and he has voluntarily chosen to be an agent of the government. How shall he ever know well what he is and does as an officer of the government, or as a man, until he is obliged to consider whether he shall treat me, his neighbor, for whom he has respect, as a neighbor and well-disposed man, or as a maniac and disturber of the peace, and see if he can get over this obstruction to his neighborliness without a ruder and more impetuous thought or speech corresponding with his action? I know this well, that if one thousand, if one hundred, if ten men whom I could name — if ten honest men only — aye, if one HONEST man, in this State of Massachusetts, ceasing to hold slaves, were actually to withdraw from this co-partnership, and be locked up in the county jail therefor, it would be the abolition of slavery in America. For it matters not how small the beginning may seem to be: what is once well done is done forever. But we love better to talk about it: that we say is our mission. Reform keeps many scores of newspapers in its service, but not one man. If my esteemed neighbor, the State's ambassador, who will devote his days to the settlement of the question of human rights in the Council Chamber, instead of being threatened with the prisons of Carolina, were to sit down the prisoner of Massachusetts, that State which is so anxious to foist the sin of slavery upon her sister, — though at present she can discover only an act of inhospitality to be the ground of a quarrel with her, — the Legislature would not wholly waive the subject the following winter.

Under a government which imprisons any unjustly, the true place for a just man is also a prison. The proper place today, the only place which Massachusetts has provided for her freer and less desponding spirits, is in her prisons, to be put out and locked out of the State by her own act, as they have already put themselves out by their principles. It is there that the fugitive slave, and the Mexican prisoner on parole, and the Indian come to plead the wrongs of his race, should find them; on that separate, but more free and honorable ground, where the State places those who are not with her, but against her — the only house in a slave-state in which a free man can abide with honor. If any think that their influence would be lost there, and their voices no longer afflict the ear of the State, that they would not be as an enemy within its walls, they do not know by how much truth is stronger than error, nor how much more eloquently and effectively he can combat injustice who has experienced a little in his own person. Cast your whole vote, not a strip of paper merely, but your whole influence. A minority is powerless while it conforms to the majority; it is not even a minority then; but it is irresistible when it clogs by its whole weight. If the alternative is to keep all just men in prison, or give up war and slavery, the State will not hesitate which to choose. If a thousand men were not to pay their tax-bills this year, that would not be a violent and bloody measure, as it would be to pay them, and enable the State to commit violence and shed innocent blood. This is, in fact, the definition of a peaceable revolution, if any such is possible. If the tax-gatherer, or any other public officer, asks me, as one has done, "But what shall I do?" my answer is, "If you really wish to do anything, resign your office." When the subject has refused allegiance, and the officer has resigned his office, then the revolution is accomplished. But even suppose blood should flow. Is there not a sort of blood shed when the conscience is wounded? Through this wound a man's real manhood and immortality flow out, and he bleeds to an everlasting death. I see this blood flowing now.

I have contemplated the imprisonment of the offender, rather than the seizure of his goods — though both will serve the same purpose, — because they who assert the purest right, and consequently are the most dangerous to a corrupt State, commonly have not spent much time in accumulating property. To such the State renders comparatively small service, and a slight tax is wont to appear exorbitant, particularly if they are obliged to earn it by special labor with their hands. If there were one who lived wholly without the use of money, the State itself would hesitate to demand it of him. But the rich man — not to make any invidious comparison — is always sold to the institution which makes him rich. Absolutely speaking, the more money, the less virtue; for money comes between a man and his objects, and obtains them for him; and it was certainly no great virtue to obtain it. It puts to rest many questions which he would otherwise be taxed to answer; while the only new question which it puts is the hard but superfluous one, how to spend it. Thus his moral ground is taken from under his feet. The opportunities of living are diminished in proportion as what are called the "means" are increased. The best thing a man can do for his culture when he is rich is to endeavor to carry out those schemes which he entertained when he was poor. Christ answered the Herodians according to their condition. "Show me the tribute-money," said he; — and one took a penny out of his pocket; — if you use money which has the image of Caesar on it, and which he has made current and valuable, that is, if you are men of the State, and gladly enjoy the advantages of Caesar's government, then pay him back some of his own when he demands it; "Render therefore to Caesar that which is Caesar's, and to God those things which are God's," — leaving them no wiser than before as to which was which; for they did not wish to know.

When I converse with the freest of my neighbors, I perceive that, whatever they may say about the magnitude and seriousness of the question, and their regard for the public tranquility, the long and the short of the matter is, that they cannot spare the protection of the existing government, and they dread the consequences to their property and families. For my own part, I should not like to think that I ever rely on the protection of the State. But, if I deny the authority of the State when it presents its tax-bill, it will soon take and waste all my property, and so harass me and my children without end. This is hard. This makes it impossible for a man to live honestly, and at the same time comfortably in outward respects. It will not be worth the while to accumulate property; that would be sure to go again. You must hire or squat somewhere, and raise but a small crop, and eat that soon. You must live within yourself, and depend upon yourself always tucked up and ready for a start, and not have many affairs. A man may grow rich in Turkey even, if he will be in all respects a good subject of the Turkish government. Confucius said, "If a state is governed by the principles of reason, poverty and misery are subjects of shame; if a state is not governed by the principles of reason, riches and honors are the subjects of shame." No: until I want the protection of Massachusetts to be extended to me in some distant southern port, where my liberty is endangered, or until I am bent solely on building up an estate at home by peaceful enterprise, I can afford to refuse allegiance to Massachusetts, and her right to my property and life. It costs me less in every sense to incur the penalty of disobedience to the State than it would to obey. I should feel as if I were worth less in that case.

Some years ago, the State met me in behalf of the church, and commanded me to pay a certain sum toward the support of a clergyman whose preaching my father attended, but never I myself. "Pay it," it said, "or be locked up in the jail." I declined to pay. But unfortunately, another man saw fit to pay it. I did not see why the schoolmaster should be taxed to support the priest, and not the priest the schoolmaster; for I was not the State's schoolmaster, but I supported myself by voluntary subscription. I did not see why the lyceum should not present its tax-bill, and have the State to back its demand, as well as the church. However, at the request of the selectmen, I condescended to make some such statement as this in writing: "Know all men by these presents, that I, Henry Thoreau, do not wish to be regarded as a member of any incorporated society which I have not joined." This I gave to the town clerk; and he has it. The State, having thus learned that I did not wish to be regarded as a member of that church, has never made a like demand on me since; though it said that it must adhere to its original presumption that time. If I had known how to name them, I should then have signed off in detail from all the societies which I never signed on to; but I did not know where to find such a complete list.

I have paid no poll-tax for six years. I was put into a jail once on this account, for one night; and, as I stood considering the walls of solid stone, two or three feet thick, the door of wood and iron, a foot thick, and the iron grating which strained the light, I could not help being struck with the foolishness of that institution which treated me as if I were mere flesh and blood and bones, to be locked up. I wondered that it should have concluded at length that this was the best use it could put me to, and had never thought to avail itself of my services in some way. I saw that, if there was a wall of stone between me and my townsmen, there was a still more difficult one to climb or break through, before they could get to be as free as I was. I did not for a moment feel confined, and the walls seemed a great waste of stone and mortar. I felt as if I alone of all my townsmen had paid my tax. They plainly did not know how to treat me, but behaved like persons who are underbred. In every threat and in every compliment there was a blunder; for they thought that my chief desire was to stand the other side of that stone wall. I could not but smile to see how industriously they locked the door on my meditations, which followed them out again without let or hindrance, and they were really all that was dangerous. As they could not reach me, they had resolved to punish my body; just as boys, if they cannot come at some person against whom they have a spite, will abuse his dog. I saw that the State was half-witted, that it was timid as a lone woman with her silver spoons, and that it did not know its friends from its foes, and I lost all my remaining respect for it, and pitied it.

Thus, the State never intentionally confronts a man's sense, intellectual or moral, but only his body, his senses. It is not armed with superior wit or honesty, but with superior physical strength. I was not born to be forced. I will breathe after my own fashion. Let us see who is the strongest. What force has a multitude? They only can force me who obey a higher law than I. They force me to become like themselves. I do not hear of men being forced to live this way or that by masses of men. What sort of life were that to live? When I meet a government which says to me, "Your money or your life," why should I be in haste to give it my money? It may be in a great strait, and not know what to do: I cannot help that. It must help itself; do as I do. It is not worth the while to snivel about it. I am not responsible for the successful working of the machinery of society. I am not the son of the engineer. I perceive that, when an acorn and a chestnut fall side by side, the one does not remain inert to make way for the other, but both obey their own laws, and spring and grow and flourish as best they can, till one, perchance, overshadows and destroys the other. If a plant cannot live according to its nature, it dies; and so a man.

The night in prison was novel and interesting enough. The prisoners in their shirt-sleeves were enjoying a chat and the evening air in the doorway, when I entered. But the jailer said, "Come, boys, it is time to lock up;" and so they dispersed, and I heard the sound of their steps returning into the hollow apartments. My room mate was introduced to me by the jailer as "a first-rate fellow and a clever man." When the door was locked, he showed me where to hang my hat, and how he managed matters there. The rooms were whitewashed once a month; and this one, at least, was the whitest, most simply furnished, and probably the neatest apartment in town. He naturally wanted to know where I came from, and what brought me there; and, when I had told him, I asked him in my turn how he came there, presuming him to be an honest man, of course; and, as the world goes, I believe he was. "Why," he said, "they accuse me of burning a barn; but I never did it." As near as I could discover, he had probably gone to bed in a barn when drunk, and smoked his pipe there; and so a barn was burnt. He had the reputation of being a clever man, had been there some three months waiting for his trial to come on, and would have to wait as much longer; but he was quite domesticated and contented, since he got his board for nothing, and thought that he was well treated.

He occupied one window, and I the other; and I saw that, if one stayed there long, his principal business would be to look out the window. I had soon read all the tracts that were left there, and examined where former prisoners had broken out, and where a grate had been sawed off, and heard the history of the various occupants of that room; for I found that even here there was a history and a gossip which never circulated beyond the walls of the jail. Probably this is the only house in the town where verses are composed, which are afterward printed in a circular form, but not published.

I was shown quite a long list of verses which were composed by some young men who had been detected in an attempt to escape, who avenged themselves by singing them.

I pumped my fellow-prisoner as dry as I could, for fear I should never see him again; but at length he showed me which was my bed, and left me to blow out the lamp.

It was like travelling into a far country, such as I had never expected to behold, to lie there for one night. It seemed to me that I never had heard the town-clock strike before, nor the evening sounds of the village; for we slept with the windows open, which were inside the grating. It was to see my native village in the light of the Middle Ages, and our Concord was turned into a Rhine stream, and visions of knights and castles passed before me. They were the voices of old burghers that I heard in the streets. I was an involuntary spectator and auditor of whatever was done and said in the kitchen of the adjacent village-inn — a wholly new and rare experience to me. It was a closer view of my native town. I was fairly inside of it. I never had seen its institutions before. This is one of its peculiar institutions; for it is a shire town. I began to comprehend what its inhabitants were about.

In the morning, our breakfasts were put through the hole in the door, in small oblong-square tin pans, made to fit, and holding a pint of chocolate, with brown bread, and an iron spoon. When they called for the vessels again, I was green enough to return what bread I had left; but my comrade seized it, and said that I should lay that up for lunch or dinner. Soon after, he was let out to work at haying in a neighboring field, whither he went every day, and would not be back till noon; so he bade me good-day, saying that he doubted if he should see me again.

When I came out of prison — for someone interfered, and paid that tax — I did not perceive that great changes had taken place on the common, such as he observed who went in a youth and emerged a tottering and gray-headed man; and yet a change had to my eyes come over the scene — the town, and State, and country — greater than any that mere time could affect. I saw yet more distinctly the State in which I lived. I saw to what extent the people among whom I lived could be trusted as good neighbors and friends; that their friendship was for summer weather only; that they did not greatly propose to do right; that they were a distinct race from me by their prejudices and superstitions; that in their sacrifices to humanity, they ran no risks, not even to their property; that after all they were not so noble but they treated the thief as he had treated them, and hoped, by a certain outward observance and a few prayers, and by walking in a particular straight though useless path from time to time, to save their souls. This may be to judge my neighbors harshly; for I believe that most of them are not aware that they have such an institution as the jail in their village.

It was formerly the custom in our village, when a poor debtor came out of jail, for his acquaintances to salute him, looking through their fingers, which were crossed to represent the grating of a jail window, "How do ye do?" My neighbors did not thus salute me, but first looked at me, and then at one another, as if I had returned from a long journey. I was put into jail as I was going to the shoemakers' to get a shoe which was mended. When I was let out the next morning, I proceeded to finish my errand, and, having put on my mended shoe, joined a huckleberry party, who were impatient to put themselves under my conduct; and in half an hour — for the horse was soon tackled — was in the midst of a huckleberry field, on one of our highest hills, two miles off; and then the State was nowhere to be seen.

This is the whole history of "My Prisons."

I have never declined paying the highway tax, because I am as desirous of being a good neighbor as I am of being a bad subject; and as for supporting schools, I am doing my part to educate my fellow-countrymen now. It is for no particular item in the tax-bill that I refuse to pay it. I simply wish to refuse allegiance to the State, to withdraw and stand aloof from it effectually. I do not care to trace the course of my dollar, if I could, till it buys a man or a musket to shoot one with — the dollar is innocent — but I am concerned to trace the effects of my allegiance. In fact, I quietly declare war with the State, after my fashion, though I will still make what use and get what advantage of her I can, as is usual in such cases.

If others pay the tax which is demanded of me, from a sympathy with the State, they do but what they have already done in their own case, or rather they abet injustice to a greater extent than the State requires. If they pay the tax from a mistaken interest in the individual taxed, to save his property, or prevent his going to jail, it is because they have not considered wisely how far they let their private feelings interfere with the public good.

This, then, is my position at present. But one cannot be too much on his guard in such a case, lest his action be biased by obstinacy or an undue regard for the opinions of men. Let him see that he does only what belongs to himself and to the hour.

I think sometimes, Why, this people mean well; they are only ignorant; they would do better if they knew how: why give your neighbors this pain to treat you as they are not inclined to? But I think, again, this is no reason why I should do as they do, or permit others to suffer much greater pain of a different kind. Again, I sometimes say to myself, when many millions of men, without heat, without ill-will, without personal feeling of any kind, demand of you a few shillings only, without the possibility, such is their constitution, of retracting or altering their present demand, and without the possibility, on your side, of appeal to any other millions, why expose yourself to this overwhelming brute force? You do not resist cold and hunger, the winds and the waves, thus obstinately; you quietly submit to a thousand similar necessities. You do not put your head into the fire. But just in proportion as I regard this as not wholly a brute force, but partly a human force, and consider that I have relations to those millions as to so many millions of men, and not of mere brute or inanimate things, I see that appeal is possible, first and instantaneously, from them to the Maker of them, and, secondly, from them to themselves. But, if I put my head deliberately into the fire, there is no appeal to fire or to the Maker of fire, and I have only myself to blame. If I could convince myself that I have any right to be satisfied with men as they are, and to treat them accordingly, and not according, in some respects, to my requisitions and expectations of what they and I ought to be, then, like a good Mussulman and fatalist, I should endeavor to be satisfied with things as they are, and say it is the will of God. And, above all, there is this difference between resisting this and a purely brute or natural force, that I can resist this with some effect; but I cannot expect, like Orpheus, to change the nature of the rocks and trees and beasts.

I do not wish to quarrel with any man or nation. I do not wish to split hairs, to make fine distinctions, or set myself up as better than my neighbors. I seek rather, I may say, even an excuse for conforming to the laws of the land. I am but too ready to conform to them. Indeed, I have reasons to suspect myself on this head; and each year, as the tax-gatherer comes around, I find myself disposed to review the acts and position of the general and state governments, and the spirit of the people, to discover a pretext for conformity.

> "We must affect our country as our parents,
> And if at any time we alienate
> Our love or industry from doing it honor,
> We must respect effects and teach the soul
> Matter of conscience and religion,
> And not desire of rule or benefit."

I believe that the State will soon be able to take all my work of this sort out of my hands, and then I shall be no better a patriot than my fellow-countrymen. Seen from a lower point of view, the Constitution, with all its faults, is very good; the law and the courts are very respectable; even this State and this American government are, in many respects, very admirable and rare things, to be thankful for, such as a great many have described them; but seen from a point of view a little higher, they are what I have described them; seen from a higher still, and the highest, who shall say what they are, or that they are worth looking at or thinking of at all?

However, the government does not concern me much, and I shall bestow the fewest possible thoughts on it. It is not many moments that I live under a government, even in this world. If a man is thought-free, fancy-free, imagination-free, that which is not never for a long time appearing to be to him, unwise rulers or reformers cannot fatally interrupt him.

I know that most men think differently from myself; but those whose lives are by profession devoted to the study of these or kindred subjects, content me as little as any. Statesmen and legislators, standing so completely within the institution, never distinctly and nakedly behold it. They speak of moving society, but have no resting-place without it. They may be men of a certain experience and discrimination, and have no doubt invented ingenious and even useful systems, for which we sincerely thank them; but all their wit and usefulness lie within certain not very wide limits. They are wont to forget that the world is not governed by policy and expediency. Webster never goes behind government, and so cannot speak with authority about it. His words are wisdom to those legislators who contemplate no essential reform in the existing government; but for thinkers, and those who legislate for all time, he never once glances at the subject. I know of those whose serene and wise speculations on this theme would soon reveal the limits of his mind's range and hospitality. Yet, compared with the cheap professions of most reformers, and the still cheaper wisdom and eloquence of politicians in general, his are almost the only sensible and valuable words, and we thank Heaven for him. Comparatively, he is always strong, original, and, above all, practical. Still, his quality is not wisdom, but prudence. The lawyer's truth is not Truth, but consistency or a consistent expediency. Truth is always in harmony with herself, and is not concerned chiefly to reveal the justice that may consist with wrong-doing. He well deserves to be called, as he has been called, the Defender of the Constitution. There are really no blows to be given by him but defensive ones. He is not a leader, but a follower. His leaders are the men of '87. "I have never made an effort," he says, "and never propose to make an effort; I have never countenanced an effort, and never mean to countenance an effort, to disturb the arrangement as originally made, by which the various States came into the Union." Still thinking of the sanction which the Constitution gives to slavery, he says, "Because it was a part of the original compact — let it stand." Notwithstanding his special acuteness and ability, he is unable to take a fact out of its merely political relations, and behold it as it lies absolutely to be disposed of by the intellect — what, for instance, it behooves a man to do here in America today with regard to slavery, but ventures, or is driven, to make some such desperate answer as the following, while professing to speak absolutely, and as a private man — from which what new and singular code of social duties might be inferred? "The manner," says he, "in which the governments of those States where slavery exists are to regulate it is for their own consideration, under their responsibility to their constituents, to the general laws of propriety, humanity, and justice, and to God. Associations formed elsewhere, springing from a feeling of humanity, or any other cause, have nothing whatever to do with it. They have never received any encouragement from me, and they never will."

They who know of no purer sources of truth, who have traced up its stream no higher, stand, and wisely stand, by the Bible and the Constitution, and drink at it there with reverence and humility; but they who behold where it comes trickling into this lake or that pool, gird up their loins once more, and continue their pilgrimage toward its fountain-head.

No man with a genius for legislation has appeared in America. They are rare in the history of the world. There are orators, politicians, and eloquent men, by the thousand; but the speaker has not yet opened his mouth to speak who is capable of settling the much-vexed questions of the day. We love eloquence for its own sake, and not for any truth which it may utter, or any heroism it may inspire. Our legislators have not yet learned the comparative value of free-trade and of freedom, of union, and of rectitude, to a nation. They have no genius or talent for comparatively humble questions of taxation and finance, commerce and manufactures and agriculture. If we were left solely to the wordy wit of legislators in Congress for our guidance, uncorrected by the seasonable experience and the effectual complaints of the people, America would not long retain her rank among the nations. For eighteen hundred years, though perchance I have no right to say it, the New Testament has been written; yet where is the legislator who has wisdom and practical talent enough to avail himself of the light which it sheds on the science of legislation?

The authority of government, even such as I am willing to submit to — for I will cheerfully obey those who know and can do better than me, and in many things even those who neither know nor can do so well — is still an impure one: to be strictly just, it must have the sanction and consent of the governed. It can have no pure right over my person and property but what I concede to it.

The progress from an absolute to a limited monarchy, from a limited monarchy to a democracy, is a progress toward a true respect for the individual. Even the Chinese philosopher was wise enough to regard the individual as the basis of the empire. Is a democracy, such as we know it, the last improvement possible in government? Is it not possible to take a step further towards recognizing and organizing the rights of man? There will never be a really free and enlightened State until the State comes to recognize the individual as a higher and independent power, from which all its own power and authority are derived, and treats him accordingly. I please myself with imagining a State at last which can afford to be just to all men, and to treat the individual with respect as a neighbor; which even would not think it inconsistent with its own repose if a few were to live aloof from it, not meddling with it, nor embraced by it, who fulfilled all the duties of neighbors and fellow-men. A State which bore this kind of fruit, and suffered it to drop off as fast as it ripened, would prepare the way for a still more perfect and glorious State, which also I have imagined, but not yet anywhere seen

4. Questions for Discussion

(1) Please sum up Thoreau's core ideas in *On the Duty of Civil Disobedience* with some examples.

(2) What are the two government policies Thoreau most objects to in this essay?

(3) In *On the Duty of Civil Disobedience*, how does Thoreau suggest people can contribute to improving the government?

Chapter 4 Consumerism

Consumption is a very important phenomenon in American culture. According to Ann Smart Martin, "The term consumption is often associated with its Latin root — to waste, to decay, to be used up. Because it is the necessary parallel to production (what is produced must be used up), consumption implies a process or means by which goods and services move through the general economy. Thus, the study of consumption ranges widely to include the institutions that produce, market, and retail those goods and services" (Martin 143). Therefore, consumption is closely related with many aspects in society such as production, marketing and fashion, etc.

Consumerism, is called a "marketing concept" by Richard H. Buskirk, meaning that "the purpose of a business is to provide customer satisfaction" (61). According to Buskirk, it is "primarily a post-World War Ⅱ development, produced largely by economic conditions which changed from a seller's market to a buyer's market" (61). Consumer behavior is not only an economic phenomenon, but also a reflection of social politics and popular culture; it is not only a personal behavior, but also a reflection of the zeitgeist. American consumerism culture is based on the belief that consumption can bring happiness. Consumption can help us build a new identity which means we are what we buy. As for consumerism culture, Jameson points out: "New types of consumption; planned obsolescence; an ever more rapid rhythm of fashion and styling changes; the penetration of advertising, television and the media generally to a hitherto unparalleled degree throughout society... these are some of the features which would seem to mark a radical break with that older pre-war society in which high modernism was still an underground force" (19 – 20).

Consumerism is a cultural phenomenon that has developed in many parts of the world, particularly in developed countries such as the United States. At its core, consumerism is the idea that personal well-being and social status can be achieved through the acquisition and consumption of goods and services. It is a way of life that is driven by a desire for material possessions, often encouraged by advertising, marketing, and other forms of media. Consumerism has had a profound impact on society, influencing everything from the economy and politics to social relationships and personal values. While consumerism has brought many benefits, such as increased material prosperity, it has also been criticized for its negative effects, including environmental degradation, social inequality, and the erosion of traditional cultural values (Day14). As such, consumerism remains a controversial and complex issue that continues to be explored and debated by scholars, policymakers, and the general public.

When the European settlers first arrived in the United States in the 17th and 18th centuries, much of this land was rich, fertile farmland. In order to survive, they had to work hard and advocate frugality. In the early days of the formation of this country, the pioneers' industrious and frugal qualities helped them accumulate a lot of wealth. During the middle and late nineteenth century the United States gradually developed into a national market. During the late 19th century and early 20th century, a profound change took place in American society and the country began to change from a production-oriented society to a consumption-oriented society. Thanks to economic growth and income growth, people began to pour into cities in large numbers. Puritanism that has dominated American ideology for centuries has been abandoned. Rural people began to follow the cosmopolitan consumption pattern and women became the main force of consumption at that time. Industrialization brought economic growth and rising incomes. Countless new consumer goods produced by mass-production, including canned soups, ready-made shirts, packaged meat, soft drinks, and watches began to enter the family. Rich people bought luxury houses, held large dancing parties, spent lavishly on goods, and conspicuous consumption became a fashion at that time①.

At that time, consumption became a vital component of the household, and women assumed major responsibility for it. Department stores became women's favorite places. With their dazzling window displays, elaborate lighting, and numerous rooms filled with goods, the big departments were magnets for residents and tourists alike. Most of the advertising was aimed at women, who made up the majority of customers.

The United States accumulated wealth rapidly after the World War Ⅰ and people's enthusiasm for consumption was high and the idea of consumerism expanded quickly. For many middle-class Americans, the 1920s was a decade of unprecedented prosperity. Rising earnings generated more disposable income for the purchase of consumer goods. Americans in the 20th century are happier than those in the 19th century. Industrialization, urbanization, economic growth, mass production, and distribution have further created possibilities for their convenient life. In his lyrical book, *The Romance of Commerce*, H. Gordon Selfridge, the American founder of the London department store Selfridges in 1909, wrote: "It (consumption) is the yeast of progress. It pictures the desirable" (321). At that time, consumer culture began to touch every corner of social life. More and more American families began to use radios, phonographs, vacuum cleaners, washing machines, and refrigerators, which gave women more opportunities to step out of the home and expand their horizons.

Nowadays, consumption remains to be the engine of economic growth in affluent America, but more and more people are beginning to realize the dangers of excessive consumption. Western affluence has caused negative consequences for consumers themselves such as stress, ill-health, traffic congestion, pollution, noise, excessive waste, etc. But people still cannot stop the pace of rapid economic development and mass production. The advertising budget for promoting consumerist spending is an estimated $435 billion per annum, and, according to a recent Human Development Report, the growth in advertisement spending now outpaces the growth of the world

① Source: Mit Press, *A Brief History of Consumer Cultur*, Kerryn Higgs.

economy by a third. But some organizations have launched a campaign against advertising and consumption. By consuming less, buying fewer things, and generally only using the resources we truly need, we can help to reduce the environmental effects and preserve the resources for those who need them.

Many American writers have explored the themes of consumerism and its impact on society. For example, F. Scott Fitzgerald's novel *The Great Gatsby* is often seen as a critique of the excesses of the Jazz Age, a period of intense consumerism and hedonism in the 1920s. The novel's characters are consumed by a desire for wealth and status, and their reckless pursuit of these goals ultimately leads to tragedy.

Another example of literature that explores consumerism is Arthur Miller's play *Death of a Salesman*. The play tells the story of Willy Loman, a traveling salesman who is consumed by a desire for success and material possessions. Despite his hard work, Loman fails to achieve his goals and ultimately succumbs to despair.

Other writers, such as Don DeLillo, have examined the impact of consumerism on modern society. DeLillo's novel *White Noise* is a satire of consumer culture and the media, depicting a world where people are bombarded with advertisements and consume goods to stave off their fears of mortality.

Overall, American literature has often reflected and critiqued the culture of consumerism that has developed in the United States. Through literature, writers have explored the impact of consumption on society and individuals, examining its promises and pitfalls.

Section One: Kate Chopin and *A Pair of Silk Stockings*

Kate Chopin was an American author known for her groundbreaking contributions to feminist literature. She is celebrated for her short stories and her novel, *The Awakening* explores themes of female independence, sexuality, and the constraints of society.

1. Introduction of Kate Chopin

Kate Chopin was born in St. Louis, Missouri, in 1851. Her mother, Eliza Faris O'Flaherty, was a member of the prominent French-Creole community and was thus a familiar figure in exclusive social circles. Chopin's father, Thomas O'Flaherty, was an Irish immigrant who had successfully established himself as a merchant and subsequently participated in various business ventures. At age five, Kate was sent to boarding school at Sacred Heart, where she was taught by nuns, until her father was killed in a train accident. She lived with her mother and grandmother who gave her much education and moral counseling.

On June 9, 1870, Chopin married Oscar Chopin, a member of a French-Creole family from Natchitoches Parish in northwestern Louisiana. After their honeymoon the couple returned to New Orleans, where Oscar Chopin became a prosperous cotton businessman. The Chopins lived comfortably in a large house while raising their six children, born between 1871 and 1879.

Devoting herself to her family and household, she still managed to reconcile her own needs with the expectations of her conventional milieu. She liked to dress unconventionally and smoked cigarettes long before smoking was an approved behavior among women in her class.

When Oscar Chopin died of swamp fever in December 1882, he left Kate with an overwhelming amount of financial debt. Kate Chopin continued to raise her family by herself and meanwhile wrote and published stories. Her first two published stories appeared in the summer of 1889. Over the next fifteen years, until her death in 1904, she published two novels and wrote almost a hundred stories and sketches, two-thirds of them set in Louisiana and peopled with characters drawn from the rich cultural mixture of the region. she wrote realistically and outspokenly about human, especially female sexuality. She was also a prolific writer. In her short literary career that spanned no more than fourteen years, Chopin produced three novels, more than a hundred short stories, and numerous poems, essays, and translations. By the 1890s, Chopin's works were being published in famous periodicals and magazines while she did experience some harsh criticism for her then-controversial portrayal of women. When in 1899 her novel *The Awakening* was published, she was censured both locally and nationally. *Daily Mirror* confessed to "a sick feeling" (Dimock 63) upon reading the book. *The St. Louis Republic* thought that something as dangerous as *The Awakening* "should be labeled poison" (ibid). When she died of a cerebral hemorrhage in August 1904, she pitifully lost her fame in American literary scene. But critics later acknowledge that she is a female writer who possesses true literary genius. The 1970s and 1980s saw something of "a Chopin revival" — a revival to which many influential critics contributed to praising her genius, including famous critics like Sandra Gilbert and Elaine Showalter.

2. Introduction of *A Pair of Silk Stockings*

The story was written by Kate Chopin in 1897. It is about a woman, Mrs. Sommers, who is very devoted to her family and for whom her children were of prior concern. When she spends money, she always puts her children's needs as her first priority. But one day, when she gets 15 dollars, she decides to spend all the money on herself. By this act, Chopin implies that Mrs. Sommers seems to be almost in the grip of some consumerist mania. It's possible to analyze the short story as a commentary on American consumerism during this period, which saw the rise of the department store and advertising. Therefore, the story can be read as a direct response to the birth of American consumerism that promised women an escape from their mundane domestic lives through the thrill of shopping. Throughout the story, Mrs. Sommers uses consumerism to avoid the mundanity of everyday life and tries to reclaim her subjectivity as a woman. In shopping she becomes an active consumer rather than a passive woman who always focuses on her children and family. For Mrs. Sommers, her consumption behavior gives her an illusion that she is equal to those wealthy and fashionable class, but we know that her sense of belonging is ultimately an empty dream. Through this story, Chopin exposes the absurdity of American consumerism, and the superficiality of the social class system.

3. Reading Material: *A Pair of Silk Stockings*

Little Mrs. Sommers one day found herself the unexpected possessor of fifteen dollars. It seemed to her a very large amount of money, and the way in which it stuffed and bulged her worn old *porte-monnaie* gave her a feeling of importance such as she had not enjoyed for years.

The question of investment was one that occupied her greatly. For a day or two she walked about apparently in a dreamy state, but really absorbed in speculation and calculation. She did not wish to act hastily, to do anything she might afterward regret. But it was during the still hours of the night when she lay awake revolving plans in her mind that she seemed to see her way clearly toward a proper and judicious use of the money.

A dollar or two should be added to the price usually paid for Janie's shoes, which would insure their lasting an appreciable time longer than they usually did. She would buy so and so many yards of percale for new shirt waists for the boys and Janie and Mag. She had intended to make the old ones do by skillful patching. Mag should have another gown. She had seen some beautiful patterns, veritable bargains in the shop windows. And still there would be left enough for new stockings — two pairs apiece — and what darning that would save for a while! She would get caps for the boys and sailor-hats for the girls. The vision of her little brood looking fresh and dainty and new for once in their lives excited her and made her restless and wakeful with anticipation.

The neighbors sometimes talked of certain "better days" that little Mrs. Sommers had known before she had ever thought of being Mrs. Sommers. She herself indulged in no such morbid retrospection. She had no time — no second of time to devote to the past. The needs of the present absorbed her every faculty. A vision of the future like some dim, gaunt monster sometimes appalled her, but luckily tomorrow never comes.

Mrs. Sommers was one who knew the value of bargains; who could stand for hours making her way inch by inch toward the desired object that was selling below cost. She could elbow her way if need be; she had learned to clutch a piece of goods and hold it and stick to it with persistence and determination till her turn came to be served, no matter when it came.

But that day she was a little faint and tired. She had swallowed a light luncheon — no! when she came to think of it, between getting the children fed and the place righted, and preparing herself for the shopping bout, she had actually forgotten to eat any luncheon at all!

She sat herself upon a revolving stool before a counter that was comparatively deserted, trying to gather strength and courage to charge through an eager multitude that was besieging breast-works of shirting and figured lawn. An all-gone limp feeling had come over her and she rested her hand aimlessly upon the counter. She wore no gloves. By degrees she grew aware that her hand had encountered something very soothing, very pleasant to touch. She looked down to see that her hand lay upon a pile of silk stockings. A placard nearby announced that they had been reduced in price from two dollars and fifty cents to one dollar and ninety-eight cents; and a young girl who stood behind the counter asked her if she wished to examine their line of silk hosiery. She smiled, just as if she had been asked to inspect a tiara of diamonds with the ultimate view of purchasing it. But she went on feeling the soft, sheeny luxurious things — with both hands now, holding them up to see them glisten, and to feel them glide serpent-like through her fingers.

Two hectic blotches came suddenly into her pale cheeks. She looked up at the girl.

"Do you think there are any eights-and-a-half among these?"

There were any number of eights-and-a-half. In fact, there were more of that size than any other. Here was a light-blue pair; there were some lavender, some all black and various shades of tan and gray. Mrs. Sommers selected a black pair and looked at them very long and closely. She pretended to be examining their texture, which the clerk assured her was excellent.

"A dollar and ninety-eight cents," she mused aloud. "Well, I'll take this pair." She handed the girl a five-dollar bill and waited for her change and for her parcel. What a very small parcel it was! It seemed lost in the depths of her shabby old shopping-bag.

Mrs. Sommers after that did not move in the direction of the bargain counter. She took the elevator, which carried her to an upper floor into the region of the ladies' waiting-rooms. Here, in a retired corner, she exchanged her cotton stockings for the new silk ones which she had just bought. She was not going through any acute mental process or reasoning with herself, nor was she striving to explain to her satisfaction the motive of her action. She was not thinking at all. She seemed for the time to be taking a rest from that laborious and fatiguing function and to have abandoned herself to some mechanical impulse that directed her actions and freed her of responsibility.

How good was the touch of the raw silk to her flesh! She felt like lying back in the cushioned chair and reveling for a while in the luxury of it. She did for a little while. Then she replaced her shoes, rolled the cotton stockings together and thrust them into her bag. After doing this she crossed straight over to the shoe department and took her seat to be fitted.

She was fastidious. The clerk could not make her out; he could not reconcile her shoes with her stockings, and she was not too easily pleased. She held back her skirts and turned her feet one way and her head another way as she glanced down at the polished, pointed-tipped boots. Her foot and ankle looked very pretty. She could not realize that they belonged to her and were a part of herself. She wanted an excellent and stylish fit, she told the young fellow who served her, and she did not mind the difference of a dollar or two more in the price so long as she got what she desired.

It was a long time since Mrs. Sommers had been fitted with gloves. On rare occasions when she had bought a pair they were always "bargains," so cheap that it would have been preposterous and unreasonable to have expected them to be fitted to the hand.

Now she rested her elbow on the cushion of the glove counter, and a pretty, pleasant young creature, delicate and deft of touch, drew a long-wristed "kid" over Mrs. Sommers' hand. She smoothed it down over the wrist and buttoned it neatly, and both lost themselves for a second or two in admiring contemplation of the little symmetrical gloved hand. But there were other places where money might be spent.

There were books and magazines piled up in the window of a stall a few paces down the street. Mrs. Sommers bought two high-priced magazines such as she had been accustomed to read in the days when she had been accustomed to other pleasant things. She carried them without wrapping. As well as she could she lifted her skirts at the crossings. Her stockings and boots and well-fitting gloves had worked marvels in her bearing — had given her a feeling of assurance, a sense of belonging to the well-dressed multitude.

She was very hungry. Another time she would have stilled the cravings for food until reaching her own home, where she would have brewed herself a cup of tea and taken a snack of anything that was available. But the impulse that was guiding her would not suffer her to entertain any such thought.

There was a restaurant at the corner. She had never entered its doors; from the outside she had sometimes caught glimpses of spotless damask and shining crystal, and soft-stepping waiters serving people of fashion.

When she entered her appearance created no surprise, no consternation, as she had half feared it might. She seated herself at a small table alone, and an attentive waiter at once approached to take her order. She did not want a profusion; she craved a nice and tasty bite — a half dozen blue-points, a plump chop with cress, a something sweet — a *crème-frappé*, for instance; a glass of Rhine wine, and after all a small cup of black coffee.

While waiting to be served she removed her gloves very leisurely and laid them beside her. Then she picked up a magazine and glanced through it, cutting the pages with a blunt edge of her knife. It was all very agreeable. The damask was even more spotless than it had seemed through the window, and the crystal more sparkling. There were quiet ladies and gentlemen, who did not notice her, lunching at the small tables like her own. A soft, pleasing strain of music could be heard, and a gentle breeze was blowing through the window. She tasted a bite, and she read a word or two, and she sipped the amber wine and wiggled her toes in the silk stockings. The price of it made no difference. She counted the money out to the waiter and left an extra coin on his tray, whereupon he bowed before her as before a princess of royal blood.

There was still money in her purse, and her next temptation presented itself in the shape of a matinée poster.

It was a little later when she entered the theatre, the play had begun and the house seemed to her to be packed. But there were vacant seats here and there, and into one of them she was ushered, between brilliantly dressed women who had gone there to kill time and eat candy and display their gaudy attire. There were many others who were there solely for the play and acting. It is safe to say there was no one present who bore quite the attitude which Mrs. Sommers did to her surroundings. She gathered in the whole — stage and players and people in one wide impression, and absorbed it and enjoyed it. She laughed at the comedy and wept — she and the gaudy woman next to her wept over the tragedy. And they talked a little together over it. And the gaudy woman wiped her eyes and sniffled on a tiny square of filmy, perfumed lace and passed little Mrs. Sommers her box of candy.

The play was over, the music ceased, the crowd filed out. It was like a dream ended. People scattered in all directions. Mrs. Sommers went to the corner and waited for the cable car.

A man with keen eyes, who sat opposite to her, seemed to like the study of her small, pale face. It puzzled him to decipher what he saw there. In truth, he saw nothing — unless he were wizard enough to detect a poignant wish, a powerful longing that the cable car would never stop anywhere, but go on and on with her forever.

4. Questions for Discussion

(1) What role does advertising play in Mrs. Sommers' decision to indulge in luxury items?

(2) Why does Mrs. Sommers spend all of her money on herself? How do you understand the story in relation to American consumerism?

(3) In what ways does Mrs. Sommers' experience challenge or reinforce traditional gender roles in terms of consumption?

(4) What commentary does the story offer about the relationship between consumerism and personal fulfillment or satisfaction?

Section Two: Don DeLillo and *The White Noise*

Don DeLillo is an American author known for his innovative and provocative novels, which explore some of the most pressing concerns of contemporary society. *The White Noise* remains to be his representative work. Jay Parini commented that "Few American novelists have been as ambitious or playful as Don DeLillo in recording the complex currents of our time, an era in which electronic images have usurped primal reality, and society has become organized around the consumption of commercial commodities" (1). In a rich fictional oeuvre whose characters inhabit the microcosms of advertising, sports, pop music, science, espionage, academe, and waste management, among others, DeLillo becomes an ambitious writer who tries to decipher America in the era following World War Ⅱ.

1. Introduction of Don DeLillo

Don DeLillo was born on November 20, 1936, in the Bronx, New York City, and grew up in an Italian-American family. He attended Fordham University, where he earned a degree in communication arts, and later worked as an advertising copywriter before devoting himself to writing full-time.

DeLillo's literary career began in the late 1960s, with the publication of his first novel, *Americana*, in 1971. However, it was his breakthrough novel, *White Noise*, published in 1985, that established him as a major voice in American literature. The novel won the National Book Award and is considered a seminal work of postmodern fiction. His subsequent novels, such as *Libra*, *Mao II*, *Underworld*, and *Cosmopolis*, have continued to explore contemporary themes such as the impact of technology, the effects of consumerism, and the complexities of political and cultural power.

DeLillo's writing style is known for its linguistic experimentation, intellectual depth, and complex structure. He often employs unconventional narrative techniques, such as fragmented storytelling, stream-of-consciousness, and multiple narrators, to challenge traditional notions of storytelling and explore the subjective nature of reality.

DeLillo has been recognized with numerous awards and honors, including the PEN/Faulkner Award for Fiction, the Library of Congress Prize for American Fiction, and the National Book Foundation Medal for Distinguished Contribution to American Letters. In addition to his novels, DeLillo has written several plays, including *The Day Room* and *Valparaiso*, which have been produced both in the United States and abroad.

DeLillo's work has had a significant impact on contemporary literature and culture, influencing writers, filmmakers, and artists around the world. His novels are frequently taught in universities and are the subject of numerous critical studies and scholarly articles. With a career spanning over five decades, DeLillo remains one of the most important and influential writers of our time.

2. Introduction of *White Noise*

White Noise is a postmodern work of fiction written by Don DeLillo and published in 1985. The story is set in a small college town in the United States and follows the life of Jack Gladney, a professor of Hitler studies and his family.

The novel mixes different elements such as death, environmental catastrophe, dehumanizing technology, and Adolf Hitler. Stephen Amidon commented that "*White Noise* is also a deliriously funny satire on our media-soaked world and a very warm portrait of a splintered yet stubbornly coherent American family. That DeLillo was able to mix these seemingly disparate elements into a coherent fictional whole is testament to his status as one of the most acute, intelligent, and sane of America's postwar novelists. *White Noise* stands in the front rank of his body of work." (Amidon 285).

The title *White Noise* is a reference to the constant hum of background noise that surrounds us in modern life, whether it be from electronic devices, advertising, or other sources. Consumerism is one of the most important themes in the novel. "*White Noise* is glutted with consumerism and consumer goods. The novel's characters are acutely conscious of the fact that they live in a society that bombards them with a superabundance of products and the advertising needed to make these often useless objects desirable" (295).

The story begins with an "airborne toxic event" that occurs near the town, causing a sense of panic and uncertainty among the population. As the Gladney family navigates the aftermath of the event, they are forced to confront their own mortality and the fragility of their existence in a world dominated by media and technology. As the novel progresses, the Gladneys encounter a series of surreal and bizarre events, including a trip to a tourist attraction called "The Most Photographed Barn in America" and a confrontation with a man who claims to have created a pill that cures fear of death.

Throughout the novel, DeLillo employs a satirical tone and a fragmented narrative structure, highlighting the absurdity and uncertainty of contemporary life. *White Noise* has been praised for its social commentary, exploration of the human condition, and innovative use of language and structure (Carter 115).

3. Reading Material: *White Noise* (excerpt)

Waves and Radiation

1

The station wagons arrived at noon, a long shining line that coursed through the west campus. In single file they eased around the orange I-beam sculpture and moved toward the dormitories. The roofs of the station wagons were loaded down with carefully secured suitcases full of light and heavy clothing; with boxes of blankets, boots and shoes, stationery and books, sheets, pillows, quilts; with rolled-up rugs and sleeping bags; with bicycles, skis, rucksacks, English and Western saddles, inflated rafts. As cars slowed to a crawl and stopped, students sprang out and raced to the rear doors to begin removing the objects inside; the stereo sets, radios, personal computers; small refrigerators and table ranges; the cartons of phonograph records and cassettes; the hairdryers and styling irons; the tennis rackets, soccer balls, hockey and lacrosse sticks, bows and arrows; the controlled substances, the birth control pills and devices; the junk food still in shopping bags — onion-and-garlic chips, nacho thins, peanut creme patties, Waffelos and Kabooms, fruit chews and toffee popcorn; the Dum-Dum pops, the Mystic mints.

I've witnessed this spectacle every September for twenty-one years. It is a brilliant event, invariably. The students greet each other with comic cries and gestures of sodden collapse. Their summer has been bloated with criminal pleasures, as always. The parents stand sun-dazed near their automobiles, seeing images of themselves in every direction. The conscientious suntans. The well-made faces and wry looks. They feel a sense of renewal, of communal recognition. The women crisp and alert, in diet trim, knowing people's names. Their husband's content to measure out the time, distant but ungrudging, accomplished in parenthood, something about them suggesting massive insurance coverage. This assembly of station wagons, as much as anything they might do in the course of the year, more than formal liturgies or laws, tells the parents they are a collection of the like-minded and the spiritually akin, a people, a nation.

I left my office and walked down the hill and into town. There are houses in town with turrets and two-story porches where people sit in the shade of ancient maples. There are Greek revival and Gothic churches. There is an insane asylum with an elongated portico, ornamented dormers and a steeply pitched roof topped by a pineapple finial. Babette and I and our children by previous marriages live at the end of a quiet street in what was once a wooded area with deep ravines. There is an expressway beyond the backyard now, well below us, and at night as we settle into our brass bed the sparse traffic washes past, a remote and steady murmur around our sleep, as of dead souls babbling at the edge of a dream.

I am chairman of the department of Hitler studies at the College-on-the-Hill. I invented Hitler studies in North America in March of 1968. It was a cold bright day with intermittent winds out of the east. When I suggested to the chancellor that we might build a whole department around Hitler's life and work, he was quick to see the possibilities. It was an immediate and electrifying success. The chancellor went on to serve as adviser to Nixon, Ford and Carter before his death on a ski lift in Austria.

At Fourth and Elm, cars turn left for the supermarket. A policewoman crouched inside a boxlike vehicle patrols the area looking for cars parked illegally, for meter violations, lapsed inspection stickers. On telephone poles all over town there are homemade signs concerning lost dogs and cats, sometimes in the handwriting of a child.

2

Babette is tall and fairly ample; there is a girth and heft to her. Her hair is a fanatical blond mop, a particular tawny hue that used to be called dirty blond. If she were a petite woman, the hair would be too cute, too mischievous and contrived. Size gives her tousled aspect a certain seriousness. Ample women do not plan such things. They lack the guile for conspiracies of the body.

"You should have been there," I said to her.

"Where?"

"It's the day of the station wagons."

"Did I miss it again? You're supposed to remind me."

"They stretched all the way down past the music library and onto the interstate. Blue, green, burgundy, brown. They gleamed in the sun like a desert caravan."

"You know I need reminding, Jack."

Babette, disheveled, has the careless dignity of someone too preoccupied with serious matters to know or care what she looks like. Not that she is a gift-bearer of great things as the world generally reckons them. She gathers and tends the children, teaches a course in an adult education program, belongs to a group of volunteers who read to the blind. Once a week she reads to an elderly man named Treadwell who lives on the edge of town. He is known as Old Man Treadwell, as if he were a landmark, a rock formation or brooding swamp. She reads to him from the National Enquirer, the National Examiner, the National Express, the Globe, the World, the Star. The old fellow demands his weekly dose of cult mysteries. Why deny him? The point is that Babette, whatever she is doing, makes me feel sweetly rewarded, bound up with a full-souled woman, a lover of daylight and dense life, the miscellaneous swarming air of families. I watch her all the time doing things in measured sequence, skillfully, with seeming ease, unlike my former wives, who had a tendency to feel estranged from the objective world — a self-absorbed and high-strung bunch, with ties to the intelligence community.

"It's not the station wagons I wanted to see. What are the people like? Do the women wear plaid skirts, cable-knit sweaters? Are the men in hacking jackets? What's a hacking jacket?"

"They've grown comfortable with their money," I said. "They genuinely believe they're entitled to it. This conviction gives them a kind of rude health. They glow a little."

"I have trouble imagining death at that income level," she said.

"Maybe there is no death as we know it. Just documents changing hands."

"Not that we don't have a station wagon ourselves."

"It's small, it's metallic gray, it has one whole rusted door."

"Where is Wilder?" she said, routinely panic-stricken, calling out to the child, one of hers, sitting motionless on his tricycle in the backyard.

Babette and I do our talking in the kitchen. The kitchen and the bedroom are the major chambers around here, the power haunts, the sources. She and I are alike in this, that we regard the rest of the house as storage space for furniture, toys, all the unused objects of earlier marriages and different sets of children, the gifts of lost in-laws, the hand-me-downs and rummages. Things, boxes. Why do these possessions carry such sorrowful weight? There is a darkness attached to them, a foreboding. They make me wary not of personal failure and defeat but of something more general, something large in scope and content.

She came in with Wilder and seated him on the kitchen counter. Denise and Steffie came downstairs and we talked about the school supplies they would need. Soon it was time for lunch. We entered a period of chaos and noise. We milled about, bickered a little, dropped utensils. Finally, we were all satisfied with what we'd been able to snatch from the cupboards and refrigerator or swipe from each other and we began quietly plastering mustard or mayonnaise on our brightly colored food. The mood was one of deadly serious anticipation, a reward hard-won. The table was crowded and Babette and Denise elbowed each other twice, although neither spoke. Wilder was still seated on the counter surrounded by open cartons, crumpled tinfoil, shiny bags of potato chips, bowls of pasty substances covered with plastic wrap, flip-top rings and twist ties, individually wrapped slices of orange cheese. Heinrich came in, studied the scene carefully, my only son, then walked out the back door and disappeared.

"This isn't the lunch I'd planned for myself," Babette said. "I was seriously thinking yogurt and wheat germ."

"Where have we heard that before?" Denise said.

"Probably right here," Steffie said.

"She keeps buying that stuff."

"But she never eats it," Steffie said.

"Because she thinks if she keeps buying it, she'll have to eat it just to get rid of it. It's like she's trying to trick herself."

"It takes up half the kitchen."

"But she throws it away before she eats it because it goes bad," Denise said. "So then she starts the whole thing all over again."

"Wherever you look," Steffie said, "there it is."

"She feels guilty if she doesn't buy it, she feels guilty if she buys it and doesn't eat it, she feels guilty when she sees it in the fridge, she feels guilty when she throws it away."

"It's like she smokes but she doesn't," Steffie said.

Denise was eleven, a hard-nosed kid. She led a more or less daily protest against those of her mother's habits that struck her as wasteful or dangerous. I defended Babette. I told her I was the one who needed to show discipline in matters of diet. I reminded her how much I liked the way she looked. I suggested there was an honesty inherent in bulkiness if it is just the right amount. People trust a certain amount of bulk in others.

But she was not happy with her hips and thighs, walked at a rapid clip, ran up the stadium steps at the neoclassical high school. She said I made virtues of her flaws because it was my nature to shelter loved ones from the truth. Something lurked inside the truth, she said.

The smoke alarm went off in the hallway upstairs, either to let us know the battery had just died or because the house was on fire. We finished our lunch in silence.

3

Department heads wear academic robes at the College-on-the-Hill. Not grand sweeping full-length affairs but sleeveless tunics puckered at the shoulders. I like the idea. I like clearing my arm from the folds of the garment to look at my watch. The simple act of checking the time is transformed by this flourish. Decorative gestures add romance to a life. Idling students may see time itself as a complex embellishment, a romance of human consciousness, as they witness the chairman walking across campus, crook'd arm emerging from his medieval robe, the digital watch blinking in late summer dusk. The robe is black, of course, and goes with almost anything.

There is no Hitler building as such. We are quartered in Centenary Hall, a dark brick structure we share with the popular culture department, known officially as American environments. A curious group. The teaching staff is composed almost solely of New York émigrés, smart, thuggish, movie-mad, trivia-crazed. They are here to decipher the natural language of the culture, to make a formal method of the shiny pleasures they'd known in their Europe-shadowed childhoods — an Aristotelianism of bubble gum wrappers and detergent jingles. The department head is Alfonse (Fast Food) Stompanato, a broad-chested glowering man whose collection of prewar soda pop bottles is on permanent display in an alcove. All his teachers are male, wear rumpled clothes, need haircuts, cough into their armpits. Together they look like teamster officials assembled to identify the body of a mutilated colleague. The impression is one of pervasive bitterness, suspicion and intrigue.

An exception to some of the above is Murray Jay Siskind, an ex-sportswriter who asked me to have lunch with him in the dining room, where the institutional odor of vaguely defined food aroused in me an obscure and gloomy memory. Murray was new to the Hill, a stoop-shouldered man with little round glasses and an Amish beard. He was a visiting lecturer on living icons and seemed embarrassed by what he'd gleaned so far from his colleagues in popular culture.

"I understand the music, I understand the movies, I even see how comic books can tell us things. But there are full professors in this place who read nothing but cereal boxes."

"It's the only avant-garde we've got."

"Not that I'm complaining. I like it here. I'm totally enamored of this place. A small-town setting. I want to be free of cities and sexual entanglements. Heat. This is what cities mean to me. You get off the train and walk out of the station and you are hit with the full blast. The heat of air, traffic and people. The heat of food and sex. The heat of tall buildings. The heat that floats out of the subways and the tunnels. It's always fifteen degrees hotter in the cities. Heat rises from the sidewalks and falls from the poisoned sky. The buses breathe heat. Heat emanates from crowds of shoppers and office workers. The entire infrastructure is based on heat, desperately uses up heat, breeds more heat. The eventual heat death of the universe that scientists love to talk about is already well underway and you can feel it happening all around you in any large or medium-sized city. Heat and wetness."

"Where are you living, Murray?"

"In a rooming house. I'm totally captivated and intrigued. It's a gorgeous old crumbling house near the insane asylum. Seven or eight boarders, more or less permanent except for me. A woman who harbors a terrible secret. A man with a haunted look. A man who never comes out of his room. A woman who stands by the letter box for hours, waiting for something that never seems to arrive. A man with no past. A woman with a past. There is a smell about the place of unhappy lives in the movies that I really respond to."

"Which one are you?" I said.

"I'm the Jew. What else would I be?"

There was something touching about the fact that Murray was dressed almost totally in corduroy. I had the feeling that since the age of eleven in his crowded plot of concrete he'd associated this sturdy fabric with higher learning in some impossibly distant and tree-shaded place.

"I can't help being happy in a town called Blacksmith," he said. "I'm here to avoid situations. Cities are full of situations, sexually cunning people. There are parts of my body I no longer encourage women to handle freely. I was in a situation with a woman in Detroit. She needed my semen in a divorce suit. The irony is that I love women. I fall apart at the sight of long legs, striding, briskly, as a breeze carries up from the river, on a weekday, in the play of morning light. The second irony is that it's not the bodies of women that I ultimately crave but their minds. The mind of a woman. The delicate chambering and massive unidirectional flow, like a physics experiment. What fun it is to talk to an intelligent woman wearing stockings as she crosses her legs. That little staticky sound of rustling nylon can make me happy on several levels. The third and related irony is that it's the most complex and neurotic and difficult women that I am invariably drawn to. I like simple men and complicated women."

Murray's hair was tight and heavy-looking. He had dense brows, wisps of hair curling up the sides of his neck. The small stiff beard, confined to his chin and unaccompanied by a mustache, seemed an optional component, to be stuck on or removed as circumstances warranted.

"What kind of lectures do you plan giving?"

"That's exactly what I want to talk to you about," he said. "You've established a wonderful thing here with Hitler. You created it, you nurtured it, you made it your own. Nobody on the faculty of any college or university in this part of the country can so much as utter the word Hitler without a nod in your direction, literally or metaphorically. This is the center, the unquestioned source. He is now your Hitler, Gladney's Hitler. It must be deeply satisfying for you. The college is internationally known as a result of Hitler studies. It has an identity, a sense of achievement. You've evolved an entire system around this figure, a structure with countless substructures and interrelated fields of study, a history within history. I marvel at the effort. It was masterful, shrewd and stunningly preemptive. It's what I want to do with Elvis."

Several days later Murray asked me about a tourist attraction known as the most photographed barn in America. We drove twenty-two miles into the country around Farmington. There were meadows and apple orchards. White fences trailed through the rolling fields. Soon the signs started appearing. THE MOST PHOTOGRAPHED BARN IN AMERICA. We counted five signs before we reached the site. There were forty cars and a tour bus in the makeshift lot. We walked along a cowpath to the slightly elevated spot set aside for viewing and photographing. All the people had cameras; some had tripods, telephoto lenses, filter kits. A man in a booth sold postcards and slides — pictures of the barn taken from the elevated spot. We stood near a grove of trees and watched the photographers. Murray maintained a prolonged silence, occasionally scrawling some notes in a little book.

"No one sees the barn," he said finally.

A long silence followed.

"Once you've seen the signs about the barn, it becomes impossible to see the barn."

He fell silent once more. People with cameras left the elevated site, replaced at once by others.

"We're not here to capture an image, we're here to maintain one. Every photograph reinforces the aura. Can you feel it, Jack? An accumulation of nameless energies."

There was an extended silence. The man in the booth sold postcards and slides.

"Being here is a kind of spiritual surrender. We see only what the others see. The thousands who were here in the past, those who will come in the future. We've agreed to be part of a collective perception. This literally colors our vision. A religious experience in a way, like all tourism."

Another silence ensued.

"They are taking pictures of taking pictures," he said.

He did not speak for a while. We listened to the incessant clicking of shutter release buttons, the rustling crank of levers that advanced the film.

"What was the barn like before it was photographed?" he said. "What did it look like, how was it different from other barns, how was it similar to other barns? We can't answer these questions because we've read the signs, seen the people snapping the pictures. We can't get outside the aura. We're part of the aura. We're here, we're now."

He seemed immensely pleased by this.

4

When times are bad, people feel compelled to overeat. Blacksmith is full of obese adults and children, baggy-pantsed, short-legged, waddling. They struggle to emerge from compact cars; they wear sweatsuits and run in families across the landscape; they walk down the street with food in their faces; they eat in stores, cars, parking lots, on bus lines and movie lines, under the stately trees.

Only the elderly seems exempt from the fever of eating. If they are sometimes absent from their own words and gestures, they are also slim and healthy-looking, the women carefully groomed, the men purposeful and well dressed, selecting shopping carts from the line outside the supermarket.

I crossed the high school lawn and walked to the rear of the building and toward the small open stadium. Babette was running up the stadium steps. I sat across the field in the first row of stone seats. The sky was full of streaking clouds. When she reached the top of the stadium she stopped and paused, putting her hands to the high parapet and leaning into it to rest diagonally. Then she turned and walked back down, breasts chugging. The wind rippled her oversized suit. She walked with her hands on her hips, fingers spread. Her face was tilted up, catching the cool air, and she didn't see me. When she reached the bottom step, she turned to face the seats and did some kind of neck stretching exercise. Then she started running up the steps.

Three times she ascended the steps, walked slowly down. There was no one around. She worked hard, hair floating, legs and shoulders working. Every time she reached the top she leaned into the wall, head down, upper body throbbing. After the last descent I met her at the edge of the playing field and embraced her, putting my hands inside the sweatband of her gray cotton pants. A small plane appeared over the trees. Babette was moist and warm, emitting a creaturely hum.

She runs, she shovels snow, she caulks the tub and sink. She plays word games with Wilder and reads erotic classics aloud in bed at night. What do I do? I twirl the garbage bags and twist-tie them, swim laps in the college pool. When I go walking, joggers come up soundlessly behind me, appearing at my side, making me jump in idiotic fright. Babette talks to dogs and cats. I see colored spots out of the corner of my right eye. She plans ski trips that we never take, her face bright with excitement. I walk up the hill to school, noting the whitewashed stones that line the driveways of newer homes.

Who will die first?

This question comes up from time to time, like where are the car keys. It ends a sentence, prolongs a glance between us. I wonder if the thought itself is part of the nature of physical love, a reverse Darwinism that awards sadness and fear to the survivor. Or is it some inert element in the air we breathe, a rare thing like neon, with a melting point, an atomic weight? I held her in my arms on the cinder track. Kids came running our way, thirty girls in bright shorts, an improbable bobbing mass. The eager breathing, the overlapping rhythms of their footfalls. Sometimes I think our love is inexperienced. The question of dying becomes a wise reminder. It cures us of our innocence of the future. Simple things are doomed, or is that a superstition? We watched the girls come round again. They were strung out now, with faces and particular gaits, almost weightless in their craving, able to land lightly.

The Airport Marriott, the Downtown Travelodge, the Sheraton Inn and Conference Center.

On our way home I said, "Bee wants to visit at Christmas. We can put her in with Steffie."

"Do they know each other?"

"They met at Disney World. It'll be all right."

"When were you in Los Angeles?"

"You mean Anaheim."

"When were you in Anaheim?"

"You mean Orlando. It's almost three years now."

"Where was I?" she said.

My daughter Bee, from my marriage to Tweedy Browner, was just starting seventh grade in a Washington suburb and was having trouble readjusting to life in the States after two years in the Republic of Korea. She took taxis to school, made phone calls to friends in Seoul and Tokyo. Abroad she'd wanted to eat ketchup sandwiches with Trix sticks. Now she cooked fierce sizzling meals of scallion bushes and baby shrimp, monopolizing Tweedy's restaurant-quality range.

That night, a Friday, we ordered Chinese food and watched television together, the six of us. Babette had made it a rule. She seemed to think that if kids watched television one night a week with parents or stepparents, the effect would be to de-glamorize the medium in their eyes, make it wholesome domestic sport. Its narcotic undertow and eerie diseased brain-sucking power would be gradually reduced. I felt vaguely slighted by this reasoning. The evening in fact was a subtle form of punishment for us all. Heinrich sat silent over his egg rolls. Steffie became upset every time something shameful or humiliating seemed about to happen to someone on the screen. She had a vast capacity for being embarrassed on other people's behalf. Often, she would leave the room until Denise signaled to her that the scene was over. Denise used these occasions to counsel the younger girl on toughness, the need to be mean in the world, thick-skinned.

It was my own formal custom on Fridays, after an evening in front of the TV set, to read deeply in Hitler well into the night.

On one such night I got into bed next to Babette and told her how the chancellor had advised me, back in 1968, to do something about my name and appearance if I wanted to be taken seriously as a Hitler innovator. Jack Gladney would not do, he said, and asked me what other names I might have at my disposal. We finally agreed that I should invent an extra initial and call myself J. A. K. Gladney, a tag I wore like a borrowed suit.

The chancellor warned against what he called my tendency to make a feeble presentation of self. He strongly suggested I gain weight. He wanted me to "grow out" into Hitler. He himself was tall, paunchy, ruddy, jowly, big-footed and dull. A formidable combination. I had the advantages of substantial height, big hands, big feet, but badly needed bulk, or so he believed — an air of unhealthy excess, of padding and exaggeration, hulking massive-ness. If I could become uglier, he seemed to be suggesting, it would help my career enormously.

So Hitler gave me something to grow into and develop toward, tentative as I have sometimes been in the effort. The glasses with thick black heavy frames and dark lenses were my own idea, an alternative to the bushy beard that my wife of the period didn't want me to grow. Babette said she liked the series J. A. K. and didn't think it was attention-getting in a cheap sense. To her it intimated dignity, significance and prestige.

I am the false character that follows the name around.

5

Let's enjoy these aimless days while we can, I told myself, I fearing some kind of deft acceleration.

At breakfast, Babette read all our horoscopes aloud, using her storytelling voice. I tried not to listen when she got to mine, although I think I wanted to listen, I think I sought some clues.

After dinner, on my way upstairs, I heard the TV say: "Let's sit half lotus and think about our spines."

That night, seconds after going to sleep, I seemed to fall through myself, a shallow heart stopping plunge. Jarred awake, I stared into the dark, realizing I'd experienced the more or less normal muscular contraction known as the myoclonic jerk. Is this what it's like, abrupt, peremptory? Shouldn't death, I thought, be a swan dive, graceful, white-winged and smooth, leaving the surface undisturbed?

Blue jeans tumbled in the dryer.

We ran into Murray Jay Siskind at the supermarket. His basket held generic food and drink, nonbrand items in plain white packages with simple labeling. There was a white can labeled CANNED PEACHES. There was a white package of bacon without a plastic window for viewing a representative slice. A jar of roasted nuts had a white wrapper bearing the words IRREGULAR PEANUTS. Murray kept nodding to Babette as I introduced them.

"This is the new austerity," he said. "Flavorless packaging. It appeals to me. I feel I'm not only saving money but contributing to some kind of spiritual consensus. It's like World War Ⅱ. Everything is white. They'll take our bright colors away and use them in the war effort."

He was staring into Babette's eyes, picking up items from our cart and smelling them.

"I've bought these peanuts before. They're round, cubical, pockmarked, seamed. Broken peanuts. A lot of dust at the bottom of the jar. But they taste good. Most of all I like the packages themselves. You were right, Jack. This is the last avant-garde. Bold new forms. The power to shock."

A woman fell into a rack of paperback books at the front of the store. A heavyset man emerged from the raised cubicle in the far corner and moved warily toward her, head tilted to get a clearer sightline. A checkout girl said, "Leon, parsley," and he answered as he approached the fallen woman, "Seventy-nine." His breast pocket was crammed with felt-tip pens.

"So then you cook at the rooming house," Babette said.

"My room is zoned for a hot plate. I'm happy there. I read the TV listings, I read the ads in Ufologist Today. I want to immerse myself in American magic and dread. My seminar is going well. The students are bright and responsive. They ask questions and I answer them. They jot down notes as I speak. It's quite a surprise in my life."

He picked up our bottle of extra-strength pain reliever and sniffed along the rim of the child-proof cap. He smelled our honeydew melons, our bottles of club soda and ginger ale. Babette went down the frozen food aisle, an area my doctor had advised me to stay out of.

"Your wife's hair is a living wonder," Murray said, looking closely into my face as if to communicate a deepening respect for me based on this new information.

"Yes, it is," I said.

"She has important hair."

"I think I know what you mean."

"I hope you appreciate that woman."

"Absolutely."

"Because a woman like that doesn't just happen."

"I know it."

"She must be good with children. More than that, I'll bet she's great to have around in a family tragedy. She'd be the type to take control, show strength and affirmation."

"Actually she falls apart. She fell apart when her mother died."

"Who wouldn't?"

"She fell apart when Steffie called from camp with a broken bone in her hand. We had to drive all night. I found myself on a lumber company road. Babette weeping."

"Her daughter, far away, among strangers, in pain. Who wouldn't?"

"Not her daughter. My daughter."

"Not even her own daughter."

"No."

"Extraordinary. I have to love it."

The three of us left together, trying to maneuver our shopping carts between the paperback books scattered across the entrance. Murray wheeled one of our carts into the parking lot and then helped us heave and push all our double-bagged merchandise into the back of the station wagon. Cars entered and exited. The policewoman in her zippered minicab scouted the area for red flags on the parking meters. We added Murray's single lightweight bag of white items to our load and headed across Elm in the direction of his rooming house. It seemed to me that Babette and I, in the mass and variety of our purchases, in the sheer plenitude those crowded bags suggested, the weight and size and number, the familiar package designs and vivid lettering, the giant sizes, the family bargain packs with Day-Glo sale stickers, in the sense of replenishment we felt, the sense of well-being, the security and contentment these products brought to some snug home in our souls — it seemed we had achieved a fullness of being that is not known to people who need less, expect less, who plan their lives around lonely walks in the evening.

Murray took Babette's hand on leaving.

"I'd ask you to visit my room but it's too small for two people unless they're prepared to be intimate."

Murray is able to produce a look that is sneaky and frank at the same time. It is a look that gives equal credence to disaster and lecherous success. He says that in the old days of his urban entanglements he believed there was only one way to seduce a woman, with clear and open desire. He took pains to avoid self-depreciation, self-mockery, ambiguity, irony, subtlety, vulnerability, a civilized world-weariness and a tragic sense of history — the very things, he says, that are most natural to him. Of these he has allowed only one element, vulnerability, to insert itself gradually into his program of straightforward lust. He is trying to develop a vulnerability that women will find attractive. He works at it consciously, like a man in a gym with weights and a mirror. But his efforts so far have produced only this half sneaky look, sheepish and wheedling.

He thanked us for the lift. We watched him walk toward the lopsided porch, propped with cinder blocks, where a man in a rocker stared into space.

6

Heinrich's hairline is beginning to recede. I wonder about this. Did his mother consume some kind of gene-piercing substance when she was pregnant? Am I at fault somehow? Have I raised him, unwittingly, in the vicinity of a chemical dump site, in the path of air currents that carry industrial wastes capable of producing scalp degeneration, glorious sunsets? (People say the sunsets around here were not nearly so stunning thirty or forty years ago.) Man's guilt in history and in the tides of his own blood has been complicated by technology, the daily seeping falsehearted death.

The boy is fourteen, often evasive and moody, at other times disturbingly compliant. I have a sense that his ready yielding to our wishes and demands is a private weapon of reproach. Babette is afraid he will end up in a barricaded room, spraying hundreds of rounds of automatic fire across an empty mall before the SWAT teams come for him with their heavy-barreled weapons, their bullhorns and body armor.

"It's going to rain tonight."

"It's raining now," I said.

"The radio said tonight."

I drove him to school on his first day back after a sore throat and fever. A woman in a yellow slicker held up traffic to let some children cross. I pictured her in a soup commercial taking off her oilskin hat as she entered the cheerful kitchen where her husband stood over a pot of smoky lobster bisque, a smallish man with six weeks to live.

"Look at the windshield," I said. "Is that rain or isn't it?"

"I'm only telling you what they said."

"Just because it's on the radio doesn't mean we have to suspend belief in the evidence of our senses."

"Our senses? Our senses are wrong a lot more often than they're right.

This has been proved in the laboratory. Don't you know about all those theorems that say nothing is what it seems? There's no past, present or future outside our own mind. The so-called laws of motion are a big hoax. Even sound can trick the mind. Just because you don't hear a sound doesn't mean it's not out there. Dogs can hear it. Other animals. And I'm sure there are sounds even dogs can't hear. But they exist in the air, in waves. Maybe they never stop. High, high, high-pitched. Coming from somewhere."

"Is it raining," I said, "or isn't it?"

"I wouldn't want to have to say."

"What if someone held a gun to your head?"

"Who, you?"

"Someone. A man in a trench coat and smoky glasses. He holds a gun to your head and says, "'Is it raining, or isn't it? All you have to do is tell the truth and I'll put away my gun and take the next flight out of here.'"

"What truth does he want? Does he want the truth of someone traveling at almost the speed of light in another galaxy? Does he want the truth of someone in orbit around a neutron star? Maybe if these people could see us through a telescope, we might look like we were two feet two inches tall and it might be raining yesterday instead of today."

"He's holding the gun to your head. He wants your truth."

"What good is my truth? My truth means nothing. What if this guy with the gun comes from a planet in a whole different solar system? What we call rain he calls soap. What we call apples he calls rain. So, what am I supposed to tell him?"

"His name is Frank J. Smalley and he comes from St. Louis."

"He wants to know if it's raining now, at this very minute?"

"Here and now. That's right."

"Is there such a thing as now? 'Now' comes and goes as soon as you say it. How can I say it's raining now if your so-called 'now' becomes 'then' as soon as I say it?"

"You said there was no past, present, or future."

"Only in our verbs. That's the only place we find it."

"Rain is a noun. Is there rain here, in this precise locality, at whatever time within the next two minutes that you choose to respond to the question?"

"If you want to talk about this precise locality while you're in a vehicle that's obviously moving, then I think that's the trouble with this discussion."

"Just give me an answer, okay, Heinrich?"

"The best I could do is make a guess."

"Either it's raining or it isn't," I said.

"Exactly. That's my whole point. You'd be guessing. Six of one, half dozen of the other."

"But you see it's raining."

"You see the sun moving across the sky. But is the sun moving across the sky or is the earth turning?"

"I don't accept the analogy."

"You're so sure that's rain. How do you know it's not sulfuric acid from factories across the river? How do you know it's not fallout from a war in China? You want an answer here and now. Can you prove, here and now, that this stuff is rain? How do I know that what you call rain is really rain? What is rain anyway?"

"It's the stuff that falls from the sky and gets you what is called wet."

"I'm not wet. Are you wet?"

"All right," I said. "Very good."

"No, seriously, are you wet?"

"First-rate," I told him. "A victory for uncertainty, randomness and chaos. Science's finest hour."

"Be sarcastic."

"The sophists and the hairsplitters enjoy their finest hour."

"Go ahead, be sarcastic, I don't care."

Heinrich's mother lives in an ashram now. She has taken the name Mother Devi and runs the business end of things. The ashram is located on the outskirts of the former copper-smelting town of Tubb, Montana, now called Dharamsalapur. The usual rumors abound of sexual freedom, sexual slavery, drugs, nudity, mind control, poor hygiene, tax evasion, monkey-worship, torture, prolonged and hideous death.

I watched him walk through the downpour to the school entrance. He moved with deliberate slowness, taking off his camouflage cap ten yards from the doorway. At such moments I find I love him with an animal desperation, a need to take him under my coat and crush him to my chest, keep him there, protect him. He seems to bring a danger to him. It collects in the air, follows him from room to room. Babette bakes his favorite cookies. We watch him at his desk, an unpainted table covered with books and magazines. He works well into the night, plotting chess moves in a game he plays by mail with a convicted killer in the penitentiary.

It was warm and bright the next day and students on the Hill sat on lawns and in dorm windows, playing their tapes, sunbathing. The air was a reverie of wistful summer things, the last languorous day, a chance to go bare-limbed once more, smell the mown clover. I went into the Arts Duplex, our newest building, a winged affair with a facade of anodized aluminum, sea green, cloud-catching. On the lower level was the movie theater, a sloped and dark-carpeted space with two hundred plush seats. I sat in shallow light at the end of the first row and waited for my seniors to arrive.

They were all Hitler majors, members of the only class I still taught, Advanced Nazism, three hours a week, restricted to qualified seniors, a course of study designed to cultivate historical perspective, theoretical rigor and mature insight into the continuing mass appeal of fascist tyranny, with special emphasis on parades, rallies and uniforms, three credits, written reports.

Every semester I arranged for a screening of background footage. This consisted of propaganda films, scenes shot at party congresses, outtakes from mystical epics featuring parades of gymnasts and mountaineers — a collection I'd edited into an impressionistic eighty-minute documentary. Crowd scenes predominated. Close-up jostled shots of thousands of people outside a stadium after a Goebbels speech, people surging, massing, bursting through the traffic. Halls hung with swastika banners, with mortuary wreaths and death's-head insignia. Ranks of thousands of flagbearers arrayed before columns of frozen light, a hundred and thirty antiaircraft searchlights aimed straight up — a scene that resembled a geometric longing, the formal notation of some powerful mass desire. There was no narrative voice. Only chants, songs, arias, speeches, cries, cheers, accusations, shrieks.

I got to my feet and took up a position at the front of the theater, middle aisle, facing the entranceway.

They came in out of the sun in their poplin walk shorts and limited-edition T-shirts, in their easy-care knits, their polo styling and rugby stripes. I watched them take their seats, noting the subdued and reverent air, the uncertain anticipation. Some had notebooks and pencil lights; some carried lecture material in bright binders. There were whispers, rustling paper, the knocking sound of seats dropping as one by one the students settled in. I leaned against the front of the apron, waiting for the last few to enter, for someone to seal the doors against our voluptuous summer day.

Soon there was a hush. It was time for me to deliver the introductory remarks. I let the silence deepen for a moment, then cleared my arms from the folds of the academic robe in order to gesture freely.

When the showing ended, someone asked about the plot to kill Hitler. The discussion moved to plots in general. I found myself saying to the assembled heads, "All plots tend to move deathward. This is the nature of plots. Political plots, terrorist plots, lovers' plots, narrative plots, plots that are part of children's games. We edge nearer death every time we plot. It is like a contract that all must sign, the plotters as well as those who are the targets of the plot."

Is this true? Why did I say it? What does it mean?

4. Questions for Discussion

(1) How does the supermarket serve as a symbol of consumerism in *White Noise*?

(2) What role does advertising play in *White Noise*? How does the constant barrage of advertisements and media messages affect the characters' perceptions of reality, and how does the advertisement influence consumer culture in this novel?

(3) How does consumerism shape the characters' lives in *White Noise*? What specific products or brands are mentioned in the novel, and how do they impact the characters' behavior and identity?

Chapter 5 Racial Problems

The historian Oscar Handlin in his now-classic study *The Uprooted* declared that the "immigrants were American history" (3). As a country of immigrants, the United States has a wide variety of races and nationalities. White Americans account for the majority, about two thirds, while the remaining one-third of the ethnic minorities are mostly concentrated in coastal or metropolitan areas.

The black people were first brought as slaves in the Sixteenth and Seventeenth century into America. They worked in southern plantation where they were treated as animals. Their hard work has brought great wealth for the slave owners. In the middle of the 19th century, when the free capitalism of the United States began to develop rapidly, the slavery system became an obstacle to the economic development of the United States, and also became the focus of the contradictions between the South and the North. The War of Independence led by Lincoln ended with the victory of the North and the abolition of slavery. But after the abolition of slavery, it was not easy for African Americans to integrate into American culture. Most stayed in the south, where they had no land and were banned from voting. To make it worse, Jim Crow Laws supported the segregation of the black from the white people. The policy of apartheid deprives the black Americans of their equal right to education and job opportunities, making their economic status worse and worse.

This situation did not improve until the civil rights movement in the 1960s. In today's American society, although the situation of African Americans has been greatly improved, invisible racial discrimination still exists. In some big cities, black people often live in slums or downtown areas with high crime rates. The quality of black schools is often poor, and black children's educational opportunities are not as good as white children's. At the same time, black people have many hidden barriers to job opportunities. Sometimes for black people equal pay for equal work is hard to realize. Just as former American president Barack Obama once said in an interview in 2015 "the legacy of slavery, Jim Crow, discrimination in almost every institution in our lives ... that's still part of our DNA that's passed on" (Singh 103).

African American literature refers to the body of literature written by Americans of African descent. "The literature has constantly documented the struggles of African Americans with race and (anti-black) racism, African heritage and Euro-American influence, slavery and freedom, constitutional enfranchisement and educational progress, political agency and social assimilation, as well as the specters of history and modernity" (Jarrett 1). The development of African American literature has experienced different stages. The first published works of African American literature came about in the 18th century, when the United States was just coming into being. As slaves, who suffered from maltreatment both physically and mentally, the earliest African American writers sought to demonstrate the proposition that "all men are created equal" in the Declaration of Independence. They produced a certain genre of writing — slave narratives. In 1789, Olaudah Equiano published his two-volume autobiography, *The Interesting Narrative of the Life of Olaudah Equiano*. The memoir wasn't a key text in the abolitionist movement in America but it did stir some anti-slavery sentiments in Britain. As the abolitionist movement gained support in America, African Americans began to actively create some literary works against slavery. For instance, Frederick Douglass's autobiography, *Narrative of the Life of Frederick Douglass* (1845), immediately became a commercial success. By the time the Civil War began, Harriet Jacobs, a female slave, had created another significant slave narrative, *Incidents in the Life of a Slave Girl* (1861) which had to publish under a pseudonym in order to write about the gender-based violence the author experienced as a slave. The text was published originally in serial form in a New York newspaper.

After the Civil War ended, American government passed Jim Crow laws which dimmed the black people's hope of freedom and equality. Some important black political leaders like Booker T. Washington① and W.E.B. DuBois② penned important essays concerning social mobility and access to equal education. In the 1910s and 1920s, black writers grew more prominent in genres of fiction and poetry. The black writers, at that time, questioned traditional "white" aesthetic standards and tried to cultivate personal self-expression, racial pride, and literary experimentation. The movement, lasting roughly from the 1910s through the mid-1930s, is considered as an important event in African American literature, with important figures including Langston Hughes, Zora Neale Hurston, and Jean Toomer.

Just before World War II broke out, Richard Wright, a famous African American writer, published *Native Son* (1940). Narrating the violent life and death of a Chicago ghetto youth, *Native Son* revived the protest tradition of 19th century African American literature. The novel addressed the results of racial prejudice and segregation, suggesting that legal violence to individual rights ultimately could lead to murder and death. The book also shows that the country and institution should be responsible for the violence of the black people. By the early 1950s, Ralph Ellison had published *Invisible Man* (1952). This novel, different from protest novel, deals with a brand-new theme of a modern Odysseus. It follows an African American narrator from social and political struggles in the American South up to Harlem. There, he finally learns that racism is not geographically confined, but rather pervades the American consciousness.

African American literature since the 1970s features a return to African American history and focuses on relationships within the African American community. Significant female writers have emerged on the literary scene, such as Alice Walker and Toni Morrison. In her early 1980s epistolary novel *The Color Purple* (1982), Walker depicted segregated existence in 1930s Georgia.

---

① Booker Taliaferro Washington (1856 — 1915) was an American educator, author, orator, and adviser to several presidents of the United States.

② W.E.B. DuBois was an American-born Ghanaian sociologist, socialist, historian, and Pan-Africanist civil rights activist.

The book won the Pulitzer Prize for fiction, and it was later adapted into a film that was nominated for eleven Academy Awards. The novel was praised as "one of the best examples for a woman's novel as it carries an identified tradition of women's writing in terms of narrative strategy, themes addressed, and the presence of female black voices" (Benarioua 5). Morrison, the first African American to receive the Nobel Prize for literature, has transformed America's view of history and literature. Her *Beloved* (1987), recounted the injuries of slavery during the period of the American Civil War. Both writers believed that African Americans must own their history in order to understand their lives in the present.

The history of African American literature is vast and varied, covering a long period and focusing on different themes. The readings in this unit will take you back into history to explore the suffering and pains of African Americans. The excerpt from *Uncle Tomes Cabin* reveals the racial contradictions and conflicts in the United States in the 19th century. Forced to be separate from their families, the slaves were treated as animals, lacking basic human right and dignity. *Invisible Man* concentrates on the black people's dilemma of searching for identity and the injury of institutionalized slavery.

Section One: Harriet Beecher Stowe and *Uncle Tom's Cabin*

Harriet Beecher Stowe was an important American author and abolitionist. *Uncle Tom's Cabin* is a seminal novel that confronts the cruelty and immorality of slavery, presenting a powerful critique of the institution and its impact on enslaved individuals.

1. Introduction of Harriet Beecher Stowe

Harriet Beecher Stowe was born on June 14, 1811 in Litchfield, Connecticut, the seventh child of famed Congregational minister Lyman Beecher and Roxana Foote Beecher. Her famous siblings include elder sister Catherine (11 years her senior), and Henry Ward Beecher, a famous preacher and reformer. When she was 11 years old, her mother died and her father remarried. Her sister Catherine became her main caregiver. At the age of eight, she attended the Litchfield Female Academy and later she attended Catherine Beecher's Hartford Female Seminary, where she learned the courses for boys. Stowe became a teacher, working from 1829 to 1832 at the Hartford Female Seminary. In 1832, Stowe went with her father to Cincinnati, Ohio where she worked as president of the esteemed Lane Seminary. In 1836, she met and married Calvin Stowe, who was a professor at the Lane Seminary. Stowe lived for 18 years in Cincinnati, separated only by the Ohio River from a slave-holding community. She came in contact with fugitive slaves and learned about life in the South from friends and from her own visits there. Her husband encouraged her to continue with her writing after marriage. The passage of the Fugitive Slave Act of 1850, which legally compelled Northerners to return runaway slaves to southern owners, infuriated Stowe and many in the North. She began to write *Uncle Tome's Cabin*, originally serialized in the *National Era,* a magazine. *Uncle Tome's Cabin* was released as a book in March 1852, selling 300,000 copies in the US in the first year. The book aroused people's strong sympathy towards slaves. *Uncle Tomes Cabin* and the Civil War made Harriet Beecher Stowe a celebrity and her name a household word. Stowe became famous and used her fame to petition to end slavery. She toured around the country and became the most visible writer during the Civil War. Her book was important to call on people to fight against slavery. President Abraham Lincoln, upon meeting Stowe in 1862, said, "So you're the woman who wrote the book that started this great war." In 1873, Stowe and her family moved to Hartford, Connecticut, where she remained until her death in 1896.

2. Introduction of *Uncle Tom's Cabin*

Published in 1852, *Uncle Tom's Cabin* was the most famous abolitionist novel in American history. The book has been translated into every civilized language from Welsh to Bengali, and Samuel Warren has praised the author as "a woman of unaffected and profound piety, and an ardent friend of the unhappy black... Every word in her pages issues glistening and warm from the mint of woman's love and sympathy, refined and purified by Christianity. We never saw in any other work, so many and such sudden irresistible appeals to the reader's heart — appeals which, moreover, only a wife and a mother could make" (1).

Harriet Beecher Stowe's *Uncle Tom's Cabin* sought to build opposition to slavery and sympathy for fugitive slaves in the wake of the broadened Fugitive Slave Law. Stowe is a woman who has strong sympathy and a sense of justice. She saw firsthand the effects of Northern racial prejudice when living in Cincinnati. Located on the Ohio River just across from the slave state of Kentucky, the city became a destination for both runaway slaves and free blacks. Her book was based on her careful observation and firsthand experience. The sentimental novel has two major plot lines. The first follows the dark-skinned Uncle Tom as he is sold farther and farther south, where he encounters increasingly harsh treatment and eventually dies at the hands of his last master, Simon Legree. The second traces the separate journeys northward of fugitive biracial slaves George and Eliza Harris and their son, Harry. The Harrises eventually escape to Canada, reunited with long-lost relatives, and make plans to seek education in Europe before traveling to Africa as missionaries.

As an immediate best seller in the northern United States and England, *Uncle Tom's Cabin* was welcomed by abolitionists who felt that it accurately exposed the fundamental evils of slavery and was criticized by southern reviewers for supposedly exaggerating the harshness of most slaves' lives. Abraham Lincoln famously praised the novel to spark the American Civil War. As a sentimental novel, *Uncle Tom's Cabin* seeks to arouse the emotions of readers. The novel discloses the pains and sufferings the slave received including physical, psychological cruelty and sexual exploitation. The novel also reveals the racial contradictions and conflicts in the United States in the 19th century. But Stowe's idea of sending black people back to Africa to solve racial conflicts has some historical limitations.

3. Reading Material: *Uncle Tom's Cabin* (excerpt)

Select Incident of Lawful Trade

Mr. Haley and Tom jogged onward in their wagon, each, for a time, absorbed in his own reflections. Now, the reflections of two men sitting side by side are a curious thing, — seated on the same seat, having the same eyes, ears, hands and organs of all sorts, and having passed before their eyes the same objects, — it is wonderful what a variety we shall find in these same reflections!

For example, Mr. Haley: he thought first of Tom's length, and breadth, and height, and what he would sell for, if he was kept fat and in good case till he got him into market. He thought of how he should make out his gang; he thought of the respective market value of certain supposititious men and women and children who were to compose it, and other kindred topics of the business; then he thought of himself, and how humane he was, that whereas other men chained their "niggers" hand and foot both, he only put fetters on the feet, and left Tom the use of his hands, as long as he behaved well; and he sighed to think how ungrateful human nature was, so that there was even room to doubt whether Tom appreciated his mercies. He had been taken in so by "niggers" whom he had favored; but still he was astonished to consider how good-natured he yet remained!

As to Tom, he was thinking over some words of an unfashionable old book, which kept running through his head, again and again, as follows: "We have here no continuing city, but we seek one to come; wherefore God himself is not ashamed to be called our God; for he hath prepared for us a city." These words of an ancient volume, got up principally by "ignorant and unlearned men," have, through all time, kept up, somehow, a strange sort of power over the minds of poor, simple fellows, like Tom. They stir up the soul from its depths, and rouse, as with trumpet call, courage, energy, and enthusiasm, where before was only the blackness of despair.

Mr. Haley pulled out of his pocket sundry newspapers, and began looking over their advertisements, with absorbed interest. He was not a remarkably fluent reader, and was in the habit of reading in a sort of recitative half-aloud, by way of calling in his ears to verify the deductions of his eyes. In this tone he slowly recited the following paragraph:

> "EXECUTOR'S SALE, — NEGROES! — Agreeably to order of court, will be sold, on Tuesday, February 20, before the Court-house door, in the town of Washington, Kentucky, the following negroes: Hagar, aged 60; John, aged 30; Ben, aged 21; Saul, aged 25; Albert, aged 14. Sold for the benefit of the creditors and heirs of the estate of Jesse Blutchford, Esq.
>
> Samuel Morris, Thomas Flint,
> Executors.

"This yer I must look at," said he to Tom, for want of somebody else to talk to.

"Ye see, I'm going to get up a prime gang to take down with ye, Tom; it'll make it sociable and pleasant like, — good company will, ye know. We must drive right to Washington first and foremost, and then I'll clap you into jail, while I do the business."

Tom received this agreeable intelligence quite meekly; simply wondering, in his own heart, how many of these doomed men had wives and children, and whether they would feel as he did about leaving them. It is to be confessed, too, that the naive, off-hand information that he was to be thrown into jail by no means produced an agreeable impression on a poor fellow who had always prided himself on a strictly honest and upright course of life. Yes, Tom, we must confess it, was rather proud of his honesty, poor fellow, — not having very much else to be proud of; — if he had belonged to some of the higher walks of society, he, perhaps, would never have been reduced to such straits. However, the day wore on, and the evening saw Haley and Tom comfortably accommodated in Washington, — the one in a tavern, and the other in a jail.

About eleven o'clock the next day, a mixed throng was gathered around the court-house steps, — smoking, chewing, spitting, swearing, and conversing, according to their respective tastes and turns, — waiting for the auction to commence. The men and women to be sold sat in a group apart, talking in a low tone to each other. The woman who had been advertised by the name of Hagar was a regular African in feature and figure. She might have been sixty, but was older than that by hard work and disease, was partially blind, and somewhat crippled with rheumatism. By her side stood her only remaining son, Albert, a bright-looking little fellow of fourteen years. The boy was the only survivor of a large family, who had been successively sold away from her to a southern market. The mother held on to him with both her shaking hands, and eyed with intense trepidation everyone who walked up to examine him.

"Don't be feared, Aunt Hagar," said the oldest of the men, "I spoke to Mas'r Thomas 'bout it, and he thought he might manage to sell you in a lot both together."

"Dey needn't call me worn out yet," said she, lifting her shaking hands. "I can cook yet, and scrub, and scour, — I'm wuth a buying, if I do come cheap; — tell 'em dat ar, — you *tell* em," She added, earnestly.

Haley here forced his way into the group, walked up to the old man, pulled his mouth open and looked in, felt of his teeth, made him stand and straighten himself, bend his back, and perform various evolutions to show his muscles; and then passed on to the next, and put him through the same trial. Walking up last to the boy, he felt of his arms, straightened his hands, and looked at his fingers, and made him jump, to show his agility.

"He an't gwine to be sold widout me!" said the old woman, with passionate eagerness; "he and I goes in a lot together; I's rail strong yet, Mas'r and can do heaps of work, — heaps on it, Mas'r."

"On plantation?" said Haley, with a contemptuous glance. "Likely story!" and, as if satisfied with his examination, he walked out and looked, and stood with his hands in his pocket, his cigar in his mouth, and his hat cocked on one side, ready for action.

"What think of 'em?" said a man who had been following Haley's examination, as if to make up his own mind from it.

"Wal," said Haley, spitting, "I shall put in, I think, for the youngerly ones and the boy."

"They want to sell the boy and the old woman together," said the man.

"Find it a tight pull; — why, she's an old rack o' bones, — not worth her salt."

"You wouldn't then?" said the man.

"Anybody'd be a fool't would. She's half blind, crooked with rheumatism, and foolish to boot."

"Some buys up these year old critters, and sees there's a sight more wear in'em than a body'd think," said the man, reflectively.

"No go't all," said Haley; "wouldn't take her for a present, — fact, — I've seen, now."

"Wal, it is kinder pity, now, not to buy her with her son, — her heart seems so sot on him, — suppose they fling her in cheap."

"Them that's got money to spend that ar way, it's all well enough. I shall bid off on that ar boy for a plantation-hand; — wouldn't be bothered with her, no way, — not if they'd give her to me," said Haley.

"She'll take on desp't," said the man.

"Nat'lly, she will," said the trader, coolly.

The conversation was here interrupted by a busy hum in the audience; and the auctioneer, a short, bustling, important fellow, elbowed his way into the crowd. The old woman drew in her breath, and caught instinctively at her son.

"Keep close to yer mammy, Albert, — close, — dey'll put us up together," she said.

"O, mammy, I'm feared they won't," said the boy.

"Dey must, child; I can't live, no ways, if they don't." said the old creature, vehemently.

The stentorian tones of the auctioneer, calling out to clear the way, now announced that the sale was about to commence. A place was cleared, and the bidding began. The different men on the list were soon knocked off at prices which showed a pretty brisk demand in the market; two of them fell to Haley.

"Come, now, young un," said the auctioneer, giving the boy a touch with his hammer, "be up and show your springs, now."

"Put us two up together, together, — do please, Mas'r," said the old woman, holding fast to her boy.

"Be off," said the man, gruffly, pushing her hands away; "you come last. Now, darkey, spring;" and, with the word, he pushed the boy toward the block, while a deep, heavy groan rose behind him. The boy paused, and looked back; but there was no time to stay, and, dashing the tears from his large, bright eyes, he was up in a moment.

His fine figure, alert limbs, and bright face, raised an instant competition, and half a dozen bids simultaneously met the ear of the auctioneer. Anxious, half-frightened, he looked from side to side, as he heard the clatter of contending bids, — now here, now there, — till the hammer fell. Haley had got him. He was pushed from the block toward his new master, but stopped one moment, and looked back, when his poor old mother, trembling in every limb, held out her shaking hands toward him.

"Buy me too, Mas'r, for de dear Lord's sake! — buy me, — I shall die if you don't!"

"You'll die if I do, that's the kink of it," said Haley, — "no!" And he turned on his heel.

The bidding for the poor old creature was summary. The man who had addressed Haley, and who seemed not destitute of compassion, bought her for a trifle, and the spectators began to disperse.

The poor victims of the sale, who had been brought up in one place together for years, gathered round the despairing old mother, whose agony was pitiful to see.

"Couldn't dey leave me one? Mas'r allers said I should have one, — he did," she repeated over and over, in heart-broken tones.

"Trust in the Lord, Aunt Hagar," said the oldest of the men, sorrowfully.

"What good will it do?" said she, sobbing passionately.

"Mother, mother, — don't! don't!" said the boy. "They say you's got a good Mas'r."

"I don't care, — I don't care. O, Albert! oh, my boy! you's my last baby. Lord, how ken I?"

"Come, take her off, can't some of ye?" said Haley, dryly; "don't do no good for her to go on that ar way."

The old men of the company, partly by persuasion and partly by force, loosed the poor creature's last despairing hold, and, as they led her off to her new master's wagon, strove to comfort her.

"Now!" said Haley, pushing his three purchases together, and producing a bundle of handcuffs, which he proceeded to put on their wrists; and fastening each handcuff to a long chain, he drove them before him to the jail.

A few days saw Haley, with his possessions, safely deposited on one of the Ohio boats. It was the commencement of his gang, to be augmented, as the boat moved on, by various other merchandise of the same kind, which he, or his agent, had stored for him in various points along shore.

The La Belle Rivière, as brave and beautiful a boat as ever walked the waters of her namesake river, was floating gayly down the stream, under a brilliant sky, the stripes and stars of free America waving and fluttering overhead; the guards crowded with well-dressed ladies and gentlemen walking and enjoying the delightful day. All was full of life, buoyant and rejoicing; — all but Haley's gang, who were stored, with other freight, on the lower deck, and who, somehow, did not seem to appreciate their various privileges, as they sat in a knot, talking to each other in low tones.

"Boys," said Haley, coming up, briskly, "I hope you keep up good heart, and are cheerful. Now, no sulks, ye see; keep stiff upper lip, boys; do well by me, and I'll do well by you."

The boys addressed responded the invariable "Yes, Mas'r," for ages the watchword of poor Africa; but it's to be owned they did not look particularly cheerful; they had their various little prejudices in favor of wives, mothers, sisters, and children, seen for the last time, — and though "they that wasted them required of them mirth," it was not instantly forthcoming.

"I've got a wife," spoke out the article enumerated as "John, aged thirty," and he laid his chained hand on Tom's knee, — "and she don't know a word about this, poor girl!"

"Where does she live?" said Tom.

"In a tavern a piece down here," said John; "I wish, now, I could see her once more in this world," he added.

Poor John! It was rather natural; and the tears that fell, as he spoke, came as naturally as if he had been a white man. Tom drew a long breath from a sore heart, and tried, in his poor way, to comfort him.

And over head, in the cabin, sat fathers and mothers, husbands and wives; and merry, dancing children moved round among them, like so many little butterflies, and everything was going on quite easy and comfortable.

"O, mamma," said a boy, who had just come up from below, "there's a negro trader on board, and he's brought four or five slaves down there."

"Poor creatures!" said the mother, in a tone between grief and indignation.

"What's that?" said another lady.

"Some poor slaves below," said the mother.

"And they've got chains on," said the boy.

"What a shame to our country that such sights are to be seen!" said another lady.

"O, there's a great deal to be said on both sides of the subject," said a genteel woman, who sat at her state-room door sewing, while her little girl and boy were playing round her. "I've been south, and I must say I think the negroes are better off than they would be to be free."

"In some respects, some of them are well off, I grant," said the lady to whose remark she had answered. "The most dreadful part of slavery, to my mind, is its outrages on the feelings and affections, — the separating of families, for example."

"That is a bad thing, certainly," said the other lady, holding up a baby's dress she had just completed, and looking intently on its trimmings; "but then, I fancy, it doesn't occur often."

"O, it does," said the first lady, eagerly; "I've lived many years in Kentucky and Virginia both, and I've seen enough to make any one's heart sick. Suppose, ma'am, your two children, there, should be taken from you, and sold?"

"We can't reason from our feelings to those of this class of persons," said the other lady, sorting out some worsteds on her lap.

"Indeed, ma'am, you can know nothing of them, if you say so," answered the first lady, warmly. "I was born and brought up among them. I know they do feel, just as keenly, — even more so, perhaps, — as we do."

The lady said "Indeed!" yawned, and looked out the cabin window, and finally repeated, for a finale, the remark with which she had begun, — "After all, I think they are better off than they would be to be free."

"It's undoubtedly the intention of Providence that the African race should be servants, — kept in a low condition," said a grave-looking gentleman in black, a clergyman, seated by the cabin door. “Cursed be Canaan; a servant of servants shall he be,” the scripture says.

“I say, stranger, is that ar what that text means?” said a tall man, standing by.

“Undoubtedly. It pleased Providence, for some inscrutable reason, to doom the race to bondage, ages ago; and we must not set up our opinion against that.”

“Well, then, we’ll all go ahead and buy up niggers,” said the man, “if that’s the way of Providence, — won’t we, Squire?” said he, turning to Haley, who had been standing, with his hands in his pockets, by the stove and intently listening to the conversation.

“Yes,” continued the tall man, “we must all be resigned to the decrees of Providence. Niggers must be sold, and trucked round, and kept under; it’s what they’s made for. “Pears like this yer view’s quite refreshing, an’t it, stranger?” said he to Haley.

“I never thought on’t,” said Haley, “I couldn’t have said as much, myself; I ha’nt no laming. I took up the trade just to make a living; if it an’t right, I calculated to pent on’t in time, ye know.”

“And now you’ll save yourself the trouble, won’t ye?” said the tall man. “See what it is, now, to know scripture. If ye’d only studied your Bible, like this yer good man, ye might have know’d it before, and saved ye a heap of trouble. Ye could just have said, ‘Cussed be’ — what’s his name? — ‘and it would all have come right.’” And the stranger, who was no other than the honest drover whom we introduced to our readers in the Kentucky tavern, sat down, and began smoking, with a curious smile on his long, dry face.

A tall, slender young man, with a face expressive of great feeling and intelligence, here broke in, and repeated the words, “All things whatsoever ye would that men should do unto you, do ye even so unto them. I suppose,” he added, “that is scripture, as much as ‘Cursed be Canaan’”.

“Wal, it seems quite as plain a text, stranger,” said John the drover, “to poor fellows like us, now;” and John smoked on like a volcano.

The young man paused, looked as if he was going to say more, when suddenly the boat stopped, and the company made the usual steamboat rush, to see where they were landing.

“Both them are chaps parsons?” said John to one of the men, as they were going out. The man nodded.

As the boat stopped, a black woman came running wildly up the plank, darted into the crowd, flew up to where the slave gang sat, and threw her arms round that unfortunate piece of merchandise before enumerated — “John, aged thirty,” and with sobs and tears bemoaned him as her husband.

But what needs tell the story, told too oft, — every day told, — of heart-strings rent and broken, — the weak broken and torn for the profit and convenience of the strong! It needs not to be told; — every day is telling it, — telling it, too, in the ear of One who is not deaf, though he be long silent.

The young man who had spoken for the cause of humanity and God before stood with folded arms, looking on this scene. He turned, and Haley was standing at his side. “My friend,” he said, speaking with thick utterance, “how can you, how dare you, carry on a trade like this? Look at those poor creatures! Here I am, rejoicing in my heart that I am going home to my wife and child;

and the same bell which is a signal to carry me onward towards them will part this poor man and his wife forever. Depend upon it, God will bring you into judgement for this."

The trader turned away in silence.

"I say, now," said the drover, touching his elbow, "there's differences in parsons, an't there? "Cussed be Canaan' don't seem to go down with this'un, does it?"

Haley gave an uneasy growl.

"And that aren't the worst on't," said John; "maybe it won't go down with the Lord, neither, when ye come to settle with Him, one o' these days, as all on us must, I reckon."

Haley walked reflectively to the other end of the boat.

"If I make pretty handsomely on one or two next gangs," he thought, "I reckon I'll stop off this year; it's really getting dangerous." And he took out his pocket-book, and began adding over his accounts, — a process which many gentlemen besides Mr. Haley have found a specific for an uneasy conscience.

The boat swept proudly away from the shore, and all went on merrily, as before. Men talked, and loafed, and read, and smoked. Women sewed, and children played, and the boat passed on her way.

One day, when she lay to for a while at a small town in Kentucky, Haley went up into the place on a little matter of business.

Tom, whose fetters did not prevent his taking a moderate circuit, had drawn near the side of the boat, and stood listlessly gazing over the railing. After a time, he saw the trader returning, with an alert step, in company with a colored woman, bearing in her arms a young child. She was dressed quite respectably, and a colored man followed her, bringing along a small trunk. The woman came cheerfully on-ward, talking, as she came, with the man who bore her trunk, and so passed up the plank into the boat. The bell rung, the steamer whizzed, the engine groaned and coughed, and away swept the boat down the river.

The woman walked forward among the boxes and bales of the lower deck, and, sitting down, busied herself with chirruping to her baby.

Haley made a turn or two about the boat, and then, coming up, seated himself near her, and began saying something to her in an indifferent undertone.

Tom soon noticed a heavy cloud passing over the woman's brow; and that she answered rapidly, and with great vehemence.

"I don't believe it, — I won't believe it!" he heard her say. "You're just a foolin with me."

"If you won't believe it, look here!" said the man, drawing out a paper; "this yer's the bill of sale, and there's your master's name to it; and I paid down good solid cash for it, too, I can tell you, — so, now!" "I don't believe Maser would cheat me so; it can't be true!" said the woman, with increasing agitation.

"You can ask any of these men here, that can read writing. Here!" he said, to a man that was passing by, "just read this yer, won't you! This yer gal won't believe me, when I tell her what it is."

"Why, it's a bill of sale, signed by John Fosdick," said the man, "making over to you the girl

Lucy and her child. It's all straight enough, for aught I see."

The woman's passionate exclamations collected a crowd around her, and the trader briefly explained to them the cause of the agitation.

"He told me that I was going down to Louisville, to hire out as cook to the same tavern where my husband works, — that's what Maser told me, his own self; and I can't believe he'd lie to me." said the woman.

"But he has sold you, my poor woman, there's no doubt about it," said a good-natured looking man, who had been examining the papers: "he has done it, and no mistake."

"Then it's no account talking," said the woman, suddenly growing quite calm; and, clasping her child tighter in her arms, she sat down on her box, turned her back round, and gazed listlessly into the river.

"Going to take it easy, after all!" said the trader. "Gal's got grit, I see."

The woman looked calm, as the boat went on; and a beautiful soft summer breeze passed like a compassionate spirit over her head, — the gentle breeze, that never inquires whether the brow is dusky or fair that it fans. And she saw sunshine sparkling on the water, in golden ripples, and heard gay voices, full of ease and pleasure, talking around her everywhere; but her heart lay as if a great stone had fallen on it. Her baby raised himself up against her, and stroked her cheeks with his little hands; and, springing up and down, crowing and chatting, seemed determined to arouse her. She strained him suddenly and tightly in her arms, and slowly one tear after another fell on his wondering, unconscious face; and gradually she seemed, and little by little, to grow calmer, and busied herself with tending and nursing him.

The child, a boy of ten months, was uncommonly large and strong of his age, and very vigorous in his limbs. Never, for a moment, still, he kept his mother constantly busy in holding him, and guarding his springing activity.

"That's a fine chap!" said a man, suddenly stopping opposite to him, with his hands in his pockets. "How old is he?"

"Ten months and a half," said the mother.

The man whistled to the boy, and offered him part of a stick of candy, which he eagerly grabbed at, and very soon had it in a baby's general depository, to wit, his mouth.

"Rum fellow!" said the man "Knows what's what!" and he whistled, and walked on. When he had got to the other side of the boat, he came across Haley, who was smoking on top of a pile of boxes.

The stranger produced a match, and lighted a cigar, saying, as he did so,

"Decentish kind o'wench you've got round there, stranger."

"Why, I reckon she is tolerable fair," said Haley, blowing the smoke out of his mouth.

"Taking her down south?" said the man.

Haley nodded, and smoked on.

"Plantation hand?" said the man.

"Wal," said Haley, "I'm filling out an order for a plantation, and I think I shall put her in. They telled me she was a good cook; and they can use her for that, or set her at the cotton-picking. She's got the right fingers for that; I looked at'em. Sell well, either way." and Haley resumed his cigar.

"They won't want the young 'un on the plantation," said the man.

"I shall sell him, first chance I find," said Haley, lighting another cigar.

"S'pose you'd be selling him tolerable cheap," said the stranger, mounting the pile of boxes, and sitting down comfortably.

"Don't know 'bout that," said Haley, "he's pretty smart young, — straight, fat, strong; flesh as hard as a brick!"

"Very true, but then there's the bother and expense of raisin".

"Nonsense!" said Haley; "they are raised as easy as any kind of critter there is going; they an't a bit more trouble than pups. This yer chap will be running all around, in a month."

"I've got a good place for raisin", and I thought of taking in a little more stock," said the man. "One cook lost a young son last week, — got drowned in a wash-tub, while she was hanging out clothes, — and I reckon it would be well enough to set her to raisin this yer."

Haley and the stranger smoked a while in silence, neither seeming willing to broach the test question of the interview. At last, the man resumed:

"You wouldn't think of wanting more than ten dollars for that ar chap, seeing you must get him off yer hand, any how?"

Haley shook his head, and spit impressively.

"That won't do, no ways," he said, and began his smoking again.

"Well, stranger, what will you take?"

"Well, now," said Haley, "I could raise that ar chap myself, or get him raised; he's common likely and healthy, and he'd fetch a hundred dollars, six months hence; and, in a year or two, he'd bring two hundred, if I had him in the right spot; — so I shan't take a cent less nor fifty for him now."

"O, stranger! that's ridiculous, altogether." said the man.

"Fact!" said Haley, with a decisive nod of his head.

"I'll give thirty for him," said the stranger, "but not a cent more."

"Now, I'll tell ye what I will do," said Haley, spitting again, with renewed decision. "I'll split the difference, and say forty-five, and that's the most I will do."

"Well, agreed!" said the man, after an interval.

"Done!" said Haley. "Where do you land?"

"At Louisville," said the man.

"Louisville," said Haley. "Very fair, we get there about dusk. Chap will be asleep, — all fair, — get him off quietly, and no screaming, — happens beautiful, — I like to do everything quietly, — I hates all kind of agitation and fluster." And so, after a transfer of certain bills had passed from the man's pocket-book to the trader's, he resumed his cigar.

It was a bright, tranquil evening when the boat stopped at the wharf at Louisville. The woman had been sitting with her baby in her arms, now wrapped in a heavy sleep. When she heard the name of the place called out, she hastily laid the child down in a little cradle formed by the hollow among the boxes, first carefully spreading under it her cloak; and then she sprung to the side of the boat, in hopes that, among the various hotel-waiters who thronged the wharf, she might see her husband. In this hope, she pressed forward to the front rails, and, stretching far over them, strained her eyes intently on the moving heads on the shore, and the crowd pressed in between her and the child.

"Now's your time," said Haley, taking the sleeping child up, and handing him to the stranger. "Don't wake him up, and set him to crying, now; it would make a devil of a fuss with the gal." The man took the bundle carefully, and was soon lost in the crowd that went up the wharf.

When the boat, creaking, and groaning, and puffing, had loosed from the wharf, and was beginning slowly to strain herself along, the woman returned to her old seat. The trader was sitting there, — the child was gone!

"Why, why, — where?" she began, in bewildered surprise.

"Lucy," said the trader, "your child's gone; you may as well know it first as last. You see, I know you couldn't take him down south; and I got a chance to sell him to a first-rate family, that'll raise him better than you can."

The trader had arrived at that stage of Christian and political perfection which has been recommended by some preachers and politicians of the north, lately, in which he had completely overcome every humane weakness and prejudice. His heart was exactly where yours, sir, and mine could be brought, with proper effort and cultivation. The wild look of anguish and utter despair that the woman cast on him might have disturbed one less practiced; but he was used to it. He had seen that same look hundreds of times. You can get used to such things, too, my friend; and it is the great object of recent efforts to make our whole northern community used to them, for the glory of the Union. So, the trader only regarded the mortal anguish which he saw working in those dark features, those clenched hands, and suffocating breathings, as necessary incidents of the trade, and merely calculated whether she was going to scream, and get up a commotion on the boat; for, like other supporters of our peculiar institution, he decidedly disliked agitation.

But the woman did not scream. The shot had passed too straight and direct through the heart, for cry or tear.

Dizzily she sat down. Her slack hands feel lifeless by her side. Her eyes looked straight forward, but she saw nothing. All the noise and hum of the boat, the groaning of the machinery, mingled dreamily to her bewildered ear; and the poor, dumb-stricken heart had neither cry not tear to show for its utter misery. She was quite calm.

The trader, who, considering his advantages, was almost as humane as some of our politicians, seemed to feel called on to administer such consolation as the case admitted of.

"I know this yer comes kinder hard, at first, Lucy," he said; "but such a smart, sensible gal as you are, won't give way to it. You see it's necessary, and can't be helped!"

"O! don't, Maser, don't!" said the woman, with a voice like one that is smothering.

"You're a smart wench, Lucy," he persisted; "I mean to do well by ye, and get ye a nice place down river; and you'll soon get another husband, — such a likely gal as you — "

"O! Maser, if you only won't talk to me now," said the woman, in a voice of such quick and living anguish that the trader felt that there was something at present in the case beyond his style of operation. He got up, and the woman turned away, and buried her head in her cloak.

The trader walked up and down for a time, and occasionally stopped and looked at her.

"Takes it hard, rather," he soliloquized, "but quiet, tho'; — let her sweat a while; she'll come right, by and by!"

Tom had watched the whole transaction from first to last, and had a perfect understanding of its results. To him, it looked like something unutterably horrible and cruel, because, poor, ignorant black soul! he had not learned to generalize, and to take enlarged views. If he had only been instructed by certain ministers of Christianity, he might have thought better of it, and seen in it an everyday incident of a lawful trade; a trade which is the vital support of an institution which an American divine tells us "no evils but such as are inseparable from any other relations in social and domestic life." But Tom, as we see, being a poor, ignorant fellow, whose reading had been confined entirely to the New Testament, could not comfort and solace himself with views like these. His very soul bled within him for what seemed to him the wrongs of the poor suffering thing that lay like a crushed reed on the boxes; the feeling, living, bleeding, yet immortal thing, which American state law coolly classes with the bundles, and bales, and boxes, among which she is lying.

Tom drew near, and tried to say something; but she only groaned. Honestly, and with tears running down his own cheeks, he spoke of a heart of love in the skies, of a pitying Jesus, and an eternal home; but the ear was deaf with anguish, and the palsied heart could not feel.

Night came on, — night calm, unmoved, and glorious, shining down with her innumerable and solemn angel eyes, twinkling, beautiful, but silent. There was no speech nor language, no pitying voice or helping hand, from that distant sky. One after another, the voices of business or pleasure died away; all on the boat were sleeping, and the ripples at the prow were plainly heard. Tom stretched himself out on a box, and there, as he lay, he heard, ever and anon, a smothered sob or cry from the prostrate creature, — "O! What shall I do? O Lord! O good Lord, do help me! and so, ever and anon, until the murmur died away in silence.

At midnight, Tom waked, with a sudden start. Something black passed quickly by him to the side of the boat, and he heard a splash in the water. No one else saw or heard anything. He raised his head, — the woman's place was vacant! He got up, and sought about him in vain. The poor bleeding heart was still, at last, and the river rippled and dimpled just as brightly as if it had not closed above it.

Patience! Patience! ye whose hearts swell indignant at wrongs like these. Not one throb of anguish, not one tear of the oppressed, is forgotten by the Man of Sorrows, the Lord of Glory. In his patient, generous bosom he bears the anguish of a world. Bear thou, like him, in patience, and labor in love; for sure as he is God, "the year of his redeemed shall come."

The trader waked up bright and early, and came out to see to his live stock. It was now his turn to look about in perplexity.

"Where alive is that gal?" he said to Tom.

Tom, who had learned the wisdom of keeping counsel, did not feel called upon to state his observations and suspicions, but said he did not know.

"She surely couldn't have got off in the night at any of the landings, for I was awake, and on the look-out, whenever the boat stopped. I never trust these yer things to other folks."

This speech was addressed to Tom quite confidentially, as if it was something that would be specially interesting to him. Tom made no answer.

The trader searched the boat from stem to stern, among boxes, bales and barrels, around the machinery, by the chimneys, in vain.

"Now, I say, Tom, be fair about this yer," he said, when, after a fruitless search, he came where Tom was standing. "You know something about it, now. Don't tell me, — I know you do. I saw the gal stretched out here about ten o'clock, and again at twelve, and again between one and two; and then at four she was gone, and you were a sleeping right there all the time. Now, you know something, — you can't help it."

"Well, Maser," said Tom, "towards morning something brushed by me, and I kinder half woke; and then I hear a great splash, and then I clare woke up, and the gal was gone. That's all I know."

The trader was not shocked nor amazed; because, as we said before, he was used to a great many things that you are not used to. Even the awful presence of death struck no solemn chill upon him. He had seen Death many times, — met him in the way of trade, and got acquainted with him, — and he only thought of him as a hard customer, that embarrassed his property operations very unfairly; and so, he only swore that the gal was a baggage, and that he was devilish unlucky, and that, if things went on in this way, he should not make a cent on the trip. In short, he seemed to consider himself an ill-used man, decidedly; but there was no help for it, as the woman had escaped into a state which never will give up a fugitive, — not even at the demand of the whole glorious Union. The trader, therefore, sat discontentedly down, with his little account-book, and put down the missing body and soul under the head of losses!

"He's a shocking creature, isn't he, — this trader? So unfeeling! It's dreadful, really!"

"Oh, but nobody thinks anything of these traders! They are universally despised, — never received into any decent society."

But who, sir, makes the trader? Who is most to blame? The enlightened, cultivated, intelligent man, who supports the system of which the trader is the inevitable result, or the poor trader himself? You make the public statement that calls for his trade, that debauches and depraves him, till he feels no shame in it; and in what are you better than he?

Are you educated and he ignorant, you high and he low, you refined and he coarse, you talented and he simple?

In the day of a future judgment, these very considerations may make it more tolerable for him than for you.

In concluding these little incidents of lawful trade, we must beg the world not to think that

American legislators are entirely destitute of humanity, as might, perhaps, be unfairly inferred from the great efforts made in our national body to protect and perpetuate this species of traffic.

Who does not know how our great men are outdoing themselves, in declaiming against the foreign slave-trade. There are a perfect host of Clarksons and Wilberforces risen up among us on that subject, most edifying to hear and behold. Trading negroes from Africa, dear reader, is so horrid! It is not to be thought of! But trading them from Kentucky, — that's quite another thing!

4. Questions for Discussion

(1) Describe how Tom is represented as a Christ-like figure.

(2) In what ways does Stowe present the incompatibility of slavery with the Christian ethics of love and tolerance?

(3) What effect did *Uncle Tom's Cabin* have on slavery?

(4) Can you describe the two black mothers in this chapter? Do you think how their suffering makes slavery more inhuman?

Section Two: Ralph Waldo Ellison and *Invisible Man*

1. Introduction of Ralph Waldo Ellison

Ralph Waldo Ellison was an African American novelist, literary critic, and scholar best known for his novel *Invisible Man*, which won him the National Book Award in 1953.

Ralph Waldo Ellison was born on March 1, 1914, in Oklahoma City, Oklahoma, to Lewis Alfred Ellison, a construction foreman and Ida Millsap Ellison. Ralph Waldo Ellison's father died when he was only three years old. His mother supported the family by doing cleaning work. He began playing the trumpet at the age of eight and, at the age of eighteen, attended Tuskegee Institute in Montgomery, Alabama, studying music from 1933 to 1936. During that time, he worked at a variety of jobs including janitor, shoeshine boy, jazz musician, and freelance photographer. He also became a game hunter, a skill he learned from reading Hemingway. Studying only three years majoring in music at Tuskegee, Ellison sometimes referred to himself as a college dropout. Moving to New York in 1936, Ellison met writers like Richard Wright and Langston Hughes, who encouraged him to take up writing and prompted his move to Harlem where he lived for more than 40 years with his wife, Fanny McConnell.

Ralph Waldo Ellison started writing *Invisible Man* while at a friend's farm in Vermont. Published in 1952, the book became a bestseller and won the National Book Award the following year. Ellison traveled throughout Europe in the mid-1950s, and lived in Rome for two years after becoming an American Academy fellow. He later taught at several colleges and universities and lectured extensively at such prestigious institutions as Yale University, the Library of Congress, and the US Military Academy. Ralph Waldo Ellison also published two important volumes of nonfiction, *Shadow and Act* (1964) and *Going to the Territory* (1986). These two works, together with numerous unpublished speeches and writings, were published in 1995 as *The Collected Essays of Ralph Ellison*.

Ralph Waldo Ellison died of cancer on April 16, 1994, at his home in New York City. Ralph Waldo Ellison is renowned not only as an author and a master of black vernacular, but as a critic of literature, culture, and race. A renowned author and critic Louis Gates Jr. once wrote that Ralph Waldo Ellison, Richard Wright and James Baldwin comprised "the holy male trinity of the black tradition." (Washington 5)

2. Introduction of *Invisible Man*

Invisible Man, written in the first person, is a kind of bildungsroman about an idealistic young Negro (Ellison never gives him a name) who tries to pursue for his identity in American society. Warren French has called the novel a psychological one and commented that "Arguably the most comprehensive fictional probing of the twentieth-century American psyche, it is entitled to a place beside the ninetieth-century *Moby-Dick*" (1). The protagonist begins as a student at a black college in the South but a naive mistake leads to his expulsion, and he then makes his way to Harlem. There, instead of eventually finding and forging an identity by which he can be recognized by others, he is subjected to a series of adventures which finally leave him with the realization that he is in fact invisible to everyone around him, whether black or white. They all want to make use of him for whatever ends they happen to be pursuing, but nobody wants to see or know him as an individual human being. So disillusioned does he become that he winds up living all by himself in an abandoned cellar. But in the closing pages he decides to end his hibernation and reemerge from the underground cellar. The book ends with the narrator's awareness that "even an invisible man has a socially responsible role to play".

Told in the first-person narrative, the story traces the nameless narrator's journey from blind ignorance to enlightened awareness. The narrator tries to look for his own identity all his life and finally realizes that as a black person his fate is controlled by the white people. The story was set in the US during the pre-Civil Rights era when segregation laws barred black Americans from enjoying the same basic human rights as their white counterparts did. The concluding section of the book is important because the narrator has transcended the physical limits of an African American individuality and becomes every man and his dilemma becomes the difficulty of all human beings who try to deal with identity crisis and seek for belonging in a community. This shows that he is concerned with not only African American individuals or communities but the whole human being. As F. H. Langman mentioned, "Although it tells the story of a black man's search for himself — his name is never given — it represents more than the quest for black identity. It is at once more specific, a very individual story, and more general, dramatizing the identity-crisis of a whole society" (1). Ellison has achieved a great success in turning the impressive story of a young American boy's life into an odyssey of modern man's quest for self-realization and identity, which is the major contribution of Ellison and the book.

3. Reading Material: *Invisible Man* (Chapter 1)

It goes a long way back, some twenty years. All my life I had been looking for something, and everywhere I turned someone tried to tell me what it was. I accepted their answers too, though they were often in contradiction and even selfcontradictory. I was naive. I was looking for myself and asking everyone except myself questions which I, and only I, could answer. It took me a long time and much painful boomeranging of my expectations to achieve a realization everyone else appears to have been born with: That I am nobody but myself. But first I had to discover that I am an invisible man!

And yet I am no freak of nature, nor of history. I was in the cards, other things having been equal (or unequal) eighty-five years ago. I am not ashamed of my grandparents for having been slaves. I am only ashamed of myself for having at one time been ashamed. About eighty-five years ago they were told that they were free, united with others of our country in everything pertaining to the common good, and, in everything social, separate like the fingers of the hand. And they believed it. They exulted in it. They stayed in their place, worked hard, and brought up my father to do the same. But my grandfather is the one. He was an odd old guy, my grandfather, and I am told I take after him. It was he who caused the trouble. On his deathbed he called my father to him and said, "Son, after I'm gone, I want you to keep up the good fight. I never told you, but our life is a war and I have been a traitor all my born days, a spy in the enemy's country ever since I give up my gun back in the Reconstruction. Live with your head in the lion's mouth. I want you to overcome th'm with yeses, undermine them with grins, agree them to death and destruction, let them swoller you till they vomit or bust wide open." They thought the old man had gone out of his mind. He had been the meekest of men. The younger children were rushed from the room, the shades drawn and the flame of the lamp turned so low that it sputtered on the wick like the old man's breathing. "Learn it to the younguns," he whispered fiercely; then he died.

But my folks were more alarmed over his last words than over his dying. It was as though he had not died at all, his words caused so much anxiety. I was warned emphatically to forget what he had said and, indeed, this is the first time it has been mentioned outside the family circle. It had a tremendous effect upon me, however. I could never be sure of what he meant. Grandfather had been a quiet old man who never made any trouble, yet on his deathbed he had called himself a traitor and a spy, and he had spoken of his meekness as a dangerous activity. It became a constant puzzle which lay unanswered in the back of my mind. And whenever things went well for me, I remembered my grandfather and felt guilty and uncomfortable. It was as though I was carrying out his advice in spite of myself. And to make it worse, everyone loved me for it. I was praised by the most lily-white men of the town. I was considered an example of desirable conduct — just as my grandfather had been. And what puzzled me was that the old man had defined it as treachery. When I was praised for my conduct, I felt a guilt that in some way I was doing something that was really against the wishes of the white folks, that if they had understood they would have desired me to act just the opposite, that I should have been sulky and mean, and that that really would have been what they wanted, even though they were fooled and thought they wanted me to act as I did. It made me afraid that someday they would look upon me as a traitor and I would be lost. Still, I was more afraid to act any other way because they didn't like that at all. The old man's words were like a curse. On my graduation day I delivered an oration in which I showed that humility was the secret, indeed, the very essence of progress. (Not that I believed this — how could I, remembering my grandfather? — I only believed that it worked.) It was a great success. Everyone praised me and I was invited to give the speech at a gathering of the town's leading white citizens. It was a triumph for our whole community.

It was in the main ballroom of the leading hotel. When I got there, I discovered that it was on the occasion of a smoker, and I was told that since I was to be there anyway, I might as well take part in the battle royal to be fought by some of my schoolmates as part of the entertainment. The battle royal came first.

All of the town's big shots were there in their tuxedoes, wolfing down the buffet foods, drinking beer and whiskey and smoking black cigars. It was a large room with a high ceiling. Chairs were arranged in neat rows around three sides of a portable boxing ring. The fourth side was clear, revealing a gleaming space of polished floor. I had some misgivings over the battle royal, by the way. Not from a distaste for fighting, but because I didn't care too much for the other fellows who were to take part. They were tough guys who seemed to have no grandfather's curse worrying their minds. No one could mistake their toughness. And besides, I suspected that fighting a battle royal might detract from the dignity of my speech. In those pre-invisible days, I visualized myself as a potential Booker T. Washington①. But the other fellows didn't care too much for me either, and there were nine of them. I felt superior to them in my way, and I didn't like the manner in which we were all crowded together into the servants' elevator. Nor did they like my being there. In fact, as the warmly lighted floors flashed past the elevator, we had words over the fact that I, by taking part in the fight, had knocked one of their friends out of a night's work.

We were led out of the elevator through a rococo hall into an anteroom and told to get into our fighting togs. Each of us was issued a pair of boxing gloves and ushered out into the big mirrored hall, which we entered looking cautiously about us and whispering, lest we might accidentally be heard above the noise of the room. It was foggy with cigar smoke. And already the whiskey was taking effect. I was shocked to see some of the most important men of the town quite tipsy. They were all there — bankers, lawyers, judges, doctors, fire chiefs, teachers, merchants. Even one of the more fashionable pastors. Something we could not see was going on up front. A clarinet was vibrating sensuously and the men were standing up and moving eagerly forward. We were a small tight group, clustered together, our bare upper bodies touching and shining with anticipatory sweat; while up front the big shots were becoming increasingly excited over something we still could not see. Suddenly I heard the school superintendent, who had told me to come, yell, "Bring up the shines, gentlemen! Bring up the little shines!"

---

① Booker T. Washington was a civil rights movement leader, an American educator, author, orator, adviser to several presidents of the United States.

We were rushed up to the front of the ballroom, where it smelled even more strongly of tobacco and whiskey. Then we were pushed into place. I almost wet my pants. A sea of faces, some hostile, some amused, ringed around us, and in the center, facing us, stood a magnificent blonde — stark naked. There was dead silence. I felt a blast of cold air chill me. I tried to back away, but they were behind me and around me. Some of the boys stood with lowered heads, trembling. I felt a wave of irrational guilt and fear. My teeth chattered, my skin turned to goose flesh, my knees knocked. Yet I was strongly attracted and looked in spite of myself. Had the price of looking been blindness, I would have looked. The hair was yellow like that of a circus kewpie doll, the face heavily powdered and rouged, as though to form an abstract mask, the eyes hollow and smeared a cool blue, the color of a baboon's butt. I felt a desire to spit upon her as my eyes brushed slowly over her body. Her breasts were firm and round as the domes of East Indian temples, and I stood so close as to see the fine skin texture and beads of pearly perspiration glistening like dew around the pink and erected buds of her nipples. I wanted at one and the same time to run from the room, to sink through the floor, or go to her and cover her from my eyes and the eyes of the others with my body; to feel the soft thighs, to caress her and destroy her, to love her and murder her, to hide from her, and yet to stroke where below the small American flag tattooed upon her belly her thighs formed a capital V. I had a notion that of all in the room she saw only me with her impersonal eyes.

And then she began to dance, a slow sensuous movement; the smoke of a hundred cigars clinging to her like the thinnest of veils. She seemed like a fair bird-girl girdled in veils calling to me from the angry surface of some gray and threatening sea. I was transported. Then I became aware of the clarinet playing and the big shots yelling at us. Some threatened us if we looked and others if we did not. On my right I saw one boy faint. And now a man grabbed a silver pitcher from a table and stepped close as he dashed ice water upon him and stood him up and forced two of us to support him as his head hung and moans issued from his thick bluish lips. Another boy began to plead to go home. He was the largest of the group, wearing dark red fighting trunks much too small to conceal the erection which projected from him as though in answer to the insinuating low-registered moaning of the clarinet. He tried to hide himself with his boxing gloves.

And all the while the blonde continued dancing, smiling faintly at the big shots who watched her with fascination, and faintly smiling at our fear. I noticed a certain merchant who followed her hungrily, his lips loose and drooling. He was a large man who wore diamond studs in a shirtfront which swelled with the ample paunch underneath, and each time the blonde swayed her undulating hips he ran his hand through the thin hair of his bald head and, with his arms upheld, his posture clumsy like that of an intoxicated panda, wound his belly in a slow and obscene grind. This creature was completely hypnotized. The music had quickened. As the dancer flung herself about with a detached expression on her face, the men began reaching out to touch her. I could see their beefy fingers sink into the soft flesh. Some of the others tried to stop them and she began to move around the floor in graceful circles, as they gave chase, slipping and sliding over the polished floor. It was mad. Chairs went crashing, drinks were spilt, as they ran laughing and howling after her. They caught her just as she reached a door, raised her from the floor, and tossed her as college boys are tossed at a hazing, and above her red, fixed-smiling lips I saw the terror and disgust in her eyes, almost like my own terror and that which I saw in some of the other boys. As I watched, they tossed her twice and her soft breasts seemed to flatten against the air and her legs flung wildly as she spun. Some of the more sober ones helped her to escape. And I started off the floor, heading for the anteroom with the rest of the boys.

Some were still crying and in hysteria. But as we tried to leave, we were stopped and ordered to get into the ring. There was nothing to do but what we were told. All ten of us climbed under the ropes and allowed ourselves to be blindfolded with broad bands of white cloth. One of the men seemed to feel a bit sympathetic and tried to cheer us up as we stood with our backs against the ropes. Some of us tried to grin. "See that boy over there?" one of the men said. "I want you to run across at the bell and give it to him right in the belly. If you don't get him, I'm going to get you. I don't like his looks." Each of us was told the same. The blindfolds were put on. Yet even then I had been going over my speech. In my mind each word was as bright as flame. I felt the cloth pressed into place, and frowned so that it would be loosened when I relaxed.

But now I felt a sudden fit of blind terror. I was unused to darkness. It was as though I had suddenly found myself in a dark room filled with poisonous cottonmouths. I could hear the bleary voices yelling insistently for the battle royal to begin.

"Get going in there!"

"Let me at that big nigger!"

I strained to pick up the school superintendent's voice, as though to squeeze some security out of that slightly more familiar sound.

"Let me at those black sonsabitches!" someone yelled.

"No, Jackson, no!" another voice yelled. "Here, somebody, help me hold Jack."

"I want to get at that ginger-colored nigger. Tear him limb from limb," the first voice yelled.

I stood against the ropes trembling. For in those days, I was what they called ginger-colored, and he sounded as though he might crunch me between his teeth like a crisp ginger cookie.

Quite a struggle was going on. Chairs were being kicked about and I could hear voices grunting as with a terrific effort. I wanted to see, to see more desperately than ever before. But the blindfold was as tight as a thick skin-puckering scab and when I raised my gloved hands to push the layers of white aside a voice yelled, "Oh, no you don't, black bastard! Leave that alone!"

"Ring the bell before Jackson kills him a coon!" someone boomed in the sudden silence. And I heard the bell clang and the sound of the feet scuffling forward.

A glove smacked against my head. I pivoted, striking out stiffly as someone went past, and felt the jar ripple along the length of my arm to my shoulder. Then it seemed as though all nine of the boys had turned upon me at once. Blows pounded me from all sides while I struck out as best I could. So many blows landed upon me that I wondered if I were not the only blindfolded fighter in the ring, or if the man called Jackson hadn't succeeded in getting me after all.

Blindfolded, I could no longer control my motions. I had no dignity. I stumbled about like a baby or a drunken man. The smoke had become thicker and with each new blow it seemed to sear and further restrict my lungs. My saliva became like hot bitter glue. A glove connected with my head, filling my mouth with warm blood. It was everywhere. I could not tell if the moisture I felt upon my body was sweat or blood. A blow landed hard against the nape of my neck. I felt myself going over, my head hitting the floor. Streaks of blue light filled the black world behind the blindfold. I lay prone, pretending that I was knocked out, but felt myself seized by hands and yanked to my feet. "Get going, black boy! Mix it up!" My arms were like lead, my head smarting from blows. I managed to feel my way to the ropes and held on, trying to catch my breath. A glove landed in my mid-section and I went over again, feeling as though the smoke had become a knife jabbed into my guts. Pushed this way and that by the legs milling around me, I finally pulled erect and discovered that I could see the black, sweat-washed forms weaving in the smoky-blue atmosphere like drunken dancers weaving to the rapid drum-like thuds of blows.

Everyone fought hysterically. It was complete anarchy. Everybody fought everybody else. No group fought together for long. Two, three, four, fought one, then turned to fight each other, were themselves attacked. Blows landed below the belt and in the kidney, with the gloves open as well as closed, and with my eye partly opened now there was not so much terror. I moved carefully, avoiding blows, although not too many to attract attention, fighting from group to group. The boys groped about like blind, cautious crabs crouching to protect their mid-sections, their heads pulled in short against their shoulders, their arms stretched nervously before them, with their fists testing the smoke-filled air like the knobbed feelers of hypersensitive snails. In one corner I glimpsed a boy violently punching the air and heard him scream in pain as he smashed his hand against a ring post. For a second, I saw him bent over holding his hand, then going down as a blow caught his unprotected head. I played one group against the other, slipping in and throwing a punch then stepping out of range while pushing the others into the melee to take the blows blindly aimed at me. The smoke was agonizing and there were no rounds, no bells at three-minute intervals to relieve our exhaustion. The room spun round me, a swirl of lights, smoke, sweating bodies surrounded by tense white faces. I bled from both nose and mouth, the blood spattering upon my chest.

The men kept yelling, "Slug him, black boy! Knock his guts out!"

"Uppercut him! Kill him! Kill that big boy!"

Taking a fake fall, I saw a boy going down heavily beside me as though we were felled by a single blow, saw a sneaker-clad foot shoot into his groin as the two who had knocked him down stumbled upon him. I rolled out of range, feeling a twinge of nausea.

The harder we fought the more threatening the men became. And yet, I had begun to worry about my speech again. How would it go? Would they recognize my ability? What would they give me?

I was fighting automatically when suddenly I noticed that one after another of the boys was leaving the ring. I was surprised, filled with panic, as though I had been left alone with an unknown danger. Then I understood. The boys had arranged it among themselves. It was the custom for the two men left in the ring to slug it out for the winner's prize. I discovered this too late. When the bell sounded two men in tuxedoes leaped into the ring and removed the blindfold. I found myself facing Tatlock, the biggest of the gang. I felt sick at my stomach. Hardly had the bell stopped ringing in my ears than it clanged again and I saw him moving swiftly toward me. Thinking of nothing else to do I hit him smash on the nose. He kept coming, bringing the rank sharp violence of stale sweat. His face was a black blank of a face, only his eyes alive — with hate of me and aglow with a feverish terror from what had happened to us all. I became anxious. I wanted to deliver my speech and he came at me as though he meant to beat it out of me. I smashed him again and again, taking his blows as they came. Then on a sudden impulse I struck him lightly and as we clinched, I whispered, "Fake like I knocked you out, you can have the prize."

"I'll break you behind," he whispered hoarsely.

"For them?"

"For me, sonofabitch!"

They were yelling for us to break it up and Tatlock spun me half around with a blow, and as a joggled camera sweeps in a reeling scene, I saw the howling red faces crouching tense beneath the cloud of blue-gray smoke. For a moment the world wavered, unraveled, flowed, then my head cleared and Tatlock bounced before me. That fluttering shadow before my eyes was his jabbing left hand. Then falling forward, my head against his damp shoulder, I whispered, "I'll make it five dollars more."

"Go to hell!"

But his muscles relaxed a trifle beneath my pressure and I breathed, "Seven?"

"Give it to your ma," he said, ripping me beneath the heart.

And while I still held him, I butted him and moved away. I felt myself bombarded with punches. I fought back with hopeless desperation. I wanted to deliver my speech more than anything else in the world, felt that only these men could judge truly my ability, and now this stupid clown was ruining my chances. I began fighting carefully now, moving in to punch him and out again with my greater speed. A lucky blow to his chin and I had him going too — until I heard a loud voice yell, "I got my money on the big boy."

Hearing this, I almost dropped my guard. I was confused: Should I try to win against the voice out there? Would not this go against my speech, and was not this a moment for humility, for nonresistance? A blow to my head as I danced about sent my right eye popping like a jack-in-the-box and settled my dilemma. The room went red as I fell. It was a dream fall, my body languid and fastidious as to where to land, until the floor became impatient and smashed up to meet me. A moment later I came to. A hypnotic voice said FIVE emphatically. And I lay there, hazily watching a dark red spot of my own blood shaping itself into a butterfly, glistening and soaking into the soiled gray world of the canvas.

When the voice drawled TEN, I was lifted up and dragged to a chair. I sat dazed. My eye pained and swelled with each throb of my pounding heart and I wondered if now I would be allowed to speak. I was wringing wet, my mouth still bleeding. We were grouped along the wall now. The other boys ignored me as they congratulated Tatlock and speculated as to how much they would be paid. One boy whimpered over his smashed hand. Looking up front, I saw attendants in white jackets rolling the portable ring away and placing a small square rug in the vacant space surrounded by chairs. Perhaps, I thought, I will stand on the rug to deliver my speech.

Then the M.C. called to us, "Come on up here boys and get your money."

We ran forward to where the men laughed and talked in their chairs, waiting. Everyone seemed friendly now.

"There it is on the rug," the man said. I saw the rug covered with coins of all dimensions and a few crumpled bills. But what excited me, scattered here and there, were the gold pieces.

"Boys, it's all yours," the man said. "You get all you grab."

"That's right, Sambo," a blond man said, winking at me confidentially.

I trembled with excitement, forgetting my pain. I would get the gold and the bills, I thought. I would use both hands. I would throw my body against the boys nearest me to block them from the gold.

"Get down around the rug now," the man commanded, "and don't anyone touch it until I give the signal."

"This ought to be good," I heard.

As told, we got around the square rug on our knees. Slowly the man raised his freckled hand as we followed it upward with our eyes.

I heard, "These niggers look like they're about to pray!"

Then, "Ready," the man said. "Go!"

I lunged for a yellow coin lying on the blue design of the carpet, touching it and sending a surprised shriek to join those rising around me. I tried frantically to remove my hand but could not let go. A hot, violent force tore through my body, shaking me like a wet rat. The rug was electrified. The hair bristled up on my head as I shook myself free. My muscles jumped, my nerves jangled, writhed. But I saw that this was not stopping the other boys. Laughing in fear and embarrassment, some were holding back and scooping up the coins knocked off by the painful contortions of the others. The men roared above us as we struggled.

"Pick it up, goddanmit, pick it up!" someone called like a bass-voiced parrot. "Go on, get it!"

I crawled rapidly around the floor, picking up the coins, trying to avoid the coppers and to get greenbacks and the gold. Ignoring the shock by laughing, as I brushed the coins off quickly, I discovered that I could contain the electricity — a contradiction, but it works. Then the men began to push us onto the rug. Laughing embarrassedly, we struggled out of their hands and kept after the coins. We were all wet and slippery and hard to hold. Suddenly I saw a boy lifted into the air, glistening with sweat like a circus seal, and dropped, his wet back landing flush upon the charged rug, heard him yell and saw him literally dance upon his back, elbows beating a frenzied tattoo upon the floor, his muscles twitching like the flesh of a horse stung my many flies. When he finally rolled off, his face was gray and no one stopped him when he ran from the floor amid booming laughter.

"Get the money," the M.C. called. "That's good hard American cash!"

And we snatched and grabbed, snatched and grabbed. I was careful not to come too close to the rug now, and when I felt the hot whiskey breath descend upon me like a cloud of foul air I reached out and grabbed the leg of a chair. It was occupied and I held on desperately.

"Leggo, nigger! Leggo!"

The huge face wavered down to mine as he tried to push me free. But my body was slippery and he was too drunk. It was Mr. Colcord, who owned a chain of movie houses and "entertainment palaces". Each time he grabbed me I slipped out of his hands. It became a real struggle. I feared the rug more than I did the drunk, so I held on, surprising myself for a moment by trying to topple him upon the rug. It was such an enormous idea that I found myself actually carrying it out. I tried not to be obvious, yet when I grabbed his leg, trying to tumble him out of the chair, he raised up roaring with laughter, and, looking at me with soberness dead in the eye, kicked me viciously in the chest. The chair leg flew out of my hand and I felt myself going and rolled. It was as though I had rolled through a bed of hot coals. It seemed a whole century would pass before I would roll free, a century in which I was seared through the deepest levels of my body to the fearful breath within me and the breath seared and heated to the point of explosion. It'll all be over in a flash, I thought as I rolled clear. It'll all be over in a flash.

But not yet, the men on the other side were waiting, red faces swollen as though from apoplexy as they bent forward in their chairs. Seeing their fingers coming toward me I rolled away as a fumbled football rolls off the receiver's fingertips, back into the coals. That time I luckily sent the rug sliding out of place and heard the coins ringing against the floor and the boys scuffling to pick them up and the M.C. calling, "All right, boys, that's all. Go get dressed and get your money."

I was limp as a dish rag. My back felt as though it had been beaten with wires.

When we had dressed the M.C. came in and gave us each five dollars, except Tatlock, who gotten for being last in the ring. Then he told us to leave. I was not to get a chance to deliver my speech, I thought. I was going out into the dim alley in despair when I was stopped and told to go back. I returned to the ballroom, where the men were pushing back their chairs and gathering in groups to talk.

The M.C. knocked on a table for quiet. "Gentlemen," he said, "we almost forgot an important part of the program. A most serious part, gentlemen. This boy was brought here to deliver a speech which he made at his graduation yesterday ..."

"Bravo!"

"I'm told that he is the smartest boy we've got out there in Greenwood. I'm told that he knows more big words than a pocket-sized dictionary."

Much applause and laughter.

"So now, gentlemen, I want you to give him your attention."

There was still laughter as I faced them, my mouth dry, my eye throbbing. I began slowly, but evidently my throat was tense, because they began shouting, "Louder! Louder!"

"We of the younger generation extol the wisdom of that great leader and educator," I shouted, "who first spoke these flaming words of wisdom: A ship lost at sea for many days suddenly sighted a friendly vessel. From the mast of the unfortunate vessel was seen a signal: "Water, water; we die of thirst!" The answer from the friendly vessel came back: "Cast down your bucket where you are." The captain of the distressed vessel, at last heeding the injunction, cast down his bucket, and it came up full of fresh sparkling water from the mouth of the Amazon River." And like him I say, and in his words, "To those of my race who depend upon bettering their condition in a foreign land, or who underestimate the importance of cultivating friendly relations with the Southern white man, who is his next-door neighbor, I would say: "Cast down your bucket where you are — cast it down in making friends in every manly way of the people of all races by whom we are surrounded ..."

I spoke automatically and with such fervor that I did not realize that the men were still talking and laughing until my dry mouth, filling up with blood from the cut, almost strangled me. I coughed, wanting to stop and go to one of the tall brass, sand-filled spittoons to relieve myself, but a few of the men, especially the superintendent, were listening and I was afraid. So, I gulped it down, blood, saliva and all, and continued. (What powers of endurance I had during those days! What enthusiasm! What a belief in the rightness of things!) I spoke even louder in spite of the pain. But still they talked and still they laughed, as though deaf with cotton in dirty ears. So, I spoke with greater emotional emphasis. I closed my ears and swallowed blood until I was nauseated. The speech seemed a hundred times as long as before, but I could not leave out a single word. All had to be said, each memorized nuance considered, rendered. Nor was that all. Whenever I uttered a word of three or more syllables a group of voices would yell for me to repeat it. I used the phrase "social responsibility" and they yelled:

"What's that word you say, boy?"

"Social responsibility," I said.

"What?"

"Social ..."

"Louder."

"... responsibility."

"More!"

"Respon ... "

"Repeat!"

"... sibility."

The room filled with the uproar of laughter until, no doubt, distracted by having to gulp down my blood, I made a mistake and yelled a phrase I had often seen denounced in newspaper editorials, heard debated in private.

"Social..."

"What?" they yelled.

"...equality — "

The laughter hung smoke-like in the sudden stillness. I opened my eyes, puzzled. Sounds of displeasure filled the room. The M.C. rushed forward. They shouted hostile phrases at me. But I did not understand.

A small dry mustached man in the front row blared out, "Say that slowly, son!"

"What sir?"

"What you just said!"

"Social responsibility, sir," I said.

"You weren't being smart, were you, boy?" he said, not unkindly.

"No, sir!"

"You sure that about "equality" was a mistake?"

"Oh, yes, sir," I said. "I was swallowing blood."

"Well, you had better speak more slowly so we can understand. We mean to do right by you, but you've got to know your place at all times. All right, now, go on with your speech."

I was afraid. I wanted to leave but I wanted also to speak and I was afraid they'd snatch me down.

"Thank you, sir," I said, beginning where I had left off, and having them ignore me as before.

Yet when I finished there was a thunderous applause. I was surprised to see the superintendent come forth with a package wrapped in white tissue paper, and, gesturing for quiet, address the men.

"Gentlemen, you see that I did not overpraise this boy. He makes a good speech and some day he'll lead his people in the proper paths. And I don't have to tell you that that is important in these days and times. This is a good, smart boy, and so to encourage him in the right direction, in the name of the Board of Education I wish to present him a prize in the form of this ..."

He paused, removing the tissue paper and revealing a gleaming calfskin brief case.

"... in the form of this first-class article from Shad Whitmore's shop."

"Boy," he said, addressing me, "take this prize and keep it well. Consider it a badge of office. Prize it. Keep developing as you are and some day it will be filled with important papers that will help shape the destiny of your people."

I was so moved that I could hardly express my thanks. A rope of bloody saliva forming a shape like an undiscovered continent drooled upon the leather and I wiped it quickly away. I felt an importance that I had never dreamed.

"Open it and see what's inside," I was told.

My fingers trembled, I complied, smelling the fresh leather and finding an official-looking document inside. It was a scholarship to the state college for Negroes. My eyes filled with tears and I ran awkwardly off the floor.

I was overjoyed; I did not even mind when I discovered that the gold pieces, I had scrambled for were brass pocket tokens advertising a certain make of automobile.

When I reached home, everyone was excited. Next day the neighbors came to congratulate me. I even felt safe from grandfather, whose deathbed curse usually spoiled my triumphs. I stood beneath his photograph with my brief case in hand and smiled triumphantly into his stolid black peasant's face. It was a face that fascinated me. The eyes seemed to follow everywhere I went.

That night I dreamed I was at a circus with him and that he refused to laugh at the clowns no matter what they did. Then later he told me to open my brief case and read what was inside and I did, finding an official envelope stamped with the state seal; and inside the envelope I found another and another, endlessly, and I thought I would fall of weariness. "them's years," he said. "Now open that one." And I did and in it I found an engraved document containing a short message in letters of gold. "Read it," my grandfather said. "Out loud."

"To Whom It May Concern," I intoned. "Keep This Nigger-Boy Running."

I awoke with the old man's laughter ringing in my ears.

(It was a dream I was to remember and dream again for many years after. But at that time, I had no insight into its meaning. First, I had to attend college.)

4. Questions for Discussion

(1) How does the Battle Royal illuminate to the narrator the differences between Blacks and Whites?

(2) How does the Battle Royal symbolize the plight of Blacks in that time period when the novel was written?

(3) Please describe how the black people were treated with violence both physically and mentally in the Battle Royal.

(4) In the chapter the word "blind" is used repeatedly. Please list all references to the image of blindness and explain their meanings.

Chapter 6 Feminism

In Lucy Mangan's *Feminism Book*, she traced the origin of the word "feminism". "Feminism as a concept did not emerge until 1837, when Frenchmen Charles Fourier first used the term "feminism". Its use caught on in Britain and the US during the ensuing decades, where it was used to describe a movement that aimed to achieve legal, economic, and social equality between the sexes, and to end sexism and the oppression of women by men" (5).

American feminism refers to a series of movements and ideologies aimed at defining, establishing, and defending equal political, economic, cultural, and social rights for women in the United States. The Feminist movement in the United States has experienced four waves. The first wave of feminism took place in the late nineteenth and early twentieth centuries. The goal of this wave was to open up opportunities for women, with a focus on suffrage. The second wave began in the 1960s and continued into the 1990s. This wave developed in the context of the anti-war and Civil Rights Movements and the growing self-consciousness of a variety of minority groups around the world. Sexuality and reproductive rights were dominant issues. The feminists at that time rejected the traditional gender roles of women as wives and mothers. In Lucy Mangan's *Feminism Book*, she traced the origin of the word "feminism".

The third wave of feminism which began in the mid-1990s was informed by post-colonial and post-modern thinking. Involving more women and girls of color, the third wave redefined women and girls as assertive, powerful. They controlled their own sexuality, challenging the stereotypical images of women as passive, weak, virginal and faithful. Some say the fourth feminist movement began in 2012, focusing on the empowerment of women, opposition to sexual harassment, body shaming, and rape culture, among other issues. A key component was the use of social media to highlight and address these concerns. All in all, feminism in the United States has gone through different stages of development, and it is believed that through the endless efforts, women will have a brighter future.

American feminism and literature have been intertwined for centuries. Literature has been a powerful tool for feminist expression, both in terms of representing feminist perspectives and challenging traditional gender norms. As early as the 19th century, writers such as Margaret Fuller and Harriet Beecher Stowe used their literary works to advocate for women's rights and challenge societal expectations of women. In the 20th century, feminist literature became more widespread and diverse, as writers from diverse backgrounds explored themes of gender, race, class, and sexuality. Some notable feminist writers include Virginia Woolf, Kate Chopin, Alice Walker, Audre Lorde, Toni Morrison, and Sylvia Plath, etc.

In addition to feminist literature, American feminism has also been shaped by literary criticism and theory. Feminist literary criticism emerged in the 1960s and 1970s, with scholars such as Kate Millett and Elaine Showalter exploring the ways in which literature reflects and reinforces gender roles and stereotypes. Feminist theory has also influenced literary studies more broadly, encouraging scholars to question dominant cultural narratives and consider the perspectives of marginalized groups.

Section One: William Faulkner and *A Rose for Emily*

William Faulkner is an American novelist and short-story writer who was awarded the 1949 Nobel Prize for Literature. Faulkner's works frequently reflect the tumultuous history of the South while developing perceptive explorations of the human character. Wagner commented that "Faulkner portrays in his fiction all the qualities he finds necessary for truly human and humane existence honor, respect, love; bravery, loyalty, humor; responsibility, reverence, fear. The vividness of his characterizations places him with such writers as Shakespeare, Dostoevski, and Dickens; his moral point of view places him with these and other less likely compatriots — Milton, for one, and perhaps Dante" (Wagner1). *A Rose for Emily* remains to be one of his most classical short stories.

1. Introduction of William Faulkner

William Faulkner was born in the small town of New Albany, Mississippi, on September 25, 1897. His parents, Murry Faulkner and Maud Butler Faulkner, named him after his paternal great-grandfather, William Clark Falkner, an adventurous and shrewd man. Raised in nearby Oxford as the oldest of four sons of an old-line southern family, William Faulkner dropped out of school in 1915 and began to work in his father's bank. He joined the Canadian Air Force, and later the British Royal Air Force during the First World War. Back home, he studied for a while at the University of Mississippi as a veteran, and temporarily worked for a New York bookstore and a New Orleans newspaper. Except for some trips to Europe and Asia, and a few brief stays in Hollywood as a scriptwriter, he worked on his novels and short stories on a farm in Oxford.

William Faulkner finished his first book, *The Marble Faun,* in 1924. The following year, he moved to New Orleans and met Sherwood Anderson who encouraged him to write about his own hometown. Inspired by Anderson, William Faulkner began writing about the places and people of his childhood, developing a great many colorful characters based on real people he had grown up with or heard about, including his great-grandfather, William Clark Falkner. In *Sartoris*, he patterned the character Colonel Sartoris after his own great-grandfather. For his famous 1929 novel, *The Sound and the Fury*, he developed the fictional Yoknapatawpha County — a setting William Faulkner created based on his hometown. The novel is an account of the tragical downfall of the Compson family through the minds of several characters. The novel *Sanctuary* (1931) is about the degeneration of Temple Drake, a young girl from a distinguished southern family. *Light in August* (1932) tells the story of Yoknapatawpha County outcasts. The story focuses on several important themes, such as race and sex, class and religion, etc. The theme of racial prejudice is brought up again in *Absalom, Absalom!* (1936), in which a young man is rejected by his father and brother because of his mixed blood. In 1946, the critic Malcolm Cowley published *The Portable Faulkner* and interest in Faulkner's works was revived.

One of Faulkner's greatest professional moments came when he was awarded the 1949 Nobel Prize in Literature, receiving the award the following year. The committee deemed him one of the most important writers of American literature. Later he was given the 1951 National Book Award for *The Collected Stories of William Faulkner*. A few years later, William Faulkner was awarded the 1955 Pulitzer Prize for Fiction along with another National Book Award. William Faulkner died of a heart attack on July 6, 1962.

William Faulkner has created an impressive literary legacy and remained a revered writer of American South. He has a very contradictory feeling towards American South, loving its beauty and meanwhile criticizing its dark past. He has created a multigenerational saga in his novels and successfully advanced the two literary devices: stream of consciousness and multiple point of view. He will be forever remembered for his achievement in American literature.

2. Introduction of *A Rose for Emily*

Published on April 30, 1930, *A Rose for Emily* is a short story by William Faulkner. Hans H. Skei commented that "*A Rose for Emily* is not Faulkner's best story, but it may well be regarded as the central one in his short-story career." (Skei 3). The story takes place in Faulkner's fictional city Jefferson, Mississippi, in the southern county of Yoknapatawpha. It's generally categorized as a southern Gothic novel.

The story describes the life of a southern spinster, Emily Grierson, who is regarded as "a tradition, a duty" in her family. She is motherless and grows up under the stifling influence of her father, who does not allow her to mix with other men. She is deprived of the chance to love by her father when she is young. When her father dies, she falls in love with a Northerner, Homer Barron. She kills him and keeps his rotting corpse in her bedroom and sleeps next to it for many years when she realizes that her lover is reluctant to marry her.

A Rose for Emily reflects feminist ideals by portraying the protagonist, Emily, as a woman who has been oppressed by a patriarchal society to the detriment of her mental health. Emily is expected to follow the traditional gender roles and become a docile daughter and wife. In the story, Emily's father with strong patriarchal chauvinism tries to dominate over her destiny. Deprived of her individuality, she is a victim of patriarchal society that regards women as weak and powerless. She is described as feeble, unintelligent and impure, which is the result of unfair treatment she has received.

3. Reading Material: *A Rose for Emily*

I

When Miss Emily Grierson died, our whole town went to her funeral: the men through a sort of respectful affection for a fallen monument, the women mostly out of curiosity to see the inside of her house, which no one save an old man-servant — a combined gardener and cook — had seen in at least ten years.

It was a big, squarish frame house that had once been white, decorated with cupolas and spires and scrolled balconies in the heavily lightsome style of the 1970s, set on what had once been our most select street. But garages and cotton gins had encroached and obliterated even the august names of that neighborhood; only Miss Emily's house was left, lifting its stubborn and coquettish decay above the cotton wagons and the gasoline pumps — an eyesore among eyesores. And now Miss Emily had gone to join the representatives of those august names where they lay in the cedar-bemused cemetery among the ranked and anonymous graves of Union and Confederate soldiers who fell at the battle of Jefferson.

Alive, Miss Emily had been a tradition, a duty, and a care; a sort of hereditary obligation upon the town, dating from that day in 1894 when Colonel Sartoris, the mayor — he who fathered the edict that no Negro woman should appear on the streets without an apron-remitted her taxes, the dispensation dating from the death of her father on into perpetuity. Not that Miss Emily would have accepted charity. Colonel Sartoris invented an involved tale to the effect that Miss Emily's father had loaned money to the town, which the town, as a matter of business, preferred this way of repaying. Only a man of Colonel Sartoris' generation and thought could have invented it, and only a woman could have believed it.

When the next generation, with its more modern ideas, became mayors and aldermen, this arrangement created some little dissatisfaction. On the first of the year, they mailed her a tax notice. February came, and there was no reply. They wrote her a formal letter, asking her to call at the sheriff's office at her convenience. A week later the mayor wrote her himself, offering to call or to send his car for her, and received in reply a note on paper of an archaic shape, in a thin, flowing calligraphy in faded ink, to the effect that she no longer went out at all. The tax notice was also enclosed, without comment.

They called a special meeting of the Board of Aldermen. A deputation waited upon her, knocked at the door through which no visitor had passed since she ceased giving china-painting lessons eight or ten years earlier. They were admitted by the old Negro into a dim hall from which a stairway mounted into still more shadow. It smelled of dust and disuse — a close, dank smell. The Negro led them into the parlor. It was furnished in heavy, leather-covered furniture. When the Negro opened the blinds of one window, they could see that the leather was cracked; and when they sat down, a faint dust rose sluggishly about their thighs, spinning with slow motes in the single sun-ray. On a tarnished gilt easel before the fireplace stood a crayon portrait of Miss Emily's father.

They rose when she entered — a small, fat woman in black, with a thin gold chain descending to her waist and vanishing into her belt, leaning on an ebony cane with a tarnished gold head. Her skeleton was small and spare; perhaps that was why what would have been merely plumpness in another was obesity in her. She looked bloated, like a body long submerged in motionless water, and of that pallid hue. Her eyes, lost in the fatty ridges of her face, looked like two small pieces of coal pressed into a lump of dough as they moved from one face to another while the visitors stated their errand.

She did not ask them to sit. She just stood in the door and listened quietly until the spokesman came to a stumbling halt. Then they could hear the invisible watch ticking at the end of the gold chain.

Her voice was dry and cold. "I have no taxes in Jefferson. Colonel Sartoris explained it to me. Perhaps one of you can gain access to the city records and satisfy yourselves."

"But we have. We are the city authorities, Miss Emily. Didn't you get a notice from the sheriff, signed by him?"

"I received a paper, yes," Miss Emily said. "Perhaps he considers himself the sheriff ... I have no taxes in Jefferson."

"But there is nothing on the books to show that, you see We must go by the—"

"See Colonel Sartoris. I have no taxes in Jefferson."

"But, Miss Emily—"

"See Colonel Sartoris." (Colonel Sartoris had been dead almost ten years.) "I have no taxes in Jefferson. Tobe!" The Negro appeared. "Show these gentlemen out."

Ⅱ

So, she vanquished them, horse and foot, just as she had vanquished their fathers thirty years before about the smell.

That was two years after her father's death and a short time after her sweetheart — the one we believed would marry her — had deserted her. After her father's death she went out very little; after her sweetheart went away, people hardly saw her at all. A few of the ladies had the temerity to call, but were not received, and the only sign of life about the place was the Negro man — a young man then — going in and out with a market basket.

"Just as if a man — any man — could keep a kitchen properly, " the ladies said; so they were not surprised when the smell developed. It was another link between the gross, teeming world and the high and mighty Griersons.

A neighbor, a woman, complained to the mayor, Judge Stevens, eighty years old.

"But what will you have me do about it, madam?" he said.

"Why, send her word to stop it," the woman said. "Isn't there a law? "

"I'm sure that won't be necessary," Judge Stevens said. "It's probably just a snake or a rat that nigger of hers killed in the yard. I'll speak to him about it."

The next day he received two more complaints, one from a man who came in diffident deprecation. "We really must do something about it, Judge. I'd be the last one in the world to bother Miss Emily, but we've got to do something." That night the Board of Aldermen met — three graybeards and one younger man, a member of the rising generation.

"It's simple enough," he said. "Send her word to have her place cleaned up. Give her a certain time to do it in, and if she doesn't."

"Dammit, sir," Judge Stevens said, "will you accuse a lady to her face of smelling bad?"

So, the next night, after midnight, four men crossed Miss Emily's lawn and slunk about the house like burglars, sniffing along the base of the brickwork and at the cellar openings while one of them performed a regular sowing motion with his hand out of a sack slung from his shoulder. They broke open the cellar door and sprinkled lime there, and in all the outbuildings. As they recrossed the lawn, a window that had been dark was lighted and Miss Emily sat in it, the light behind her, and her upright torso motionless as that of an idol. They crept quietly across the lawn and into the shadow of the locusts that lined the street. After a week or two the smell went away.

That was when people had begun to feel really sorry for her. People in our town, remembering how old lady Wyatt, her great-aunt, had gone completely crazy at last, believed that the Griersons held themselves a little too high for what they really were. None of the young men were quite good enough for Miss Emily and such. We had long thought of them as a tableau, Miss Emily a slender figure in white in the background, her father a spraddled silhouette in the foreground, his back to her and clutching a horsewhip, the two of them framed by the back-flung front door. So when she got to be thirty and was still single, we were not pleased exactly, but vindicated; even with insanity in the family she wouldn't have turned down all of her chances if they had really materialized.

When her father died, it got about that the house was all that was left to her; and in a way, people were glad. At last they could pity Miss Emily. Being left alone, and a pauper, she had become humanized. Now she too would know the old thrill and the old despair of a penny more or less.

The day after his death all the ladies prepared to call at the house and offer condolence and aid, as is our custom Miss Emily met them at the door, dressed as usual and with no trace of grief on her face. She told them that her father was not dead. She did that for three days, with the ministers calling on her, and the doctors, trying to persuade her to let them dispose of the body. Just as they were about to resort to law and force, she broke down, and they buried her father quickly.

We did not say she was crazy then. We believed she had to do that. We remembered all the young men her father had driven away, and we knew that with nothing left, she would have to cling to that which had robbed her, as people will.

Ⅲ

She was sick for a long time. When we saw her again, her hair was cut short, making her look like a girl, with a vague resemblance to those angels in colored church windows — sort of tragic and serene.

The town had just let the contracts for paving the sidewalks, and in the summer after her father's death they began the work. The construction company came with riggers and mules and machinery, and a foreman named Homer Barron, a Yankee — a big, dark, ready man, with a big voice and eyes lighter than his face. The little boys would follow in groups to hear him cuss the niggers, and the niggers singing in time to the rise and fall of picks. Pretty soon he knew everybody in town. Whenever you heard a lot of laughing anywhere about the square, Homer Barron would be in the center of the group. Presently we began to see him and Miss Emily on Sunday afternoons driving in the yellow-wheeled buggy and the matched team of bays from the livery stable.

At first, we were glad that Miss Emily would have an interest, because the ladies all said, "Of course a Grierson would not think seriously of a Northerner, a day laborer." But there were still others, older people, who said that even grief could not cause a real lady to forget *noblesse oblige* — without calling it *noblesse oblige*. They just said, "Poor Emily. Her kinsfolk should come to her." She had some kin in Alabama; but years ago her father had fallen out with them over the estate of old lady Wyatt, the crazy woman, and there was no communication between the two families. They had not even been represented at the funeral.

And as soon as the old people said, "Poor Emily," the whispering began. "Do you suppose it's really so?" they said to one another. "Of course it is. What else could ..." This behind their hands; rustling of craned silk and satin behind jalousies closed upon the sun of Sunday afternoon as the thin, swift clop-clop-clop of the matched team passed: "Poor Emily."

She carried her head high enough — even when we believed that she was fallen. It was as if she demanded more than ever the recognition of her dignity as the last Grierson; as if it had wanted that touch of earthiness to reaffirm her imperviousness. Like when she bought the rat poison, the arsenic. That was over a year after they had begun to say "Poor Emily," and while the two female cousins were visiting her.

"I want some poison," she said to the druggist. She was over thirty then, still a slight woman, though thinner than usual, with cold, haughty black eyes in a face the flesh of which was strained across the temples and about the eye sockets as you imagine a lighthouse-keeper's face ought to look. "I want some poison," she said.

"Yes, Miss Emily. What kind? For rats and such? I'd recom—"

"I want the best you have. I don't care what kind."

The druggist named several. "They'll kill anything up to an elephant. But what you want is —"

"Arsenic," Miss Emily said. "Is that a good one?"

"Is ... arsenic? Yes, ma'am. But what you want—"

"I want arsenic."

The druggist looked down at her. She looked back at him, erect, her face like a strained flag. "Why, of course," the druggist said. "If that's what you want. But the law requires you to tell what you are going to use it for."

Miss Emily just stared at him, her head tilted back in order to look him eye for eye, until he looked away and went and got the arsenic and wrapped it up. The Negro delivery boy brought her the package; the druggist didn't come back. When she opened the package at home there was written on the box, under the skull and bones: "For rats."

Ⅳ

So, the next day we all said, "She will kill herself"; and we said it would be the best thing. When she had first begun to be seen with Homer Barron, we had said, "She will marry him." Then we said, "She will persuade him yet," because Homer himself had remarked — he liked men, and it was known that he drank with the younger men in the Elks' Club — that he was not a marrying man. Later we said, "Poor Emily" behind the jalousies as they passed on Sunday afternoon in the glittering buggy, Miss Emily with her head high and Homer Barron with his hat cocked and a cigar in his teeth, reins and whip in a yellow glove.

Then some of the ladies began to say that it was a disgrace to the town and a bad example to the young people. The men did not want to interfere, but at last the ladies forced the Baptist minister — Miss Emily's people were Episcopal — to call upon her. He would never divulge what happened during that interview, but he refused to go back again. The next Sunday they again drove about the streets, and the following day the minister's wife wrote to Miss Emily's relations in Alabama.

So, she had blood-kin under her roof again and we sat back to watch developments. At first nothing happened. Then we were sure that they were to be married. We learned that Miss Emily had been to the jeweler's and ordered a man's toilet set in silver, with the letters H. B. on each piece. Two days later we learned that she had bought a complete outfit of men's clothing, including a nightshirt, and we said, "They are married." We were really glad. We were glad because the two female cousins were even more Grierson than Miss Emily had ever been.

So we were not surprised when Homer Barron — the streets had been finished some time since — was gone. We were a little disappointed that there was not a public blowing-off, but we believed that he had gone on to prepare for Miss Emily's coming, or to give her a chance to get rid of the cousins. (By that time it was a cabal, and we were all Miss Emily's allies to help circumvent the cousins.) Sure enough, after another week they departed. And, as we had expected all along, within three days Homer Barron was back in town. A neighbor saw the Negro man admit him at the kitchen door at dusk one evening.

And that was the last we saw of Homer Barron. And of Miss Emily for some time. The Negro man went in and out with the market basket, but the front door remained closed. Now and then we would see her at a window for a moment, as the men did that night when they sprinkled the lime, but for almost six months she did not appear on the streets. Then we knew that this was to be expected too; as if that quality of her father which had thwarted her woman's life so many times had been too virulent and too furious to die.

When we next saw Miss Emily, she had grown fat and her hair was turning gray. During the next few years it grew grayer and grayer until it attained an even pepper-and-salt iron-gray, when it ceased turning. Up to the day of her death at seventy-four it was still that vigorous iron-gray, like the hair of an active man.

From that time on her front door remained closed, save for a period of six or seven years, when she was about forty, during which she gave lessons in china-painting. She fitted up a studio in one of the downstairs rooms, where the daughters and granddaughters of Colonel Sartoris' contemporaries were sent to her with the same regularity and in the same spirit that they were sent to church on Sundays with a twenty-five-cent piece for the collection plate. Meanwhile her taxes had been remitted.

Then the newer generation became the backbone and the spirit of the town, and the painting pupils grew up and fell away and did not send their children to her with boxes of color and tedious brushes and pictures cut from the ladies' magazines. The front door closed upon the last one and remained closed for good. When the town got free postal delivery, Miss Emily alone refused to let them fasten the metal numbers above her door and attach a mailbox to it. She would not listen to them.

Daily, monthly, yearly we watched the Negro grow grayer and more stooped, going in and out with the market basket. Each December we sent her a tax notice, which would be returned by the post office a week later, unclaimed. Now and then we would see her in one of the downstairs windows — she had evidently shut up the top floor of the house — like the carven torso of an idol in a niche, looking or not looking at us, we could never tell which. Thus she passed from generation to generation — dear, inescapable, impervious, tranquil, and perverse.

And so she died. Fell ill in the house filled with dust and shadows, with only a doddering Negro man to wait on her. We did not even know she was sick; we had long since given up trying to get any information from the Negro. He talked to no one, probably not even to her, for his voice had grown harsh and rusty, as if from disuse.

She died in one of the downstairs rooms, in a heavy walnut bed with a curtain, her gray head propped on a pillow yellow and moldy with age and lack of sunlight.

V

The Negro met the first of the ladies at the front door and let them in, with their hushed, sibilant voices and their quick, curious glances, and then he disappeared. He walked right through the house and out the back and was not seen again.

The two female cousins came at once. They held the funeral on the second day, with the town coming to look at Miss Emily beneath a mass of bought flowers, with the crayon face of her father musing profoundly above the bier and the ladies sibilant and macabre; and the very old men — some in their brushed Confederate uniforms — on the porch and the lawn, talking of Miss Emily as if she had been a contemporary of theirs, believing that they had danced with her and courted her perhaps, confusing time with its mathematical progression, as the old do, to whom all the past is not a diminishing road but, instead, a huge meadow which no winter ever quite touches, divided from them now by the narrow bottle-neck of the most recent decade of years.

Already we knew that there was one room in that region above stairs which no one had seen in forty years, and which would have to be forced. They waited until Miss Emily was decently in the ground before they opened it.

The violence of breaking down the door seemed to fill this room with pervading dust. A thin, acrid pall as of the tomb seemed to lie everywhere upon this room decked and furnished as for a bridal: upon the valance curtains of faded rose color, upon the rose-shaded lights, upon the dressing table, upon the delicate array of crystal and the man's toilet things backed with tarnished silver, silver so tarnished that the monogram was obscured. Among them lay a collar and tie, as if they had just been removed, which, lifted, left upon the surface a pale crescent in the dust. Upon a chair hung the suit, carefully folded; beneath it the two mute shoes and the discarded socks.

The man himself lay in the bed.

For a long while we just stood there, looking down at the profound and fleshless grin. The body had apparently once lain in the attitude of an embrace, but now the long sleep that outlasts love, that conquers even the grimace of love, had cuckolded him. What was left of him, rotted beneath what was left of the nightshirt, had become inextricable from the bed in which he lay; and upon him and upon the pillow beside him lay that even coating of the patient and biding dust.

Then we noticed that in the second pillow was the indentation of a head. One of us lifted something from it, and leaning forward, that faint and invisible dust dry and acrid in the nostrils, we saw a long strand of iron-gray hair.

4. Questions for Discussion

(1) What does the narrator mean when he describes Emily Grierson as "a fallen monument" in Part 1 of *A Rose for Emily*?

(2) What does Homer Barron represent in *A Rose for Emily*?

(3) Do you think Miss Emily is a victim of patriarchy? Why or why not?

Section Two: Charlotte Perkins Gilman and *The Yellow Wallpaper*

1. Introduction of Charlotte Gilman

Born on July 3, 1860, in Hartford, Connecticut, Gilman was a writer and social activist during the late 1800s and early 1900s. When she was young, she had a difficult childhood. Her father Frederick Beecher Perkins abandoned the family, leaving Charlotte's mother to raise two children on her own. In order to survive, Gilman had to move around a lot and her education was influenced by that, but she did attend the Rhode Island School of Design for a time.

In her early adulthood, Gilman supported herself as a teacher and also as a commercial artist. In 1884 Gilman married Charles Stetson who was himself an artist. After the birth of a daughter named Katherine, Gilman entered into a period of profound depression. She suffered from serious postpartum depression and underwent a series of unusual treatments for it. Under the advice of a noted neurologist, S. Weir Mitchell, Gilman undertook a rest cure which deprived her of all the creative activities. This experience inspired her to write best-known short story *The Yellow Wallpaper*.

The couple separated in 1888 when Gilman moved with her young daughter to Pasadena, California. Eventually, Perkins Gilman got officially divorced from her husband. In June 1900 she married her cousin, Houghton Gilman with whom she lived in New York City until 1922 and this marriage claimed to be satisfied. Besides a writer, Gilman was also a successful feminist, lecturer and intellectual. She published *Women and Economics* in 1898 and called for women to gain economic independence. Perkins Gilman also made a living as a lecturer on women's issues, labor issues, and social reform. She toured Europe and the US as a lecturer, and founded her own magazine, *The Forerunner*. She committed suicide on August 17, 1935 after she found that her breast cancer was incurable.

2. Introduction of *The Yellow Wallpaper*

Published in 1892, Charlotte Perkins Gilman's classic short story, *The Yellow Wallpaper* tells the story of a young woman's gradual descent into madness. It is often cited as an early feminist work that predates a woman's right to vote in the United States. The author was involved in first-wave feminism, and her other works questioned the origins of the subjugation of women, particularly in marriage. The short story is concerned about women's role in society, their mental health and right to autonomy and self-identity. In the story, when the heroine is experiencing postpartum depression, she is on a "rest cure" on a rented summer country estate where she is expected to recover from her "temporary nervous depression". Her husband John is a doctor who watches her action carefully. She is forbidden to create in spite of her love for writing. Her confinement in the room makes her fascinated with the yellow wallpaper. She believes that there is a woman locked in it and tried her best to free her.

The novel was written before the first wave of feminism and enlightened the reader on women's health, motherhood, mental breakdown and its treatment, as well as gender relations in late 19th century America. The author questions the role of women in marriage. Women at that time were expected to be subordinate to their husbands and completely obedient and took on domestic roles at home. Women had no say in anything in their life, even including their health.

The Yellow Wallpaper illuminated the challenges of being a woman of ambition in the late 19th century. All women were seen vulnerable at that time, so those who fought for suffrage, or who took on male roles and challenged female dress codes, or who sought higher education or creative lives could be accused of defying female conventions and placing themselves at risk of mental illness. Perkins Gilman clearly disagreed with this situation for women and considered it harmful for women's growth and health.

3. Reading Material: *The Yellow Wallpaper*

I

It is very seldom that mere ordinary people like John and myself secure ancestral halls for the summer.

A colonial mansion, a hereditary estate, I would say a haunted house, and reach the height of romantic felicity — but that would be asking too much of fate!

Still, I will proudly declare that there is something queer about it.

Else, why should it be let so cheaply? And why have stood so long untenanted?

John laughs at me, of course, but one expects that in marriage.

John is practical in the extreme. He has no patience with faith, an intense horror of superstition, and he scoffs openly at any talk of things not to be felt and seen and put down in figures.

John is a physician, and PERHAPS — (I would not say it to a living soul, of course, but this is dead paper and a great relief to my mind) — PERHAPS that is one reason I do not get well faster.

You see, he does not believe I am sick!

And what can one do?

If a physician of high standing, and one's own husband, assures friends and relatives that there is really nothing the matter with one but temporary nervous depression — a slight hysterical tendency — what is one to do?

My brother is also a physician, and also of high standing, and he says the same thing.

So, I take phosphates or phosphites — whichever it is, and tonics, and journeys, and air, and exercise, and am absolutely forbidden to "work" until I am well again.

Personally, I disagree with their ideas.

Personally, I believe that congenial work, with excitement and change, would do me good.

But what is one to do?

I did write for a while in spite of them; but it DOES exhaust me a good deal — having to be so sly about it, or else meet with heavy opposition.

I sometimes fancy that in my condition if I had less opposition and more society and stimulus — but John says the very worst thing I can do is to think about my condition, and I confess it always makes me feel bad.

So, I will let it alone and talk about the house.

The most beautiful place! It is quite alone, standing well back from the road, quite three miles from the village. It makes me think of English places that you read about, for there are hedges and walls and gates that lock, and lots of separate little houses for the gardeners and people.

There is a DELICIOUS garden! I never saw such a garden — large and shady, full of box-bordered paths, and lined with long grape-covered arbors with seats under them.

There were greenhouses, too, but they are all broken now.

There was some legal trouble, I believe, something about the heirs and coheirs; anyhow, the place has been empty for years.

That spoils my ghostliness, I am afraid, but I don't care — there is something strange about the house — I can feel it.

I even said so to John one moonlight evening, but he said what I felt was a DRAUGHT, and shut the window.

I get unreasonably angry with John sometimes. I'm sure I never used to be so sensitive. I think it is due to this nervous condition.

But John says if I feel so, I shall neglect proper self-control; so I take pains to control myself — before him, at least, and that makes me very tired.

I don't like our room a bit. I wanted one downstairs that opened on the piazza and had roses all over the window, and such pretty old-fashioned chintz hangings! But John would not hear of it.

He said there was only one window and not room for two beds, and no near room for him if he took another.

He is very careful and loving, and hardly lets me stir without special direction.

I have a schedule prescription for each hour in the day; he takes all care from me, and so I feel basely ungrateful not to value it more.

He said we came here solely on my account, that I was to have perfect rest and all the air I could get. "Your exercise depends on your strength, my dear," he said, "and your food somewhat on your appetite; but air you can absorb all the time." So we took the nursery at the top of the house.

It is a big, airy room, the whole floor nearly, with windows that look all ways, and air and sunshine galore. It was nursery first and then playroom and gymnasium, I should judge; for the windows are barred for little children, and there are rings and things in the walls.

The paint and paper look as if a boy's school had used it. It is stripped off — the paper — in great patches all around the head of my bed, about as far as I can reach, and in a great place on the other side of the room low down. I never saw a worse paper in my life.

One of those sprawling flamboyant patterns committing every artistic sin.

It is dull enough to confuse the eye in following, pronounced enough to constantly irritate and provoke study, and when you follow the lame uncertain curves for a little distance, they suddenly commit suicide — plunge off at outrageous angles, destroy themselves in unheard of contradictions.

The color is repellent, almost revolting; a smoldering unclean yellow, strangely faded by the slow-turning sunlight.

It is a dull yet lurid orange in some places, a sickly sulphur tint in others.

No wonder the children hated it! I should hate it myself if I had to live in this room long.

There comes John, and I must put this away, — he hates to have me write a word.

We have been here two weeks, and I haven't felt like writing before, since that first day.

I am sitting by the window now, up in this atrocious nursery, and there is nothing to hinder my writing as much as I please, save lack of strength.

John is away all day, and even some nights when his cases are serious.

I am glad my case is not serious!

But these nervous troubles are dreadfully depressing.

John does not know how much I really suffer. He knows there is no REASON to suffer, and that satisfies him.

Of course it is only nervousness. It does weigh on me so not to do my duty in any way!

I meant to be such a help to John, such a real rest and comfort, and here I am a comparative burden already!

Nobody would believe what an effort it is to do what little I am able, — to dress and entertain, and order things.

It is fortunate that Mary is so good with the baby. Such a dear baby!

And yet I cannot be with him, it makes me so nervous.

I suppose John never was nervous in his life. He laughs at me so about this wall-paper!

At first he meant to repaper the room, but afterwards he said that I was letting it get the better of me, and that nothing was worse for a nervous patient than to give way to such fancies.

He said that after the wall-paper was changed it would be the heavy bedstead, and then the barred windows, and then that gate at the head of the stairs, and so on.

"You know the place is doing you good," he said, "and really, dear, I don't care to renovate the house just for a three months' rental."

"Then do let us go downstairs," I said, "there are such pretty rooms there."

Then he took me in his arms and called me a blessed little goose, and said he would go down to the cellar, if I wished, and have it whitewashed into the bargain.

But he is right enough about the beds and windows and things.

It is an airy and comfortable room as any one need wish, and, of course, I would not be so silly as to make him uncomfortable just for a whim.

I'm really getting quite fond of the big room, all but that horrid paper.

Out of one window I can see the garden, those mysterious deep-shaded arbors, the riotous old-fashioned flowers, and bushes and gnarly trees.

Out of another I get a lovely view of the bay and a little private wharf belonging to the estate. There is a beautiful shaded lane that runs down there from the house. I always fancy I see people walking in these numerous paths and arbors, but John has cautioned me not to give way to fancy in the least. He says that with my imaginative power and habit of story-making, a nervous weakness like mine is sure to lead to all manner of excited fancies, and that I ought to use my will and good sense to check the tendency. So, I try.

I think sometimes that if I were only well enough to write a little it would relieve the press of ideas and rest me.

But I find I get pretty tired when I try.

It is so discouraging not to have any advice and companionship about my work. When I get really well, John says we will ask Cousin Henry and Julia down for a long visit; but he says he would as soon put fireworks in my pillow-case as to let me have those stimulating people about now.

I wish I could get well faster.

But I must not think about that. This paper looks to me as if it knew what a vicious influence it had!

There is a recurrent spot where the pattern lolls like a broken neck and two bulbous eyes stare at you upside down.

I get positively angry with the impertinence of it and the everlastingness. Up and down and sideways they crawl, and those absurd, unblinking eyes are everywhere. There is one place where two breadths didn't match, and the eyes go all up and down the line, one a little higher than the other.

I never saw so much expression in an inanimate thing before, and we all know how much expression they have! I used to lie awake as a child and get more entertainment and terror out of blank walls and plain furniture than most children could find in a toy store.

I remember what a kindly wink the knobs of our big, old bureau used to have, and there was one chair that always seemed like a strong friend.

I used to feel that if any of the other things looked too fierce. I could always hop into that chair and be safe.

The furniture in this room is no worse than inharmonious, however, for we had to bring it all from downstairs. I suppose when this was used as a playroom they had to take the nursery things out, and no wonder! I never saw such ravages as the children have made here.

The wall-paper, as I said before, is torn off in spots, and it sticketh closer than a brother — they must have had perseverance as well as hatred.

Then the floor is scratched and gouged and splintered, the plaster itself is dug out here and there, and this great heavy bed which is all we found in the room, looks as if it had been through the wars.

But I don't mind it a bit — only the paper.

There comes John's sister. Such a dear girl as she is, and so careful of me! I must not let her find me writing.

She is a perfect and enthusiastic housekeeper, and hopes for no better profession. I verily believe she thinks it is the writing which made me sick!

But I can write when she is out, and see her a long way off from these windows.

There is one that commands the road, a lovely shaded winding road, and one that just looks off over the country. A lovely country, too, full of great elms and velvet meadows.

This wall-paper has a kind of sub-pattern in a different shade, a particularly irritating one, for you can only see it in certain lights, and not clearly then.

But in the places where it isn't faded and where the sun is just so — I can see a strange, provoking, formless sort of figure, that seems to skulk about behind that silly and conspicuous front design.

There's sister on the stairs!

Well, the Fourth of July is over! The people are gone and I am tired out. John thought it might do me good to see a little company, so we just had mother and Nellie and the children down for a week.

Of course, I didn't do a thing. Jennie sees to everything now.

But it tired me all the same.

John says if I don't pick up faster he shall send me to Weir Mitchell in the fall.

But I don't want to go there at all. I had a friend who was in his hands once, and she says he is just like John and my brother, only more so!

Besides, it is such an undertaking to go so far.

I don't feel as if it was worthwhile to turn my hand over for anything, and I'm getting dreadfully fretful and querulous.

I cry at nothing, and cry most of the time.

Of course I don't when John is here, or anybody else, but when I am alone.

And I am alone a good deal just now. John is kept in town very often by serious cases, and Jennie is good and lets me alone when I want her to.

So, I walk a little in the garden or down that lovely lane, sit on the porch under the roses, and lie down up here a good deal.

I'm getting really fond of the room in spite of the wall-paper. Perhaps because of the wall-paper.

It dwells in my mind so!

I lie here on this great immovable bed — it is nailed down, I believe — and follow that pattern about by the hour. It is as good as gymnastics, I assure you. I start, we'll say, at the bottom, down in the corner over there where it has not been touched, and I determine for the thousandth time that I will follow that pointless pattern to some sort of a conclusion.

I know a little of the principle of design, and I know this thing was not arranged on any laws of radiation, or alternation, or repetition, or symmetry, or anything else that I ever heard of.

It is repeated, of course, by the breadths, but not otherwise.

Looked at in one way each breadth stands alone, the bloated curves and flourishes — a kind of "debased Romanesque" with delirium tremens — go waddling up and down in isolated columns of fatuity.

But, on the other hand, they connect diagonally, and the sprawling outlines run off in great slanting waves of optic horror, like a lot of wallowing seaweeds in full chase.

The whole thing goes horizontally, too, at least it seems so, and I exhaust myself in trying to distinguish the order of its going in that direction.

They have used a horizontal breadth for a frieze, and that adds wonderfully to the confusion.

There is one end of the room where it is almost intact, and there, when the cross-lights fade and the low sun shines directly upon it, I can almost fancy radiation after all, — the interminable grotesques seem to form around a common center and rush off in headlong plunges of equal distraction.

It makes me tired to follow it. I will take a nap, I guess.

I don't know why I should write this.

I don't want to.

I don't feel able.

And I know John would think it absurd. But I MUST say what I feel and think in some way — it is such a relief!

But the effort is getting to be greater than the relief.

Half the time now I am awfully lazy, and lie down ever so much.

John says I mustn't lose my strength, and has me take cod liver oil and lots of tonics and things, to say nothing of ale and wine and rare meat.

Dear John! He loves me very dearly, and hates to have me sick. I tried to have a real earnest reasonable talk with him the other day, and tell him how I wish he would let me go and make a visit to Cousin Henry and Julia.

But he said I wasn't able to go, nor able to stand it after I got there; and I did not make out a very good case for myself, for I was crying before I had finished.

It is getting to be a great effort for me to think straight. Just this nervous weakness I suppose.

And dear John gathered me up in his arms, and just carried me upstairs and laid me on the bed, and sat by me and read to me till it tired my head.

He said I was his darling and his comfort and all he had, and that I must take care of myself for his sake, and keep well.

He says no one but myself can help me out of it, that I must use my will and self-control and not let any silly fancies run away with me.

There's one comfort, the baby is well and happy, and does not have to occupy this nursery with the horrid wall-paper.

If we had not used it, that blessed child would have! What a fortunate escape! Why, I wouldn't have a child of mine, an impressionable little thing, live in such a room for worlds.

I never thought of it before, but it is lucky that John kept me here after all, I can stand it so much easier than a baby, you see.

Of course, I never mention it to them any more — I am too wise, — but I keep watch of it all the same.

There are things in that paper that nobody knows but me, or ever will.

Behind that outside pattern the dim shapes get clearer every day.

It is always the same shape, only very numerous.

And it is like a woman stooping down and creeping about behind that pattern. I don't like it a bit. I wonder — I begin to think — I wish John would take me away from here!

It is so hard to talk with John about my case, because he is so wise, and because he loves me so.

But I tried it last night.

It was moonlight. The moon shines in all around just as the sun does.

I hate to see it sometimes, it creeps so slowly, and always comes in by one window or another.

John was asleep and I hated to waken him, so I kept still and watched the moonlight on that undulating wall-paper till I felt creepy.

The faint figure behind seemed to shake the pattern, just as if she wanted to get out.

I got up softly and went to feel and see if the paper DID move, and when I came back John was awake.

"What is it, little girl?" he said. "Don't go walking about like that — you'll get cold."

I thought it was a good time to talk, so I told him that I really was not gaining here, and that I wished he would take me away.

"Why darling!" said he, "our lease will be up in three weeks, and I can't see how to leave before.

"The repairs are not done at home, and I cannot possibly leave town just now. Of course if you were in any danger, I could and would, but you really are better, dear, whether you can see it or not. I am a doctor, dear, and I know. You are gaining flesh and color, your appetite is better, I feel really much easier about you."

"I don't weigh a bit more,"I said, "nor as much; and my appetite may be better in the evening when you are here, but it is worse in the morning when you are away!"

"Bless her little heart!" said he with a big hug, "she shall be as sick as she pleases! But now let's improve the shining hours by going to sleep, and talk about it in the morning!"

"And you won't go away?" I asked gloomily.

"Why, how can I, dear? It is only three weeks more and then we will take a nice little trip of a few days while Jennie is getting the house ready. Really dear you are better!"

"Better in body perhaps —" I began, and stopped short, for he sat up straight and looked at me with such a stern, reproachful look that I could not say another word.

"My darling," he said, "I beg of you, for my sake and for our child's sake, as well as for your own, that you will never for one instant let that idea enter your mind! There is nothing so dangerous, so fascinating, to a temperament like yours. It is a false and foolish fancy. Can you not trust me as a physician when I tell you so?"

So of course I said no more on that score, and we went to sleep before long. He thought I was asleep first, but I wasn't, and lay there for hours trying to decide whether that front pattern and the back pattern really did move together or separately.

On a pattern like this, by daylight, there is a lack of sequence, a defiance of law, that is a constant irritant to a normal mind.

The color is hideous enough, and unreliable enough, and infuriating enough, but the pattern is torturing.

You think you have mastered it, but just as you get well underway in following, it turns a back-somersault and there you are. It slaps you in the face, knocks you down, and tramples upon you. It is like a bad dream.

The outside pattern is a florid arabesque, reminding one of a fungus. If you can imagine a toadstool in joints, an interminable string of toadstools, budding and sprouting in endless convolutions — why, that is something like it.

That is, sometimes!

There is one marked peculiarity about this paper, a thing nobody seems to notice but myself, and that is that it changes as the light changes.

When the sun shoots in through the east window — I always watch for that first long, straight ray — it changes so quickly that I never can quite believe it.

That is why I watch it always.

By moonlight — the moon shines in all night when there is a moon — I wouldn't know it was the same paper.

At night in any kind of light, in twilight, candle light, lamplight, and worst of all by moonlight, it becomes bars! The outside pattern I mean, and the woman behind it is as plain as can be.

I didn't realize for a long time what the thing was that showed behind, that dim sub-pattern, but now I am quite sure it is a woman.

By daylight she is subdued, quiet. I fancy it is the pattern that keeps her so still. It is so puzzling. It keeps me quiet by the hour.

I lie down ever so much now. John says it is good for me, and to sleep all I can.

Indeed, he started the habit by making me lie down for an hour after each meal.

It is a very bad habit I am convinced, for you see I don't sleep.

And that cultivates deceit, for I don't tell them I'm awake — O no!

The fact is I am getting a little afraid of John.

He seems very queer sometimes, and even Jennie has an inexplicable look.

It strikes me occasionally, just as a scientific hypothesis, — that perhaps it is the paper!

I have watched John when he did not know I was looking, and come into the room suddenly on the most innocent excuses, and I've caught him several times LOOKING AT THE PAPER! And Jennie too. I caught Jennie with her hand on it once.

She didn't know I was in the room, and when I asked her in a quiet, a very quiet voice, with the most restrained manner possible, what she was doing with the paper — she turned around as if she had been caught stealing, and looked quite angry — asked me why I should frighten her so!

Then she said that the paper stained everything it touched, that she had found yellow smooches on all my clothes and John's, and she wished we would be more careful!

Did not that sound innocent? But I know she was studying that pattern, and I am determined that nobody shall find it out but myself!

Life is very much more exciting now than it used to be. You see I have something more to expect, to look forward to, to watch. I really do eat better, and am quieter than I was.

John is so pleased to see me improve! He laughed a little the other day, and said I seemed to be flourishing in spite of my wall-paper.

I turned it off with a laugh. I had no intention of telling him it was BECAUSE of the wall-paper — he would make fun of me. He might even want to take me away.

I don't want to leave now until I have found it out. There is a week more, and I think that will be enough.

I'm feeling ever so much better! I don't sleep much at night, for it is so interesting to watch developments; but I sleep a good deal in the daytime.

In the daytime it is tiresome and perplexing.

There are always new shoots on the fungus, and new shades of yellow all over it. I cannot keep count of them, though I have tried conscientiously.

It is the strangest yellow, that wall-paper! It makes me think of all the yellow things I ever saw — not beautiful ones like buttercups, but old foul, bad yellow things.

But there is something else about that paper — the smell! I noticed it the moment we came into the room, but with so much air and sun it was not bad. Now we have had a week of fog and rain, and whether the windows are open or not, the smell is here.

It creeps all over the house.

I find it hovering in the dining-room, skulking in the parlor, hiding in the hall, lying in wait for me on the stairs.

It gets into my hair.

Even when I go to ride, if I turn my head suddenly and surprise it — there is that smell!

Such a peculiar odor, too! I have spent hours in trying to analyze it, to find what it smelled like.

It is not bad — at first, and very gentle, but quite the subtlest, most enduring odor I ever met.

In this damp weather it is awful, I wake up in the night and find it hanging over me.

It used to disturb me at first. I thought seriously of burning the house — to reach the smell.

But now I am used to it. The only thing I can think of that it is like is the COLOR of the paper! A yellow smell.

There is a very funny mark on this wall, low down, near the mopboard. A streak that runs round the room. It goes behind every piece of furniture, except the bed, a long, straight, even SMOOCH, as if it had been rubbed over and over.

I wonder how it was done and who did it, and what they did it for. Round and round and round — round and round and round — it makes me dizzy!

I really have discovered something at last.

Through watching so much at night, when it changes so, I have finally found out.

The front pattern DOES move — and no wonder! The woman behind shakes it!

Sometimes I think there are a great many women behind, and sometimes only one, and she crawls around fast, and her crawling shakes it all over.

Then in the very bright spots she keeps still, and in the very shady spots she just takes hold of the bars and shakes them hard.

And she is all the time trying to climb through. But nobody could climb through that pattern — it strangles so; I think that is why it has so many heads.

They get through, and then the pattern strangles them off and turns them upside down, and makes their eyes white!

If those heads were covered or taken off it would not be half so bad.

I think that woman gets out in the daytime!

And I'll tell you why — privately — I've seen her!

I can see her out of every one of my windows!

It is the same woman, I know, for she is always creeping, and most women do not creep by daylight.

I see her on that long road under the trees, creeping along, and when a carriage comes, she hides under the blackberry vines.

I don't blame her a bit. It must be very humiliating to be caught creeping by daylight!

I always lock the door when I creep by daylight. I can't do it at night, for I know John would suspect something at once.

And John is so queer now, that I don't want to irritate him. I wish he would take another room! Besides, I don't want anybody to get that woman out at night but myself.

I often wonder if I could see her out of all the windows at once.

But, turn as fast as I can, I can only see out of one at a time.

And though I always see her, she MAY be able to creep faster than I can turn!

I have watched her sometimes away off in the open country, creeping as fast as a cloud shadow in a high wind.

If only that top pattern could be gotten off from the under one! I mean to try it, little by little.

I have found out another funny thing, but I shan't tell it this time! It does not trust people too much.

There are only two more days to get this paper off, and I believe John is beginning to notice. I don't like the look in his eyes.

And I heard him ask Jennie a lot of professional questions about me. She had a very good report to give.

She said I slept a good deal in the daytime.

John knows I don't sleep very well at night, for all I'm so quiet!

He asked me all sorts of questions, too, and pretended to be very loving and kind.

As if I couldn't see through him!

Still, I don't wonder he acts so, sleeping under this paper for three months.

It only interests me, but I feel sure John and Jennie are secretly affected by it.

Hurrah! This is the last day, but it is enough. John is to stay in town overnight, and won't be out until this evening.

Jennie wanted to sleep with me — the sly thing! but I told her I should undoubtedly rest better for a night all alone.

That was clever, for really I wasn't alone a bit! As soon as it was moonlight and that poor thing began to crawl and shake the pattern, I got up and ran to help her.

I pulled and she shook, I shook and she pulled, and before morning we had peeled off yards of that paper.

A strip about as high as my head and half around the room.

And then when the sun came and that awful pattern began to laugh at me, I declared I would finish it today!

We go away tomorrow, and they are moving all my furniture down again to leave things as they were before.

Jennie looked at the wall in amazement, but I told her merrily that I did it out of pure spite at the vicious thing.

She laughed and said she wouldn't mind doing it herself, but I must not get tired.

How she betrayed herself that time!

But I am here, and no person touches this paper but me — not ALIVE!

She tried to get me out of the room — it was too patent! But I said it was so quiet and empty and clean now that I believed I would lie down again and sleep all I could; and not to wake me even for dinner — I would call when I woke.

So now she is gone, and the servants are gone, and the things are gone, and there is nothing left but that great bedstead nailed down, with the canvas mattress we found on it.

We shall sleep downstairs tonight, and take the boat home tomorrow.

I quite enjoy the room, now it is bare again.

How those children did tear about here!

This bedstead is fairly gnawed!

But I must get to work.

I have locked the door and thrown the key down into the front path.

I don't want to go out, and I don't want to have anybody come in, till John comes.

I want to astonish him.

I've got a rope up here that even Jennie did not find. If that woman does get out, and tries to get away, I can tie her!

But I forgot I could not reach far without anything to stand on!

This bed will NOT move!

I tried to lift and push it until I was lame, and then I got so angry I bit off a little piece at one corner — but it hurt my teeth.

Then I peeled off all the paper I could reach standing on the floor. It sticks horribly and the pattern just enjoys it! All those strangled heads and bulbous eyes and waddling fungus growths just shriek with derision!

I am getting angry enough to do something desperate. To jump out of the window would be admirable exercise, but the bars are too strong even to try.

Besides I wouldn't do it. Of course not. I know well enough that a step like that is improper and might be misconstrued.

I don't like to LOOK out of the windows even — there are so many of those creeping women, and they creep so fast.

I wonder if they all come out of that wall-paper as I did?

But I am securely fastened now by my well-hidden rope — you don't get ME out in the road there!

I suppose I shall have to get back behind the pattern when it comes night, and that is hard!

It is so pleasant to be out in this great room and creep around as I please!

I don't want to go outside. I won't, even if Jennie asks me to.

For outside you have to creep on the ground, and everything is green instead of yellow.

But here I can creep smoothly on the floor, and my shoulder just fits in that long smooch around the wall, so I cannot lose my way.

Why there's John at the door!

It is no use, young man, you can't open it!

How he does call and pound!

Now he's crying for an axe.

It would be a shame to break down that beautiful door!

"John dear!" said I in the gentlest voice, "the key is down by the front steps, under a plantain leaf!"

That silenced him for a few moments.

Then he said — very quietly indeed, "Open the door, my darling!"

"I can't," said I. "The key is down by the front door under a plantain leaf!"

And then I said it again, several times, very gently and slowly, and said it so often that he had to go and see, and he got it of course, and came in. He stopped short by the door.

"What is the matter?" he cried. "For God's sake, what are you doing!"

I kept on creeping just the same, but I looked at him over my shoulder.

"I've got out at last," said I, "in spite of you and Jane. And I've pulled off most of the paper, so you can't put me back!"

Now why should that man have fainted? But he did, and right across my path by the wall, so that I had to creep over him every time!

4. Questions for Discussion

(1) In *The Yellow Wallpaper*, is the narrator reliable or unreliable? Can we believe everything that she says? Why or why not?

(2) What does the woman behind the wallpaper represent? How does the narrator come to identify with her?

(3) What does the wallpaper represent in the story *The Yellow Wallpaper*?

(4) What is the significance of the fact that the narrator's room in *The Yellow Wallpaper* was once a nursery?

(5) What does the story *The Yellow Wallpaper* suggest about middle-class women's place and roles in the society?

Chapter 7 Multiculturalism

American multiculturalism and literature are closely intertwined, as literature has often been used as a way to explore and showcase the diverse cultures and experiences of many American communities.

According to Ali Rattansi, "Multiculturalism entered public discourses in the late 1960s and early 1970s, when both Australia and Canada began to declare their support for it...Immigrants were encouraged to integrate rather than required to assimilate. This meant that they were to be enabled to retain elements of their 'home culture', and ethnic community associations were seen as important vehicles of integration" (5). Multiculturalism is a concept that recognizes the diversity of cultural backgrounds and promotes the idea that different cultural groups can coexist and thrive together. It has been an important topic in American literature for many decades. American literature reflects the country's diverse population, which includes people from various ethnic, racial, and cultural backgrounds.

A survey of American multiculturalism and literature would necessarily include a wide range of authors and works, as well as the historical and cultural context in which they were produced. Some of the key themes and topics that have been explored in multicultural literature include race, ethnicity, gender, sexuality, religion, and class.

One of the earliest examples of multicultural literature in America is the slave narrative, which told the stories of enslaved Africans and their experiences of bondage and liberation. Prominent examples of these works include *Narrative of the Life of Frederick Douglass, an American Slave* by Frederick Douglass and *Incidents in the Life of a Slave Girl* by Harriet Jacobs.

In the early 20th century, American literature focused mostly on the experiences of white, middle-class Americans. However, with the increasing visibility of minority communities, writers began to explore the cultural differences and the experiences of marginalized groups in America. As a result, multiculturalism became an important theme in American literature. Many writers from diverse backgrounds have made significant contributions to American literature.

For example, African American writers such as Langston Hughes, Zora Neale Hurston, and Richard Wright, among others, explored the experiences of black Americans in a country that was still grappling with racism and discrimination.

Similarly, Latino writers like Sandra Cisneros and Junot Diaz have explored issues of identity, immigration, and cultural heritage in their work. Asian American writers such as Maxine Hong Kingston and Amy Tan have explored the experiences of Asian Americans in America, highlighting the challenges of assimilation and the tensions between tradition and modernity.

Indian American writers have also made significant contributions to American literature, and their work has been recognized both in India and the United States. Some of the most well-known Indian American writers include Jhumpa Lahiri, Salman Rushdie, and Amitav Ghosh, among many others.

In recent years, the concept of multiculturalism has expanded to include a wider range of identities and experiences, including LGBTQ① and disabled communities. Multiculturalism has played an important role in shaping American literature, art, music, and other cultural expressions.

In addition to cultural expressions, multiculturalism has also influenced American social and political life. Efforts to promote diversity, inclusion, and equality have been at the forefront of social and political movements throughout American history. These efforts have resulted in legislative and policy changes that have helped to address systemic discrimination and promote greater understanding and acceptance of different cultures. Overall, multiculturalism has played a significant role in American literature and culture, giving voice to diverse perspectives and enriching the literary landscape of the country.

The readings in this unit include Amy Tan's *Joy Luck Club* and Jhumpa Lahir's short story *The Third and Final Continent*. Focusing on the relationships between four Chinese immigrant mothers and their American-born daughters, *The Joy Luck Club* explores themes of mother-daughter relationships, identity, cultural conflict, and the immigrant experience. *The Third and Final Continent* is a short story by Jhumpa Lahiri, first published in *The New Yorker* in 1999. It is a story about the immigrant experience and the struggles and joys of starting a new life in a foreign country. It also explores themes of cultural identity, homesickness, and the importance of human connection in navigating the challenges of life.

Section One: Amy Tan and *The Joy Luck Club*

Amy Tan is a bestselling American author known for her novels and essays that explore the complex relationships between mothers and daughters, and the experiences of Chinese American immigrants. *The Joy Luck Club* is a critically acclaimed novel written by Amy Tan and was published in 1989. The book explores the complex relationships between four Chinese immigrant women and their American-born daughters, delving into themes of culture, identity, mother-daughter dynamics, and the power of storytelling. It remains a significant and influential novel in Chinese American literature.

1. Introduction of Amy Tan

Amy Tan was born on February 19, 1952, in Oakland, California, to Chinese immigrant parents.

Tan grew up in a bilingual household, speaking both English and Mandarin, and she

① LGBTQ is an initialism that stands for "lesbian, gay, bisexual, and transgender and queer".

frequently visited her family in China during her childhood. She attended San Jose State University and later the University of California, Berkeley, where she earned a master's degree in linguistics.

After working as a language development consultant and freelance writer, Tan published her debut novel, *The Joy Luck Club*, in 1989. The novel became a bestseller and was adapted into a successful film, and it helped establish Tan as a major literary voice. She has since published several more novels, including *The Kitchen God's Wife, The Bonesetter's Daughter*, and *Saving Fish from Drowning*, as well as a number of non-fictional works.

Tan's writing often explores the complexities of the immigrant experience and the challenges of cultural assimilation, while also delving into issues of family, identity. Her work has earned numerous awards and honors, including the National Endowment for the Arts fellowship, the Guggenheim fellowship, and the Commonwealth Gold Award. Tan is also a vocal advocate for issues related to social justice and has been involved in various charitable organizations throughout her career.

2. Introduction of *The Joy Luck Club*

Published in 1989, *The Joy Luck Club* is a novel by Amy Tan that explores the relationships between four Chinese immigrant mothers and their American-born daughters. Feng, Pin-Chia commented that "Tan's skillful storytelling not only provides culturally-specific experiences of Chinese-American women but also powerfully appeals to the universal emotions of general readers". The novel is divided into four parts, with each section narrated by a different character, and each character telling her own story and revealing her own struggles with the cultural divide between China and the United States.

The story begins with Jing-Mei (June Woo), an American-born daughter, who is asked to take her mother's place in a weekly mahjong game with her mother's three best friends. As the four women play mahjong, they share stories about their lives, their cultural heritage, and the challenges they faced as immigrants in the United States.

Through the stories of these eight women, *The Joy Luck Club* explores themes of mother-daughter relationships, identity, cultural conflicts, and the immigrant experience. The novel is widely acclaimed for its insightful portrayal of the complexities of the Chinese American experience, and has been adapted into a successful film and stage play. Analyzing *The Joy Luck Club* from a multicultural perspective involves examining how the novel portrays the intersections of culture, gender, and history, and how these factors shape the experiences of its characters.

3. Reading Material: *The Joy Luck Club* (excerpt)

Chapter One: Feathers from a Thousand Li Away

The old woman remembered a swan she had bought many years ago in Shanghai for a foolish sum. This bird, boasted the market vendor, was once a duck that stretched its neck in hopes of becoming a goose, and now look! — it is too beautiful to eat.

Then the woman and the swan sailed across an ocean many thousands of li wide, stretching their necks toward America. On her journey she cooed to the swan: "In America I will have a daughter just like me. But over there nobody will say her worth is measured by the loudness of her husband's belch. Over there nobody will look down on her, because I will make her speak only perfect American English. And over there she will always be too full to swallow any sorrow! She will know my meaning, because I will give her this swan — a creature that became more than what was hoped for."

But when she arrived in the new country, the immigration of officials pulled her swan away from her, leaving the woman fluttering her arms and with only one swan feather for a memory. And then she had to fill out so many forms she forgot why she had come and what she had left behind.

Now the woman was old. And she had a daughter who grew up speaking only English and swallowing more Coca-Cola than sorrow. For a long time now, the woman had wanted to give her daughter the single swan feather and tell her, "This feather may look worthless, but it comes from afar and carries with it all my good intentions." And she waited, year after year, for the day she could tell her daughter this in perfect American English.

Jing-Mei Woo: *The Joy Luck Club*

My father has asked me to be the fourth corner at the Joy Luck Club. I am to replace my mother, whose seat at the mah jong table has been empty since she died two months ago. My father thinks she was killed by her own thoughts.

"She had a new idea inside her head," said my father. "But before it could come out of her mouth, the thought grew too big and burst. It must have been a very bad idea."

The doctor said she died of a cerebral aneurysm. And her friends at the Joy Luck Club said she died just like a rabbit: quickly and with unfinished business left behind. My mother was supposed to host the next meeting of the Joy Luck Club.

The week before she died, she called me, full of pride, full of life: "Auntie Lin cooked red bean soup for Joy Luck. I'm going to cook black sesame-seed soup."

"Don't show off," I said.

"It's not showoff." She said the two soups were almost the same, *chabudwo*. Or maybe she said *butong*, not the same thing at all. It was one of those Chinese expressions that means the better half of mixed intentions. I can never remember things I didn't understand in the first place.

My mother started the San Francisco version of the Joy Luck Club in 1949, two years before I was born. This was the year my mother and father left China with one stiff leather trunk filled only with fancy silk dresses. There was no time to pack anything else, my mother had explained to my father after they boarded the boat. Still his hands swam frantically between the slippery silks, looking for his cotton shirts and wool pants.

When they arrived in San Francisco, my father made her hide those shiny clothes. She wore the same brown-checked Chinese dress until the Refugee Welcome Society gave her two hand-me-down dresses, all too large in sizes for American women. The society was composed of a group of white-haired American missionary ladies from the First Chinese Baptist Church. And because of their gifts, my parents could not refuse their invitation to join the church. Nor could they ignore the old ladies' practical advice to improve their English through Bible study class on Wednesday nights and, later, through choir practice on Saturday mornings. This was how my parents met the Hsus, the Jongs, and the St. Clairs. My mother could sense that the women of these families also had unspeakable tragedies they had left behind in China and hopes they couldn't begin to express in their fragile English. Or at least, my mother recognized the numbness in these women's faces. And she saw how quickly their eyes moved when she told them her idea for the Joy Luck Club.

Joy Luck was an idea my mother remembered from the days of her first marriage in Kweilin, before the Japanese came. That's why I think of Joy Luck as her Kweilin story. It was the story she would always tell me when she was bored, when there was nothing to do, when every bowl had been washed and the Formica table had been wiped down twice, when my father sat reading the newspaper and smoking one Pall Mall cigarette after another, a warning not to disturb him. This is when my mother would take out a box of old ski sweaters sent to us by unseen relatives from Vancouver. She would snip the bottom of a sweater and pull out a kinky thread of yarn, anchoring it to a piece of cardboard. And as she began to roll with one sweeping rhythm, she would start her story. Over the years, she told me the same story, except for the ending, which grew darker, casting long shadows into her life, and eventually into mine.

"I dreamed about Kweilin before I ever saw it," my mother began, speaking Chinese. "I dreamed of jagged peaks lining a curving river, with magic moss greening the banks. At the tops of these peaks were white mists. And if you could float down this river and eat the moss for food, you would be strong enough to climb the peak. If you slipped, you would only fall into a bed of soft moss and laugh. And once you reached the top, you would be able to see everything and feel such happiness it would be enough to never have worries in your life ever again.

"In China, everybody dreamed about Kweilin. And when I arrived, I realized how shabby my dreams were, how poor my thoughts. When I saw the hills, I laughed and shuddered at the same time. The peaks looked like giant fried fish heads trying to jump out of a vat of oil. Behind each hill, I could see shadows of another fish, and then another and another. And then the clouds would move just a little and the hills would suddenly become monstrous elephants marching slowly toward me! Can you see this? And at the root of the hill were secret caves. Inside grew hanging rock gardens in the shapes and colors of cabbage, winter melons, turnips, and onions. These were things so strange and beautiful you can't ever imagine them.

"But I didn't come to Kweilin to see how beautiful it was. The man who was my husband brought me and our two babies to Kweilin because he thought we would be safe. He was an officer with the Kuomintang, and after he put us down in a small room in a two-story house, he went off to the northwest, to Chungking.

"We knew the Japanese were winning, even when the newspapers said they were not. Every day, every hour, thousands of people poured into the city, crowding the sidewalks, looking for places to live. They came from the East, West, North, and South. They were rich and poor, Shanghainese, Cantonese, northerners, and not just Chinese, but foreigners and missionaries of every religion. And there was, of course, the Kuomintang and their army officers who thought they were top level to everyone else.

"We were a city of leftovers mixed together. If it hadn't been for the Japanese, there would have been plenty of reason for fighting to break out among these different people. Can you see it? Shanghai people with north-water peasants, bankers with barbers, rickshaw pullers with Burma refugees. Everybody looked down on someone else. It didn't matter that everybody shared the same sidewalk to spit on and suffered the same fast-moving diarrhea. We all had the same stink, but everybody complained someone else smelled the worst. Me? Oh, I hated the American air force officers who said habba-habba sounds to make my face turn red. But the worst were the northern peasants who emptied their noses into their hands and pushed people around and gave everybody their dirty diseases.

"So you can see how quickly Kweilin lost its beauty for me. I no longer climbed the peaks to say, how lovely are these hills! I only wondered which hills the Japanese had reached. I sat in the dark corners of my house with a baby under each arm, waiting with nervous feet. When the sirens cried out to warn us of bombers, my neighbors and I jumped to our feet and scurried to the deep caves to hide like wild animals. But you can't stay in the dark for so long. Something inside of you starts to fade and you become like a starving person, crazy-hungry for light. Outside I could hear the bombing. Boom! Boom! And then the sound of raining rocks. And inside I was no longer hungry for the cabbage or the turnips of the hanging rock garden. I could only see the dripping bowels of an ancient hill that might collapse on top of me. Can you imagine how it is, to want to be neither inside nor outside, to want to be nowhere and disappear?

"So when the bombing sounds grew farther away, we would come back out like newborn kittens scratching our way back to the city. And always, I would be amazed to find the hills against the burning sky had not been torn apart.

"I thought up Joy Luck on a summer night that was so hot even the moths fainted to the ground, their wings were so heavy with the damp heat. Every place was so crowded there was no room for fresh air. Unbearable smells from the sewers rose up to my second-story window and the stink had nowhere else to go but into my nose. At all hours of the night and day, I heard screaming sounds. I didn't know if it was a peasant slitting the throat of a runaway pig or an officer beating a half-dead peasant for lying in his way on the sidewalk. I didn't go to the window to find out. What use would it have been? And that's when I thought I needed something to do to help me move.

"My idea was to have a gathering of four women, one for each corner of my mah jong table. I knew which women I wanted to ask. They were all young like me, with wishful faces. One was an army officer's wife, like myself. Another was a girl with very fine manners from a rich family in Shanghai. She had escaped with only a little money. And there was a girl from Nanking who had the blackest hair I have ever seen. She came from a low-class family, but she was pretty and pleasant and had married well, to an old man who died and left her with a better life.

"Each week one of us would host a party to raise money and to raise our spirits. The hostess had to serve special *dyansyin* foods to bring good fortune of all kinds — dumplings shaped like silver money ingots, long rice noodles for long life, boiled peanuts for conceiving sons, and of course, many good-luck oranges for a plentiful, sweet life.

"What fine food we treated ourselves to with our meager allowances! We didn't notice that the dumplings were stuffed mostly with stringy squash and that the oranges were spotted with wormy holes. We ate sparingly, not as if we didn't have enough, but to protest how we could not eat another bite, we had already bloated ourselves from earlier in the day. We knew we had luxuries few people could afford. We were the lucky ones.

"After filling our stomachs, we would then fill a bowl with money and put it where everyone could see. Then we would sit down at the mah jong table. My table was from my family and was of a very fragrant red wood, not what you call rosewood, but *hong mu,* which is so fine there's no English word for it. The table had a very thick pad, so that when the mah jong pai were spilled onto the table the only sound was of ivory tiles washing against one another.

"Once we started to play, nobody could speak, except to say "*Pung*!" or "*Chr*!" when taking a tile. We had to play with seriousness and think of nothing else but adding to our happiness through winning. But after sixteen rounds, we would again feast, this time to celebrate our good fortune. And then we would talk into the night until the morning, saying stories about good times in the past and good times yet to come.

"Oh, what good stories! Stories spilling out all over the place! We almost laughed to death. A rooster that ran into the house screeching on top of dinner bowls, the same bowls that held him quietly in pieces the next day! And one about a girl who wrote love letters for two friends who loved the same man. And a silly foreign lady who fainted on a toilet when firecrackers went off next to her.

"People thought we were wrong to serve banquets every week while many people in the city were starving, eating rats and, later, the garbage that the poorest rats used to feed on. Others thought we were possessed by demons — to celebrate when even within our own families we had lost generations, had lost homes and fortunes, and were separated, husband from wife, brother from sister, daughter from mother. Hnnnh! How could we laugh, people asked.

"It's not that we had no heart or eyes for pain. We were all afraid. We all had our miseries. But to despair was to wish back for something already lost. Or to prolong what was already unbearable. How much can you wish for a favorite warm coat that hangs in the closet of a house that burned down with your mother and father inside of it? How long can you see in your mind arms and legs hanging from telephone wires and starving dogs running down the streets with half-chewed hands dangling from their jaws? What was worse, we asked among ourselves, to sit and wait for our own deaths with proper somber faces? Or to choose our own happiness?

"So, we decided to hold parties and pretend each week had become the new year. Each week we could forget past wrongs done to us. We weren't allowed to think a bad thought. We feasted, we laughed, we played games, lost and won, we told the best stories. And each week, we could hope to be lucky. That hope was our only joy. And that's how we came to call our little parties Joy Luck.

My mother used to end the story on a happy note, bragging about her skill at the game. "I won many times and was so lucky the others teased that I had learned the trick of a clever thief," she said. "I won tens of thousands of *yuan*. But I wasn't rich. No. By then paper money had become worthless. Even toilet paper was worth more. And that made us laugh harder, to think a thousand-*yuan* note wasn't even good enough to rub on our bottoms.

I never thought my mother's Kweilin story was anything but a Chinese fairy tale. The endings always changed. Sometimes she said she used that worthless thousand-*yuan* note to buy a half-cup of rice. She turned that rice into a pot of porridge. She traded that gruel for two feet from a pig. Those two feet became six eggs, those eggs six chickens. The story always grew and grew.

And then one evening, after I had begged her to buy me a transistor radio, after she refused and I had sulked in silence for an hour, she said, "Why do you think you are missing something you never had?" And then she told me a completely different ending to the story.

"An army officer came to my house early one morning," she said, "and told me to go quickly to my husband in Chungking. And I knew he was telling me to run away from Kweilin. I knew what happened to officers and their families when the Japanese arrived. How could I go? There were no trains leaving Kweilin. My friend from Nanking, she was so good to me. She bribed a man to steal a wheelbarrow used to haul coal. She promised to warn our other friends.

"I packed my things and my two babies into this wheelbarrow and began pushing to Chungking four days before the Japanese marched into Kweilin. On the road I heard news of the slaughter from people running past me. It was terrible. Up to the last day, the Kuomintang insisted that Kweilin was safe, protected by the Chinese army. But later that day, the streets of Kweilin were strewn with newspapers reporting great Kuomintang victories, and on top of these papers, like fresh fish from a butcher, lay rows of people — men, women, and children who had never lost hope, but had lost their lives instead. When I heard this news, I walked faster and faster, asking myself at each step, Were they foolish? Were they brave?

"I pushed toward Chungking, until my wheel broke. I abandoned my beautiful mah jong table of *hong mu*. By then I didn't have enough feeling left in my body to cry. I tied scarves into slings and put a baby on each side of my shoulder. I carried a bag in each hand, one with clothes, the other with food. I carried these things until deep grooves grew in my hands. And I finally dropped one bag after the other when my hands began to bleed and became too slippery to hold onto anything.

"Along the way, I saw others had done the same, gradually given up hope. It was like a pathway inlaid with treasures that grew in value along the way. Bolts of fine fabric and books. Paintings of ancestors and carpenter tools. Until one could see cages of ducklings now quiet with thirst and, later still, silver urns lying in the road, where people had been too tired to carry them for any kind of future hope. By the time I arrived in Chungking I had lost everything except for three fancy silk dresses which I wore one on top of the other.

"What do you mean by 'everything'?" I gasped at the end. I was stunned to realize the story had been true all along. "What happened to the babies?"

She didn't even pause to think. She simply said in a way that made it clear there was no more to the story: "Your father is not my first husband. You are not those babies."

When I arrive at the Hsus' house, where the Joy Luck Club is meeting tonight, the first person I see is my father. "There she is! Never on time!" he announces. And it's true. Everybody's already here, seven family friends in their sixties and seventies. They look up and laugh at me, always tardy, a child still at thirty-six.

I'm shaking, trying to hold something inside. The last time I saw them, at the funeral, I had broken down and cried big gulping sobs. They must wonder now how someone like me can take my mother's place. A friend once told me that my mother and I were alike, that we had the same wispy hand gestures, the same girlish laugh and sideways look. When I shyly told my mother this, she seemed insulted and said, "You don't even know little percent of me! How can you be me?" And she's right. How can I be my mother at Joy Luck?

"Auntie, Uncle," I say repeatedly, nodding to each person there. I have always called these old family friends Auntie and Uncle. And then I walk over and stand next to my father.

He's looking at the Jongs' pictures from their recent China trip. "Look at that," he says politely, pointing to a photo of the Jongs' tour group standing on wide slab steps. There is nothing in this picture that shows it was taken in China rather than San Francisco, or any other city for that matter. But my father doesn't seem to be looking at the picture anyway. It's as though everything were the same to him, nothing stands out. He has always been politely indifferent. But what's the Chinese word that means indifferent because you can't *see* any differences? That's how troubled I think he is by my mother's death.

"Will you look at that," he says, pointing to another nondescript picture.

The Hsus' house feels heavy with greasy odors. Too many Chinese meals cooked in a too small kitchen, too many once fragrant smells compressed onto a thin layer of invisible grease. I remember how my mother used to go into other people's houses and restaurants and wrinkle her nose, then whisper very loudly: "I can see and feel the stickiness with my nose."

I have not been to the Hsus' house in many years, but the living room is exactly the same as I remember it. When Auntie An-mei and Uncle George moved to the Sunset district from Chinatown twenty-five years ago, they bought new furniture. It's all there, still looking mostly new under yellowed plastic. The same turquoise couch shaped in a semicircle of nubby tweed. The colonial end tables made out of heavy maple. A lamp of fake cracked porcelain. Only the scroll-length calendar, free from the Bank of Canton, changes every year.

I remember this stuff, because when we were children, Auntie An-mei didn't let us touch any of her new furniture except through the clear plastic coverings. On Joy Luck nights, my parents brought me to the Hsus'. Since I was the guest, I had to take care of all the younger children, so many children it seemed as if there were always one baby who was crying from having bumped its head on a table leg.

"You are responsible," said my mother, which meant I was in trouble if anything was spilled, burned, lost, broken, or dirty. I was responsible, no matter who did it. She and Auntie An-mei were dressed up in funny Chinese dresses with stiff stand-up collars and blooming branches of embroidered silk sewn over their breasts. These clothes were too fancy for real Chinese people, I thought, and too strange for American parties. In those days, before my mother told me her Kweilin story, I imagined Joy Luck was a shameful Chinese custom, like the secret gathering of the Ku Klux Klan or the tom-tom dances of TV Indians preparing for war.

But tonight, there's no mystery. The Joy Luck aunties are all wearing slacks, bright print blouses, and different versions of sturdy walking shoes. We are all seated around the dining room table under a lamp that looks like a Spanish candelabra. Uncle George puts on his bifocals and starts the meeting by reading the minutes:

"Our capital account is $24,825, or about $6,206 a couple, $3,103 per person. We sold Subaru for a loss at six and three-quarters. We bought a hundred shares of Smith International at seven. Our thanks to Lindo and Tin Jong for the goodies. The red bean soup was especially delicious. The March meeting had to be canceled until further notice. We were sorry to have to bid a fond farewell to our dear friend Suyuan and extended our sympathy to the Canning Woo family. Respectfully submitted, George Hsu, president and secretary."

That's it. I keep thinking the others will start talking about my mother, the wonderful friendship they shared, and why I am here in her spirit, to be the fourth corner and carry on the idea my mother came up with on a hot day in Kweilin.

But everybody just nods to approve the minutes. Even my father's head bobs up and down routinely. And it seems to me my mother's life has been shelved for new business.

Auntie An-mei heaves herself up from the table and moves slowly to the kitchen to prepare the food. And Auntie Lin, my mother's best friend, moves to the turquoise sofa, crosses her arms, and watches the men still seated at the table. Auntie Ying, who seems to shrink even more every time I see her, reaches into her knitting bag and pulls out the start of a tiny blue sweater.

The Joy Luck uncles begin to talk about stocks they are interested in buying. Uncle Jack, who is Auntie Ying's younger brother, is very keen on a company that mines gold in Canada.

"It's a great hedge on inflation," he says with authority. He speaks the best English, almost accentless. I think my mother's English was the worst, but she always thought her Chinese was the best. She spoke Mandarin slightly blurred with a Shanghai dialect.

"Weren't we going to play mah jong tonight?" I whisper loudly to Auntie Ying, who's slightly deaf.

"Later," she says, "after midnight."

"Ladies, are you at this meeting or not?" says Uncle George.

After everybody votes unanimously for the Canada gold stock, I go into the kitchen to ask Auntie An-mei why the Joy Luck Club started investing in stocks.

"We used to play mah jong, winner take all. But the same people were always winning, the same people always losing," she says. She is stuffing wonton, one chopstick jab of gingery meat dabbed onto a thin skin and then a single fluid turns with her hand that seals the skin into the shape of a tiny nurse's cap. "You can't have luck when someone else has skill. So long time ago, we decided to invest in the stock market. There's no skill in that. Even your mother agreed."

Auntie An-mei takes count of the tray in front of her. She's already made five rows of eight wonton each. "Forty wonton, eight people, ten each, five row more," she says aloud to herself, and then continues stuffing. "We got smart. Now we can all win and lose equally. We can have stock market luck. And we can play mah jong for fun, just for a few dollars, winner take all. Losers take home leftovers! So everyone can have some joy. Smart-hanh?"

I watch Auntie An-mei make more wonton. She has quick, expert fingers. She doesn't have to think about what she is doing. That's what my mother used to complain about, that Auntie An-mei never thought about what she was doing.

"She's not stupid," said my mother on one occasion, "but she has no spine. Last week, I had a good idea for her. I said to her, Let's go to the consulate and ask for papers for your brother. And she almost wanted to drop her things and go right then. But later she talked to someone. Who knows who? And that person told her she can get her brother in bad trouble in China. That person said FBI will put her on a list and give her trouble in the US the rest of her life. That person said, you ask for a house loan and they say no loan, because your brother is a communist. I said, you already have a house! But still she was scared.

"Aunti An-mei runs this way and that," said my mother, "and she doesn't know why."

As I watch Auntie An-mei, I see a short-bent woman in her seventies, with a heavy bosom and thin, shapeless legs. She has the flattened soft fingertips of an old woman. I wonder what Auntie An-mei did to inspire a lifelong stream of criticism from my mother. Then again, it seemed my mother was always displeased with all her friends, with me, and even with my father. Something was always missing. Something always needed improving. Something was not in balance. This one or that had too much of one element, not enough of another.

The elements were from my mother's own version of organic chemistry. Each person is made of five elements, she told me.

Too much fire and you had a bad temper. That was like my father, whom my mother always criticized for his cigarette habit and who always shouted back that she should keep her thoughts to herself. I think he now feels guilty that he didn't let my mother speak her mind.

Too little wood and you bent too quickly to listen to other people's ideas, unable to stand on your own. This was like my Auntie An mei.

Too much water and you flowed in too many directions, like myself, for having started half a degree in biology, then half a degree in art, and then finishing neither when I went off to work for a small ad agency as a secretary, later becoming a copywriter.

I used to dismiss her criticisms as just more of her Chinese superstitions, beliefs that conveniently fit the circumstances. In my twenties, while taking Introduction to Psychology, I tried to tell her why she shouldn't criticize so much, why it didn't lead to a healthy learning environment.

"There's a school of thought," I said, "that parents shouldn't criticize children. They should encourage instead. You know, people rise to other people's expectations. And when you criticize, it just means you're expecting failure."

"That's the trouble," my mother said. "You never rise. Lazy to get up. Lazy to rise to expectations."

"Time to eat," Auntie An-mei happily announces, bringing out a steaming pot of the wonton she was just wrapping. There are piles of food on the table, served buffet style, just like at the Kweilin feasts. My father is digging into the chow mein, which still sits in an oversize aluminum pan surrounded by little plastic packets of soy sauce. Auntie An-mei must have bought this on Clement Street. The wonton soup smells wonderful with delicate sprigs of cilantro floating on top. I'm drawn first to a large platter of *chaswei*, sweet barbecued pork cut into coin-sized slices, and then to a whole assortment of what I've always called finger goodies — thin-skinned pastries filled with chopped pork, beef, shrimp, and unknown stuffings that my mother used to describe as "nutritious things."

Eating is not a gracious event here. It's as though everybody had been starving. They push large forkfuls into their mouths, jab at more pieces of pork, one right after the other. They are not like the ladies of Kweilin, who I always imagined savored their food with a certain detached delicacy.

And then, almost as quickly as they started, the men get up and leave the table. As if on cue, the women peck at last morsels and then carry plates and bowls to the kitchen and dump them in the sink. The women take turns washing their hands, scrubbing them vigorously. Who started this ritual? I too put my plate in the sink and wash my hands. The women are talking about the Jongs' China trip, then they move toward a room in the back of the apartment. We pass another room, what used to be the bedroom shared by the four Hsu sons. The bunk beds with their scuffed, splintery ladders are still there. The Joy Luck uncles are already seated at the card table. Uncle George is dealing out cards fast, as though he learned this technique in a casino. My father is passing out Pall Mall cigarettes, with one already dangling from his lips.

And then we get to the room in the back, which was once shared by the three Hsu girls. We were all childhood friends. And now they've all grown and married and I'm here to play in their room again. Except for the smell of camphor, it feels the same — as if Rose, Ruth, and Janice might soon walk in with their hair rolled up in big orange-juice cans and plop down on their identical narrow beds. The white chenille bedspreads are so worn they are almost translucent. Rose and I used to pluck the nubs out while talking about our boy problems. Everything is the same, except now a mahogany-colored mah jong table sits in the center. And next to it is a floor lamp, a long black pole with three oval spotlights attached like the broad leaves of a rubber plant.

Nobody says to me, "Sit here, this is where your mother used to sit." But I can tell even before everyone sits down. The chair closest to the door has an emptiness to it. But the feeling doesn't really have to do with the chair. It's her place on the table. Without having anyone tell me, I know her corner on the table was the East.

The East is where things begin, my mother once told me, the direction from which the sun rises, where the wind comes from.

Auntie An-mei, who is sitting on my left, spills the tiles onto the green felt tabletop and then says to me, "Now we wash tiles." We swirl them with our hands in a circular motion. They make a cool swishing sound as they bump into one another.

"Do you win like your mother?" asks Auntie Lin across from me. She is not smiling.

"I only played a little in college with some Jewish friends."

"Annh! Jewish mah jong," she says in disgusted tones. "Not the same thing." This is what my mother used to say, although she could never explain exactly why.

"Maybe I shouldn't play tonight. I'll just watch," I offer.

Auntie Lin looks exasperated, as though I were a simple child: "How can we play with just three people? Like a table with three legs, no balance. When Auntie Ying's husband died, she asked her brother to join. Your father asked you. So, it's decided."

"What's the difference between Jewish and Chinese mah jong?" I once asked my mother. I couldn't tell by her answer if the games were different or just her attitude toward Chinese and Jewish people.

"Entirely different kind of playing," she said in her English explanation voice. "Jewish mah jong, they watch only for their own tile, play only with their eyes."

Then she switched to Chinese: "Chinese mah jong, you must play using your head, very tricky. You must watch what everybody else throws away and keep that in your head as well. And if nobody plays well, then the game becomes like Jewish mah jong. Why play? There's no strategy. You're just watching people make mistakes."

These kinds of explanations made me feel my mother and I spoke two different languages, which we did. I talked to her in English, she answered back in Chinese.

"So what's the difference between Chinese and Jewish mah jong?" I ask Auntie Lin.

"Aii-ya," she exclaims in a mock scolding voice. "Your mother did not teach you anything?"

Auntie Ying pats my hand. "You a smart girl. You watch us, do the same. Help us stack the tiles and make four walls."

I follow Auntie Ying, but mostly I watch Auntie Lin. She is the fastest, which means I can almost keep up with the others by watching what she does first. Auntie Ying throws the dice and I'm told that Auntie Lin has become the East wind. I've become the North wind, the last hand to play. Auntie Ying is the South and Auntie An-mei is the West. And then we start taking tiles, throwing the dice, counting back on the wall to the right number of spots where our chosen tiles lie. I rearrange my tiles, sequences of bamboo and balls, doubles of colored number tiles, odd tiles that do not fit anywhere.

"Your mother was the best, like a pro," says Auntie An-mei while slowly sorting her tiles, considering each piece carefully.

Now we begin to play, looking at our hands, casting tiles, picking up others at an easy, comfortable pace. The Joy Luck aunties begin to make small talk, not really listening to each other. They speak in their special language, half in broken English, half in their own Chinese dialect. Auntie Ying mentions she bought yarn at half price, somewhere out in the avenues. Auntie An-mei brags about a sweater she made for her daughter Ruth's new baby. "She thought it was store-bought," she says proudly.

Auntie Lin explains how mad she got at a store clerk who refused to let her return a skirt with a broken zipper. "I was *chiszle*," she says, still fuming, "mad to death."

"But Lindo, you are still with us. You didn't die," teases Auntie Ying, and then as she laughs Auntie Lin says 'Pung!' and 'Mah jong!' and then spreads her tiles out, laughing back at Auntie Ying while counting up her points. We start washing tiles again and it grows quiet. I'm getting bored and sleepy.

"Oh, I have a story," says Auntie Ying loudly, startling everybody. Auntie Ying has always been the weird auntie, someone lost in her own world. My mother used to say, "Auntie Ying is not hard of hearing. She is hard of listening."

"Police arrested Mrs. Emerson's son last weekend," Auntie Ying says in a way that sounds as if she were proud to be the first with this big news. "Mrs. Chan told me at church. Too many TV set found in his car."

Auntie Lin quickly says, "Aii-ya, Mrs. Emerson good lady," meaning Mrs. Emerson didn't deserve such a terrible son. But now I see this is also said for the benefit of Auntie An-mei, whose own youngest son was arrested two years ago for selling stolen car stereos. Auntie An-mei is rubbing her tile carefully before discarding it. She looks pained.

"Everybody has TVs in China now," says Auntie Lin, changing the subject. "Our family there all has TV sets — not just black-and-white, but color and remote! They have everything. So when we asked them what we should buy them, they said nothing, it was enough that we would come to visit them. But we bought them different things anyway, VCR and Sony Walkman for the kids. They said, No, don't give it to us, but I think they liked it."

Poor Auntie An-mei rubs her tiles ever harder. I remember my mother telling me about the Hsus' trip to China three years ago. Auntie An-mei had saved two thousand dollars, all to spend on her brother's family. She had shown my mother the insides of her heavy suitcases. One was crammed with See's Nuts & Chews, M & M's, candy-coated cashews, instant hot chocolate with miniature marshmallows. My mother told me the other bag contained the most ridiculous clothes, all new: bright California-style beachwear, baseball caps, cotton pants with elastic waists, bomber jackets, Stanford sweatshirts, crew socks.

My mother had told her, "Who wants those useless things? They just want money." But Auntie An-mei said her brother was so poor and they were so rich by comparison. So, she ignored my mother's advice and took the heavy bags and their two thousand dollars to China. And when their China tour finally arrived in Hangzhou, the whole family from Ningbo was there to meet them. It wasn't just Auntie An-mei's little brother, but also his wife's stepbrothers and stepsisters, and a distant cousin, and that cousin's husband and that husband's uncle. They had all brought their mothers-in-law and children, and even their village friends who were not lucky enough to have overseas Chinese relatives to show off.

As my mother told it, "Auntie An-mei had cried before she left for China, thinking she would make her brother very rich and happy by communist standards. But when she got home, she cried to me that everyone had a palm out and she was the only one who left with an empty hand."

My mother confirmed her suspicions. Nobody wanted the sweatshirts, those useless clothes. The M & M were thrown in the air, gone. And when the suitcases were emptied, the relatives asked what else the Hsus had brought.

Auntie An-mei and Uncle George were shaken down, not just for two thousand dollars' worth of TVs and refrigerators but also for a night's lodging for twenty-six people in the Overlooking the Lake Hotel, for three banquet tables at a restaurant that catered to rich foreigners, for three special gifts for each relative, and finally, for a loan of five thousand *yuan* in foreign exchange to a cousin's so-called uncle who wanted to buy a motorcycle but who later disappeared for good along with the money. When the train pulled out of Hangzhou the next day, the Hsus found themselves depleted of some nine thousand dollars' worth of goodwill. Months later, after an inspiring Christmastime service at the First Chinese Baptist Church, Auntie An-mei tried to recoup her loss by saying it truly was more blessed to give than to receive, and my mother agreed, her longtime friend had blessings for at least several lifetimes.

Listening now to Auntie Lin bragging about the virtues of her family in China, I realize that Auntie Lin is oblivious to Auntie An-mei's pain. Is Auntie Lin being mean, or is it that my mother never told anybody but me the shameful story of Auntie Anmei's greedy family?

"So, Jing-mei, you go to school now?" says Auntie Lin.

"Her name is June. They all go by their American names," says Auntie Ying.

"That's okay," I say, and I really mean it. In fact, it's even becoming fashionable for American-born Chinese to use their Chinese names.

"I'm not in school anymore, though," I say. "That was more than ten years ago."

Auntie Lin's eyebrows arch. "Maybe I'm thinking of someone else's daughter," she says, but I know right away she's lying. I know my mother probably told her I was going back to school to finish my degree, because somewhere back, maybe just six months ago, we were again having this argument about my being a failure, a "college drop-off," about my going back to finish.

Once again I had told my mother what she wanted to hear: "You're right. I'll look into it."

I had always assumed we had an unspoken understanding about these things: that she didn't really mean I was a failure, and I really meant I would try to respect her opinions more. But listening to Auntie Lin tonight reminds me once again: My mother and I never really understood one another. We translated each other's meanings and I seemed to hear less than what was said, while my mother heard more. No doubt she told Auntie Lin I was going back to school to get a doctorate.

Auntie Lin and my mother were both best friends and arch enemies who spent a lifetime comparing their children. I was one month older than Waverly Jong, Auntie Lin's prized daughter. From the time we were babies, our mothers compared the creases in our belly buttons, how shapely our earlobes were, how fast we healed when we scraped our knees, how thick and dark our hair, how many shoes we wore out in one year, and later, how smart Waverly was at playing chess, how many trophies she had won last month, how many newspapers had printed her name, how many cities she had visited.

I know my mother resented listening to Auntie Lin talk about Waverly when she had nothing to come back with. At first my mother tried to cultivate some hidden genius in me. She did housework for an old retired piano teacher down the hall who gave me lessons and free use of a piano to practice on in exchange. When I failed to become a concert pianist, or even an accompanist for the church youth choir, she finally explained that I was late-blooming, like Einstein, who everyone thought was retarded until he discovered a bomb.

Now it is Auntie Ying who wins this hand of mah jong, so we count points and begin again.

"Did you know Lena move to Woodside?" asks Auntie Ying with obvious pride, looking down at the tiles, talking to no one in particular. She quickly erases her smile and tries for some modesty. "Of course, it's not best house in neighborhood, not million-dollar house, not yet. But it's good investment. Better than paying rent. Better than somebody putting you under their thumb to rub you out."

So now I know Auntie Ying's daughter, Lena, told her about my being evicted from my apartment on lower Russian Hill. Even though Lena and I are still friends, we have grown naturally cautious about telling each other too much. Still, what little we say to one another often comes back in another guise. It's the same old game, everybody talking in circles.

"It's getting late," I say after we finish the round. I start to stand up, but Auntie Lin pushes me back down into the chair.

"Stay, stay. We talk awhile, get to know you again," she says. "Been a long time."

I know this is a polite gesture on the Joy Luck aunties' part — a protest when actually they are just as eager to see me go as I am to leave. "No, I really must go now, thank you, thank you," I say, glad I remembered how the pretense goes.

"But you must stay! We have something important to tell you, from your mother," Auntie Ying blurts out in her too-loud voice. The others look uncomfortable, as if this were not how they intended to break some sort of bad news to me.

I sit down. Auntie An-mei leaves the room quickly and returns with a bowl of peanuts, then quietly shuts the door. Everybody is quiet, as if nobody knew where to begin.

It is Auntie Ying who finally speaks. "I think your mother die with an important thought on her mind," she says in halting English. And then she begins to speak in Chinese, calmly, softly.

"Your mother was a very strong woman, a good mother. She loved you very much, more than her own life. And that's why you can understand why a mother like this could never forget her other daughters. She knew they were alive, and before she died, she wanted to find her daughters in China."

The babies in Kweilin, I think. I was not those babies. The babies in a sling on her shoulder. Her other daughters. And now I feel as if I were in Kweilin amidst the bombing and I can see these babies lying on the side of the road, their red thumbs popped out of their mouths, screaming to be reclaimed. Somebody took them away. They're safe. And now my mother's left me forever, gone back to China to get these babies. I can barely hear Auntie Ying's voice.

"She had searched for years, written letters back and forth," says Auntie Ying. "And last year she got an address. She was going to tell your father soon. Aii-ya, what a shame. A lifetime of waiting."

Auntie An-mei interrupts with an excited voice: "So your aunties and I, we wrote to this address," she says. "We say that a certain party, your mother, want to meet another certain party. And this party write back to us. They are your sisters, Jing-mei."

My sisters, I repeat to myself, saying these two words together for the first time.

Auntie An-mei is holding a sheet of paper as thin as wrapping tissue. In perfectly straight vertical rows I see Chinese characters written in blue fountain-pen ink. A word is smudged. A tear? I take the letter with shaking hands, marveling at how smart my sisters must be to be able to read and write Chinese.

The aunties are all smiling at me, as though I had been a dying person who has now miraculously recovered. Auntie Ying is handing me another envelope. Inside is a check made out to June Woo for $1,200. I can't believe it.

"My sisters are sending me money?" I ask.

"No, no," says Auntie Lin with her mock exasperated voice. "Every year we save our mah jong winnings for big banquet at fancy restaurant. Most times your mother win, so most is her money. We add just a little, so you can go Hong Kong, take a train to Shanghai, see your sisters. Besides, we all getting too rich, too fat." she pats her stomach for proof.

"See my sisters," I say numbly. I am awed by this prospect, trying to imagine what I would see. And I am embarrassed by the end-of-the-year-banquet lie my aunties have told to mask their generosity. I am crying now, sobbing and laughing at the same time, seeing but not understanding this loyalty to my mother.

"You must see your sisters and tell them about your mother's death," says Auntie Ying. "But most important, you must tell them about her life. The mother they did not know, they must now know."

"See my sisters, tell them about my mother," I say, nodding. "What will I say? What can I tell them about my mother? I don't know anything. She was my mother."

The aunties are looking at me as if I had become crazy right before their eyes.

"Not know your own mother?" cries Auntie An-mei with disbelief. "How can you say? Your mother is in your bones!"

"Tell them stories of your family here. How she became success," offers Auntie Lin.

"Tell them stories she told you, lessons she taught, what you know about her mind that has become your mind," says Auntie Ying. "You mother very smart lady."

I hear more choruses of "Tell them, tell them" as each Auntie frantically tries to think what should be passed on.

"Her kindness."

"Her smartness."

"Her dutiful nature to family."

"Her hopes, things that matter to her."

"The excellent dishes she cooked."

"Imagine, a daughter not knowing her own mother!"

And then it occurs to me. They are frightened. In me, they see their own daughters, just as ignorant, just as unmindful of all the truths and hopes they have brought to America. They see daughters who grow impatient when their mothers talk in Chinese, who think they are stupid when they explain things in fractured English. They see that joy and luck do not mean the same to their daughters, that to these closed American-born minds "joy luck" is not a word, it does not exist. They see daughters who will bear grandchildren born without any connecting hope passed from generation to generation.

"I will tell them everything," I say simply, and the aunties look at me with doubtful faces.

"I will remember everything about her and tell them," I say more firmly. And gradually, one by one, they smile and pat my hand. They still look troubled, as if something were out of balance. But they also look hopeful that what I say will become true. What more can they ask? What more can I promise?

They go back to eating their soft-boiled peanuts, saying stories among themselves. They are young girls again, dreaming of good times in the past and good times yet to come. A brother from Ningbo who makes his sister cry with joy when he returns nine thousand dollars plus interest. A youngest son whose stereo and TV repair business is so good he sends leftovers to China. A daughter whose babies are able to swim like fish in a fancy pool in Woodside. Such good stories. The best. They are the lucky ones.

And I am sitting at my mother's place at the mah jong table, on the East, where things begin.

4. Questions for Discussion

(1) One of the themes in this novel is the Americanized daughters' inability to understand their Chinese mothers. Find an example of this conflict between Suyuan and her daughter.

(2) In the story Jing-mei Woo is talking about her problems of communicating with her mother. She says, "My mother and I never really understood one another. We translated each other's meanings and I seemed to hear less than what was said, while my mother heard more." Find an incident from the story which supports Jing-mei's statement.

(3) In Amy Tan's *The Joy Luck Club*, what does the swan represent in Prologue?

(4) An important theme in the novel is the divide between the immigrant generation and their American-born children. Please analyze how this divide is portrayed in the novel, and how it reflects broader cultural and social tensions between Chinese and American cultures.

(5) The novel touches on the Chinese Civil War, the Japanese occupation of China. Please analyze how these events shape the characters' perspectives and experiences, and how they reflect larger historical and cultural trends.

Section Two: Jhumpa Lahiri and *The Third and Final Continent*

Jhumpa Lahiri is a very important Indian American writer and a professor of creative writing at Princeton University. She has been recognized with numerous awards and honors, including the National Humanities Medal. *The Third and Final Continent* is a short story by Jhumpa Lahiri, first published in *The New Yorker* in 1999, and later included in Lahiri's Pulitzer Prize-winning collection, *Interpreter of Maladies*.

1. Introduction of Jhumpa Lahiri

Jhumpa Lahiri was born on July 11, 1967, in London, England, to Bengali Indian parents. Her family moved to the United States when she was just two years old, and she grew up in Rhode Island. Lahiri's parents were both librarians, and her childhood was filled with books and a deep appreciation for literature.

Lahiri attended Barnard College, where she studied English literature and graduated with a Bachelor of Arts degree in 1989. She then went on to earn a Master of Arts degree in English, and a Doctor of Philosophy degree in Renaissance Studies, both from Boston University. It was during her time at Boston University that Lahiri began to hone her writing skills and develop her distinctive voice.

Lahiri's debut collection of short stories, *Interpreter of Maladies* was published in 1999 to critical acclaim. The collection won the Pulitzer Prize for Fiction in 2000, making Lahiri the first Asian American woman to receive the award. Her subsequent works, including the novel *The Namesake* and the short story collection *Unaccustomed Earth*, have also been widely praised for their vivid and poignant portrayals of the immigrant experience. In 2013, Lahiri published *The Lowland* which is set primarily in Kolkata (formerly Calcutta), India, and follows the lives of two brothers, Subhash and Udayan, as they come of age during a time of political upheaval in India. As the story unfolds, Lahiri explores themes of family, love, grief, and the search for identity. *The Lowland* is a complex and moving portrait of the immigrant experience, as well as a powerful meditation on the forces that shape our lives and the legacies we leave behind. The book was a finalist for the Man Booker Prize in 2013 and was named a New York Times Notable Book of the Year.

Lahiri's writing often deals with themes of cultural displacement, the search for identity, and the struggle to find a sense of belonging. Her work draws on her personal experiences as a second-generation immigrant, and explores the complexities and contradictions of growing up between two cultures.

2. Introduction of *The Third and Final Continent*

The Third and Final Continent follows an unnamed narrator, an Indian man who has just arrived in Cambridge, Massachusetts, to start a new life with his wife.

The story is divided into three parts, each representing a different continent. The first part recounts the narrator's experiences in Calcutta, where he meets and marries his wife, Mala. The second part describes the narrator's time in London, where he works and saves money to bring Mala to the United States. The third and final part takes place in Cambridge, where the narrator and Mala build a home in the US through their own effort.

Throughout the story, Lahiri explores themes of displacement, identity, and the search for a sense of belonging. The narrator is acutely aware of the cultural differences between his homeland of India and the various countries he visits, and his struggle to adjust to his new surroundings is a central theme of the story. The story is also a reflection on the universal experience of migration and the challenges that come with building a new life in a foreign land. *The Third and Final Continent* is widely regarded as a masterpiece of contemporary short fictions and has been anthologized in numerous collections.

3. Reading Material: *The Third and Final Continent* (from *The Interpreter of Maladies)*

I left India in 1964 with a certificate in commerce and the equivalent, in those days, of ten dollars to my name. For three weeks I sailed on the S.S. Roma, an Italian cargo vessel, in a cabin next to the ship's engine, across the Arabian Sea, the Red Sea, the Mediterranean, and finally to England. I lived in London, in Finsbury Park, in a house occupied entirely by penniless Bengali bachelors like myself, at least a dozen and sometimes more, all struggling to educate and establish ourselves abroad.

I attended lectures at L.S.E. and worked at the university library to get by. We lived three or four to a room, shared a single, icy toilet, and took turns cooking pots of egg curry, which we ate with our hands on a table covered with newspapers. Apart from our jobs we had few responsibilities. On weekends we lounged barefoot in drawstring pajamas, drinking tea and smoking Rothmans, or set out to watch cricket at Lord's. Some weekends the house was crammed with still more Bengalis, to whom we had introduced ourselves at the greengrocer, or on the Tube, and we made yet more egg curry, and played Mukesh on a Grundig reel-to-reel, and soaked our dirty dishes in the bathtub. Every now and then someone in the house moved out, to live with a woman whom his family back in Calcutta had determined he was to wed. In 1969, when I was thirty-six years old, my own marriage was arranged. Around the same time, I was offered a full-time job in America, in the processing department of a library at M.I.T. The salary was generous enough to support a wife, and I was honored to be hired by a world-famous university, and so I obtained a green card, and prepared to travel farther still.

By then I had enough money to go by plane. I flew first to Calcutta, to attend my wedding, and a week later to Boston, to begin my new job. During the flight I read *The Student Guide to North America*, for although I was no longer a student, I was on a budget all the same. I learned that Americans drove on the right side of the road, not the left, and that they called a lift an elevator and an engaged phone busy. "The pace of life in North America is different from Britain, as you will soon discover," the guidebook informed me. "Everybody feels he must get to the top. Don't expect an English cup of tea." As the plane began its descent over Boston Harbor, the pilot announced the weather and the time, and that President Nixon had declared a national holiday: two American men had landed on the moon. Several passengers cheered. "God bless America!" one of them hollered. Across the aisle, I saw a woman praying.

I spent my first night at the Y.M.C.A. in Central Square, Cambridge, an inexpensive accommodation recommended by my guidebook which was within walking distance of M.I.T. The room contained a cot, a desk, and a small wooden cross on one wall. A sign on the door said that cooking was strictly forbidden. A bare window overlooked Massachusetts Avenue. Car horns, shrill and prolonged, blared one after another. Sirens and flashing lights heralded endless emergencies, and a succession of buses rumbled past, their doors opening and closing with a powerful hiss, throughout the night. The noise was constantly distracting, at times suffocating. I felt it deep in my ribs, just as I had felt the furious drone of the engine on the S.S. Roma. But there was no ship's deck to escape to, no glittering ocean to thrill my soul, no breeze to cool my face, no one to talk to. I was too tired to pace the gloomy corridors of the Y.M.C.A. in my pajamas. Instead, I sat at the desk and stared out the window. In the morning I reported to my job at the Dewey Library, a beige fortlike building by Memorial Drive. I also opened a bank account, rented a post-office box, and bought a plastic bowl and a spoon. I went to a supermarket called Purity Supreme, wandering up and down the aisles, comparing prices with those in England. In the end I bought a carton of milk and a box of cornflakes. This was my first meal in America. Even the simple chore of buying milk was new to me; in London we'd had bottles delivered each morning to our door.

In a week I had adjusted, more or less. I ate cornflakes and milk morning and night, and bought some bananas for variety, slicing them into the bowl with the edge of my spoon. I left my carton of milk on the shaded part of the windowsill, as I had seen other residents at the Y.M.C.A. do. To pass the time in the evenings I read the Boston Globe downstairs, in a spacious room with stained-glass windows. I read every article and advertisement, so that I would grow familiar with things, and when my eyes grew tired, I slept. Only I did not sleep well. Each night I had to keep the window wide open; it was the only source of air in the stifling room, and the noise was intolerable. I would lie on the cot with my fingers pressed into my ears, but when I drifted off to sleep my hands fell away, and the noise of the traffic would wake me up again. Pigeon feathers drifted onto the windowsill, and one evening, when I poured milk over my cornflakes, I saw that it had soured. Nevertheless, I resolved to stay at the Y.M.C.A. for six weeks, until my wife's passport and green card were ready. Once she arrived, I would have to rent a proper apartment, and from time to time I studied the classified section of the newspaper, or stopped in at the housing office at M.I.T. during my lunch break to see what was available. It was in this manner that I discovered a room for immediate occupancy, in a house on a quiet street, the listing said, for eight dollars per week. I dialed the number from a pay telephone, sorting through the coins, with which I was still unfamiliar, smaller and lighter than shillings, heavier and brighter than paisas.

"Who is speaking?" a woman demanded. Her voice was bold and clamorous.

"Yes, good afternoon, Madam. I am calling about the room for rent."

"Harvard or Tech?"

"I beg your pardon?"

"Are you from Harvard or Tech?"

Gathering that Tech referred to the Massachusetts Institute of Technology, I replied, "I work at Dewey Library," adding tentatively, "at Tech."

"I only rent rooms to boys from Harvard or Tech!"

"Yes, Madam."

I was given an address and an appointment for seven o'clock that evening. Thirty minutes before the hour I set out, my guidebook in my pocket, my breath fresh with Listerine. I turned down a street shaded with trees, perpendicular to Massachusetts Avenue. In spite of the heat, I wore a coat and tie, regarding the event as I would any other interview; I had never lived in the home of a person who was not Indian. The house, surrounded by a chain-link fence, was off-white with dark-brown trim, with a tangle of forsythia bushes plastered against its front and sides. When I pressed the bell, the woman with whom I had spoken on the phone hollered from what seemed to be just the other side of the door, "One minute, please!"

Several minutes later the door was opened by a tiny, extremely old woman. A mass of snowy hair was arranged like a small sack on top of her head. As I stepped into the house, she sat down on a wooden bench positioned at the bottom of a narrow-carpeted staircase. Once she was settled on the bench, in a small pool of light, she peered up at me, giving me her undivided attention. She wore a long black skirt that spread like a stiff tent to the floor, and a starched white shirt edged with ruffles at the throat and cuffs. Her hands, folded together in her lap, had long pallid fingers, with swollen knuckles and tough yellow nails. Age had battered her features so that she almost resembled a man, with sharp, shrunken eyes and prominent creases on either side of her nose. Her lips, chapped and faded, had nearly disappeared, and her eyebrows were missing altogether. Nevertheless, she looked fierce.

"Lock up!" she commanded. She shouted even though I stood only a few feet away. "Fasten the chain and firmly press that button on the knob! This is the first thing you shall do when you enter, is that clear?"

I locked the door as directed and examined the house. Next to the bench was a small round table, its legs fully concealed, much like the woman's, by a skirt of lace. The table held a lamp, a transistor radio, a leather change purse with a silver clasp, and a telephone. A thick wooden cane was propped against one side. There was a parlor to my right, lined with bookcases and filled with shabby claw-footed furniture. In the corner of the parlor I saw a grand piano with its top down, piled with papers. The piano's bench was missing; it seemed to be the one on which the woman was sitting. Somewhere in the house a clock chimed seven times.

"You're punctual!" the woman proclaimed. "I expect you shall be so with the rent!"

"I have a letter, Madam." In my jacket pocket was a letter from M.I.T. confirming my employment, which I had brought along to prove that I was indeed from Tech.

She stared at the letter, then handed it back to me carefully, gripping it with her fingers as if it were a plate heaped with food. She did not wear glasses, and I wondered if she'd read a word of it. "The last boy was always late! Still owes me eight dollars! Harvard boys aren't what they used to be! Only Harvard and Tech in this house! How's Tech, boy?"

"It is very well."

"You checked the lock?"

"Yes, Madam."

She unclasped her fingers, slapped the space beside her on the bench with one hand, and told me to sit down. For a moment she was silent. Then she intoned, as if she alone possessed this knowledge:

"There is an American flag on the moon!"

"Yes, Madam." Until then I had not thought very much about the moon shot. It was in the newspaper, of course, article upon article. The astronauts had landed on the shores of the Sea of Tranquility, I had read, travelling farther than anyone in the history of civilization. For a few hours they explored the moon's surface. They gathered rocks in their pockets, described their surroundings (a magnificent desolation, according to one astronaut), spoke by phone to the President, and planted a flag in lunar soil. The voyage was hailed as man's most awesome achievement.

The woman bellowed, "A flag on the moon, boy! I heard it on the radio! Isn't that splendid?"

"Yes, Madam."

But she was not satisfied with my reply. Instead, she commanded, "Say 'Splendid'!"

I was both baffled and somewhat insulted by the request. It reminded me of the way I was taught multiplication tables as a child, repeating after the master, sitting cross-legged on the floor of my one-room Tollygunge school. It also reminded me of my wedding, when I had repeated endless Sanskrit verses after the priest, verses I barely understood, which joined me to my wife. I said nothing.

"Say 'Splendid'!" the woman bellowed once again.

"Splendid," I murmured. I had to repeat the word a second time at the top of my lungs, so she could hear. I was reluctant to raise my voice to an elderly woman, but she did not appear to be offended. If anything, the reply pleased her, because her next command was:

"Go see the room!"

I rose from the bench and mounted the narrow staircase. There were five doors, two on either side of an equally narrow hallway, and one at the opposite end. Only one door was open. The room contained a twin bed under a sloping ceiling, a brown oval rug, a basin with an exposed pipe, and a chest of drawers. One door led to a closet, another to a toilet and a tub. The window was open; net curtains stirred in the breeze. I lifted them away and inspected the view: a small back yard, with a few fruit trees and an empty clothesline. I was satisfied.

When I returned to the foyer the woman picked up the leather change purse on the table, opened the clasp, fished about with her fingers, and produced a key on a thin wire hoop. She informed me that there was a kitchen at the back of the house, accessible through the parlor. I was welcome to use the stove as long as I left it as I found it. Sheets and towels were provided, but keeping them clean was my own responsibility. The rent was due Friday mornings on the ledge above the piano keys. "And no lady visitors!"

"I am a married man, Madam." It was the first time I had announced this fact to anyone.

But she had not heard. "No lady visitors!" she insisted. She introduced herself as Mrs. Croft.

My wife's name was Mala. The marriage had been arranged by my older brother and his wife. I regarded the proposition with neither objection nor enthusiasm. It was a duty expected of me, as it was expected of every man. She was the daughter of a schoolteacher in Beleghata. I was told that she could cook, knit, embroider, sketch landscapes, and recite poems by Tagore, but these talents could not make up for the fact that she did not possess a fair complexion, and so a string of men had rejected her to her face. She was twenty-seven, an age when her parents had begun to fear that she would never marry, and so they were willing to ship their only child halfway across the world in order to save her from spinsterhood.

For five nights we shared a bed. Each of those nights, after applying cold cream and braiding her hair, she turned from me and wept; she missed her parents. Although I would be leaving the country in a few days, custom dictated that she was now a part of my household, and for the next six weeks she was to live with my brother and his wife, cooking, cleaning, serving tea and sweets to guests. I did nothing to console her. I lay on my own side of the bed, reading my guidebook by flashlight. At times I thought of the tiny room on the other side of the wall which had belonged to my mother. Now the room was practically empty; the wooden pallet on which she'd once slept was piled with trunks and old bedding. Nearly six years ago, before leaving for London, I had watched her die on that bed, had found her playing with her excrement in her final days. Before we cremated her, I had cleaned each of her fingernails with a hairpin, and then, because my brother could not bear it, I had assumed the role of eldest son, and had touched the flame to her temple, to release her tormented soul to heaven.

The next morning, I moved into Mrs. Croft's house. When I unlocked the door, I saw that she was sitting on the piano bench, on the same side as the previous evening. She wore the same black skirt, the same starched white blouse, and had her hands folded together the same way in her lap. She looked so much the same that I wondered if she'd spent the whole night on the bench. I put my suitcase upstairs and then headed off to work. That evening when I came home from the university, she was still there.

"Sit down, boy!" She slapped the space beside her.

I perched on the bench. I had a bag of groceries with me — more milk, more cornflakes, and more bananas, for my inspection of the kitchen earlier in the day had revealed no spare pots or pans. There were only two saucepans in the refrigerator, both containing some orange broth, and a copper kettle on the stove.

"Good evening, Madam."

She asked me if I had checked the lock. I told her I had.

For a moment she was silent. Then suddenly she declared, with the equal measures of disbelief and delight as the night before, “There’s an American flag on the moon, boy!”

“Yes, Madam.”

“A flag on the moon! Isn’t that splendid?”

I nodded, dreading what I knew was coming. “Yes, Madam.”

“Say ‘Splendid’! ”

This time I paused, looking to either side in case anyone was there to overhear me, though I knew perfectly well that the house was empty. I felt like an idiot. But it was a small enough thing to ask. “Splendid!” I cried out.

Within days it became our routine. In the mornings when I left for the library Mrs. Croft was either hidden away in her bedroom, on the other side of the staircase, or sitting on the bench, oblivious of my presence, listening to the news or classical music on the radio. But each evening when I returned the same thing happened: she slapped the bench, ordered me to sit down, declared that there was a flag on the moon, and declared that it was splendid. I said it was splendid, too, and then we sat in silence. As awkward as it was, and as endless as it felt to me then, the nightly encounter lasted only about ten minutes; inevitably she would drift off to sleep, her head falling abruptly toward her chest, leaving me free to retire to my room. By then, of course, there was no flag standing on the moon. The astronauts, I read in the paper, had seen it fall before they flew back to Earth. But I did not have the heart to tell her.

Friday morning, when my first week’s rent was due, I went to the piano in the parlor to place my money on the ledge. The piano keys were dull and discolored. When I pressed one, it made no sound at all. I had put eight-dollar bills in an envelope and written Mrs. Croft’s name on the front of it. I was not in the habit of leaving money unmarked and unattended. From where I stood, I could see the profile of her tent-shaped skirt in the hall. It seemed unnecessary to make her get up and walk all the way to the piano. I never saw her walking about, and assumed, from the cane propped against the round table, that she did so with difficulty. When I approached the bench, she peered up at me and demanded:

“What is your business?”

“The rent, Madam.”

“On the ledge above the piano keys!”

“I have it here.” I extended the envelope toward her, but her fingers, folded together in her lap, did not budge. I bowed slightly and lowered the envelope, so that it hovered just above her hands. After a moment she accepted it, and nodded her head. That night when I came home, she did not slap the bench, but out of habit I sat beside her as usual. She asked me if I had checked the lock, but she mentioned nothing about the flag on the moon. Instead, she said:

“It was very kind of you!”

“I beg your pardon, Madam?”

“Very kind of you!”

She was still holding the envelope in her hands.

On Sunday there was a knock on my door. An elderly woman introduced herself: she was Mrs.

Croft's daughter, Helen. She walked into the room and looked at each of the walls as if for signs of change, glancing at the shirts that hung in the closet, the neckties draped over the doorknob, the box of cornflakes on the chest of drawers, the dirty bowl and spoon in the basin. She was short and thick-waisted, with cropped silver hair and bright pink lipstick. She wore a sleeveless summer dress, a necklace of white plastic beads, and spectacles on a chain that hung like a swing against her chest. The backs of her legs were mapped with dark-blue veins, and her upper arms sagged like the flesh of a roasted eggplant. She told me she lived in Arlington, a town farther up Massachusetts Avenue. "I come once a week to bring Mother groceries. Has she sent you packing yet?"

"It is very well, Madam."

"Some of the boys run screaming. But I think she likes you. You're the first boarder she's ever referred to as a gentleman.

"She looked at me, noticing my bare feet. (I still felt strange wearing shoes indoors, and always removed them before entering my room.) "Are you new to Boston?"

"New to America, Madam."

"From?" She raised her eyebrows.

"I am from Calcutta, India."

"Is that right? We had a Brazilian fellow, about a year ago. You'll find Cambridge a very international city."

I nodded, and began to wonder how long our conversation would last. But at that moment we heard Mrs. Croft's electrifying voice rising up the stairs.

"You are to come downstairs immediately!"

"What is it?" Helen cried back.

"Immediately!"

I put on my shoes. Helen sighed.

I followed Helen down the staircase. She seemed to be in no hurry, and complained at one point that she had a bad knee. "Have you been walking without your cane?" Helen called out. "You know you're not supposed to walk without that cane." She paused, resting her hand on the banister, and looked back at me. "She slips sometimes."

For the first time Mrs. Croft seemed vulnerable. I pictured her on the floor in front of the bench, flat on her back, staring at the ceiling, her feet pointing in opposite directions. But when we reached the bottom of the staircase she was sitting there as usual, her hands folded together in her lap. Two grocery bags were at her feet. She did not slap the bench, or ask us to sit down. She glared.

"What is it, Mother?"

"It's improper!"

"What's improper?"

"It is improper for a lady and gentleman who are not married to one another to hold a private conversation without a chaperone!"

Helen said she was sixty-eight years old, old enough to be my mother, but Mrs. Croft insisted that Helen and I speak to each other downstairs, in the parlor. She added that it was also improper for a lady of Helen's station to reveal her age, and to wear a dress so high above the ankle.

"For your information, Mother, it's 1969. What would you do if you actually left the house one day and saw a girl in a miniskirt?"

Mrs. Croft sniffed. "I'd have her arrested."

Helen shook her head and picked up one of the grocery bags. I picked up the other one, and followed her through the parlor and into the kitchen. The bags were filled with cans of soup, which Helen opened up one by one with a few cranks of a can opener. She tossed the old soup into the sink, rinsed the saucepans under the tap, filled them with soup from the newly opened cans, and put them back in the refrigerator." A few years ago, she could still open the cans herself," Helen said. "She hates that I do it for her now. But the piano killed her hands." She put on her spectacles, glanced at the cupboards, and spotted my tea bags. "Shall we have a cup?"

I filled the kettle on the stove. "I beg your pardon, Madam. The piano?"

"She used to give lessons for forty years. It was how she raised us after my father died." Helen put her hands on her hips, staring at the open refrigerator. She reached into the back, pulled out a wrapped stick of butter, frowned, and tossed it into the garbage. "That ought to do it," she said, and put the unopened cans of soup in the cupboard. I sat at the table and watched as Helen washed the dirty dishes, tied up the garbage bag, and poured boiling water into two cups. She handed one to me without milk, and sat down at the table.

"Excuse me, Madam, but is it enough?"

Helen took a sip of her tea. Her lipstick left a smiling pink stain on the rim of the cup. "Is that enough?"

"The soup in the pans. Is it enough food for Mrs. Croft?"

"She won't eat anything else. She stopped eating solids after she turned one hundred. That was, let's see, three years ago."

I was mortified. I had assumed Mrs. Croft was in her eighties, perhaps as old as ninety. I had never known a person who had lived for over a century. That this person was a widow who lived alone mortified me further still. Widowhood had driven my own mother insane. My father, who worked as a clerk at the General Post Office of Calcutta, died of encephalitis when I was sixteen. My mother refused to adjust to life without him; instead, she sank deeper into a world of darkness from which neither I, nor my brother, nor concerned relatives, nor psychiatric clinics on Rash Behari Avenue could save her. What pained me most was to see her so unguarded, to hear her burp after meals or expel gas in front of company without the slightest embarrassment. After my father's death my brother abandoned his schooling and began to work in the jute mill, he would eventually manage, in order to keep the household running. And so, it was my job to sit by my mother's feet and study for my exams as she counted and recounted the bracelets on her arm as if they were the beads of an abacus. We tried to keep an eye on her. Once she had wandered half naked to the tram depot before we were able to bring her inside again.

"I am happy to warm Mrs. Croft's soup in the evenings," I suggested. "It is no trouble."

Helen looked at her watch, stood up, and poured the rest of her tea into the sink. "I wouldn't if I were you. That's the sort of thing that would kill her altogether."

That evening, when Helen had gone and Mrs. Croft and I were alone again, I began to worry. Now that I knew how very old, she was, I worried that something would happen to her in the middle of the night, or when I was out during the day. As vigorous as her voice was, and imperious as she seemed, I knew that even a scratch or a cough could kill a person that old; each day she lived, I knew, was something of a miracle. Helen didn't seem concerned. She came and went, bringing soup for Mrs. Croft, one Sunday after the next.

In this manner the six weeks of that summer passed. I came home each evening, after my hours at the library, and spent a few minutes on the piano bench with Mrs. Croft. Some evenings I sat beside her long after she had drifted off to sleep, still in awe of how many years she had spent on this earth. At times I tried to picture the world she had been born into, in 1866 — a world, I imagined, filled with women in long black skirts, and chaste conversations in the parlor. Now, when I looked at her hands with their swollen knuckles folded together in her lap, I imagined them smooth and slim, striking the piano keys. At times I came downstairs before going to sleep, to make sure she was sitting upright on the bench, or was safe in her bedroom. On Fridays I put the rent in her hands. There was nothing I could do for her beyond these simple gestures. I was not her son, and, apart from those eight dollars, I owed her nothing.

At the end of August, Mala's passport and green card were ready. I received a telegram with her flight information; my brother's house in Calcutta had no telephone. Around that time, I also received a letter from her, written only a few days after we had parted. There was no salutation; addressing me by name would have assumed an intimacy we had not yet discovered. It contained only a few lines. "I write in English in preparation for the journey. Here I am very much lonely. I sit very cold there. Is there snow. Yours, Mala."

I was not touched by her words. We had spent only a handful of days in each other's company. And yet we were bound together; for six weeks she had worn an iron bangle on her wrist, and applied vermillion powder to the part in her hair, to signify to the world that she was a bride. In those six weeks I regarded her arrival as I would the arrival of a coming month, or season — something inevitable, but meaningless at the time. So little did I know her that, while details of her face sometimes rose to my memory, I could not conjure up the whole of it.

A few days after receiving the letter, as I was walking to work in the morning, I saw an Indian woman on Massachusetts Avenue, wearing a sari with its free end nearly dragging on the footpath, and pushing a child in a stroller. An American woman with a small black dog on a leash was walking to one side of her. Suddenly the dog began barking. I watched as the Indian woman, startled, stopped in her path, at which point the dog leaped up and seized the end of the sari between its teeth. The American woman scolded the dog, appeared to apologize, and walked quickly away, leaving the Indian woman to fix her sari, and quiet her crying child. She did not see me standing there, and eventually she continued on her way. Such a mishap, I realized that morning, would soon be my concern. It was my duty to take care of Mala, to welcome her and protect her. I would have to buy her first pair of snow boots, her first winter coat. I would have to tell her which streets to avoid, which way the traffic came, tell her to wear her sari so that the free end did not drag on the footpath. A five-mile separation from her parents, I recalled with some irritation, had caused her to weep.

Unlike Mala, I was used to it all by then: used to cornflakes and milk, used to Helen's visits, used to sitting on the bench with Mrs. Croft. The only thing I was not used to was Mala. Nevertheless, I did what I had to do. I went to the housing office at M.I.T. and found a furnished apartment a few blocks away, with a double bed and a private kitchen and bath, for forty dollars a week. One last Friday I handed Mrs. Croft eight-dollar bills in an envelope, brought my suitcase downstairs, and informed her that I was moving. She put my key into her change purse. The last thing she asked me to do was hand her the cane propped against the table, so that she could walk to the door and lock it behind me. "Goodbye, then," she said, and retreated back into the house. I did not expect any display of emotion, but I was disappointed all the same. I was only a boarder, a man who paid her a bit of money and passed in and out of her home for six weeks. Compared with a century, it was no time at all.

At the airport I recognized Mala immediately. The free end of her sari did not drag on the floor, but was draped in a sign of bridal modesty over her head, just as it had draped my mother until the day my father died. Her thin brown arms were stacked with gold bracelets, a small red circle was painted on her forehead, and the edges of her feet were tinted with a decorative red dye. I did not embrace her, or kiss her, or take her hand. Instead, I asked her, speaking Bengali for the first time in America, if she was hungry.

She hesitated, then nodded yes.

I told her I had prepared some egg curry at home. "What did they give you to eat on the plane?"

"I didn't eat."

"All the way from Calcutta?"

"The menu said oxtail soup."

"But surely there were other items."

"The thought of eating an ox's tail made me lose my appetite."

When we arrived home, Mala opened up one of her suitcases, and presented me with two pullover sweaters, both made with bright-blue wool, which she had knitted in the course of our separation, one with a V neck, the other covered with cables. I tried them on; both were tight under the arms. She had also brought me two new pairs of drawstring pajamas, a letter from my brother, and a packet of loose Darjeeling tea. I had no present for her apart from the egg curry. We sat at a bare table, staring at our plates. We ate with our hands, another thing I had not yet done in America.

"The house is nice," she said. "Also, the egg curry." With her left hand she held the end of her sari to her chest, so it would not slip off her head.

"I don't know many recipes."

She nodded, peeling the skin off each of her potatoes before eating them. At one point the sari slipped to her shoulders. She readjusted it at once."

There is no need to cover your head," I said. "I don't mind. It doesn't matter here."

She kept it covered anyway.

I waited to get used to her, to her presence at my side, at my table and in my bed, but a week later we were still strangers. I still was not used to coming home to an apartment that smelled of steamed rice, and finding that the basin in the bathroom was always wiped clean, our two toothbrushes lying side by side, a cake of pears soap residing in the soap dish. I was not used to the fragrance of the coconut oil she rubbed every other night into her scalp, or the delicate sound her bracelets made as she moved about the apartment. In the mornings she was always awake before I was. The first morning when I came into the kitchen, she had heated up the leftover sand set a plate with a spoonful of salt on its edge, assuming I would eat rice for breakfast, as most Bengali husbands did. I told her cereal would do, and the next morning when I came into the kitchen, she had already poured the cornflakes into my bowl. One morning she walked with me to M.I.T., where I gave her a short tour of the campus. The next morning before I left for work, she asked me for a few dollars. I parted with them reluctantly, but I knew that this, too, was now normal. When I came home from work there was a potato peeler in the kitchen drawer, and a tablecloth on the table, and chicken curry made with fresh garlic and ginger on the stove. After dinner I read the newspaper, while Mala sat at the kitchen table, working on a cardigan for herself with more of the blue wool, or writing letters home.

On Friday, I suggested going out. Mala set down her knitting and disappeared into the bathroom. When she emerged, I regretted the suggestion; she had put on a silk sari and extra bracelets, and coiled her hair with a flattering side part on top of her head. She was prepared as if for a party, or at the very least for the cinema, but I had no such destination in mind. The evening was balmy. We walked several blocks down Massachusetts Avenue, looking into the windows of restaurants and shops. Then, without thinking, I led her down the quiet street where for so many nights I had walked alone.

"This is where I lived before you came," I said, stopping at Mrs. Croft's chain-link fence.

"In such a big house?"

"I had a small room upstairs. At the back."

"Who else lives there?"

"A very old woman."

"With her family?"

"Alone."

"But who takes care of her?"

I opened the gate. "For the most part she takes care of herself."

I wondered if Mrs. Croft would remember me; I wondered if she had a new boarder to sit with her each evening. When I pressed the bell, I expected the same long wait as that day of our first meeting, when I did not have a key. But this time the door was opened almost immediately, by

Helen. Mrs. Croft was not sitting on the bench. The bench was gone.

"Hello there," Helen said, smiling with her bright pink lips at Mala. "Mother's in the parlor. Will you be visiting awhile?"

"As you wish, Madam."

"Then I think I'll run to the store, if you don't mind. She had a little accident. We can't leave her alone these days, not even for a minute."

I locked the door after Helen and walked into the parlor. Mrs. Croft was lying flat on her back, her head on a peach-colored cushion, a thin white quilt spread over her body. Her hands were folded together on her chest. When she saw me, she pointed at the sofa, and told me to sit down. I took my place as directed, but Mala wandered over to the piano and sat on the bench, which was now positioned where it belonged.

"I broke my hip!" Mrs. Croft announced, as if no time had passed.

"Oh dear, Madam."

"I fell off the bench!"

"I am so sorry, Madam."

"It was the middle of the night! Do you know what I did, boy?"

I shook my head.

"I called the police!"

She stared up at the ceiling and grinned sedately, exposing a crowded row of long gray teeth. "What do you say to that, boy?"

As stunned as I was, I knew what I had to say. With no hesitation at all, I cried out, "Splendid!"

Mala laughed then. Her voice was full of kindness, her eyes bright with amusement. I had never heard her laugh before, and it was loud enough so that Mrs. Croft heard, too. She turned to Mala and glared.

"Who is she, boy?"

"She is my wife, Madam."

Mrs. Croft pressed her head at an angle against the cushion to get a better look. "Can you play the piano?"

"No, Madam," Mala replied.

"Then stand up!"

Mala rose to her feet, adjusting the end of her sari over her head and holding it to her chest, and, for the first time since her arrival, I felt sympathy. I remembered me first days in London, learning how to take the tube to Russell Square, riding an escalator for the first time, unable to understand that when the man cried "piper" it meant "paper," unable to decipher, for a whole year, that the conductor said "Mind the gap" as the train pulled away from each station. Like me, Mala had travelled far from home, not knowing where she was going, or what she would find, for no reason other than to be my wife. As strange as it seemed, I knew in my heart that one day her death would affect me, and stranger still, that mine would affect her. I wanted somehow to explain this to

Mrs. Croft, who was still scrutinizing Mala from top to toe with what seemed to be placid disdain. I wondered if Mrs. Croft had ever seen a woman in a sari, with a dot painted on her forehead and bracelets stacked on her wrists. I wondered what she would object to. I wondered if she could see the red dye still vivid on Mala's feet, all but obscured by the bottom edge of her sari. At last Mrs. Croft declared, with the equal measures of disbelief and delight I knew well:

"She is a perfect lady!"

Now it was I who laughed. I did so quietly, and Mrs. Croft did not hear me. But Mala had heard, and, for the first time, we looked at each other and smiled.

I like to think of that moment in Mrs. Croft's parlor as the moment when the distance between Mala and me began to lessen. Although we were not yet fully in love, I like to think of the months that followed as a honeymoon of sorts. Together we explored the city and met other Bengalis, some of whom are still friends today. We discovered that a man named Bill sold fresh fish on Prospect Street, and that a shop in Harvard Square called Cardullo's sold bay leaves and cloves. In the evenings we walked to the Charles River to watch sailboats drift across the water, or had ice-cream cones in Harvard Yard. We bought a camera with which to document our life together, and I took pictures of her posing in front of the Prudential Building, so that she could send them to her parents. At night we kissed, shy at first but quickly bold, and discovered pleasure and solace in each other's arms. I told her about my voyage on the S.S. Roma, and about Finsbury Park and the Y.M.C.A., and my evenings on the bench with Mrs. Croft. When I told her stories about my mother, she wept. It was Mala who consoled me when, reading the Globe one evening, I came across Mrs. Croft's obituary. I had not thought of her in several months — by then those six weeks of the summer were already a remote interlude in my past — but when I learned of her death I was stricken, so much so that when Mala looked up from her knitting, she found me staring at the wall, unable to speak. Mrs. Croft's was the first death I mourned in America, for hers was the first life I had admired; she had left this world at last, ancient and alone, never to return.

As for me, I have not strayed much farther. Mala and I live in a town about twenty miles from Boston, on a tree-lined street much like Mrs. Croft's, in a house we own, with room for guests, and a garden that saves us from buying tomatoes in summer. We are American citizens now, so that we can collect Social Security when it is time. Though we visit Calcutta every few years, we have decided to grow old here. I work in a small college library. We have a son who attends Harvard University. Mala no longer drapes the end of her sari over her head, or weeps at night for her parents, but occasionally she weeps for our son. So, we drive to Cambridge to visit him, or bring him home for a weekend, so that he can eat rice with us with his hands, and speak in Bengali, things we sometimes worry he will no longer do after we die.

Whenever we make that drive, I always take Massachusetts Avenue, in spite of the traffic. I barely recognize the buildings now, but each time I am there I return instantly to those six weeks as if they were only the other day, and I slow down and point to Mrs. Croft's Street, saying to my son, here was my first home in America, where I lived with a woman who was a hundred and three. "Remember?" Mala says, and smiles, amazed, as I am, that there was ever a time that we were strangers. My son always expresses his astonishment, not at Mrs. Croft's age but at how little I paid in rent, a fact nearly as inconceivable to him as a flag on the moon was to a woman born in 1866. In my son's eyes I see the ambition that had first hurled me across the world. In a few years he will graduate and pave his own way, alone and unprotected. But I remind myself that he has a father who is still living, a mother who is happy and strong. Whenever he is discouraged, I tell him that if I can survive on three continents, then there is no obstacle he cannot conquer. While the astronauts, heroes forever, spent mere hours on the moon, I have remained in this new world for nearly thirty years. I know that my achievement is quite ordinary. I am not the only man to seek his fortune far from home, and certainly I am not the first. Still, there are times I am bewildered by each mile I have travelled, each meal I have eaten, each person I have known, each room in which I have slept. As ordinary as it all appears, there are times when it is beyond my imagination.

4. Questions for Discussion

(1) In the story, the narrator has transcended different countries physically and mentally. How can you analyze the influence of different cultural backgrounds on the narrator?

(2) Explain how Lahiri communicates her ideas about the negotiation between two cultures in the story.

(3) Although many of Lahiri's characters live abroad, their connections with their place of birth cannot be broken. How is this shown in this short story?

Chapter 8 Social Violence

Americans have a complex relationship with violence, and violence occupies a special place in American literature. Genocide, terrorism, war, torture, slavery, rape, and murder are major themes. Violence is the use of physical force so as to injure, abuse, damage, or destroy others. Other definitions are also used, such as the World Health Organization's definition of violence as "the intentional use of physical force or power, threatened or actual, against oneself, another person, or against a group or community, which either results in or has a high likelihood of resulting in injury, death, psychological harm, maldevelopment, or deprivation."[①] In her 1969 study entitled *On Violence* political theorist Hannah Arendt describes the 1900s as a century of violence. The philosopher views the phenomenon as a part of the timeless struggle for power.

As we all know, America has a long history of violence. The pervasiveness of violence in US history is one of the undisputed aspects of the American past. Violence has almost become a feature of life. "The United States was born in a revolution, torn asunder by the Civil War, made dominant through global wars, and reborn through a tumultuous civil rights era. Violence has played a role in some of the most progressive events, such as the emancipation of slaves, as well as the most troubling, such as the decimation of indigenous populations" (Gac385).

Violence has played a role in some of the most progressive events, such as the emancipation of slaves, as well as the most troubling thing, such as the massacre of Indians. Along the way, individual Americans have often embraced a violent ethos. In terms of classification, violence can also be categorized as war violence, racial violence, gender-based violence and violence against children, etc.

The United States has the highest homicide-by-firearms rate among the world's most developed nations. The country also has the most guns per capita and the weakest gun control laws of any developed country. It is estimated that at least 30% of American adults own a gun, and an additional 11% live with someone who does. American kids grow in an environment which is exposed to violence and shooting. Children often watch movies and TV programs which glorify violence.

American literature has shown a peculiar fascination with violence. Ever since the Puritans arrived in North America in the 17th century they had to fight against nature with violence. Early American writers like James Fenimore Cooper often depicts pioneers who use violence to survive in their works. They fought with violence against nature and the Indians. The violent American

① from wiki https://en.wikipedia.org/wiki/Violence

cowboy also represents the spirit of independent heroism. Edgar Allan Poe, a Romantic writer, likes to describe a gallery of dark and ghastly crime, such as domestic violence and psycho killers. Mark Twain, an American writer in the 19th century, is good at describing violent executions, feud and fights in the American West. Huck Finn is an eye-witness of two unforgettable murders in American literature. Ernest Hemingway is skilled at writing about violence and death in war. The code hero in his works like drinking, watching bullfights and showing masculine violence. William Faulkner also excels at writing about violence and murder in the American South, especially racial violence.

In the contemporary American literature, violence remains to be an important theme. It is a reflection of the cultural identity of American society and will continue to shape American society in the future.

Section One: Flannery O'Connor and *A Good Man Is Hard to Find*

Flannery O'Connor is considered one of the foremost short story writers in American literature. She was a unique writer among post-World War II authors — a Roman Catholic from the Bible-belt South with a purpose to reveal the mystery of God's grace in everyday life. Her religion and regional upbringing greatly contributed to her themes and writing style. *A Good Man Is Hard to Find* is one of the most-read short stories by Flannery O'Connor and remains one of her classics.

1. Introduction of Flannery O'Connor

Flannery O'Connor was born on March 25, 1925, in Savannah, Georgia, Flannery O'Connor was the only child of devout Roman Catholics from prominent Georgia families. She attended parochial schools in Savannah and public high schools in Milledgeville, where the family moved after her father developed disseminated lupus, a degenerative blood disease. During her high school and college years, O'Connor demonstrated a talent for cartooning and writing. But O'Connor later proved to inherit the degenerative disease. Soon after her father's death when she was nearly sixteen, O'Connor entered the nearby Georgia State College for Women, where she majored in social sciences. In her spare time, she edited and wrote for school publications. O'Connor then enrolled in the graduate writing program at Iowa State University, where she earned her master's degree in 1947 with six stories. Throughout her career, O'Connor's stories were readily published in prestigious literary journals including *Sewanee Review* and *Kenyon Review*.

O'Connor began writing her first novel, *Wise Blood*, in 1947. However, O'Connor's independent lifestyle ended abruptly at age twenty-five when she suffered her first attack of lupus. From that point onward, O'Connor lived with her mother at Andalusia, on a small dairy farm outside Milledgeville. She maintained a steady writing pace, publishing *Wise Blood* in 1952. The novel was followed by the story collection *A Good Man Is Hard to Find* in 1955, and a second novel, *The Violent Bear It Away*, in 1960. Each volume attracted significant critical attention, and she was awarded three O. Henry awards for her short stories in addition to several grants and two honorary degrees. As her reputation grew, when her health permitted, she traveled to give readings and lectures. O'Connor also enjoyed such pastimes as oil-painting and raising exotic fowls — peacocks, which, as her particular favorites, bears significant symbolic weight in some of her stories.

Religion is a central topic in O'Connor's writing. In her fiction O'Connor frequently criticizes materialism and spiritual apathy of contemporary society. Critics have described O'Connor's protagonists as grotesque in personality, inclining to violence, and isolated and frustrated by their spiritual struggle. Her novels often depict divine grace descending in a violent way, causing the hero a sudden awakening.

During the fourteen years after her diagnosis, O'Connor continued with her writing and was given a number of awards, including O. Henry Memorial Awards in 1957, 1963, and 1964, a Ford Foundation grant in 1959, a National Catholic Book award in 1966, and the National Book Award in 1972. O'Connor died of lupus-related renal failure on August 3, 1964, in Atlanta, Georgia.

2. Introduction of *A Good Man Is Hard to Find*

A Good Man Is Hard to Find is the most-read short story by Flannery O'Connor. It tells the story of a road trip which went horribly wrong. The story begins as a southern American family — a husband, a wife, children, and the children's grandmother — set out on a driving vacation from their home in Georgia to Florida. The entire family is portrayed as comically vapid, ill-tempered, and self-centered, but Grandmother, with her smug pretensions about "breeding", her racial prejudice, and unceasing chatter is singled out as a particularly hollow, if harmless, character. Grandmother has insisted that the family visit relatives in East Tennessee rather than go to Florida, making the excuse that a notorious escaped murderer, The Misfit, is believed to be headed south. When her son ignores her urging, Grandmother manipulates him to turn off the highway onto a desolate dirt road to visit a mansion she remembers from her girlhood. When she realizes that the house is in Tennessee, not Georgia, Grandmother inadvertently causes an accident that lands the car, overturned, in a ditch. The family emerges to find themselves confronted by three men, and Grandmother carelessly blurts the name of one she recognizes from a newspaper photograph: The Misfit. The whole family are finally killed by The Misfit and his gangs.

O'Connor is a regional writer who focuses on American South. She uses violence in a rhetorical manner in this short story where grace and violence are intertwined. For the author, violence as a powerful and simple way to embody conflict, is redemptive and transformative. It is a force which can be used for good or evil. She is concerned with the ordinariness of evil as the character the Misfit who looks like a common person in everyday life.

3. Reading Material: *A Good Man Is Hard to Find*

The grandmother didn't want to go to Florida. She wanted to visit some of her connections in east Tennessee and she was seizing at every chance to change Bailey's mind. Bailey was the son she lived with, her only boy. He was sitting on the edge of his chair at the table, bent over the orange sports section of the *Journal*. "Now look here, Bailey," she said, "see here, read this," and she stood with one hand on her thin hip and the other rattling the newspaper at his bald head. "Here this fellow that calls himself The Misfit is aloose from the Federal Pen and headed toward Florida and you read here what it says he did to these people. Just you read it. I wouldn't take my children in any direction with a criminal like that aloose in it. I couldn't answer to my conscience if I did."

Bailey didn't look up from his reading so she wheeled around then and faced the children's mother, a young woman in slacks, whose face was as broad and innocent as a cabbage and was tied around with a green head-kerchief that had two points on the top like rabbit's ears. She was sitting on the sofa, feeding the baby his apricots out of a jar. "The children have been to Florida before," the old lady said. "You all ought to take them somewhere else for a change so they would see different parts of the world and be broad. They never have been to east Tennessee."

The children's mother didn't seem to hear her but the eight-year-old boy, John Wesley, a stocky child with glasses, said, "If you don't want to go to Florida, why dontcha stay at home?" He and the little girl, June Star, were reading the funny papers on the floor.

"She wouldn't stay at home to be queen for a day," June Star said without raising her yellow head.

"Yes and what would you do if this fellow, The Misfit, caught you?" the grandmother asked.

"I'd smack his face," John Wesley said.

"She wouldn't stay at home for a million bucks," June Star said. "Afraid she'd miss something. She has to go everywhere we go."

"All right, Miss," the grandmother said. "Just remember that the next time you want me to curl your hair."

June Star said her hair was naturally curly.

The next morning the grandmother was the first one in the car, ready to go. She had her big black valise that looked like the head of a hippopotamus in one corner, and underneath it she was hiding a basket with Pitty Sing, the cat, in it. She didn't intend for the cat to be left alone in the house for three days because he would miss her too much and she was afraid he might brush against one of her gas burners and accidentally asphyxiate himself. Her son, Bailey, didn't like to arrive at a motel with a cat.

She sat in the middle of the back seat with John Wesley and June Star on either side of her. Bailey and the children's mother and the baby sat in front and they left Atlanta at eight forty-five with the mileage on the car at 55890. The grandmother wrote this down because she thought it would be interesting to say how many miles they had been when they got back. It took them twenty minutes to reach the outskirts of the city.

The old lady settled herself comfortably, removing her white cotton gloves and putting them up with her purse on the shelf in front of the back window. The children's mother still had on slacks and still had her head tied up in a green kerchief, but the grandmother had on a navy-blue straw sailor hat with a bunch of white violets on the brim and a navy-blue dress with a small white dot in the print. Her collars and cuffs were white organdy trimmed with lace and at her neckline she had pinned a purple spray of cloth violets containing a sachet. In case of an accident, anyone seeing her dead on the highway would know at once that she was a lady.

She said she thought it was going to be a good day for driving, neither too hot nor too cold, and she cautioned Bailey that the speed limit was fifty-five miles an hour and that the patrolmen hid themselves behind billboards and small clumps of trees and sped out after you before you had a chance to slow down. She pointed out interesting details of the scenery: Stone Mountain; the blue granite that in some places came up to both sides of the highway; the brilliant red clay banks slightly streaked with purple; and the various crops that made rows of green lace-work on the ground. The trees were full of silver-white sunlight and the meanest of them sparkled. The children were reading comic magazines and their mother had gone back to sleep.

"Let's go through Georgia fast so we won't have to look at it much," John Wesley said.

"If I were a little boy," said the grandmother, "I wouldn't talk about my native state that way. Tennessee has the mountains and Georgia has the hills."

"Tennessee is just a hillbilly dumping ground," John Wesley said, "and Georgia is a lousy state too."

"You said it," June Star said.

"In my time," said the grandmother, folding her thin veined fingers, "children were more respectful of their native states and their parents and everything else. People did right then. Oh, look at the cute little pickaninny!" she said and pointed to a Negro child standing in the door of a shack. "Wouldn't that make a picture, now?" she asked and they all turned and looked at the little Negro out of the back window. He waved.

"He didn't have any britches on," June Star said.

"He probably didn't have any," the grandmother explained. "Little niggers in the country don't have things like we do. If I could paint, I'd paint that picture," she said.

The children exchanged comic books.

The grandmother offered to hold the baby and the children's mother passed him over the front seat to her. She set him on her knee and bounced him and told him about the things they were passing. She rolled her eyes and screwed up her mouth and stuck her leathery thin face into his smooth bland one. Occasionally he gave her a faraway smile. They passed a large cotton field with five or fix graves fenced in the middle of it, like a small island. "Look at the graveyard!" the grandmother said, pointing it out. "That was the old family burying ground. That belonged to the plantation."

"Where's the plantation?" John Wesley asked.

"Gone with the Wind," said the grandmother. "Ha. Ha."

When the children finished all the comic books they had brought, they opened the lunch and ate it. The grandmother ate a peanut butter sandwich and an olive and would not let the children throw the box and the paper napkins out the window. When there was nothing else to do, they played a game by choosing a cloud and making the other two guess what shape it suggested. John

Wesley took one the shape of a cow and June Star guessed a cow and John Wesley said, no, an automobile, and June Star said he didn't play fair, and they began to slap each other over the grandmother.

The grandmother said she would tell them a story if they would keep quiet. When she told a story, she rolled her eyes and waved her head and was very dramatic. She said once when she was a maiden lady, she had been courted by a Mr. Edgar Atkins Teagarden from Jasper, Georgia. She said he was a very good-looking man and a gentleman and that he brought her a watermelon every Saturday afternoon with his initials cut in it, E. A. T. Well, one Saturday, she said, Mr. Teagarden brought the watermelon and there was nobody at home and he left it on the front porch and returned in his buggy to Jasper, but she never got the watermelon, she said, because a nigger boy ate it when he saw the initials, E. A. T.! This story tickled John Wesley's funny bone and he giggled and giggled but June Star didn't think it was any good. She said she wouldn't marry a man that just brought her a watermelon on Saturday. The grandmother said she would have done well to marry Mr. Teagarden because he was a gentle man and had bought Coca-Cola stock when it first came out and that he had died only a few years ago, a very wealthy man.

They stopped at The Tower for barbecued sandwiches. The Tower was a part stucco and part wood filling station and dance hall set in a clearing outside of Timothy. A fat man named Red Sammy Butts ran it and there were signs stuck here and there on the building and for miles up and down the highway saying, TRY RED SAMMY' S FAMOUS BARBECUE. NONE LIKE FAMOUS RED SAMMY' S! RED SAM! THE FAT BOY WITH THE HAPPY LAUGH. A VETERAN! RED SAMMY' S YOUR MAN!

Red Sammy was lying on the bare ground outside The Tower with his head under a truck while a gray monkey about a foot high, chained to a small chinaberry tree, chattered nearby. The monkey sprang back into the tree and got on the highest limb as soon as he saw the children jump out of the car and run toward him.

Inside, The Tower was a long dark room with a counter at one end and tables at the other and dancing space in the middle. They all sat down at a board table next to the nickelodeon and Red Sam's wife, a tall burnt-brown woman with hair and eyes lighter than her skin, came and took their order. The children's mother put a dime in the machine and played "The Tennessee Waltz," and the grandmother said that tune always made her want to dance. She asked Bailey if he would like to dance but he only glared at her. He didn't have a naturally sunny disposition like she did and trips made him nervous. The grandmother's brown eyes were very bright. She swayed her head from side to side and pretended she was dancing in her chair. June Star said play something she could tap to so the children's mother put in another dime and played a fast number and June Star stepped out onto the dance floor and did her tap routine.

"Ain't she cute?" Red Sam's wife said, leaning over the counter. "Would you like to come be my little girl?"

"No, I certainly wouldn't," June Star said. "I wouldn't live in a broken-down place like this for a million bucks!" and she ran back to the table.

“Ain’t she cute?” the woman repeated, stretching her mouth politely.

“Ain’t you ashamed?” hissed the grandmother.

Red Sam came in and told his wife to quit lounging on the counter and hurry up with these people’s order. His khaki trousers reached just to his hip bones and his stomach hung over them like a sack of meal swaying under his shirt. He came over and sat down at a table nearby and let out a combination sigh and yodel. “You can’t win,” he said. “You can’t win,” and he wiped his sweating red face off with a gray handkerchief. “These days you don’t know who to trust,” he said. “Ain’t that the truth?”

“People are certainly not nice like they used to be,” said the grandmother.

“Two fellers come in here last week,” Red Sammy said, “driving a Chrysler. It was an old beat-up car but it was a good one and these boys looked all right to me. Said they worked at the mill and you know I let them fellers charge the gas they bought? Now why did I do that?”

“Because you’re a good man!” the grandmother said at once.

“Yes, I suppose so,” Red Sam said as if he were struck with this answer.

His wife brought the orders, carrying the five plates all at once without a tray, two in each hand and one balanced on her arm. “It isn’t a soul in this green world of God’s that you can trust,” she said. “And I don’t count nobody out of that, not nobody,” she repeated, looking at Red Sammy.

“Did you read about that criminal, The Misfit, that’s escaped?” asked the grandmother.

“I wouldn’t be a bit surprised if he didn’t attack this place right here,” said the woman. “If he hears about it being here, I wouldn’t be none surprised to see him. If he hears it’s two cent in the cash register, I wouldn’t be a tall surprised if he ...”

“That’ll do,” Red Sam said. “Go bring these people their Co’-Colas,” and the woman went off to get the rest of the order.

“A good man is hard to find,” Red Sammy said. “Everything is getting terrible. I remember the day you could go off and leave your screen door unlatched. Not no more.”

He and the grandmother discussed better times. The old lady said that in her opinion Europe was entirely to blame for the way things were now. She said the way Europe acted you would think we were made of money and Red Sam said it was no use talking about it, she was exactly right. The children ran outside into the white sunlight and looked at the monkey in the lacy chinaberry tree. He was busy catching fleas on himself and biting each one carefully between his teeth as if it were a delicacy.

They drove off again into the hot afternoon. The grandmother took cat naps and woke up every few minutes with her own snoring. Outside of Toombsboro she woke up and recalled an old plantation that she had visited in this neighborhood once when she was a young lady. She said the house had six white columns across the front and that there was an avenue of oaks leading up to it and two little wooden trellis arbors on either side in front where you sat down with your suitor after a stroll in the garden. She recalled exactly which road to turn off to get to it. She knew that Bailey would not be willing to lose any time looking at an old house, but the more she talked about it, the more she wanted to see it once again and find out if the little twin arbors were still standing. “There was a secret panel in this house," she said craftily, not telling the truth but wishing that she were, "and the story went that all the family silver was hidden in it when Sherman came through but it was never found ..."

"Hey!" John Wesley said. "Let's go see it! We'll find it! We'll poke all the woodwork and find it! Who lives there? Where do you turn off at? Hey Pop, can't we turn off there?"

"We never have seen a house with a secret panel!" June Star shrieked. "Let's go to the house with the secret panel! Hey Pop, can't we go see the house with the secret panel!"

"It's not far from here, I know," the grandmother said. "It wouldn't take over twenty minutes."

Bailey was looking straight ahead. His jaw was as rigid as a horseshoe. "No," he said.

The children began to yell and scream that they wanted to see the house with the secret panel. John Wesley kicked the back of the front seat and June Star hung over her mother's shoulder and whined desperately into her ear that they never had any fun even on their vacation, that they could never do what THEY wanted to do. The baby began to scream and John Wesley kicked the back of the seat so hard that his father could feel the blows in his kidney.

"All right!" he shouted and drew the car to a stop at the side of the road. "Will you all shut up? Will you all just shut up for one second? If you don't shut up, we won't go anywhere."

"It would be very educational for them," the grandmother murmured.

"All right," Bailey said, "but get this: this is the only time we're going to stop for anything like this. This is the one and only time."

"The dirt road that you have to turn down is about a mile back," the grandmother directed. "I marked it when we passed."

"A dirt road," Bailey groaned.

After they had turned around and were headed toward the dirt road, the grandmother recalled other points about the house, the beautiful glass over the front doorway and the candle-lamp in the hall. John Wesley said that the secret panel was probably in the fireplace.

"You can't go inside this house," Bailey said. "You don't know who lives there."

"While you all talk to the people in front, I'll run around behind and get in a window," John Wesley suggested.

"We'll all stay in the car," his mother said.

They turned onto the dirt road and the car raced roughly along in a swirl of pink dust. The grandmother recalled the times when there were no paved roads and thirty miles was a day's journey. The dirt road was hilly and there were sudden washes in it and sharp curves on dangerous embankments. All at once they would be on a hill, looking down over the blue tops of trees for miles around, then the next minute, they would be in a red depression with the dust-coated trees looking down on them.

"This place had better turn up in a minute," Bailey said, "or I'm going to turn around."

The road looked as if no one had traveled on it in months.

"It's not much farther," the grandmother said and just as she said it, a horrible thought came to her. The thought was so embarrassing that she turned red in the face and her eyes dilated and her feet jumped up, upsetting her valise in the corner. The instant the valise moved, the newspaper top she had over the basket under it rose with a snarl and Pitty Sing, the cat, sprang onto Bailey's shoulder.

The children were thrown to the floor and their mother, clutching the baby, was thrown out the door onto the ground; the old lady was thrown into the front seat. The car turned over once and landed right-side-up in a gulch off the side of the road. Bailey remained in the driver's seat with the cat gray-striped with a broad white face and an orange nose clinging to his neck like a caterpillar.

As soon as the children saw they could move their arms and legs, they scrambled out of the car, shouting, "We've had an ACCIDENT!" The grandmother was curled up under the dashboard, hoping she was injured so that Bailey's wrath would not come down on her all at once. The horrible thought she had had before the accident was that the house she had remembered so vividly was not in Georgia but in Tennessee.

Bailey removed the cat from his neck with both hands and flung it out the window against the side of a pine tree. Then he got out of the car and started looking for the children's mother. She was sitting against the side of the red gutted ditch, holding the screaming baby, but she only had a cut down her face and a broken shoulder. "We've had an ACCIDENT!" the children screamed in a frenzy of delight.

"But nobody's killed," June Star said with disappointment as the grandmother limped out of the car, her hat still pinned to her head but the broken front brim standing up at a jaunty angle and the violet spray hanging off the side. They all sat down in the ditch, except the children, to recover from the shock. They were all shaking.

"Maybe a car will come along," said the children's mother hoarsely.

"I believe I have injured an organ," said the grandmother, pressing her side, but no one answered her. Bailey's teeth were clattering. He had on a yellow sport shirt with bright blue parrots designed in it and his face was as yellow as the shirt. The grandmother decided that she would not mention that the house was in Tennessee.

The road was about ten feet above and they could see only the tops of the trees on the other side of it. Behind the ditch they were sitting in there were more woods, tall and dark and deep. In a few minutes they saw a car some distance away on top of a hill, coming slowly as if the occupants were watching them. The grandmother stood up and waved both arms dramatically to attract their attention. The car continued to come on slowly, disappeared around a bend and appeared again, moving even slower, on top of the hill they had gone over. It was a big black battered hearse-like automobile. There were three men in it.

It came to a stop just over them and for some minutes, the driver looked down with a steady expressionless gaze to where they were sitting, and didn't speak. Then he turned his head and muttered something to the other two and they got out. One was a fat boy in black trousers and a red sweat shirt with a silver stallion embossed on the front of it. He moved around on the right side of them and stood staring, his mouth partly open in a kind of loose grin. The other had on khaki pants and a blue striped coat and a gray hat pulled down very low, hiding most of his face. He came around slowly on the left side. Neither spoke.

The driver got out of the car and stood by the side of it, looking down at them. He was an older man than the other two. His hair was just beginning to gray and he wore silver-rimmed spectacles that gave him a scholarly look. He had a long-creased face and didn't have on any shirt or undershirt. He had on blue jeans that were too tight for him and was holding a black hat and a gun. The two boys also had guns.

"We've had an ACCIDENT!" the children screamed.

The grandmother had the peculiar feeling that the bespectacled man was someone she knew. His face was as familiar to her as if she had known him all her life but she could not recall who he was. He moved away from the car and began to come down the embankment, placing his feet carefully so that he wouldn't slip. He had on tan and white shoes and no socks, and his ankles were red and thin. "Good afternoon," he said. "I see you all had you a little spill."

"We turned over twice!" said the grandmother.

"Oncet", he corrected. "We see it happen. Try their car and see will it run, Hiram," he said quietly to the boy with the gray hat.

"What you got that gun for?" John Wesley asked. "Whatcha gonna do with that gun?"

"Lady," the man said to the children's mother, "would you mind calling them children to sit down by you? Children make me nervous. I want all you all to sit down right together there where you're at."

"What are you telling US what to do for?" June Star asked.

Behind them the line of woods gaped like a dark open mouth. "Come here," said their mother.

"Look here now," Bailey began suddenly, "we're in a predicament! We're in ..."

The grandmother shrieked. She scrambled to her feet and stood staring. "You're The Misfit!" she said. "I recognized you at once!"

"Yes'm," the man said, smiling slightly as if he were pleased in spite of himself to be known, "but it would have been better for all of you, lady, if you hadn't recognized me."

Bailey turned his head sharply and said something to his mother that shocked even the children. The old lady began to cry and The Misfit reddened.

"Lady," he said, "don't you get upset. Sometimes a man says things he doesn't mean. I don't reckon he meant to talk to you thataway."

"You wouldn't shoot a lady, would you?" the grandmother said and removed a clean handkerchief from her cuff and began to slap at her eyes with it.

The Misfit pointed the toe of his shoe into the ground and made a little hole and then covered it up again. "I would hate to have to," he said.

"Listen," the grandmother almost screamed, "I know you're a good man. You don't look a bit like you have common blood. I know you must come from nice people!"

"Yes mam," he said, "finest people in the world." When he smiled, he showed a row of strong white teeth. "God never made a finer woman than my mother and my daddy's heart was pure gold," he said. The boy with the red sweat shirt had come around behind them and was standing with his gun at his hip. The Misfit squatted down on the ground. “Watch them children, Bobby Lee,” he said. “You know they make me nervous.” He looked at the six of them huddled together in front of him and he seemed to be embarrassed as if he couldn’t think of anything to say. “Ain’t a cloud in the sky,” he remarked, looking up at it. “Don’t see no sun but don’t see no cloud neither.”

“Yes, it’s a beautiful day,” said the grandmother. “Listen,” she said, “you shouldn’t call yourself The Misfit because I know you’re a good man at heart. I can just look at you and tell.”

“Hush!” Bailey yelled. “Hush! Everybody shut up and let me handle this!” He was squatting in the position of a runner about to sprint forward but he didn’t move.

“I prechate that, lady,” The Misfit said and drew a little circle in the ground with the butt of his gun.

“It’ll take a half an hour to fix this here car,” Hiram called, looking over the raised hood of it.

“Well, first you and Bobby Lee get him and that little boy to step over yonder with you,” The Misfit said, pointing to Bailey and John Wesley. “The boys want to ask you something,” he said to Bailey. “Would you mind stepping back in the woods there with them?”

“Listen,” Bailey began, “we’re in a terrible predicament! Nobody realizes what this is,” and his voice cracked. His eyes were as blue and intense as the parrots in his shirt and he remained perfectly still.

The grandmother reached up to adjust her hat brim as if she were going to the woods with him but it came off in her hand. She stood staring at it and after a second, she let it fall on the ground. Hiram pulled Bailey up by the arm as if he were assisting an old man. John Wesley caught hold of his father’s hand and Bobby Lee followed. They went off toward the woods and just as they reached the dark edge, Bailey turned and supporting himself against a gray naked pine trunk, he shouted, “I’ll be back in a minute, Mamma, wait on me!”

“Come back this instant!” his mother shrilled but they all disappeared into the woods.

“Bailey Boy!” the grandmother called in a tragic voice but she found she was looking at The Misfit squatting on the ground in front of her. “I just know you’re a good man,” she said desperately. “You’re not a bit common!”

“Nome, I ain’t a good man,” The Misfit said after a second as if he had considered her statement carefully, “but I ain’t the worst in the world neither. My daddy said I was a different breed of dog from my brothers and sisters. ‘You know,’ Daddy said, ‘it’s some that can live their whole life out without asking about it and its others has to know why it is, and this boy is one of the latters. He’s going to be into everything!’” He put on his black hat and looked up suddenly and then away deep into the woods as if he were embarrassed again. “I’m sorry I don’t have on a shirt before you ladies,” he said, hunching his shoulders slightly. “We buried our clothes that we had on when we escaped and we’re just making do until we can get better. We borrowed these from some folks we met,” he explained.

“That’s perfectly all right,” the grandmother said. “Maybe Bailey has an extra shirt in his suitcase.”

“I’ll look and see directly,” The Misfit said.

"Where are they taking him?" the children's mother screamed.

"Daddy was a card himself," The Misfit said. "You couldn't put anything over on him. He never got in trouble with the Authorities though. Just had the knack of handling them."

"You could be honest too if you'd only try," said the grandmother. "Think how wonderful it would be to settle down and live a comfortable life and not have to think about somebody chasing you all the time."

The Misfit kept scratching in the ground with the butt of his gun as if he were thinking about it. "Yes'm, somebody is always after you," he murmured.

The grandmother noticed how thin his shoulder blades were just behind his hat because she was standing up looking down on him. "Do you every pray?" she asked.

He shook his head. All she saw was the black hat wiggle between his shoulder blades. "Nome," he said.

There was a pistol shot from the woods, followed closely by another. Then silence. The old lady's head jerked around. She could hear the wind move through the tree tops like taking a long-satisfied breath. "Bailey Boy!" she called.

"I was a gospel singer for a while," The Misfit said. "I been most everything. Been in the arm service both land and sea, at home and abroad, been twice married, been an undertaker, been with the railroads, plowed Mother Earth, been in a tornado, seen a man burnt alive oncet," and he looked up at the children's mother and the little girl who were sitting close together, their faces white and their eyes glassy; "I even seen a woman flogged," he said.

"Pray, pray," the grandmother began, "pray, pray ..."

"I never was a bad boy that I remember of," The Misfit said in an almost dreamy voice, "but somewhere along the line I done something wrong and got sent to the penitentiary. I was buried alive," and he looked up and held her attention to him by a steady stare.

"That's when you should have started to pray," she said. "What did you do to get sent to the penitentiary that first time?"

"Turn to the right, it was a wall," The Misfit said, looking up again at the cloudless sky. "Turn to the left, it was a wall. Look up it was a ceiling, look down it was a floor. I forget what I done, lady. I set there and set there, trying to remember what it was I done and I ain't recalled it to this day. Once in a while, I would think it was coming to me, but it never come."

"Maybe they put you in by mistake," the old lady said vaguely.

"Nome," he said. "It wasn't no mistake. They had the papers on me."

"You must have stolen something," she said.

The Misfit sneered slightly. "Nobody had nothing I wanted," he said. "It was a head-doctor at the penitentiary said what I had done was kill my daddy but I know that for a lie. My daddy died in nineteen ought nineteen of the epidemic flu and I never had a thing to do with it. He was buried in the Mount Hopewell Baptist churchyard and you can go there and see for yourself."

"If you would pray," the old lady said, "Jesus would help you."

"That's right," The Misfit said.

"Well then, why don't you pray?" she asked trembling with delight suddenly.

"I don't want no hep," he said. "I'm doing all right by myself."

Bobby Lee and Hiram came ambling back from the woods. Bobby Lee was dragging a yellow shirt with bright blue parrots in it.

"Throw me that shirt, Bobby Lee," The Misfit said. The shirt came flying at him and landed on his shoulder and he put it on. The grandmother couldn't name what the shirt reminded her of. "No, lady," The Misfit said while he was buttoning it up, "I found out the crime don't matter. You can do one thing or you can do another, kill a man or take a tire off his car, because sooner or later you're going to forget what it was you done and just be punished for it."

The children's mother had begun to make heaving noises as if she couldn't get her breath. "Lady," he asked, "would you and that little girl like to step off yonder with Bobby Lee and Hiram and join your husband?"

"Yes, thank you," the mother said faintly. Her left arm dangled helplessly and she was holding the baby, who had gone to sleep, in the other. "Hep that lady up, Hiram," The Misfit said as she struggled to climb out of the ditch, "and Bobby Lee, you hold onto that little girl's hand."

"I don't want to hold hands with him," June Star said. "He reminds me of a pig."

The fat boy blushed and laughed and caught her by the arm and pulled her off into the woods after Hiram and her mother.

Alone with The Misfit, the grandmother found that she had lost her voice. There was not a cloud in the sky nor any sun. There was nothing around her but woods. She wanted to tell him that he must pray. She opened and closed her mouth several times before anything came out. Finally, she found herself saying, "Jesus. Jesus," meaning, Jesus will help you, but the way she was saying it, it sounded as if she might be cursing.

"Yes'm, The Misfit said as if he agreed. "Jesus shown everything off balance. It was the same case with Him as with me except He hadn't committed any crime and they could prove I had committed one because they had the papers on me. Of course," he said, "they never shown me my papers. That's why I sign myself now. I said long ago, you get you a signature and sign everything you do and keep a copy of it. Then you'll know what you done and you can hold up the crime to the punishment and see do they match and in the end, you'll have something to prove you ain't been treated right. I call myself The Misfit," he said, "because I can't make what all I done wrong fit what all I gone through in punishment."

There was a piercing scream from the woods, followed closely by a pistol report. "Does it seem right to you, lady, that one is punished a heap and another ain't punished at all?"

"Jesus!" the old lady cried. "You've got good blood! I know you wouldn't shoot a lady! I know you come from nice people! Pray! Jesus, you ought not to shoot a lady. I'll give you all the money I've got!"

"Lady," The Misfit said, looking beyond her far into the woods, "there never was a body that give the undertaker a tip."

There were two more pistol reports and the grandmother raised her head like a parched old turkey hen crying for water and called, "Bailey Boy, Bailey Boy!" as if her heart would break.

"Jesus was the only One that ever raised the dead," The Misfit continued, "and He shouldn't have done it. He thrown everything off balance. If He did what He said, then it's nothing for you to do but throw away everything and follow Him, and if He didn't, then it's nothing for you to do but enjoy the few minutes you got left the best way you can by killing somebody or burning down his house or doing some other meanness to him. No pleasure but meanness," he said and his voice had become almost a snarl.

"Maybe He didn't raise the dead," the old lady mumbled, not knowing what she was saying and feeling so dizzy that she sank down in the ditch with her legs twisted under her.

"I wasn't there so I can't say He didn't," The Misfit said. "I wish I had of been there," he said, hitting the ground with his fist. "It ain't right I wasn't there because if I had been there I would have known. Listen lady," he said in a high voice, "if I had been there I would have known and I wouldn't be like I am now." His voice seemed about to crack and the grandmother's head cleared for an instant. She saw the man's face twisted close to her own as if he were going to cry and she murmured, "Why you're one of my babies. You're one of my own children!" She reached out and touched him on the shoulder. The Misfit sprang back as if a snake had bitten him and shot her three times through the chest. Then he put his gun down on the ground and took off his glasses and began to clean them.

Hiram and Bobby Lee returned from the woods and stood over the ditch, looking down at the grandmother who half sat and half lay in a puddle of blood with her legs crossed under her, like a child's and her face smiling up at the cloudless sky.

Without his glasses, The Misfit's eyes were red-rimmed and pale and defenseless-looking. "Take her off and throw her where you've thrown the others," he said, picking up the cat that was rubbing itself against his leg.

"She was a talker, wasn't she?" Bobby Lee said, sliding down the ditch with a yodel.

"She would have been a good woman," The Misfit said, "if it had been somebody there to shoot her every minute of her life."

"Some fun!" Bobby Lee said.

"Shut up, Bobby Lee," The Misfit said. "It's no real pleasure in life."

4. Questions for Discussion

(1) What is the relationship between violence and grace in the story?

(2) What is the function of violence in the story?

(3) How do you understand the symbols like the grandmother's hat, The Misfit's automobile and the dark forest, etc.?

Section Two: Edgar Allan Poe and *The Black Cat*

Edgar Allan Poe, often referred to as simply Poe, was an American writer and poet. He is renowned for his macabre and suspenseful tales, as well as his haunting poetry, which have had a profound influence on the genres of horror, mystery, and the psychological thriller. Poe's short story *The Black Cat* was published in 1843 in *The Saturday Evening Post*. It was considered "one of his most mystifying and horrifying tales" (Piacentino153), popular with readers, but Poe did not receive instant success. However, since its publication, elements of *The Black Cat* have inspired films, television episodes, paintings, plays, comics, and novels.

1. Introduction of Allan Poe

Edgar Allan Poe was born in Boston, Massachusetts in 1809. Considered as an important writer of the Romantic Movement, he lived a life filled with tragedy. He became an accomplished poet, short story writer, editor, and literary critic, and gained worldwide fame for his dark, macabre tales of horror, practically inventing the genre of Gothic Literature.

Edgar Allan Poe became an orphan at a young age after his mother died and his father abandoned the family. He was taken in by John and Frances Allan of Richmond, Virginia, but Poe was never formally adopted by them. He went to the University of Virginia for a term before running out of money, then enlisted in the Army, where he failed and was expelled from West Point. He was married to his cousin for 12 years, until she died of tuberculosis in 1847. Throughout his life, he struggled with poverty and money.

Poe was one of the earliest American writers to focus on the short story and was credited with inventing the detective fiction genre. Poe is world famous today mostly for the great short stories he has created, including *The Pit and the Pendulum*, *The Cask of Amontillado*, *The Tell-Tale Heart*, *The Black Cat*, *The Fall of the House of Usher*, and *The Purloined Letter*. Poe died in 1849 because of poverty and unknown illness at the young age of 40.

2. Introduction of *The Black Cat*

The Black Cat is told from the perspective of a narrator who, in his own words, does not expect the reader to believe him. The man tells the reader about a cat named Pluto he used to have as a pet. He describes Pluto as a remarkably large, beautiful animal, entirely black. The narrator and Pluto have a close bond. He takes care of Pluto, and Pluto follows him everywhere around the house.

Then, everything goes wrong. One night, after a drunken rage, the narrator gouges out one of Pluto's eyes with a penknife. The narrator later kills the cat in cold blood. But months later, he comes across another cat which looks similar to Pluto. Eventually, the narrator is driven so mad by the similar cat that he tries to kill the cat with an axe. His wife intervenes, and the narrator ends up killing his wife. He decides to conceal the body inside his house, behind the wall of the basement. Later the police come to investigate about the wife's disappearance. During their investigation, the narrator raps on the wall he has rebuilt to conceal his wife's corpse. The noise of knocking causes the cat, which had accidentally been sealed inside the wall, to howl, alerting the police to the presence of the narrator's wife.

Violence and death are very important topics in Poe's writing because Poe had a tragic life himself. From an early age he learned that life can be nothing more than a series of misfortunes. The premature death of three women who were dear to him (his mother, his friend's mother and his wife), left him alone and bitter, so the violence and terror in his works are a reflection of his own tortured psyche. In this horror classic, the unnamed narrator offers us a parade of violent acts, including eye gouging, hanging, and axing. Violence is a secret beast that grows uncontrollably, destroying all the bodies and minds it touches.

3. Reading Material: *The Black Cat*

For the most wild, yet most homely narrative which I am about to pen, I neither expect nor solicit belief. Mad indeed would I be to expect it, in a case where my very senses reject their own evidence. Yet, mad am I not — and very surely do I not dream. But tomorrow I die, and today I would unburden my soul. My immediate purpose is to place before the world, plainly, succinctly, and without comment, a series of mere household events. In their consequences, these events have terrified — have tortured — have destroyed me. Yet I will not attempt to expound them. To me, they have presented little but horror — to many they will seem less terrible than baroques. Hereafter, perhaps, some intellect may be found which will reduce my phantasm to the commonplace — some intellect more calm, more logical, and far less excitable than my own, which will perceive, in the circumstances I detail with awe, nothing more than an ordinary succession of very natural causes and effects.

From my infancy I was noted for the docility and humanity of my disposition. My tenderness of heart was even so conspicuous as to make me the jest of my companions. I was especially fond of animals, and was indulged by my parents with a great variety of pets. With these I spent most of my time, and never was so happy as when feeding and caressing them. This peculiarity of character grew with my growth, and, in my manhood, I derived from it one of my principal sources of pleasure. To those who have cherished an affection for a faithful and sagacious dog, I need hardly be at the trouble of explaining the nature or the intensity of the gratification thus derivable. There is something in the unselfish and self-sacrificing love of a brute, which goes directly to the heart of him who has had frequent occasion to test the paltry friendship and gossamer fidelity of mere Man.

I married early, and was happy to find in my wife a disposition not uncongenial with my own. Observing my partiality for domestic pets, she lost no opportunity of procuring those of the most agreeable kind. We had birds, gold-fish, a fine dog, rabbits, a small monkey, and a cat.

This latter was a remarkably large and beautiful animal, entirely black, and sagacious to an astonishing degree. In speaking of his intelligence, my wife, who at heart was not a little tinctured with superstition, made frequent allusion to the ancient popular notion, which regarded all black cats as witches in disguise. Not that she was ever serious upon this point — and I mention the matter at all for no better reason than that it happens, just now, to be remembered.

Pluto — this was the cat's name — was my favorite pet and playmate. I alone fed him, and he attended me wherever I went about the house. It was even with difficulty that I could prevent him from following me through the streets.

Our friendship lasted, in this manner, for several years, during which my general temperament and character — through the instrumentality of the Fiend Intemperance — had (I blush to confess it) experienced a radical alteration for the worse. I grew, day by day, more moody, more irritable, more regardless of the feelings of others. I suffered myself to use intemperate language to my wife. At length, I even offered her personal violence. My pets, of course, were made to feel the change in my disposition. I not only neglected, but ill-used them. For Pluto, however, I still retained sufficient regard to restrain me from maltreating him, as I made no scruple of maltreating the rabbits, the monkey, or even the dog, when, by accident, or through affection, they came in my way. But my disease grew upon me — for what disease is like Alcohol! — and at length even Pluto, who was now becoming old, and consequently somewhat peevish — even Pluto began to experience the effects of my ill temper.

One night, returning home, much intoxicated, from one of my haunts about town, I fancied that the cat avoided my presence. I seized him; when, in his fright at my violence, he inflicted a slight wound upon my hand with his teeth. The fury of a demon instantly possessed me. I knew myself no longer. My original soul seemed, at once, to take its flight from my body; and a more than fiendish malevolence, gin-nurtured, thrilled every fiber of my frame. I took from my waistcoat-pocket a penknife, opened it, grasped the poor beast by the throat, and deliberately cut one of its eyes from the socket! I blush, I burn, I shudder, while I pen the damnable atrocity.

When reason returned with the morning — when I had slept off the fumes of the night's debauch — I experienced a sentiment half of horror, half of remorse, for the crime of which I had been guilty; but it was, at best, a feeble and equivocal feeling, and the soul remained untouched. I again plunged into excess, and soon drowned in wine all memory of the deed.

In the meantime, the cat slowly recovered. The socket of the lost eye presented, it is true, a frightful appearance, but he no longer appeared to suffer any pain. He went about the house as usual, but, as might be expected, fled in extreme terror at my approach. I had so much of my old heart left, as to be at first grieved by this evident dislike on the part of a creature which had once so loved me. But this feeling soon gave place to irritation. And then came, as if to my final and irrevocable overthrow, the spirit of PERVERSENESS. Of this spirit philosophy takes no account. Yet I am not more sure that my soul lives, than I am that perverseness is one of the primitive impulses of the human heart — one of the indivisible primary faculties, or sentiments, which give direction to the character of Man. Who has not, a hundred times, found himself committing a vile or a stupid action, for no other reason than because he knows he should not? Have we not a perpetual inclination, in the teeth of our best judgment, to violate that which is Law, merely because we understand it to be such? This spirit of perverseness, I say, came to my final overthrow. It was this unfathomable longing of the soul to vex itself — to offer violence to its own nature — to do wrong for the wrong's sake only — that urged me to continue and finally to consummate the injury I had inflicted upon the unoffending brute. One morning, in cold blood, I slipped a noose about its neck and hung it to the limb of a tree — hung it with the tears streaming from my eyes, and with the bitterest remorse at my heart — hung it because I knew that it had loved me, and because I felt it had given me no reason of offence — hung it because I knew that in so doing I was committing a sin — a deadly sin that would so jeopardize my immortal soul as to place it — if such a thing were possible — even beyond the reach of the infinite mercy of the Most Merciful and Most Terrible God.

On the night of the day on which this most cruel deed was done, I was aroused from sleep by the cry of fire. The curtains of my bed were in flames. The whole house was blazing. It was with great difficulty that my wife, a servant, and myself, made our escape from the conflagration. The destruction was complete. My entire worldly wealth was swallowed up, and I resigned myself thenceforward to despair.

I am above the weakness of seeking to establish a sequence of cause and effect, between the disaster and the atrocity. But I am detailing a chain of facts — and wish not to leave even a possible link imperfect. On the day succeeding the fire, I visited the ruins. The walls, with one exception, had fallen in. This exception was found in a compartment wall, not very thick, which stood about the middle of the house, and against which had rested the head of my bed. The plastering had here, in great measure, resisted the action of the fire — a fact which I attributed to its having been recently spread. About this wall a dense crowd were collected, and many persons seemed to be examining a particular portion of it with very minute and eager attention. The words "strange!" "singular!" and other similar expressions, excited my curiosity. I approached and saw, as if graven in bas-relief upon the white surface, the figure of a gigantic cat. The impression was given with an accuracy truly marvelous. There was a rope about the animal's neck.

When I first beheld this apparition — for I could scarcely regard it as less — my wonder and my terror were extreme. But at length reflection came to my aid. The cat, I remembered, had been hung in a garden adjacent to the house. Upon the alarm of fire, this garden had been immediately filled by the crowd — by some one of whom the animal must have been cut from the tree and thrown, through an open window, into my chamber. This had probably been done with the view of arousing me from sleep. The falling of other walls had compressed the victim of my cruelty into the substance of the freshly-spread plaster; the lime of which, with the flames, and the ammonia from the carcass, had then accomplished the portraiture as I saw it.

Although I thus readily accounted to my reason, if not altogether to my conscience, for the startling fact just detailed, it did not the less fail to make a deep impression upon my fancy. For months I could not rid myself of the phantasm of the cat; and, during this period, there came back into my spirit a half-sentiment that seemed, but was not, remorse. I went so far as to regret the loss of the animal, and to look about me, among the vile haunts which I now habitually frequented, for another pet of the same species, and of somewhat similar appearance, with which to supply its place.

One night as I sat, half stupefied, in a den of more than infamy, my attention was suddenly drawn to some black objects, reposing upon the head of one of the immense hogsheads of gin, or of rum, which constituted the chief furniture of the apartment. I had been looking steadily at the top of this hogshead for some minutes, and what now caused me surprise was the fact that I had not sooner perceived the object thereupon. I approached it, and touched it with my hand. It was a black cat — a very large one — fully as large as Pluto, and closely resembling him in every respect but one. Pluto had not a white hair upon any portion of his body; but this cat had a large, although indefinite splotch of white, covering nearly the whole region of the breast.

Upon my touching him, he immediately arose, purred loudly, rubbed against my hand, and appeared delighted with my notice. This, then, was the very creature of which I was in search. I at once offered to purchase it of the landlord; but this person made no claim to it — knew nothing of it — had never seen it before.

I continued my caresses, and, when I prepared to go home, the animal evinced a disposition to accompany me. I permitted it to do so; occasionally stooping and patting it as I proceeded. When it reached the house, it domesticated itself at once, and became immediately a great favorite with my wife.

For my own part, I soon found a dislike to it arising within me. This was just the reverse of what I had anticipated; but — I know not how or why it was — it's evident fondness for myself rather disgusted and annoyed me. By slow degrees, these feelings of disgust and annoyance rose into the bitterness of hatred. I avoided the creature; a certain sense of shame, and the remembrance of my former deed of cruelty, preventing me from physically abusing it. I did not, for some weeks, strike, or otherwise violently ill-use it; but gradually — very gradually — I came to look upon it with unutterable loathing, and to flee silently from its odious presence, as from the breath of a pestilence.

What added, no doubt, to my hatred of the beast, was the discovery, on the morning after I brought it home, that, like Pluto, it also had been deprived of one of its eyes. This circumstance, however, only endeared it to my wife, who, as I have already said, possessed, in a high degree, that humanity of feeling which had once been my distinguishing trait, and the source of many of my simplest and purest pleasures.

With my aversion to this cat, however, its partiality for myself seemed to increase. It followed my footsteps with a pertinacity which it would be difficult to make the reader comprehend. Whenever I sat, it would crouch beneath my chair, or spring upon my knees, covering me with its loathsome caresses. If I arose to walk, it would get between my feet and thus nearly throw me down, or, fastening its long and sharp claws in my dress, clamber, in this manner, to my breast. At such times, although I longed to destroy it with a blow, I was yet withheld from so doing, partly by a memory of my former crime, but chiefly — let me confess it at once — by absolute dread of the beast.

This dread was not exactly a dread of physical evil — and yet I should be at a loss how otherwise to define it. I am almost ashamed to own — yes, even in this felon's cell, I am almost ashamed to own — that the terror and horror with which the animal inspired me, had been heightened by one of the merest chimeras it would be possible to conceive. My wife had called my attention, more than once, to the character of the mark of white hair, of which I have spoken, and which constituted the sole visible difference between the strange beast and the one I had destroyed. The reader will remember that this mark, although large, had been originally very indefinite; but, by slow degrees — degrees nearly imperceptible, and which for a long time my reason struggled to reject as fanciful — it had, at length, assumed a rigorous distinctness of outline. It was now the representation of an object that I shudder to name — and for this, above all, I loathed, and dreaded, and would have rid myself of the monster had I dared — it was now, I say, the image of a hideous — of a ghastly thing — of the GALLOWS! — oh, mournful and terrible engine of Horror and of Crime — of Agony and of Death!

And now was I indeed wretched beyond the wretchedness of mere Humanity. And a brute beast — whose fellow I had contemptuously destroyed — a brute beast to work out for me — for me, a man fashioned in the image of the High God — so much of insufferable woe! Alas! Neither by day nor by night knew I the blessing of rest anymore! During the former the creature left me no moment alone, and in the latter, I started hourly from dreams of unutterable fear to find the hot breath of the thing upon my face, and its vast weight — an incarnate nightmare that I had no power to shake off — incumbent eternally upon my heart!

Beneath the pressure of torments such as these, the feeble remnant of the good within me succumbed. Evil thoughts became my sole intimates — the darkest and most evil of thoughts. The moodiness of my usual temper increased to hatred of all things and of all mankind; while from the sudden, frequent, and ungovernable outbursts of a fury to which I now blindly abandoned myself, my uncomplaining wife, alas, was the most usual and the most patient of sufferers.

One day she accompanied me, upon some household errand, into the cellar of the old building which our poverty compelled us to inhabit. The cat followed me down the steep stairs, and, nearly throwing me headlong, exasperated me to madness. Uplifting an axe, and forgetting, in my wrath, the childish dread which had hitherto stayed my hand, I aimed a blow at the animal, which, of course, would have proved instantly fatal had it descended as I wished. But this blow was arrested by the hand of my wife. Goaded by the interference into a rage more than demoniacal, I withdrew my arm from her grasp and buried the axe in her brain. She fell dead upon the spot without a groan.

This hideous murder accomplished, I set myself forthwith, and with entire deliberation, to the task of concealing the body. I knew that I could not remove it from the house, either by day or by night, without the risk of being observed by the neighbors. Many projects entered my mind. At one period I thought of cutting the corpse into minute fragments, and destroying them by fire. At another, I resolved to dig a grave for it in the floor of the cellar. Again, I deliberated about casting it in the well in the yard — about packing it in a box, as if merchandise, with the usual arrangements, and so getting a porter to take it from the house. Finally, I hit upon what I considered a far better expedient than either of these. I determined to wall it up in the cellar, as the monks of the Middle Ages are recorded to have walled up their victims.

For a purpose such as this the cellar was well adapted. Its walls were loosely constructed, and had lately been plastered throughout with a rough plaster, which the dampness of the atmosphere had prevented from hardening. Moreover, in one of the walls was a projection, caused by a false chimney, or fireplace, that had been filled up and made to resemble the rest of the cellar. I made no doubt that I could readily displace the bricks at this point, insert the corpse, and wall the whole up as before, so that no eye could detect anything suspicious.

And in this calculation, I was not deceived. By means of a crowbar I easily dislodged the bricks, and, having carefully deposited the body against the inner wall, I propped it in that position, while with little trouble, I relaid the whole structure as it originally stood. Having procured mortar, sand, and hair, with every possible precaution, I prepared a plaster which could not be distinguished from the old, and with this I very carefully went over the new brickwork. When I had finished, I felt satisfied that all was right. The wall did not present the slightest appearance of having been disturbed. The rubbish on the floor was picked up with the minutest care. I looked around triumphantly, and said to myself, "Here at least, then, my labor has not been in vain."

My next step was to look for the beast which had been the cause of so much wretchedness; for I had, at length, firmly resolved to put it to death. Had I been able to meet with it at the moment, there could have been no doubt of its fate; but it appeared that the crafty animal had been alarmed at the violence of my previous anger, and forbore to present itself in my present mood. It is impossible to describe or to imagine the deep, the blissful sense of relief which the absence of the detested creature occasioned in my bosom. It did not make its appearance during the night; and thus for one night, at least, since its introduction into the house, I soundly and tranquilly slept; aye, slept even with the burden of murder upon my soul!

The second and the third day passed, and still my tormentor came not. Once again, I breathed as a free man. The monster, in terror, had fled the premises forever! I should behold it no more! My happiness was supreme! The guilt of my dark deed disturbed me but little. Some few inquiries had been made, but these had been readily answered. Even a search had been instituted — but of course nothing was to be discovered. I looked upon my future felicity as secured.

Upon the fourth day of the assassination, a party of the police came, very unexpectedly, into the house, and proceeded again to make rigorous investigation of the premises. Secure, however, in the inscrutability of my place of concealment, I felt no embarrassment whatever. The officers bade me accompany them in their search. They left no nook or corner unexplored. At length, for the third or fourth time, they descended into the cellar. I quivered not in a muscle. My heart beat calmly as that of one who slumbers in innocence. I walked the cellar from end to end. I folded my arms upon my bosom, and roamed easily to and fro. The police were thoroughly satisfied and prepared to depart. The glee at my heart was too strong to be restrained. I burned to say if but one word, by way of triumph, and to render doubly sure their assurance of my guiltlessness.

"Gentlemen," I said at last, as the party ascended the steps, "I delight to have allayed your suspicions. I wish you all health and a little more courtesy. By the bye, gentlemen, this — this is a very well-constructed house." (In the rabid desire to say something easily, I scarcely knew what I uttered at all.) — "I may say an excellently well-constructed house. These walls — are you going, gentlemen? — these walls are solidly put together." and here, through the mere frenzy of bravado, I rapped heavily with a cane which I held in my hand, upon that very portion of the brickwork behind which stood the corpse of the wife of my bosom.

But may God shield and deliver me from the fangs of the Arch-Fiend! No sooner had the reverberation of my blows sunk into silence, than I was answered by a voice from within the tomb! — by a cry, at first muffled and broken, like the sobbing of a child, and then quickly swelling into one long, loud, and continuous scream, utterly anomalous and inhuman — a howl — a wailing shriek, half of horror and half of triumph, such as might have arisen only out of hell, conjointly from the throats of the damned in their agony and of the demons that exult in the damnation.

Of my own thoughts it is folly to speak. Swooning, I staggered to the opposite wall. For one instant the party upon the stairs remained motionless, through extremity of terror and awe. In the next, a dozen stout arms were toiling at the wall. It fell bodily. The corpse, already greatly decayed and clotted with gore, stood erect before the eyes of the spectators. Upon its head, with red extended mouth and solitary eye of fire, sat the hideous beast whose craft had seduced me into murder, and whose informing voice had consigned me to the hangman. I had walled the monster up within the tomb!

4. Questions for Discussion

(1) How does the narrator's abusive behavior towards his pets foreshadow the violent acts he will commit later in the story?

(2) What effect does the narrator's drinking have on his violent behavior towards his wife and pets?

(3) What is the significance of the violent act of walling up the cat alive, and how does it contribute to the story's themes of guilt and madness?

(4) In what ways does the violence in *The Black Cat* reflect the societal attitudes towards violence and cruelty during the time period in which it was written?

(5) How does the narrator explain his early behavior and disposition towards animals and others in the beginning of his story? What reasons do the narrator give for his later violence?

Chapter 9 Environmental Crisis

As we know environment plays a crucial role in the sustainability of life. All living things on the earth depend on the planet's resources to survive. If humans continue to pollute environment and overuse resources, the resources will be exhausted in a matter of years. Recently, a number of environmental issues have risen to new heights, affecting economies and policies worldwide, such as destruction of ecosystem, water damage, etc. The US is just one of many countries suffering from and contributing to these effects. From air pollution to the depletion of non-renewable resources, the nation is beginning to recognize and address environmental issues within its borders. Natural world is regarded as a resource for human beings, whether economically or culturally, so we should conserve it against overexploitation. Humans should see themselves as part of the large biosphere, rather than a dominator in nature. Anthropocentrism is dangerous for human beings.

Nature writing in America is a literary tradition that explores the natural world, its beauty, and complexity. The genre has a long history in American literature, dating back to the early days of the country when writers like Henry David Thoreau and John Muir wrote about their experiences in the wilderness. Nature writing in America is characterized by its focus on the natural environment, and the relationship between humans and nature. It is often concerned with themes of conservation, preservation, and environmental activism. Nature writers are also interested in exploring the emotional and spiritual connections that humans have with nature, and how the natural world can provide solace, inspiration, and a sense of purpose. According to Tidita Abdurrahmani, central themes of nature writing include: "landscape, animal and plant life, taxonomies of natural objects, reflections of pastoral or agrarian life, fantasies of the Golden Age of Eden." (1).

Ecocriticism as an academic discipline, can be traced back to the late 1970s. Many critics also emphasize the interdisciplinary nature of the study, which is informed by ecological science, politics, ethics, women's studies, Native American studies, and history, among other academic fields. "Ecocriticism consists of a body of work that studies links between literature, culture, and the natural environment. Ecocriticism arose from the influence of the environmental movement, and is the foremost contribution of the humanities to environmentalist thought and action" (Reed 218-219). Since the term "ecocriticism" was coined in 1978 by William Rueckert, interest in the study of nature writing grew through the 1980s, and by the early 1990s ecocriticism had emerged as a recognizable discipline within literature departments of American universities.

American literature has been shaped by the natural landscape and the way in which humans have interacted with it. From the Native American oral traditions to the contemporary environmentalist movement, the environment has played a prominent role in shaping American literature. American environmental literature has produced many excellent works. The representative classic of the 19th century is Henry David Thoreau's *Walden* (1854). The author describes his two-month experience of living in a small cabin in the woods near Walden Pond in Massachusetts. He recorded his encounters in the natural world and discussed the meaning of living in harmony with nature and one's soul. Some critics have argued that the American tradition of nature writing stems from Thoreau's *Walden*. Another landmark of American nonfiction work about nature was Ralph Waldo Emerson's *Nature*. The book is considered the "Bible of American transcendentalism" and a masterpiece of natural literature. Other writers such as James Fennimore Cooper, Nathaniel Hawthorne, and Walt Whitman, also write about nature and American wild west. However, these writers were predominantly white, male writers.

In the 20th century, the relationship between the environment and American literature became even more complex. The rise of industrialization and urbanization led to a growing concern for the environment and a sense of nostalgia for a simpler, more rural way of life. By the middle of the 20th century, environmental writers began considering human life as a part of the nonhuman world. Writers in the 20th century such as William Faulkner, Willa Cather and John Steinbeck also pay much attention to the writing of nature and environment.

Contemporary American writers show more concern about the global environmental crisis in the Anthropocene — a period in which humans have had a substantial impact on our planet. In the past 60 years in particular, human impacts have unfolded at an unprecedented rate and scale. Carbon dioxide emissions, global warming, ocean acidification, habitat destruction, animal distinction and widescale natural resource extraction are all signs that we have significantly modified our planet. Writers depict landscapes transformed by human activities, capturing the beauty and vulnerability of ecosystems threatened by climate change, pollution, and habitat destruction. They emphasize the importance of empathy, urging readers to reconsider their role as caretakers of the Earth. They explore themes of environmental justice, the interconnectedness of species, and the ethical implications of our actions. Through their narratives, American writers inspire readers to reflect on their own relationships with the natural world and advocate for a more sustainable and equitable future.

Section One: Rachel Carson and *Silent Spring*

Rachel Carson was an American biologist, writer, and environmentalist who is widely regarded as one of the most important figures in the modern environmental movement. She is best known for her book *Silent Spring*, which is considered a landmark work of environmental literature and helps to inspire the modern environmental movement.

1. Introduction of Rachel Carson

Rachel Carson was born on May 27, 1907, on a family farm near Springdale, Pennsylvania.

She earned a master's degree in zoology from Johns Hopkins University in Baltimore, Maryland, in 1932, working as an aquatic biologist in the US Bureau of Fisheries. In 1941, she published *The Sea Around Us* which won her a US National Book Award and became a bestseller. She showed her concern towards environment protection and sea conservation and later published several books on these topics. Her book, *Silent Spring,* published in 1962, raised people's concern on the abuse of DDT and led to a nationwide ban on DDT and other pesticides. In view of her great contribution, she was awarded the Presidential Medal of Freedom.

Throughout all her life, Carson continued to write and speak out on environmental issues until her death in 1964 from cancer. Her legacy continues to inspire environmental activists and writers today, and her work is widely credited with helping to shape modern environmental policies and regulations.

2. Introduction of *Silent Spring*

Silent Spring is a groundbreaking book by Rachel Carson, first published in 1962, which sparked a national conversation about the use of pesticides and their effects on the environment. The book was a seminal work in the modern environmental movement and is widely regarded as a classic of environmental literature.

Carson's book focused on the indiscriminate use of pesticides, particularly DDT, and their impact on the environment and human health. Yaakov Garb thinks "*Silent Spring*'s center of gravity lay in Carson's reworking of deeply conventional conceptions of the balance of nature and the web of life". Carson argued that the widespread use of pesticides was causing serious harm to wildlife and their habitats, as well as to human beings.

The book's title comes from the idea that the use of pesticides was causing the disappearance of birds and other wildlife, leading to a "silent spring" devoid of the sounds of nature. Carson argued that the use of pesticides was disrupting ecosystems and causing long-term damage to the natural world.

Silent Spring was a controversial book that faced opposition from the chemical industry and other opponents of environmental regulations. However, it also garnered widespread attention and helped to inspire a wave of environmental activism.

Carson's book remains a classic of environmental literature and continues to inspire environmental activists and writers today. It is a powerful reminder of the importance of preserving and protecting the natural world for future generations.

3. Reading Material: *Silent Spring* (excerpt)

Chapter 1: A Fable for Tomorrow

There was once a town in the heart of America where all life seemed to live in harmony with its surroundings. The town lay in the midst of a checkerboard of prosperous farms, with fields of grain and hillsides of orchards where, in spring, white clouds of bloom drifted above the green fields. In autumn, oak and maple and birch set up a blaze of color that flamed and flickered across a backdrop of pines. Then foxes barked in the hills and deer silently crossed the fields, half hidden in the mists of the fall mornings.

Along the roads, laurel, viburnum and alder, great ferns and wildflowers delighted the traveler's eye through much of the year. Even in winter the roadsides were places of beauty, where countless birds came to feed on the berries and on the seed heads of the dried weeds rising above the snow. The countryside was, in fact, famous for the abundance and variety of its bird life, and when the flood of migrants was pouring through in spring and fall people traveled from great distances to observe them. Others came to fish the streams, which flowed clear and cold out of the hills and contained shady pools where trout lay. So, it had been from the days many years ago when the first settlers raised their houses, sank their wells, and built their barns.

Then a strange blight crept over the area and everything began to change. Some evil spell had settled on the community: mysterious maladies swept the flocks of chickens; the cattle and sheep sickened and died. Everywhere was a shadow of death. The farmers spoke of much illness among their families. In the town the doctors had become more and more puzzled by new kinds of sickness appearing among their patients. There had been several sudden and unexplained deaths, not only among adults but even among children, who would be stricken suddenly while at play and die within a few hours.

There was a strange stillness. The birds, for example — where had they gone? Many people spoke of them, puzzled and disturbed. The feeding stations in the backyards were deserted. The few birds seen anywhere were moribund; they trembled violently and could not fly. It was a spring without voices. On the mornings that had once throbbed with the dawn chorus of robins, catbirds, doves, jays, wrens, and scores of other bird voices there was now no sound; only silence lay over the fields and woods and marsh.

On the farms the hens brooded, but no chicks hatched. The farmers complained that they were unable to raise any pigs — the litters were small and the young survived only a few days. The apple trees were coming into bloom but no bees droned among the blossoms, so there was no pollination and there would be no fruit.

The roadsides, once so attractive, were now lined with browned and withered vegetation as though swept by fire. These, too, were silent, deserted by all living things. Even the streams were now lifeless. Anglers no longer visited them, for all the fish had died.

In the gutters under the eaves and between the shingles of the roofs, a white granular powder still showed a few patches; some weeks before it had fallen like snow upon the roofs and the lawns, the fields and streams.

No witchcraft, no enemy action had silenced the rebirth of new life in this stricken world. The people had done it themselves.

This town does not actually exist, but it might easily have a thousand counterparts in America or elsewhere in the world. I know of no community that has experienced all the misfortunes I describe. Yet every one of these disasters has actually happened somewhere, and many real communities have already suffered a substantial number of them. A grim specter has crept upon us almost unnoticed, and this imagined tragedy may easily become a stark reality we all shall know.

What has already silenced the voices of spring in countless towns in America? This book is an attempt to explain.

Chapter 2: The Obligation to Endure

The history of life on earth has been a history of interaction between living things and their surroundings. To a large extent, the physical form and the habits of the earth's vegetation and its animal life have been molded by the environment. Considering the whole span of earthly time, the opposite effect, in which life actually modifies its surroundings, has been relatively slight. Only within the moment of time represented by the present century has one species — man — acquired significant power to alter the nature of his world.

During the past quarter century this power has not only increased to one of disturbing magnitude but it has changed in character. The most alarming of all man's assaults upon the environment is the contamination of air, earth, rivers, and sea with dangerous and even lethal materials. This pollution is for the most part irrecoverable; the chain of evil it initiates not only in the world that must support life but in living tissues is for the most part irreversible. In this now universal contamination of the environment, chemicals are the sinister and little-recognized partners of radiation in changing the very nature of the world — the very nature of its life. Strontium-90, released through nuclear explosions into the air, comes to earth in rain or drifts down as fallout, lodges in soil, enters into the grass or corn or wheat grown there, and in time takes up its abode in the bones of a human being, there to remain until his death. Similarly, chemicals sprayed on croplands or forests or gardens lie long in soil, entering into living organisms, passing from one to another in a chain of poisoning and death. Or they pass mysteriously by underground streams until they emerge and, through the alchemy of air and sunlight, combine into new forms that kill vegetation, sicken cattle, and work unknown harm on those who drink from once pure wells. As Albert Schweitzer has said, "Man can hardly even recognize the devils of his own creation."

It took hundreds of millions of years to produce the life that now inhabits the earth — eons of time in which that developing and evolving and diversifying life reached a state of adjustment and balance with its surroundings. The environment, rigorously shaping and directing the life it supported, contained elements that were hostile as well as supporting. Certain rocks gave out dangerous radiation; even within the light of the sun, from which all life draws its energy, there were short-wave radiations with power to injure. Given time — time not in years but in millennia — life adjusts, and a balance has been reached. For time is the essential ingredient; but in modern world there is no time.

The rapidity of change and the speed with which new situations are created follow the impetuous and heedless pace of man rather than the deliberate pace of nature. Radiation is no longer merely the background radiation of rocks, the bombardment of cosmic rays, the ultraviolet of the sun that have existed before there was any life on earth; radiation is now the unnatural creation of man's tampering with the atom. The chemicals to which life is asked to make its adjustment are no longer merely the calcium and silica and copper and all the rest of the minerals washed out of the rocks and carried in rivers to the sea; they are the synthetic creations of man's inventive mind, brewed in his laboratories, and having no counterparts in nature.

To adjust to these chemicals would require time on the scale that is nature's; it would require not merely the years of a man's life but the life of generations. And even this, were it by some miracle possible, would be futile, for the new chemicals come from our laboratories in an endless stream; almost five hundred annually find their way into actual use in the United States alone. The figure is staggering and its implications are not easily grasped — 500 new chemicals to which the bodies of men and animals are required somehow to adapt each year, chemicals totally outside the limits of biologic experience.

Among them are many that are used in man's war against nature. Since the mid-1940s over 200 basic chemicals have been created for use in killing insects, weeds, rodents, and other organisms described in the modern vernacular as "pests"; and they are sold under several thousand different brand names.

These sprays, dusts, and aerosols are now applied almost universally to farms, gardens, forests, and homes — nonselective chemicals that have the power to kill every insect, the "good" and the "bad", to still the song of birds and the leaping of fish in the streams, to coat the leaves with a deadly film, and to linger on in soil — all this though the intended target may be only a few weeds or insects. Can anyone believe it is possible to lay down such a barrage of poisons on the surface of the earth without making it unfit for all life? They should not be called "insecticides" , but "biocides".

The whole process of spraying seems caught up in an endless spiral. Since DDT was released for civilian use, a process of escalation has been going on in which ever more toxic materials must be found. This has happened because insects, in a triumphant vindication of Darwin's principle of the survival of the fittest, have evolved super races immune to the particular insecticide used, hence a deadlier one has always to be developed — and then a deadlier one than that. It has happened also because, for reasons to be described later, destructive insects often undergo a "flareback," or resurgence, after spraying, in numbers greater than before. Thus, the chemical war is never won, and all life is caught in its violent crossfire.

Along with the possibility of the extinction of mankind by nuclear war, the central problem of our age has therefore become the contamination of man's total environment with such substances of incredible potential for harm — substances that accumulate in the tissues of plants and animals and even penetrate the germ cells to shatter or alter the very material of heredity upon which the shape of the future depends.

Some would-be architects of our future look toward a time when it will be possible to alter the human germ plasm by design. But we may easily be doing so now by inadvertence, for many chemicals, like radiation, bring about gene mutations. It is ironic to think that man might determine his own future by something so seemingly trivial as the choice of an insect spray.

All this has been risked — for what? Future historians may well be amazed by our distorted sense of proportion. How could intelligent beings seek to control a few unwanted species by a method that contaminated the entire environment and brought the threat of disease and death even to their own kind? Yet this is precisely what we have done. We have done it, moreover, for reasons that collapse the moment we examine them. We are told that the enormous and expanding use of pesticides is necessary to maintain farm production. Yet is our real problem not one of *overproduction*? Our farms, despite measures to remove acreages from production and to pay farmers *not* to produce, have yielded such a staggering excess of crops that the American taxpayer in 1962 is paying out more than one billion dollars a year as the total carrying cost of the surplus-food storage program. And is the situation helped when one branch of the Agriculture Department tries to reduce production while another states, as it did in 1958, "It is believed generally that reduction of crop acreages under provisions of the Soil Bank will stimulate interest in use of chemicals to obtain maximum production on the land retained in crops."

All this is not to say there is no insect problem and no need of control. I am saying, rather, that control must be geared to realities, not to mythical situations, and that the methods employed must be such that they do not destroy us along with the insects.

The problem whose attempted solution has brought such a train of disaster in its wake is an accompaniment of our modern way of life. Long before the age of man, insects inhabited the earth — a group of extraordinarily varied and adaptable beings. Over the course of time since man's advent, a small percentage of the more than half a million species of insects have come into conflict with human welfare in two principal ways: as competitors for the food supply and as carriers of human disease.

Disease-carrying insects become important where human beings are crowded together, especially under conditions where sanitation is poor, as in time of natural disaster or war or in situations of extreme poverty and deprivation. Then control of some sort becomes necessary. It is a sobering fact, however, as we shall presently see, that the method of massive chemical control has had only limited success, and also threatens to worsen the very conditions it is intended to curb.

Under primitive agricultural conditions the farmer had few insect problems. These arose with the intensification of agriculture — the devotion of immense acreages to a single crop. Such a system set the stage for explosive increases in specific insect populations. Single-crop farming does not take advantage of the principles by which nature works; it is agriculture as an engineer might conceive it to be. Nature has introduced great variety into the landscape, but man has displayed a passion for simplifying it. Thus, he undoes the built-in checks and balances by which nature holds the species within bounds. One important natural check is a limit on the amount of suitable habitat for each species. Obviously then, an insect that lives on wheat can build up its population to much higher levels on a farm devoted to wheat than on one in which wheat is intermingled with other crops to which the insect is not adapted.

The same thing happens in other situations. A generation or more ago, the towns of large areas of the United States lined their streets with the noble elm tree. Now the beauty they hopefully created is threatened with complete destruction as disease sweeps through the elms, carried by a beetle that would have only limited chance to build up large populations and to spread from tree to tree if the elms were only occasional trees in a richly diversified planting.

Another factor in the modern insect problem is one that must be viewed against a background of geologic and human history: the spreading of thousands of different kinds of organisms from their native homes to invade new territories. This worldwide migration has been studied and graphically described by the British ecologist Charles Elton in his recent book *The Ecology of Invasions*. During the Cretaceous Period, some hundred million years ago, flooding seas cut many land bridges between continents and living things found themselves confined in what Elton calls "colossal separate nature reserves." There, isolated from others of their kind, they developed many new species. When some of the land masses were joined again, about 15 million years ago, these species began to move out into new territories — a movement that is not only still in progress but is now receiving considerable assistance from man.

The importation of plants is the primary agent in the modern spread of species, for animals have almost invariably gone along with the plants, quarantine being a comparatively recent and not completely effective innovation. The United States Office of Plant Introduction alone has introduced almost 200,000 species and varieties of plants from all over the world. Nearly half of the 180 or so major insect enemies of plants in the United States are accidental imports from abroad, and most of them have come as hitchhikers on plants.

In new territory, out of reach of the restraining hand of the natural enemies that kept down its numbers in its native land, an invading plant or animal is able to become enormously abundant. Thus it is no accident that our most troublesome insects are introduced species.

These invasions, both the naturally occurring and those dependent on human assistance, are likely to continue indefinitely. Quarantine and massive chemical campaigns are only extremely expensive ways of buying time. We are faced, according to Dr. Elton, "with a life-and-death need not just to find new technological means of suppressing this plant or that animal"; instead, we need the basic knowledge of animal populations and their relations to their surroundings that will "promote an even balance and damp down the explosive power of outbreaks and new invasions".

Much of the necessary knowledge is now available but we do not use it. We train ecologists in our universities and even employ them in our governmental agencies but we seldom take their advice. We allow the chemical death rain to fall as though there were no alternative, whereas in fact there are many, and our ingenuity could soon discover many more if given opportunity.

Have we fallen into a mesmerized state that makes us accept as inevitable that which is inferior or detrimental, as though having lost the will or the vision to demand that which is good? Such thinking, in the words of the ecologist Paul Shepard, "idealizes life with only its head out of water, inches above the limits of toleration of the corruption of its own environment... Why should we tolerate a diet of weak poisons, a home in insipid surroundings, a circle of acquaintances who are not quite our enemies, the noise of motors with just enough relief to prevent insanity? Who would want to live in a world which is just not quite fatal?"

Yet such a world is pressed upon us. The crusade to create a chemically sterile, insect-free world seems to have engendered a fanatic zeal on the part of many specialists and most of the so-called control agencies. On every hand there is evidence that those engaged in spraying operations exercise a ruthless power. "The regulatory entomologists... function as prosecutor, judge and jury, tax assessor and collector and sheriff to enforce their own orders," said Connecticut entomologist Neely Turner. The most flagrant abuses go unchecked in both state and federal agencies.

It is not my contention that chemical insecticides must never be used. I do contend that we have put poisonous and biologically potent chemicals indiscriminately into the hands of persons largely or wholly ignorant of their potentials for harm. We have subjected enormous numbers of people to contact with these poisons, without their consent and often without their knowledge. If the Bill of Rights contains no guarantee that a citizen shall be secure against lethal poisons distributed either by private individuals or by public officials, it is surely only because our forefathers, despite their considerable wisdom and foresight, could conceive of no such problem.

I contend, furthermore, that we have allowed these chemicals to be used with little or no advance investigation of their effect on soil, water, wildlife, and man himself. Future generations are unlikely to condone our lack of prudent concern for the integrity of the natural world that supports all life.

There is still very limited awareness of the nature of the threat. This is an era of specialists, each of whom sees his own problem and is unaware of or intolerant of the larger frame into which it fits. It is also an era dominated by industry, in which the right to make a dollar at whatever cost is seldom challenged. When the public protests, confronted with some obvious evidence of damaging results of pesticide applications, it is fed little tranquilizing pills of half truth. We urgently need an end to these false assurances, to the sugar coating of unpalatable facts. It is the public that is being asked to assume the risks that the insect controllers calculate. The public must decide whether it wishes to continue on the present road, and it can do so only when in full possession of the facts. In the words of Jean Rostand, "The obligation to endure gives us the right to know."

Chapter 3: Elixirs of Death

For the first time in the history of the world, every human being is now subjected to contact with dangerous chemicals, from the moment of conception until death. In less than two decades of their use, the synthetic pesticides have been so thoroughly distributed throughout the animate and inanimate world that they occur virtually everywhere. They have been recovered from most of the major river systems and even from streams of groundwater flowing unseen through the earth. Residues of these chemicals linger in soil to which they may have been applied a dozen years before. They have entered and lodged in the bodies of fish, birds, reptiles, and domestic and wild animals so universally that scientists carrying on animal experiments find it almost impossible to locate subjects free from such contamination. They have been found in fish in remote mountain lakes, in earthworms burrowing in soil, in the eggs of birds — and in man himself. For these chemicals are now stored in the bodies of the vast majority of human beings, regardless of age. They occur in the mother's milk, and probably in the tissues of the unborn child.

All this has come about because of the sudden rise and prodigious growth of an industry for the production of man-made or synthetic chemicals with insecticidal properties. This industry is a child of the Second World War. In the course of developing agents of chemical warfare, some of the chemicals created in the laboratory were found to be lethal to insects. The discovery did not come by chance: insects were widely used to test chemicals as agents of death for man.

The result has been a seemingly endless stream of synthetic insecticides. In being man-made — by ingenious laboratory manipulation of the molecules, substituting atoms, altering their arrangement — they differ sharply from the simpler insecticides of prewar days. These were derived from naturally occurring minerals and plant products — compounds of arsenic, copper, lead, manganese, zinc and other minerals, pyrethrum from dried flowers of chrysanthemums, nicotine sulphate from some of the relatives of tobacco, and rotenone from leguminous plants of the East Indies.

What sets the new synthetic insecticides apart is their enormous biological potency. They have immense power not merely to poison but to enter into the most vital processes of the body and change them in sinister and often deadly ways. Thus, as we shall see, they destroy the very enzymes whose function is to protect the body from harm, they block the oxidation processes from which the body receives its energy, they prevent the normal functioning of various organs, and they may initiate in certain cells the slow and irreversible change that leads to malignancy.

Yet new and more deadly chemicals are added to the list each year and new uses are devised so that contact with these materials has become practically worldwide. The production of synthetic pesticides in the United States soared from 124, 259,000 pounds in 1947 to 637,666,000 pounds in 1960 — more than a fivefold increase. The wholesale value of these products was well over a quarter of a billion dollars. But in the plans and hopes of the industry this enormous production is only a beginning.

A Who's Who of pesticides is therefore of concern to us all. If we are going to live so intimately with these chemicals — eating and drinking them, taking them into the very marrow of our bones — we had better know something about their nature and their power.

Although the Second World War marked a turning away from inorganic chemicals as pesticides into the wonder world of the carbon molecule, a few of the old materials persist. Chief among these is arsenic, which is still the basic ingredient in a variety of weed and insect killers. Arsenic is a highly toxic mineral occurring widely in association with the ores of various metals, and in very small amounts in volcanoes, in the sea, and in spring water. Its relations to man are varied and historic. Since many of its compounds are tasteless, it has been a favorite agent of homicide from long before the time of the Borgias to the present. Arsenic is present in English chimney soot and along with certain aromatic hydrocarbons is considered responsible for the carcinogenic (or cancer-causing) action of the soot, which was recognized nearly two centuries ago by an English physician. Epidemics of chronic arsenical poisoning involving whole populations over long periods are on record. Arsenic-contaminated environments have also caused sickness and death among horses, cows, goats, pigs, deer, fishes, and bees; despite this record arsenical sprays and dusts are widely used. In the arsenic-sprayed cotton country of southern United States beekeeping as an industry has nearly died out. Farmers using arsenic dusts over long periods have been afflicted with chronic arsenic poisoning; livestock have been poisoned by crop sprays or weed killers containing arsenic. Drifting arsenic dusts from blueberry lands have spread over neighboring farms, contaminating streams, fatally poisoning bees and cows, and causing human illness. "It is scarcely possible…to handle arsenicals with more utter disregard of the general health than that which has been practiced in our country in recent years," said Dr. W. C. Hueper, of the National Cancer Institute, an authority on environmental cancer. "Anyone who has watched the dusters and sprayers of arsenical insecticides at work must have been impressed by the almost supreme carelessness with which the poisonous substances are dispensed."

Modern insecticides are still more deadly. The vast majority fall into one of two large groups of chemicals. One, represented by DDT, is known as the "chlorinated hydrocarbons." The other group consists of the organic phosphorus insecticides, and is represented by the reasonably familiar malathion and parathion. All have one thing in common. As mentioned above, they are built on a basis of carbon atoms, which are also the indispensable building blocks of the living world, and thus classed as "organic." To understand them, we must see of what they are made, and how, although linked with the basic chemistry of all life, they lend themselves to the modifications which make them agents of death.

The basic element, carbon, is one whose atoms have an almost infinite capacity for uniting with each other in chains and rings and various other configurations, and for becoming linked with atoms of other substances. Indeed, the incredible diversity of living creatures from bacteria to the great blue whale is largely due to this capacity of carbon. The complex protein molecule has the carbon atom as its basis, as have molecules of fat, carbohydrates, enzymes, and vitamins. So, too, have enormous numbers of nonliving things, for carbon is not necessarily a symbol of life…

4. Questions for Discussion

(1) Do you agree that the project of controlling nature is arrogant, foolish, and dangerous, as Carson argues? Why? Can you think of any more recent examples that support or refute this statement?

(2) Carson's first chapter explains the title of her book. Why is it called *Silent Spring?*

(3) What were the key environmental issues that Rachel Carson raised in *Silent Spring*?

(4) In what ways did *Silent Spring* contribute to the public's understanding of the relationship between human health and the environment?

Section Two: William Faulkner and *The Bear*

William Faulkner (1897 — 1962) was an American writer and Nobel Prize laureate from Mississippi. He is widely regarded as one of the most important and influential writers of the 20th century, known for his complex and innovative narrative style and his exploration of the themes of race, class, and identity in the American South. By the time of his death in 1962, Faulkner was widely considered the most important American novelist of his generation. Considered one of the best short stories of the 20th century, *The Bear* is a coming-of-age tale that combines together themes of family, race, and the taming of the wilderness, as the young main character learns to hunt and track the huge bear known as Old Ben.

1. Introduction of William Faulkner

William Faulkner was born on September 25, 1897, New Albany, Mississippi, US and died on July 6, 1962, Byhalia, Mississippi. In his works, he fabricated Yoknapatawpha County, a small fictional town based on his real hometown Oxford and created his most famous works including *The Sound and the Fury*, *As I Lay Dying*, *Absalom, Absalom!* and so on.

Faulkner was named after his great-grandfather, Colonel William Clark Falkner, a hero who fought gallantly during the Civil War, built a local railway, and published a popular romantic novel called *The White Rose of Memphis*. As a teenager, Faulkner was taken by drawing. He also greatly enjoyed reading and writing poetry. As a reluctant student, he left high school without graduation and then worked in carpentry and sporadically as a clerk at his grandfather's bank. Later lured by the war in Europe, he joined the British Royal Flying Corps in 1918 and was trained as a pilot in the first Royal Canadian Air Force. But the First World War ended before he could join it. In 1919, Faulkner was enrolled at the University of Mississippi where he wrote for the student newspaper, *The Mississippian*. In 1926, Faulkner published his first novel, *Soldiers' Pay*. Influenced by his friend and mentor, Sherwood Anderson, Faulkner began to write about his native region of Mississippi. He later married his childhood sweetheart, Estelle Oldham, and continued to create great works like *Light in August* (1932), *Absalom, Absalom!* (1936), *The Hamlet* (1940) and *Go Down, Moses* (1942). He also wrote for Hollywood to earn money for his family. In 1946, Malcolm Cowley published *The Portable Faulkner* and interest in Faulkner's works was revived.

Faulkner's writing was characterized by its stream-of-consciousness narrative style, use of multiple narrators, and exploration of themes related to Southern history and culture, including slavery, segregation, and the Civil War. He was awarded the Nobel Prize in Literature in 1949 for his contribution to "the art of the novel".

Later he also got the awards like National Book Awards for Fiction and Pulitzer Prize. On July 6, 1962, Faulkner died of a heart attack. He was posthumously awarded his second Pulitzer in 1963. By the time of his death, Faulkner had clearly emerged not just as a major American novelist of his generation but as one of the greatest writers of the 20th century. He remains influential not only in the United States, but also throughout the world.

2. Introduction of *The Bear*

William Faulkner's short story *The Bear* was first published on the May 9, 1942. Set in the late 19th century, the story is a have hunting told from the perspective of Isaac ("Ike") McCaslin, a young man from an old family in Yoknapatawpha county.

Set in Faulkner's fictional Yoknapatawpha County, *The Bear* follows the hunting expeditions of a group of men, led by the hunter and woodsman, Ike McCaslin. As the story progresses, the group becomes obsessed with hunting down a legendary bear known as Old Ben, which has eluded them for years.

Through the hunt for the bear, Faulkner explores themes related to man's relationship with nature, the complexities of race and class in the American South, and the search for identity and meaning in a changing world. The story is also notable for its experimental use of narrative techniques, which includes multiple narrators, flashbacks, and stream-of-consciousness writing.

The story explores themes of man's relationship with nature, the role of hunting in the human experience, and the ways in which our connection to the natural world shapes our identity and sense of self. The story has also been adapted into various forms, including stage plays and films.

3. Reading Material: *The Bear*

He was ten. But it had already begun, long before that day when at last he wrote his age in two figures and he saw for the first time the camp where his father and Major de Spain and old General Compson and the others spent two weeks each November and two weeks again each June. He had already inherited then, without ever having seen it, the tremendous bear with one trap-ruined foot which, in an area almost a hundred miles deep, had earned itself a name, a definite designation like a living man.

He had listened to it for years: the long legend of corncribs rifled, of shotes and grown pigs and even calves carried bodily into the woods and devoured, of traps and deadfalls overthrown and dogs mangled and slain, and shotgun and even rifle charges delivered at point-blank range and with no more effect than so many peas blown through a tube by a boy — a corridor of wreckage and destruction beginning back before he was born, through which sped, not fast but rather with the ruthless and irresistible deliberation of a locomotive, the shaggy tremendous shape.

It ran in his knowledge before he ever saw it. It looked and towered in his dreams before he even saw the unaxed woods where it left its crooked print, shaggy, huge, red-eyed, not malevolent but just big — too big for the dogs which tried to bay it, for the horses which tried to ride it down, for the men and the bullets they fired into it, too big for the very country which was its constricting scope. He seemed to see it entire with a child's complete divination before he ever laid eyes on either — the doomed wilderness whose edges were being constantly and punily gnawed at by men with axes and plows who feared it because it was wilderness, men myriad and nameless even to one another in the land where the old bear had earned a name, through which ran not even a mortal animal but an anachronism, indomitable and invincible, out of an old dead time, a phantom, epitome and apotheosis of the old wild life at which the puny humans swarmed and hacked in a fury of abhorrence and fear, like pygmies about the ankles of a drowsing elephant: the old bear solitary, indomitable and alone, widowered, childless, and absolved of mortality — old Priam reft of his old wife and having outlived all his sons.

Until he was ten, each November he would watch the wagon containing the dogs and the bedding and food and guns and his father and Tennie's Jim, the Negro, and Sam Fathers, the Indian, son of a slave woman and a Chickasaw chief, depart on the road to town, to Jefferson, where Major de Spain and the others would join them. To the boy, at seven, eight, and nine, they were not going into the Big Bottom to hunt bear and deer, but to keep yearly rendezvous with the bear which they did not even intend to kill. Two weeks later they would return, with no trophy, no head and skin. He had not expected it. He had not even been afraid it would be in the wagon. He believed that even after he was ten and his father would let him go too, for those two weeks in November, he would merely make another one, along with his father and Major de Spain and General Compson and the others, the dogs which feared to bay at it and the rifles and shotguns which failed even to bleed it, in the yearly pageant of the old bear's furious immortality.

Then he heard the dogs. It was in the second week of his first time in the camp. He stood with Sam Fathers against a big oak beside the faint crossing where they had stood each dawn for nine days now, hearing the dogs. He had heard them once before, one morning last week — a murmur, sourceless, echoing through the wet woods, swelling presently into separate voices which he could recognize and call by name. He had raised and cocked his gun as Sam told him and stood motionless again while the uproar, the invisible course, swept up and past and faded; it seemed to him that he could actually see the deer, the buck, blond, smoke-colored, elongated with speed, fleeing, vanishing, the woods, the gray solitude, still ringing even when the cries of the dogs had died away.

"Now let the hammers down," Sam said.

"You knew they were not coming here too," he said.

"Yes," Sam said. "I want you to learn how to do when you didn't shoot. It's after the chance for the bear or the deer has done already come and gone that men and dogs get killed."

"Anyway," he said, "it was just a deer."

Then on the tenth morning he heard the dogs again. And he readied the too-long, too-heavy gun as Sam had taught him, before Sam even spoke. But this time it was no deer, no ringing chorus of dogs running strong on a free scent, but a moiling yapping an octave too high, with something more than indecision and even abjectness in it, not even moving very fast, taking a long time to pass completely out of hearing, leaving then somewhere in the air that echo, thin, slightly hysterical, abject, almost grieving, with no sense of a fleeing, unseen, smoke-colored, grass-eating shape ahead of it, and Sam, who had taught him first of all to cock the gun and take position where he could see everywhere and then never move again, had himself moved up beside him; he could hear Sam breathing at his shoulder, and he could see the arched curve of the old man's inhaling nostrils.

"Hah," Sam said. "Not even running. Walking."

"Old Ben!" the boy said. "But up here!" he cried. "Way up here!"

"He does it every year," Sam said. "Once. Maybe to see who in camp this time, if he can shoot or not. Whether we got the dog yet that can bay and hold him. He'll take them to the river, then he'll send them back home. We may as well go back too; see how they look when they come back to camp."

When they reached the camp the hounds were already there, ten of them crouching back under the kitchen, the boy and Sam squatting to peer back into the obscurity where they had huddled, quiet, the eyes luminous, glowing at them and vanishing, and no sound, only that effluvium of something more than dog, stronger than dog and not just animal, just beast, because still there had been nothing in front of that abject and almost painful yapping save the solitude, the wilderness, so that when the eleventh hound came in at noon and with all the others watching — even Old Uncle Ash, who called himself first a cook — Sam daubed the tattered ear and the raked shoulder with turpentine and axle grease, to the boy, it was still no living creature, but the wilderness which, leaning for the moment down, had patted lightly once the hound's temerity.

"Just like a man," Sam said. "Just like folks. Put off as long as she could have to be brave, knowing all the time that sooner or later she would have to be brave to keep on living with herself, and knowing all the time beforehand what was going to happen to her when she done it."

That afternoon, himself on the one-eyed wagon mule which did not mind the smell of blood nor, as they told him, of bear, and with Sam on the other one, they rode for more than three hours through the rapid, shortening winter day. They followed no path, no trail even that he could see; almost at once they were in a country which he had never seen before. Then he knew why Sam had made him ride the mule which would not spook. The sound one stopped short and tried to whirl and bolt even as Sam got down, blowing its breath, jerking and wrenching at the rein, while Sam held it, coaxing it forward with his voice, since he could not risk tying it, drawing it forward while the boy got down from the marred one.

Then, standing beside Sam in the gloom of the dying afternoon, he looked down at the rotted overturned log, gutted and scored with claw marks and, in the wet earth beside it, the print of the enormous warped two-toed foot. He knew now what he had smelled when he peered under the kitchen where the dogs huddled. He realized for the first time that the bear which had run in his listening and loomed in his dreams since before he could remember to the contrary, and which, therefore, must have existed in the listening and dreams of his father and Major de Spain and even old General Compson, too, before they began to remember in their turn, was a mortal animal, and that if they had departed for the camp each November without any actual hope of bringing its trophy back, it was not because it could not be slain, but because so far they had had no actual hope to.

"Tomorrow," he said.

"We'll try tomorrow," Sam said. "We aunt got the dog yet."

"We've got eleven. They ran him this morning."

"It won't need but one," Sam said. "He ain't here. Maybe he ain't nowhere. The only other way will be for him to run by accident over somebody that has a gun."

"That wouldn't be me," the boy said. "It will be Walter or Major or..."

"It might," Sam said. "You watch close in the morning, because he's smart. That's how come he has lived this long. If he gets hemmed up and has to pick out somebody to run over, he will pick out you."

"How?" the boy said. "How will he know..." He ceased. "You mean he already knows me, that I ain't never been here before, ain't had time to find out yet whether I... "He ceased again, looking at Sam, the old man whose face revealed nothing until it smiled. He said humbly, not even amazed, "It was me he was watching. I don't reckon he did need to come but once."

The next morning, they left the camp three hours before daylight. They rode this time because it was too far to walk, even the dogs in the wagon; again, the first gray light found him in a place which he had never seen before, where Sam had placed him and told him to stay and then departed. With the gun which was too big for him, which did not even belong to him, but to Major de Spain, and which he had fired only once — at a stump on the first day, to learn the recoil and how to reload it — he stood against a gum tree beside a little bayou whose black still water crept without movement out of a canebrake and crossed a small clearing and into cane again, where invisible, a bird — the big woodpecker called Lord-to-God by Negroes — clattered at a dead limb.

It was a stand like any other, dissimilar only in incidentals to the one where he had stood each morning for ten days; a territory new to him, yet no less familiar than that other one which, after almost two weeks, he had come to believe he knew a little — the same solitude, the same loneliness through which human beings had merely passed without altering it, leaving no mark, no scar, which looked exactly as it must have looked when the first ancestor of Sam Fathers' Chickasaw predecessors crept into it and looked about, club or stone ax or bone arrow drawn and poised; different only because, squatting at the edge of the kitchen, he smelled the hounds huddled and cringing beneath it and saw the raked ear and shoulder of the one who, Sam said, had had to be brave in order to live with herself, and saw yesterday in the earth beside the gutted log the print of the living foot.

He heard no dogs at all. He never did hear them. He heard only the drumming of the woodpecker stop short off and knew that the bear was looking at him. He never saw it. He did not know whether it was in front of him or behind him. He did not move, holding the useless gun, which he had not even had warning to cock and which even now he did not cock, tasting in his saliva that taint as of brass which he knew now because he had smelled it when he peered under the kitchen at the huddled dogs.

Then it was gone. As abruptly as it had ceased, the woodpecker's dry, monotonous clatter set up again, and after a while he even believed he could hear the dogs — a murmur, scarce a sound even, which he had probably been hearing for some time before he ever remarked it, drifting into hearing and then out again, dying away. They came nowhere near him. If it was a bear they ran, it was another bear. It was Sam himself who came out of the cane and crossed the bayou, followed by the injured bitch of yesterday. She was almost at heel, like a bird dog, making no sound. She came and crouched against his leg, trembling, staring off into the cane.

"I didn't see him," he said. "I didn't, Sam!"

"I know it," Sam said. "He done the looking. You didn't hear him neither, did you?"

"No," the boy said. "I..."

"He's smart," Sam said. "Too smart." He looked down at the hound, trembling faintly and steadily against the boy's knee. From the raked shoulder a few drops of fresh blood oozed and clung. "Too big. We ain't got the dog yet. But maybe someday. Maybe not next time. But someday."

So, I must see him, he thought. *I must look at him*. Otherwise, it seemed to him that it would go on like this forever, as it had gone on with his father and Major de Spain, who was older than his father, and even with old General Compson, who had been old enough to be a brigade commander in 1865. Otherwise, it would go on so forever, next time and next time, after and after and after. It seemed to him that he could never see the two of them, himself and the bear, shadowy in the limbo from which time emerged, becoming time; the old bear absolved of mortality and himself partaking, sharing a little of it, enough of it. And he knew now what he had smelled in the huddled dogs and tasted in his saliva. He recognized fear. *So, I will have to see him*, he thought, without dread or even hope. *I will have to look at him*.

It was in June of the next year. He was eleven. They were in camp again, celebrating Major de Spain's and General Copson's birthdays. Although the one had been born in September and the other in the depth of winter and in another decade, they had met for two weeks to fish and shoot squirrels and turkeys and run coons and wildcats with the dogs at night. That is, he and Boon Hoggenback and the Negroes fished and shot squirrels and ran the coons and cats, because the proved hunters, not only Major de Spain and old General Compson, who spent those two weeks sitting in a rocking chair before a tremendous iron pot of Brunswick stew, stirring and tasting, with old Ash to quarrel with about how he was making it and Tennie's Jim to pour whiskey from the demijohn into the tin dipper from which he drank it, but even the boy's father and Walter Ewell, who were still young enough, scorned such, other than shooting the wild gobblers with pistols for wagers on their marksmanship.

Or, that is, his father and the others believed he was hunting squirrels. Until the third day, he thought that Sam Fathers believed that too. Each morning he would leave the camp right after breakfast. He had his own gun now, a Christmas present. He went back to the tree beside the bayou where he had stood that morning. Using the compass which old General Compson had given him, he ranged from that point; he was teaching himself to be a better-than-fair woodsman without knowing he was doing it. On the second day he even found the gutted log where he had first seen the crooked print. It was almost completely crumbled now, healing with unbelievable speed, a passionate and almost visible relinquishment, back into the earth from which the tree had grown.

He ranged the summer woods now, green with gloom; if anything, actually dimmer than in November's gray dissolution, where, even at noon, the sun fell only in intermittent dappling upon the earth, which never completely dried out and which crawled with snakes — moccasins and water snakes and rattlers, themselves the color of the dappling gloom, so that he would not always see them until they moved, returning later and later, first day, second day, passing in the twilight of the third evening the little log pen enclosing the log stable where Sam was putting up the horses for the night.

"You ain't looked right yet," Sam said.

He stopped. For a moment he didn't answer. Then he said peacefully, in a peaceful rushing burst as when a boy's miniature dam in a little brook gives way, "All right. But how? I went to the bayou. I even found that log again. I..."

"I reckon that was all right. Likely he's been watching you. You never saw his foot?"

"I," the boy said... "I didn't... I never thought..."

"It's the gun," Sam said. He stood beside the fence motionless — the old man, the Indian, in the battered faded overalls and the five-cent straw hat which in the Negro's race had been the badge of his enslavement and was now the regalia of his freedom. The camp — the clearing, the house, the barn and its tiny lot with which Major de Spain in his turn had scratched punily and evanescently at the wilderness — faded in the dusk, back into the immemorial darkness of the woods. *The gun*, the boy thought. *The gun*.

"Be scared," Sam said. "You can't help that. But don't be afraid. Ain't nothing in the woods going to hurt you unless you corner it, or it smells that you are afraid. A bear or a deer, too, has got to be scared of a coward the same as a brave man has got to be."

The gun, the boy thought.

"You will have to choose," Sam said.

He left the camp before daylight, long before Uncle Ash would wake in his quilts on the kitchen floor and start the fire for breakfast. He had only the compass and a stick for snakes. He could go almost a mile before he would begin to need the compass. He says on a log, the invisible compass in his invisible hand, while the secret night sounds, fallen still at his movements, scurried again and then ceased for good, and the owls ceased and gave over to the waking of day birds, and he could see the compass. Then he went fast yet still quietly; he was becoming better and better as a woodsman, still without having yet realized it.

He jumped a doe and a fawn at sunrise, walked them out of the bed, close enough to see them — the crash of undergrowth, the white scut, the fawn scudding behind her faster than he had believed it could run. He was hunting right, upwind, as Sam had taught him; not that it mattered now. He had left the gun; of his own will and relinquishment he had accepted not a gambit, not a choice, but a condition in which not only the bear's heretofore inviolable anonymity but all the old rules and balances of hunter and hunted had been abrogated. He would not even be afraid, not even in the moment when the fear would take him completely — blood, skin, bowels, bones, memory from the long time before it became his memory — all save that thin, clear, immortal lucidity which alone differed him from this bear and from all other bear and deer he would ever kill in the humility and pride of his skill and endurance, to which Sam had spoken when he leaned in the twilight on the lot fence yesterday.

By noon he was far beyond the little bayou, farther into the new and alien country than he had ever been. He was traveling now not only by the old, heavy, biscuit-thick silver watch which had belonged to his grandfather. When he stopped at last, it was for the first time since he had risen from the log at dawn when he could see the compass. It was far enough. He had left the camp nine hours ago; nine hours from now, dark would have already been an hour old. But he didn't think that. He thought, *all right. Yes. But what?* and stood for a moment, alien and small in the green and topless solitude, answering his own question before it had formed and ceased. It was the watch, the compass, the stick — the three lifeless mechanicals with which for nine hours he had fended the wilderness off; he hung the watch and compass carefully on a bush and leaned the stick beside them and relinquished completely to it.

He had not been going very fast for the last two or three hours. He went no faster now, since distance would not matter even if he could have gone fast. And he was trying to keep a bearing on the tree where he had left the compass, trying to complete a circle which would bring him back to it or at least intersect itself, since direction would not matter now either. But the tree was not there, and he did as Sam had schooled him — made the next circle in the opposite direction, so that the two patterns would bisect somewhere, but crossing no print of his own feet, finding the tree at last, but in the wrong place — no bush, no compass, no watch — and the tree not even the tree, because there was a down log beside it and he did what Sam Fathers had told him was the next thing and the last.

As he sat down on the log he saw the crooked print — the warped, tremendous, two-toed indentation which, even as he watched it, filled with water. As he looked up, the wilderness coalesced, solidified — the glade, the tree he sought, the bush, the watch and the compass glinting where a ray of sunshine touched them. Then he saw the bear. It did not emerge, appear; it was just there, immobile, solid, fixed in the hot dappling of the green and windless noon, not as big as he had dreamed it, but as big as he had expected it, bigger, dimensionless, against the dappled obscurity, looking at him where he sat quietly on the log and looked back at it.

Then it moved. It made no sound. It did not hurry. It crossed the glade, walking for an instant into the full glare of the sun; when it reached the other side, it stopped again and looked back at him across one shoulder while his quiet breathing inhaled and exhaled three times.

Then it was gone. It didn't walk into the woods, the undergrowth. It faded, sank back into the wilderness as he had watched a fish, a huge old bass, sink and vanish into the dark depths of its pool without even any movement of its fins.

He thought, *it will be next fall.* But it was not next fall, nor the next nor the next. He was fourteen then. He had killed his buck, and Sam Fathers had marked his face with the hot blood, and in the next year he killed a bear. But even before that accolade he had become as competent in the woods as many grown men with the same experience; by his fourteenth year he was a better woodsman than most grown men with more. There was no territory within thirty miles of the camp that he did not know — bayou, ridge, brake, landmark, tree and path. He could have led anyone to any point in it without deviation, and brought them out again. He knew the game trails that even Sam Fathers did not know; in his thirteenth year he found a buck's bedding place, and unbeknown to his father he borrowed Walter Ewell's rifle and lay in wait at dawn and killed the buck when it walked back to the bed, as Sam had told him how the old Chickasaw fathers did.

But not the old bear, although by now he knew its footprints better than he did his own, and not only the crooked one. He could see any one of the three sound ones and distinguish it from any other, and not only by its size. There were other bears within these thirty miles which left tracks almost as large, but this was more than that. If Sam Fathers had been his mentor and the backyard rabbits and squirrels at his home his kindergarten, then the wilderness the old bear ran was his college, the old male bear itself, so long unwifed and childless as to have become its own ungendered progenitor, was his alma mater. But he never saw it.

He could find the crooked print now almost whenever he liked, fifteen or ten or five miles, or sometimes nearer the camp than that. Twice while on stand during the three years he heard the dogs strike its trail by accident; on the second time they jumped it seemingly, the voices high, abject, almost human in hysteria, as on that first morning two years ago. But not the bear itself. He would remember that noon three years ago, the glade, himself and the bear fixed during that moment in the windless and dappled blaze, and it would seem to him that it had never happened, that he had dreamed that too. But it had happened. They had looked at each other, they had emerged from the wilderness old as earth, synchronized to the instant by something more than the blood that that moved the flesh and bones which bore them, and touched, pledged something, affirmed something more lasting than the frail web of bones and flesh which any accident could obliterate.

Then he saw it again. Because of the very fact that he thought of nothing else, he had forgotten to look for it. He was still hunting with Walter Ewell's rifle. He saw it cross the end of a long blow-down, a corridor where a tornado had swept, rushing through rather than over the tangle of trunks and branches as a locomotive would have, faster than he had ever believed it could move, almost as fast as a deer even, because a deer would have spent most of that time in the air, faster than he could bring the rifle sights up with it. And now he knew what had been wrong during all the three years. He sat on a log, shaking and trembling as if he had never seen the woods before nor anything that ran them, wondering with incredulous amazement how he could have forgotten the very thing which Sam Fathers had told him and which the bear itself had proved the next day and had now returned after three years to reaffirm.

And now he knew what Sam Fathers had meant about the right dog, a dog in which size would mean less than nothing. So, when he returned alone in April — school was out then, so that the sons of farmers could help with the land's planting, and at last his father had granted him permission, on his promise to be back in four days — he had the dog. It was his own, a mongrel of the sort called by Negroes a fyce, a ratter, itself not much bigger than a rat and possessing that bravery which had long since stopped being courage and had become foolhardiness.

It did not take four days. Alone again, he found the trail on the first morning. It was not a stalk; it was an ambush. He timed the meeting almost as if it were an appointment with a human being. Himself holding the fyce muffled in a feed sack and Sam Fathers with two of the hounds on a piece of plowing rope, they lay down wind of the trail at dawn of the second morning. They were so close that the bear turned without even running, as if in surprised amazement at the shrill and frantic uproar of the released fyce, turning at bay against the trunk of a tree, on its hind feet; it seemed to the boy that it would never stop rising, taller and taller, and even the two hounds seemed to take a desperate and despairing courage from the fyce, following it as it went in.

Then he realized that the fyce was actually not going to stop. He flung, threw the gun away, and ran; when he overtook and grasped the frantically pin-wheeling little dog, it seemed to him that he was directly under the bear.

He could smell it, strong and hot and rank. Sprawling, he looked up to where it loomed and towered over him like a cloudburst and colored like a thunderclap, quite familiar, peacefully and even lucidly familiar, until he remembered: this was the way he had used to dream about it. Then it was gone. He didn't see it go. He knelt, holding the frantic fyce with both hands, hearing the abashed wailing of the hounds drawing farther and farther away, until Sam came up. He carried the gun. He laid it down quietly beside the boy and stood looking down at him.

"You've done seed him twice now with a gun in your hands," he said. "This time you couldn't have missed him."

The boy rose. He still held the fyce. Even in his arms and clear of the ground, it yapped frantically, straining and surging after the fading uproar of the two hounds like a tangle of wire springs. He was panting a little, but he was neither shaking nor trembling now. "Neither could you!" he said. "You had the gun! Neither did you!"

"And you didn't shoot," his father said. "How close were you?"

"I don't know, sir," he said. "There was a big wood tick inside his right hind leg. I saw that. But I didn't have the gun then."

"But you didn't shoot when you had the gun," his father said. "Why?"

But he didn't answer, and his father didn't wait for him, rising and crossing the room, across the pelt of the bear which the boy had killed two years ago and the larger one which his father had killed before he was born, to the bookcase beneath the mounted head of the boy's first buck. It was the room which his father called the office, from which all the plantation business was transacted; in it for the fourteen years of his life he had heard the best of all talking. Major de Spain would be there and sometimes old General Compson, and Walter Ewell and Boon Hoggenback and Sam Fathers and Tennie's Jim, too, were hunters, knew the woods and what ran them.

He would hear it, not talking himself, but listening — the wilderness, the big woods, bigger and older than any recorded document of white man fatuous enough to believe he had bought any fragment of it or Indian ruthless enough to pretend that any fragment of it had been his to convey. It was of the men, not white nor black nor red, but men, hunters with the will and hardihood to endure and the humility and skill to survive, and the dogs and the bear and deer juxtaposed and relieved against it, ordered and compelled by and within the wilderness in the ancient and unremitting contest by the ancient and immitigable rules which voided all regrets and brooked no quarter, the voices quiet and weighty and deliberate for retrospection and recollection and exact remembering, while he squatted in the blazing firelight as Tennie's Jim squatted, who stirred only to put more wood on the fire and to pass the bottle from one glass to another. Because the bottle was always present, so that after a while it seemed to him that those fierce instants of heart and brain and courage and wiliness and speed were concentrated and distilled into that brown liquor which not women, not boys and children, but only hunters drank, drinking not of the blood they had spilled but some condensation of the wild immortal spirit, drinking it moderately, humbly even, not with the pagan's base hope of acquiring the virtues of cunning and strength and speed, but in salute to them.

His father returned with the book and sat down again and opened it. "Listen," he said. He read the five stanzas aloud, his voice quiet and deliberate in the room where there was no fire now because it was already spring. Then he looked up. The boy watched him. "All right," his father said. "Listen." He read again, but only the second stanza this time, to the end of it, the last two lines, and closed the book and put it on the table beside him. "She cannot fade, though thou hast not thy bliss, forever wilt thou love, and she be fair," he said.

"He's talking about a girl," the boy said.

"He had to talk about something," his father said. Then he said, "He was talking about truth. Truth doesn't change. Truth is one thing. It covers all things which touch the heart — honor and pride and pity and justice and courage and love. Do you see now?"

He didn't know. Somehow it was simpler than that. There was an old bear, fierce and ruthless, not merely just to stay alive, but with the fierce pride of liberty and freedom, proud enough of the liberty and freedom to see it threatened without fear or even alarm; nay, who at times even seemed deliberately to put that freedom and liberty in jeopardy in order to savor them, to remind his old strong bones and flesh to keep supple and quick to defend and preserve them. There was an old man, son of a Negro slave and an Indian king, inheritor on the one side of the long chronicle of a people who had learned humility through suffering, and pride through the endurance which survived the suffering and injustice, and on the other side, the chronicle of a people even longer in the land than the first, yet who no longer existed in the land at all save in the solitary brotherhood of an old Negros 'alien blood and the wild and invincible spirit of an old bear. There was a boy who wished to learn humility and pride in order to become skillful and worthy in the woods, who suddenly found himself becoming so skillful so rapidly that he feared he would ever become worthy because he had not learned humility and pride, although he had tried to, until one day and as suddenly he discovered that an old man who could not have defined either had led him, as though by the hand, to that point where an old bear and a little mongrel of a dog showed him that, by possessing one thing other, he would possess them both.

And a little dog, nameless and mongrel and many-fathered, grown, yet weighing less than six pounds, saying as if to itself, "I can't be dangerous, because there's nothing much smaller than I am; I can't be fierce, because they would call it just a noise; I can't be humble, because I'm already too close to the ground to genuflect; I can't be proud, because I wouldn't be near enough to it for anyone to know who was casting the shadow, and I don't even know that I'm not going to heaven, because they have already decided that I don't possess an immortal soul. So, all I can be is brave. But it's all right. I can be that, even if they still call it just noise."

That was all. It was simple, much simpler than somebody talking in a book about youth and a girl he would never need to grieve over, because he could never approach any nearer her and would never have to get any farther away. He had heard about a bear, and finally got big enough to trail it, and he trailed it four years and at last met it with a gun in his hands and he didn't shoot. Because a little dog — but he could have shot long before the little dog covered the twenty yards to where the bear waited, and Sam Fathers could have shot at any time during that interminable minute while Old Ben stood on his hind feet over them. He stopped. His father was watching him gravely across the spring-rife twilight of the room; when he spoke, his words were as quiet as the twilight, too, not loud, because they did not need to be because they would last. "Courage, and honor, and pride," his father said, "and pity, and love of justice and of liberty. They all touch the heart, and what the heart holds to becomes truth, as far as we know the truth. Do you see now?"

Sam, and Old Ben, and Nip, he thought. And himself too. He had been all right too. His father had said so. "Yes, sir," he said.

4. Questions for Discussion

(1) How do you explain the relationship between man and nature in William Faulkner's *The Bear*?

(2) How does the character of Ike McCaslin's relationship to the woods and his experiences in nature shape his sense of identity and his understanding of the world around him?

(3) In what ways does the story challenge traditional notions of human dominion over the natural world, and what implications does this have for our understanding of environmental ethics?

(4) How does Faulkner's use of narrative technique, including multiple narrators and stream-of-consciousness writing, contribute to the story's exploration of human-nature relationships?

Chapter 10 Illness and Plague

Plague is a term referring to a deadly infectious disease more commonly in the distant past and in episodes described in the Bible. Today we are more likely to use the words like "epidemic" or "pandemic" for disease outbreaks just like Covid-19. Plague has been a recurring theme in American literature, with writers using it as a lens through which to explore a range of themes related to human nature, society, and the natural world. Literature and medicine have a close relationship with each other. "Just as ancient Greek religion united the principles of medicine and literature in Apollo, who was the god of both the healing arts and poetry, ancient Greek philosophy linked medicine and the verbal arts" (Tobbin 180). The history of American literature is filled with works that grapple with the experience of plagues, epidemics, and pandemics, from the colonial-era accounts of smallpox and yellow fever, to the contemporary works that address the COVID-19 pandemic.

According to the Bible, plague is God's punishment for human's sins. Between 1348 and the early years of the 18th century, successive waves of the plague rolled across Europe, killing millions of people and affecting every aspect of life. The most famous one is Black Death which ravaged Europe between 1347 and 1351, killing almost half of the European population.

One of the most notable works of American literature that deals with the theme of plague is *The Plague* by Albert Camus. Although Camus was a French writer, his novel has been widely read and discussed in American literary circles. *The Plague* explores the experience of a small town in Algeria that is struck by a deadly epidemic, and the ways in which the townspeople react to the crisis. The novel examines questions of morality, heroism, and the nature of human suffering, and has been interpreted as a commentary on the rise of fascism in Europe in the years leading up to World War II.

Another important novel is Daniel Defoe's *A Journal of the Plague Year*. Published in 1722, *A Journal of the Plague Year* described the tragic scene of London after the city was ravaged by the outbreak of bubonic plague. The novel is based on the true story of the Great Plague of London in 1665, which killed an estimated 75,000 people in just a few months. Defoe himself was only five years old at the time of the outbreak, but he drew on first-hand accounts and other sources to create a vivid and detailed portrayal of the epidemic. The novel is structured as a fictional journal, supposedly written by an eyewitness to the events of the plague year. The narrator describes the outbreak of the disease, the desperate efforts of authorities to control it, and the terrible suffering of the people of London. He also explores the social and psychological impact of the epidemic, examining the breakdown of social order, the rise of superstition and religious fanaticism, and the ways in which individuals and communities responded to the crisis.

Other notable works of American literature that deal with the theme of plague include Katherine Anne Porter's "*Pale Horse, Pale Rider*," which explores the 1918 influenza pandemic; Cormac McCarthy's *The Road*, which imagines a post-apocalyptic world in which a deadly plague has wiped out most of humanity; what's more, there are also some novels which focus on the experience of patients of TB (Tuberculosis). Famous ones include Thomas Mann's *The Magic Mountain* and *The Jungle* by Upton Sinclair, etc. These novels about disease and plague have greatly enriched the subject matter and content of American literature and brought us to a different side of life.

In the following sections, from the perspective of plague writing, Edgar Allan Poe's *The Masque of the Red Death* and Jack London's *The Scarlet Plague* will be introduced. Hopefully, through such reading, readers can find more resonance in today's post-COVID-19 era and have a deeper understanding of plague literature.

Section One: Edgar Allan Poe and *The Masque of the Red Death*

Edgar Allan Poe (1809 — 1849) was an American writer of Romanticism, a poet, editor, and literary critic. He is best known for his poetry and short stories, particularly for his gothic tales. He is also regarded as one of the pioneers of American detective story. *The Masque of the Red Death* was a story first published in 1842 and remains to be one of the classical short stories of him.

1. Introduction of Edgar Allan Poe

Born in a poor family, Allan Poe was the son of the English-born actress Elizabeth Arnold Poe and David Poe, Jr., an actor from Baltimore. After his parents died, he was adopted by John Allan, a Richmond merchant. He received a formal education and later went to University of Virginia. But he was expelled from the university because of poor academic performance and later his foster father helped him find a position in the US Military Academy at West Point. But he was expelled again because he refused to join the military drills. During that time, he continued to write poems and later worked as an editor for *The Southern Literary Messenger*. Poe had a talent for writing and published essays, poems, and stories in several periodicals. But his private life was dominated by poverty, unrest and a hang to gambling and alcohol. He secretly married his young cousin Virginia Clemm, who was only 13, but the marriage didn't last long. His wife some years later died of tuberculosis.

Edgar Allan Poe introduced the mystery plot and the horror story to American literature. The readers still love his thrilling and mystic narratives where strange and disturbing things happen. He was both logic and morbid with his stories full of death and tragic characters. Edgar Allan Poe remains a pioneer in today's crime literature and horror movies, and he is still among the most popular American authors.

2. Introduction of *The Masque of the Red Death*

The Masque of the Red Death is about a mysterious disease or plague which kills the sufferer within half an hour, causing pain, sudden dizziness, and profuse bleeding. In the story the disease is called the Red Death. The disease might be inspired by tuberculosis since Poe's wife Virginia was suffering from the disease at the time the story was written. In the story, the prince and his noble friends are described as a group of folly who think they can escape death by such physical barriers as high walls and iron gates. But they are actually struggling in vain to escape from the disease. Amid this plague the prince of the land, Prospero, holds a masquerade ball for his courtiers in a secluded abbey. The Red Death attends the party, bringing doom for all the people present. The story is not a realistic one with no real characters and places but its atmosphere of strangeness, bizarre situation, and evocative style all combine to make it a Poe's most effective story which is taken as an allegory for the inevitability of death of modern people.

Actually, Poe was familiar with pandemics in his times. Cholera and yellow fever killed tens of thousands across America in the 1830s and 1940s, particularly among poorer communities. It is said that Poe even caught cholera himself in 1849 and expected to die. Cholera spread through contaminated food, water and sewage, causing intense diarrhea, vomiting and muscle spasms. Sometimes death would follow within hours. These symptoms are quite similar to those Poe described in his short story. Therefore, there's a clear influence between the pandemics Poe lived through and the plague of his 1942 short story. Unfortunately, before the advances of 20th century medicine, when people had no antibiotics and little knowledge about how diseases spread, an outbreak of disease could be a terror which caused the tragedy for Poe's characters. When reading the story, we should pay attention to the important symbols like the clock, the rooms and the plague and their symbolic meaning which will be helpful for us to understand the connotations of the story if we understand these symbols.

3. Reading Material: *The Masque of the Red Death*

The "Red Death" had long devastated the country. No pestilence had ever been so fatal, or so hideous. Blood was its Avatar and its seal — the redness and the horror of blood. There were sharp pains, and sudden dizziness, and then profuse bleeding at the pores, with dissolution. The scarlet stains upon the body and especially upon the face of the victim, were the pest ban which shut him out from the aid and from the sympathy of his fellow-men. And the whole seizure, progress and termination of the disease, were the incidents of half an hour.

But the Prince Prospero was happy and dauntless and sagacious. When his dominions were half depopulated, he summoned to his presence a thousand hale and light-hearted friends from among the knights and dames of his court, and with these retired to the deep seclusion of one of his castellated abbeys. This was an extensive and magnificent structure, the creation of the prince's own eccentric yet august taste. A strong and lofty wall girdled it in. This wall had gates of iron. The courtiers, having entered, brought furnaces and massy hammers and welded the bolts. They resolved to leave means neither of ingress nor egress to the sudden impulses of despair from without or of frenzy from within. The abbey was amply provisioned. With such precautions the courtiers might bid defiance to contagion. The external world could take care of itself. In the meantime, it was folly to grieve, or to think. The prince had provided all the appliances of pleasure. There were buffoons, there were improvisatori, there were ballet-dancers, there were musicians, there was Beauty, there was wine. All these and security were within. Without was the "Red Death."

It was towards the close of the fifth or sixth month of his seclusion, and while the pestilence raged most furiously abroad, that the Prince Prospero entertained his thousand friends at a masked ball of the most unusual magnificence. It was a voluptuous scene, that masquerade.

But first let me tell of the rooms in which it was held. These were seven — an imperial suite. In many palaces, however, such suites form a long and straight vista, while the folding doors slide back nearly to the walls on either hand, so that the view of the whole extent is scarcely impeded. Here the case was very different; as might have been expected from the duke's love of the bizarre. The apartments were so irregularly disposed that the vision embraced but little more than one at a time. There was a sharp turn at every twenty or thirty yards, and at each turn a novel effect. To the right and left, in the middle of each wall, a tall and narrow Gothic window looked out upon a closed corridor which pursued the windings of the suite. These windows were of stained glass whose color varied in accordance with the prevailing hue of the decorations of the chamber into which it opened. That at the eastern extremity was hung, for example, in blue — and vividly blue were its windows. The second chamber was purple in its ornaments and tapestries, and here the panes were purple. The third was green throughout, and so were the casements. The fourth was furnished and lighted with orange — the fifth with white — the sixth with violet. The seventh apartment was closely shrouded in black velvet tapestries that hung all over the ceiling and down the walls, falling in heavy folds upon a carpet of the same material and hue. But in this chamber only, the color of the windows failed to correspond with the decorations. The panes here were scarlet — a deep blood color. Now in no one of the seven apartments was there any lamp or candelabrum, amid the profusion of golden ornaments that lay scattered to and fro or depended from the roof. There was no light of any kind emanating from lamp or candle within the suite of chambers. But in the corridors that followed the suite, there stood, opposite to each window, a heavy tripod, bearing a brazier of fire, that projected its rays through the tinted glass and so glaringly illumined the room. And thus were produced a multitude of gaudy and fantastic appearances. But in the western or black chamber the effect of the firelight that streamed upon the dark hangings through the blood-tinted panes, was ghastly in the extreme, and produced so wild a look upon the countenances of those who entered, that there were few of the company bold enough to set foot within its precincts at all.

It was in this apartment, also, that there stood against the western wall, a gigantic clock of ebony. Its pendulum swung to and fro with a dull, heavy, monotonous clang; and when the minute-hand made the circuit of the face, and the hour was to be stricken, there came from the brazen lungs of the clock a sound which was clear and loud and deep and exceedingly musical, but of so peculiar a note and emphasis that, at each lapse of an hour, the musicians of the orchestra were constrained to pause, momentarily, in their performance, to harken to the sound; and thus the waltzers perforce ceased their evolutions; and there was a brief disconcert of the whole gay company; and, while the chimes of the clock yet rang, it was observed that the giddiest turned pale, and the more aged and sedate passed their hands over their brows as if in confused reverie or meditation. But when the echoes had fully ceased, a light laughter at once pervaded the assembly; the musicians looked at each other and smiled as if at their own nervousness and folly, and made whispering vows, each to the other, that the next chiming of the clock should produce in them no similar emotion; and then, after the lapse of sixty minutes, (which embrace three thousand and six hundred seconds of the Time that flies,) there came yet another chiming of the clock, and then were the same disconcert and tremulousness and meditation as before.

But, in spite of these things, it was a gay and magnificent revel. The tastes of the duke were peculiar. He had a fine eye for colors and effects. He disregarded the decora of mere fashion. His plans were bold and fiery, and his conceptions glowed with barbaric luster. There are some who would have thought him mad. His followers felt that he was not. It was necessary to hear and see and touch him to be sure that he was not.

He had directed, in great part, the movable embellishments of the seven chambers, upon occasion of this great fête; and it was his own guiding taste which had given character to the masqueraders. Be sure they were grotesque. There were much glare and glitter and piquancy and phantasm — much of what has been since seen in "Hernani." There were arabesque figures with unsuited limbs and appointments. There were delirious fancies such as the madman fashions. There was much of the beautiful, much of the wanton, much of the bizarre, something of the terrible, and not a little of that which might have excited disgust. To and fro in the seven chambers there stalked, in fact, a multitude of dreams. And these — the dreams — writhed in and about, taking hue from the rooms, and causing the wild music of the orchestra to seem as the echo of their steps. And, anon, there strikes the ebony clock which stands in the hall of the velvet. And then, for a moment, all is still, and all is silent save the voice of the clock. The dreams are stiff-frozen as they stand. But the echoes of the chime die away — they have endured but an instant — and a light, half-subdued laughter floats after them as they depart. And now again the music swells, and the dreams live, and writhe to and fro more merrily than ever, taking hue from the many-tinted windows through which stream the rays from the tripods. But to the chamber which lies most westwardly of the seven, there are now none of the maskers who venture; for the night is waning away; and there flows a ruddier light through the blood-colored panes; and the blackness of the sable drapery appalls; and to him whose foot falls upon the sable carpet, there comes from the near clock of ebony a muffled peal more solemnly emphatic than any which reaches their ears who indulge in the more remote gaieties of the other apartments.

But these other apartments were densely crowded, and in them beat feverishly the heart of life. And the revel went whirlingly on, until at length there commenced the sounding of midnight upon the clock. And then the music ceased, as I have told; and the evolutions of the waltzes were quieted; and there was an uneasy cessation of all things as before. But now there were twelve strokes to be sounded by the bell of the clock; and thus, it happened, perhaps, that more of the thought crept, with more of time, into the meditations of the thoughtful among those who reveled. And thus, too, it happened, perhaps, that before the last echoes of the last chime had utterly sunk into silence, there were many individuals in the crowd who had found leisure to become aware of the presence of a masked figure which had arrested the attention of no single individual before. And the rumor of this new presence having spread itself whisperingly around, there arose at length from the whole company a buzz, or murmur, expressive of disapprobation and surprise — then, finally, of terror, or horror, and of disgust.

In an assembly of the phantasms such as I have painted, it may well be supposed that no ordinary appearance could have excited such sensation. In truth the masquerade license of the night was nearly unlimited; but the figure in question had out-Herolded Herod, and gone beyond the bounds of even the prince's indefinite decorum. There are chords in the hearts of the most reckless which cannot be touched without emotion. Even with the utterly lost, to whom life and death are equally jests, there are matters of which no jest can be made. The whole company, indeed, seemed now deeply to feel that in the costume and bearing of the stranger neither wit nor propriety existed. The figure was tall and gaunt, and shrouded from head to foot in the habiliments of the grave. The mask which concealed the visage was made so nearly to resemble the countenance of a stiffened corpse that the closest scrutiny must have had difficulty in detecting the cheat. And yet all this might have been endured, if not approved, by the mad revelers around. But the murmer had gone so far as to assume the type of Red Death. His vesture was dabbled in blood — and his broad brow, with all the features of the face, was besprinkled with the scarlet horror.

When the eyes of Prince Prospero fell upon this spectral image (which with a slow and solemn movement, as if more fully to sustain its role, stalked to and fro among the waltzers) he was seen to be convulsed, in the first moment with a strong shudder either of terror or distaste; but, in the next, his brow reddened with rage.

"Who dares?" he demanded hoarsely of the courtiers who stood near him, who dears insult us with this blasphemous mockery? Seize him and unmask him — that we may know whom we have to hang at sunrise, from the battlements!"

It was in the eastern or blue chamber in which stood the Prince Prospero as he uttered these words. They rang throughout the seven rooms loudly and clearly — for the prince was a bold and robust man, and the music had become hushed at the waving of his hand.

It was in the blue room where stood the prince, with a group of pale courtiers by his side. At first, as he spoke, there was a slight rushing movement of this group in the direction of the intruder, who at the moment was also near at hand, and now, with deliberate and stately step, made closer approach to the speaker. But from a certain nameless awe with which the mad assumptions of the mummer had inspired the whole party, there were found none who put forth hand to seize him; so that, unimpeded, he passed within a yard of the prince's person; and, while the vast assembly, as if with one impulse, shrank from the centers of the rooms to the walls, he made his way uninterruptedly, but with the same solemn and measured step which had distinguished him from the first, through the blue chamber to the purple — through the purple to the green — through the green to the orange — through this again to the white — and even thence to the violet, ere a decided movement had been made to arrest him. It was then, however, that the Prince Prospero, maddening with rage and the shame of his own momentary cowardice, rushed hurriedly through the six chambers while none followed him on account of a deadly terror that had seized upon all. He bore aloft a drawn dagger, and had approached, in rapid impetuosity, to within three or four feet of the retreating figure, when the latter, having attained the extremity of the velvet apartment turned suddenly and confronted his pursuer. There was a sharp cry — and the dagger dropped gleaming upon the sable carpet, upon which, instantly afterwards, fell prostrate in death Prince Prospero. Then, summoning the wild courage of despair, a throng of the revelers at once threw themselves into the black apartment, and seizing the mummer, whose tall figure stood erect and motionless within the shadow of the ebony clock, gasped in unutterable horror at finding the grave-cerements and corpse-like mask, which they handled with so violent a rudeness, untenanted by any tangible form.

And now was acknowledged the presence of the Red Death. He had come like a thief in the night. And one by one dropped the revelers in the blood-bedewed halls of their revel, and died each in the despairing posture of his fall. And the life of the ebony clock went out with that of the last of the gay. And the flames of the tripods expired. And Darkness and Decay and the Red Death held illimitable dominion over all.

4. Questions for Discussion

(1) What do the clock, the masked figure and the different rooms symbolize in *The Masque of the Red Death*?

(2) In what ways does Poe explore the theme of mortality in *The Masque of the Red Death*?

(3) What is the significance of the ending of the story?

Section Two: Jack London and *The Scarlet Plague*

Jack London was an American novelist, short-story writer, political essayist, adventurer, seaman, socialist, rancher, and war correspondent. He was a native Californian who achieved worldwide acclaim as a powerful storyteller, a legendary public figure, and one of the America's most commercially successful writers. *The Scarlet Plague*, originally published by Jack London in 1912, was one of the first examples of a post-apocalyptic fictional novel in modern literature. Jack London took his inspiration from the Bubonic Plague of the Middle Ages.

1. Introduction of Jack London

Jack London was born into a poor family in San Francisco, and his childhood was marked by poverty and hard work. He had little formal education but was a voracious reader and taught himself in many subjects. At age fourteen, London was forced to discontinue his education to work in a factory. At the age of seventeen, he sailed to Alaska to join the Klondike Gold Rush, where he endured extreme cold, hunger, and poverty. These experiences provided inspiration for many of his later works. At twenty, he joined the socialist party and, after intensive cramming, enrolled for a semester at the University of California. At twenty-two, suffering from scurvy, he returned to Oakland and launched his career as a professional writer. At twenty-three, he made his major breakthrough into the literary marketplace by publishing *An Odyssey of the North* in *the Atlantic Monthly* for $120 and a year's free subscription to the magazine. At twenty-four, he was hailed as the American Kipling with the publication of *The Son of the Wolf*, and married Bessie Mae Maddern, who became the mother of his two daughters, Joan (1901) and Becky (1902). At twenty-seven, he won worldwide acclaim as the author of *The Call of the Wild* and separated from Bessie after falling in love with Charmian Kittredge.

Jack married Charmian Kittredge in 1905, and the next decade proved to be a very productive one for the author. Being a prolific writer who reportedly wrote at least 1,000 words every day, London spent the next ten years writing well over 100 different novels, short stories, poems, and nonfiction works. He also spent this time lecturing in various venues on the evils of capitalism, having become an activist for socialism as a result of his own early socio-economic difficulties and the many impoverished people he met. His stories of high adventure were based on his own experiences at sea, and in the fields and factories of California. His writings appealed to millions worldwide. He touched upon a variety of subjects in his writing such as agronomy, alcoholism, animal and human psychology, animal training, architecture, etc.

Jack London died from kidney disease on November 22, 1916. Though only forty years old at the time of his death, London was regarded as an important American writer of his day, leaving us some beloved tales of adventure that reflect the truly bold life of their author.

2. Introduction of *The Scarlet Plague*

The novel is a dystopian science fiction novella that tells the story of a devastating epidemic that wipes out most of humanity in the year 2073. The story is set in San Francisco, where a man named James Howard Smith, also known as "Grandsir" recounts his experiences of the plague to his grandchildren. As one of the few survivors of the disease, Grandsir describes how civilization has crumbled, and people have regressed to a more primitive way of life.

Even though the novel was published more than a century ago, *The Scarlet Plague* feels contemporary because it allows modern readers to reflect on the worldwide fear of pandemics, such as Coronavirus, a fear that remains very much alive.

3. Reading Material: *The Scarlet Plague* (excerpt)

Ⅲ

The old man wiped the tears away on his grimy knuckles and took up the tale in a tremulous, piping voice that soon strengthened as he got the swing of the narrative.

"It was in the summer of 2013 that the Plague came. I was twenty-seven years old, and well do I remember it. Wireless dispatches..."

Hare-Lip spat loudly his disgust, and Granser hastened to make amends.

"We talked through the air in those days, thousands and thousands of miles. And the word came of a strange disease that had broken out in New York. There were seventeen million people living then in that noblest city of America. Nobody thought anything about the news. It was only a small thing. There had been only a few deaths. It seemed, though, that they had died very quickly, and that one of the first signs of the disease was the turning red of the face and all the body. Within twenty-four hours came the report of the first case in Chicago. And on the same day, it was made public that London, the greatest city in the world, next to Chicago, had been secretly fighting the plague for two weeks and censoring the news dispatches — that is, not permitting the word to go forth to the rest of the world that London had the plague.

"It looked serious, but we in California, like everywhere else, were not alarmed. We were sure that the bacteriologists would find a way to overcome this new germ, just as they had overcome other germs in the past. But the trouble was the astonishing quickness with which this germ destroyed human beings, and the fact that it inevitably killed any human body it entered. No one ever recovered. There was the old Asiatic cholera, when you might eat dinner with a well man in the evening, and the next morning, if you got up early enough, you would see him being hauled by your window in the death-cart. But this new plague was quicker than that — much quicker.

"From the moment of the first signs of it, a man would be dead in an hour. Some lasted for several hours. Many died within ten or fifteen minutes of the appearance of the first signs.

"The heart began to beat faster and the heat of the body to increase. Then came the scarlet rash, spreading like wildfire over the face and body. Most persons never noticed the increase in heat and heart-beat, and the first they knew was when the scarlet rash came out. Usually, they had convulsions at the time of the appearance of the rash. But these convulsions did not last long and were not very severe. If one lived through them, he became perfectly quiet, and only did he feel a numbness swiftly creeping up his body from the feet. The heels became numb first, then the legs, and hips, and when the numbness reached as high as his heart he died. They did not rave or sleep. Their minds always remained cool and calm up to the moment their heart numbed and stopped. And another strange thing was the rapidity of decomposition. No sooner was a person dead than the body seemed to fall to pieces, to fly apart, to melt away even as you looked at it. That was one of the reasons the plague spread so rapidly. All the billions of germs in a corpse were so immediately released.

"And it was because of all this that the bacteriologists had so little chance in fighting the germs. They were killed in their laboratories even as they studied the germ of the Scarlet Death. They were heroes. As fast as they perished, others stepped forth and took their places. It was in London that they first isolated it. The news was telegraphed everywhere. Trask was the name of the man who succeeded in this, but within thirty hours he was dead. Then came the struggle in all the laboratories to find something that would kill the plague germs. All drugs failed. You see, the problem was to get a drug, or serum, that would kill the germs in the body and not kill the body. They tried to fight it with other germs, to put into the body of a sick man germs that were the enemies of the plague germs —"

"And you can't see these germ-things, Granser," Hare-Lip objected, "and here you gabble, gabble, gabble about them as if they were anything, when they're nothing at all. Anything you can't see, ain't, that's what. Fighting things that ain't with things that ain't! They must have been all fools in them days. That's why they croaked. I ain't goin' to believe in such rot, I tell you that."

Granser promptly began to weep, while Edwin hotly took up his defence.

"Look here, Hare-Lip, you believe in lots of things you can't see."

Hare-Lip shook his head.

"You believe in dead men walking about. You never seen one dead man walk about."

"I tell you I've seen'm, last winter, when I was wolf-hunting with dad."

"Well, you always spit when you cross running water," Edwin challenged.

"That's to keep off bad luck," was Hare-Lip's defence.

"You believe in bad luck?"

"Sure."

"An' you ain't never seen bad luck," Edwin concluded triumphantly. "You ain't just as bad as Granser and his germs. You believe in what you don't see. Go on, Granser."

Hare-Lip, crushed by this metaphysical defeat, remained silent, and the old man went on. Often and often, though this narrative must not be clogged by the details, was Granser's tale interrupted while the boys squabbled among themselves. Also, among themselves they kept up a constant, low-voiced exchange of explanation and conjecture, as they strove to follow the old man into his unknown and vanished world.

"The Scarlet Death broke out in San Francisco. The first death came on a Monday morning. By Thursday they were dying like flies in Oakland and San Francisco. They died everywhere — in their beds, at their work, walking along the street. It was on Tuesday that I saw my first death — Miss Collbran, one of my students, sitting right there before my eyes, in my lecture-room. I noticed her face while I was talking. It had suddenly turned scarlet. I ceased speaking and could only look at her, for the first fear of the plague was already on all of us and we knew that it had come. The young women screamed and ran out of the room. So did the young men run out, all but two. Miss Collbran's convulsions were very mild and lasted less than a minute. One of the young men fetched her a glass of water. She drank only a little of it, and cried out:

"My feet! All sensation has left them."

"After a minute she said, 'I have no feet. I am unaware that I have any feet. And my knees are cold. I can scarcely feel that I have knees."

"She lay on the floor, a bundle of notebooks under her head. And we could do nothing. The coldness and the numbness crept up past her hips to her heart, and when it reached her heart, she was dead. In fifteen minutes, by the clock — I timed it — she was dead, there, in my own class-room, dead. And she was a very beautiful, strong, healthy young woman. And from the first sign of the plague to her death only fifteen minutes elapsed. That will show you how swift was the Scarlet Death.

"Yet in those few minutes I remained with the dying woman in my classroom, the alarm had spread over the university; and the students, by thousands, all of them, had deserted the lecture-room and laboratories. When I emerged, on my way to make report to the President of the Faculty, I found the university deserted. Across the campus were several stragglers hurrying for their homes. Two of them were running.

"President Hoag, I found in his office, all alone, looking very old and very gray, with a multitude of wrinkles in his face that I had never seen before. At the sight of me, he pulled himself to his feet and tottered away to the inner office, banging the door after him and locking it. You see, he knew I had been exposed, and he was afraid. He shouted to me through the door to go away. I shall never forget my feelings as I walked down the silent corridors and out across that deserted campus. I was not afraid. I had been exposed, and I looked upon myself as already dead. It was not that, but a feeling of awful depression that impressed me. Everything had stopped. It was like the end of the world to me — my world. I had been born within sight and sound of the university. It had been my predestined career. My father had been a professor there before me, and his father before him. For a century and a half had this university, like a splendid machine, been running steadily on. And now, in an instant, it had stopped. It was like seeing the sacred flame die down on some thrice-sacred altar. I was shocked, unutterably shocked.

"When I arrived home, my housekeeper screamed as I entered, and fled away. And when I rang, I found the housemaid had likewise fled. I investigated. In the kitchen I found the cook on the point of departure. But she screamed, too, and in her haste dropped a suitcase of her personal belongings and ran out of the house and across the grounds, still screaming. I can hear her scream to this day. You see, we did not act in this way when ordinary diseases smote us. We were always calm over such things, and sent for the doctors and nurses who knew just what to do. But this was different. It struck so suddenly, and killed so swiftly, and never missed a stroke. When the scarlet rash appeared on a person's face, that person was marked by death. There was never a known case of a recovery.

"I was alone in my big house. As I have told you often before, in those days we could talk with one another over wires or through the air. The telephone bell rang, and I found my brother talking to me. He told me that he was not coming home for fear of catching the plague from me, and that he had taken our two sisters to stop at Professor Bacon's home. He advised me to remain where I was, and wait to find out whether or not I had caught the plague.

"To all of this I agreed, staying in my house and for the first time in my life attempting to cook. And the plague did not come out on me. By means of the telephone I could talk with whomsoever I pleased and get the news. Also, there were the newspapers, and I ordered all of them to be thrown up to my door so that I could know what was happening with the rest of the world.

"New York City and Chicago were in chaos. And what happened with them was happening in all the large cities. A third of the New York police were dead. Their chief was also dead, likewise the mayor. All law and order had ceased. The bodies were lying in the streets unburied. All railroads and vessels carrying food and such things into the great city had ceased running, and mobs of the hungry poor were pillaging the stores and warehouses. Murder and robbery and drunkenness were everywhere. Already the people had fled from the city by millions — at first the rich, in their private motor-cars and dirigibles, and then the great mass of the population, on foot, carrying the plague with them, themselves starving and pillaging the farmers and all the towns and villages on the way.

"The man who sent this news, the wireless operator, was alone with his instrument on the top of a lofty building. The people remaining in the city — he estimated them at several hundred thousand — had gone mad from fear and drink, and on all sides of him great fires were raging. He was a hero, that man who staid by his post — an obscure newspaperman, most likely.

"For twenty-four hours, he said, no transatlantic airships had arrived, and no more messages were coming from England. He did state, though, that a message from Berlin — that's in Germany — announced that Hoffmeyer, a bacteriologist of the Metchnikoff School, had discovered the serum for the plague. That was the last word, to this day, that we of America ever received from Europe. If Hoffmeyer discovered the serum, it was too late, or otherwise, long ere this, explorers from Europe would have come looking for us. We can only conclude that what happened in America happened in Europe, and that, at the best, some several score may have survived the Scarlet Death on that whole continent.

"For one day longer, the dispatches continued to come from New York. Then they, too, ceased. The man who had sent them, perched in his lofty building, had either died of the plague or been consumed in the great conflagrations he had described as raging around him. And what had occurred in New York had been duplicated in all the other cities. It was the same in San Francisco, and Oakland, and Berkeley. By Thursday the people were dying so rapidly that their corpses could not be handled, and dead bodies lay everywhere. Thursday night the panic outrushes for the country began. Imagine, my grandsons, people, thicker than the salmon-run you have seen on the Sacramento River, pouring out of the cities by millions, madly over the country, in vain attempt to escape the ubiquitous death. You see, they carried the germs with them. Even the airships of the rich, fleeing for mountain and desert fastnesses, carried the germs.

"Hundreds of these airships escaped to Hawaii, and not only did they bring the plague with them, but they found the plague already there before them. This we learned by the dispatches, until all order in San Francisco vanished, and there were no operators left at their posts to receive or send. It was amazing, astounding, this loss of communication with the world. It was exactly as if the world had ceased, been blotted out. For sixty years that world has no longer existed for me. I know there must be such places as New York, Europe, Asia, and Africa; but not one word has been heard of them — not in sixty years. With the coming of the Scarlet Death the world fell apart, absolutely, irretrievably. Ten thousand years of culture and civilization passed in the twinkling of an eye, "lapsed like foam?'.

"I was telling about the airships of the rich. They carried the plague with them and no matter where they fled, they died. I never encountered but one survivor of any of them — Mungerson. He was afterwards a Santa Rosan, and he married my eldest daughter. He came into the tribe eight years after the plague. He was then nineteen years old, and he was compelled to wait twelve years more before he could marry. You see, there were no unmarried women, and some of the older daughters of the Santa Rosans were already bespoken. So he was forced to wait until my Mary had grown to sixteen years. It was his son, Gimp-Leg, who was killed last year by the mountain lion.

"Mungerson was eleven years old at the time of the plague. His father was one of the Industrial Magnates, a very wealthy, powerful man. It was on his airship, the Condor, that they were fleeing, with all the family, for the wilds of British Columbia, which is far to the north of here. But there was some accident, and they were wrecked near Mount Shasta. You have heard of that mountain. It is far to the north. The plague broke out amongst them, and this boy of eleven was the only survivor. For eight years he was alone, wandering over a deserted land and looking vainly for his own kind. And at last, travelling south, he picked up with us, the Santa Rosans.

"But I am ahead of my story. When the great exodus from the cities around San Francisco Bay began, and while the telephones were still working, I talked with my brother. I told him this flight from the cities was insanity, that there were no symptoms of the plague in me, and that the thing for us to do was to isolate ourselves and our relatives in some safe place. We decided on the Chemistry Building, at the university, and we planned to lay in a supply of provisions, and by force of arms to prevent any other persons from forcing their presence upon us after we had retired to our refuge.

"All this being arranged, my brother begged me to stay in my own house for at least twenty-four hours more, on the chance of the plague developing in me. To this I agreed, and he promised to come for me next day. We talked on over the details of the provisioning and the defending of the Chemistry Building until the telephone died. It died in the midst of our conversation. That evening there were no electric lights, and I was alone in my house in the darkness. No more newspapers were being printed, so I had no knowledge of what was taking place outside. I heard sounds of rioting and of pistol shots, and from my windows I could see the glare of the sky of some conflagration in the direction of Oakland. It was a night of terror. I did not sleep a wink. A man — why and how I do not know — was killed on the sidewalk in front of the house. I heard the rapid reports of an automatic pistol, and a few minutes later the wounded wretch crawled up to my door, moaning and crying out for help. Arming myself with two automatics, I went to him. By the light of a match, I ascertained that while he was dying of the bullet wounds, at the same time the plague was on him. I fled indoors, whence I heard him moan and cry out for half an hour longer.

"In the morning, my brother came to me. I had gathered into a handbag what things of value I *proposed* taking, but when I saw his face, I knew that he would never accompany me to the Chemistry Building. The plague was on him. He intended shaking my hand, but I went back hurriedly before him.

"Look at yourself in the mirror," I commanded.

"He did so, and at sight of his scarlet face, the color deepening as he looked at it, he sank down *nervelessly* in a chair.

"My God!" he said. "I've got it. Don't come near me. I am a dead man.

"Then the convulsions seized him. He was two hours in dying, and he was conscious to the last, complaining about the coldness and loss of sensation in his feet, his calves, his thighs, until at last it was his heart and he was dead.

"That was the way the Scarlet Death slew. I caught up my handbag and fled. The sights in the streets were terrible. One stumbled on bodies everywhere. Some were not yet dead. And even as you looked, you saw men sink down with the death fastened upon them. There were numerous fires burning in Berkeley, while Oakland and San Francisco were apparently being swept by vast conflagrations. The smoke of the burning filled the heavens, so that the midday was as a gloomy twilight, and, in the shifts of wind, sometimes the sun shone through dimly, a dull red orb. Truly, my grandsons, it was like the last days of the end of the world.

"There were numerous stalled motor cars, showing that the gasoline and the engine supplies of the garages had given out. I remember one such car. A man and a woman lay back dead in the seats, and on the pavement near it were two more women and a child. Strange and terrible sights there were on every hand. People slipped by silently, furtively, like ghosts — white-faced women carrying infants in their arms; fathers leading children by the hand; singly, and in couples, and in families — all fleeing out of the city of death. Some carried supplies of food, others blankets and valuables, and there were many who carried nothing.

"There was a grocery store — a place where food was sold. The man to whom it belonged — I knew him well — a quiet, sober, but stupid and obstinate fellow, was defending it. The windows and doors had been broken in, but he, inside, hiding behind a counter, was discharging his pistol at a number of men on the sidewalk who were breaking in. In the entrance were several bodies — of men, I decided, whom he had killed earlier in the day. Even as I looked on from a distance, I saw one of the robbers break the windows of the adjoining store, a place where shoes were sold, and deliberately set fire to it. I did not go to the groceryman's assistance. The time for such acts had already passed. Civilization was crumbling, and it was each for himself.

4. Questions for Discussion

(1) What is the Scarlet Plague, and how does it affect humanity in the novella?

(2) What is the significance of the character of Granser, and how does his perspective shape the narrative?

(3) How does the novella explore the themes of human nature and civilization?

(4) How does the novella use imagery and symbolism to create a sense of a world reduced to savagery?

(5) What is the meaning of the novella's title, and how does it relate to the story's themes and plot?

Bibliography

[1] ABDURRAHMANI T. Eco-criticism and nature writing: the trails of the American approaches[J]. European Journal of Social Sciences Education and Research, 2014,11(2) :1-12.

[2] ALEX Z. The roots of american individualism: political myth in the age of Jackson[M]. Princeton: Princeton University Press, 2022.

[3] AMIDON S. Don DeLillo's white noise [M/OL]. New York: Charles Scribner's Sons, 2004: 285-301. [2023-1-6]. link.gale.com/apps/doc/CX1382800026/G-Scrib?u=xmu&sid=bookmark-G-Scrib&xid=bb714ecc.

[4] BENARIOUA A. Black feminist voices and space in *The Color Purple* by Alice Walker [M/OL]. Gale Literature Resource Center, 2022, 256:1-8. [2023-6-22]. link.gale.com/apps/doc/MOSPYE904960353/LitRC?u=xmu&sid=bookmark-LitRC&xid=4b2f6eb5.

[5] BLOOM H. The American Dream[M]. New York: Infobase Publishing, 2009.

[6] CARTER S. DeLillo's *White Noise*[J/OL]. Gale Literature Resource Center, 2006,213. [2023-6-16].link.gale.com/apps/doc/H1100067958/LitRC?u=xmu&sid=bookmark-LitRC&xid=dd94da4e.

[7] DAY G S, DAVID A A. A guide to consumerism [J]. Journal of Marketing, 1970 (34.3) :12-19.

[8] WAI-CHEE D. Kate Chopin 1850—1904 [M/OL]. New York: Charles Scribner's Sons, 1991: 63-75. Gale Literature: Scribner Writer Series. [2023-6-15]. link.gale.com/apps/doc/ CX1385900015/G-Scrib?u=xmu&sid=bookmark-G-Scrib&xi，d=0b0c9c9e.

[9] EVANS D. Charlotte Perkins Gilman: overview [M/OL]. Chicago: St. James Press, 1996. [2023-6-15]. link.gale.com/apps/doc/H1420003293/LitRC?u=xmu&sid=bookmark- LitRC&xid=71a4e2c1.

[10] FELTY D. An overview of *Catch-22*[J/OL]. Gale Literature Resource Center, 2021. [2023-6-15].link.gale.com/apps/doc/H1420001498/LitRC?u=xmu&sid=bookmark-LitRC&xid=2bf3b588.

[11] FENG P C. *The Joy Luck Club*: overview [M/OL]. 3rd ed. Chicago: St. James Press, 1994. [2023-6-24].link.gale.com/apps/doc/H1420007858/LitRC?u=xmu&sid=bookmark-LitRC&xid=926a55e0.

[12] FLEXNER E, ELLEN F. Century of struggle: the woman's rights movement in the United States [M]. Cambridge: Harvard University Press, 1996.

[13] FRENCH W. *Invisible man*: overview [M/OL]. 3rd ed. Chicago: St. James Press, 1994. [2023-6-23]. link.gale.com/apps/doc/H1420002611/LitRC?u=xmu&sid=bookmarkLitRC&xid=de5c0d56.

[14] GAC S. The tradition of violence in the United States: a multidisciplinary survey [J/OL].

Choice, 2014, 52(3): 385. [2023-6-27]. link.gale.com/apps/doc/A388824486/LitRC?u=xmu&sid=bookmark-LitRC&xid=eddb1e1c.

[15] GARB Y. Rachel Carson's *Silent Spring* [J/OL]. Dissent, 1995: 539-546. [2023-6-27]. link.gale.com/apps/doc/H1420035903/LitRC?u=xmu&sid=bookmark-LitRC&xid=b695c034.

[16] GRABB E, DOUGLAS B, JAMES C. The origins of American individualism: reconsidering the historical evidence[J]. The Canadian Journal of Sociology, 24(4): 511-533.

[17] GRAY R. A history of American literature [M]. West Sussex: Wiley-Blackwell, 2012.

[18] HENRICKSON, S H. An overview of *The Joy Luck Club* [M/OL]. Gale Literature Resource Center, 2021. [2023-6-24]. link.gale.com/apps/doc/H1420004450/LitRC?u=xmu&sid=bookmark- LitRC& xid=4df10d8d.

[19] JARRETT G A. A companion to African American literature [M]. Chichester: Wiley-Blackwell, 2010.

[20] LANGMAN F H. Reconsidering *Invisible Man* [M/OL]. Gale Literature Resource Center, 1989,54. [2023-6-23]. link.gale.com/apps/doc/H1100002915/LitRC?u=xmu&sid=bookmark-LitRC&xid=d8202f5b.

[21] LAURIE C. Joseph Heller: overview [J]. Chicago: St. James Press, 1997. [2023-6-15]. link.gale.com/apps/doc/H1420003882/LitRC?u=xmu&sid=bookmark-LitRC&xid=77ca63c6.

[22] LAUTER P. A Companion to American literature and culture [M]. West Sussex: Wiley-Blackwell, 2010.

[23] LEACH W R. Transformations in a culture of consumption: women and department stores, 1890-1925[J]. The Journal of American History, 1984 (71.2): 319-342.

[24] MANGAN L. The feminism book: big ideas simply explained [M]. London: D.K. Publishing, 2019.

[25] MARTIN A S. Makers, buyers, and users: consumerism as a material culture framework[J]. Winterthur Portfolio, 1993 (28.3): 141-157.

[26] MASON A T. American individualism: fact and fiction[J]. The American Political Science Review, 1952 (46.1): 1-18.

[27] MCDONALD G. American literature and culture 1900–1960 [M]. Malden: Wiley-Blackwell, 2007.

[28] MILLER D Q. The routledge introduction to African American literature [M]. London: Routledge, 2016.

[29] MOUNT C, ERIC J. American individualism reconsidered[J]. Review of Religious Research, 1981(22.4): 362-376.

[30] PIZER D. The Cambridge companion to American realism and naturalism [M]. New York: Cambridge University Press, 1995.

[31] RATTANSI A. Multiculturalism: a very short introduction [M]. New York: Oxford University Press, 2011.

[32] RULAND R. From puritanism to postmodernism [M]. New York: Penguin Books, 1991.

[33] SCHMEINK L. The Anthropocene, the posthuman, and the animal [M]. Liverpool:

Liverpool University Press, 2016: 71-118.

[34] SCOFIELD M. The Cambridge introduction to the American short story [M]. New York: Cambridge University Press, 2006.

[35] WASHINGTON D A. Cliffsnotes on Ellison's *Invisible Man* [M]. Foster City: Houghton Mifflin Harcourt, 2001.

[36] WILLIAMS D A. Everybody's protest narrative: between the world and me and the limits of genre [J]. African American Review. 2016 (49.3):179-183.

[37] SHESTAKOV V P. American dream and American culture[J]. Gale Literature Resource Center, 2009.

[38] SOPER K. The other pleasures of post-consumerism [J]. Soundings, 2007, 35:31. [2022-7-26]. Gale Literature Resource Center. link-gale-com-s-libproxy-xmu-edu-cn-s. libproxy.xmu.edu.cn: 443/ apps/doc/A165352393/LitRC?u=xmu&sid=bookmark-LitRC& xid=e8e1f742.